Jenn plummer
was here!

ALL'S FAIR IN LOVE & MALICE

QUEENS & HEATHENS VOL 3

JENN PLUMMER

Jen Plummer

Wild Lupine
BOOKS

All's Fair in Love & Malice

Queens & Heathens, Volume Three

Published by Wild Lupine Books LLC

Editing by Katie Ducharme, Between the Covers Editorial

Cover Design by David @digital_pro_art

Typography by Emily Wittig

A NOTE FROM THE AUTHOR

Dear readers,

Welcome to the world of Queens and Heathens. All's Fair in Love and Malice is volume three in the interconnected series of Queens and Heathens. Each book can be read as a standalone and does not have to be read in order, but for the best experience, I recommend that you do.

There is no sharing, both adults are always willing participants, and there is a true HEA; this is a romance after all. The hero is completely and utterly obsessed with the heroine from the moment he lays eyes on her, and there are no lines he won't cross to make her his.

Let me be clear, this is a motorcycle romance. There will be usage of club slang and terms that are different from what you're used to if the genre is new to you.

Sending you all love.

KNOW BEFORE YOU READ

The following will have spoilers for the book. If you do not want to know, turn back now. Your mental health is important. Please read responsibly.

This book contains graphic content that includes: explicit language, on-page memories of prior childhood abuse that includes, mental, emotional, and physical (not from an MC), stalking, death of a spouse (a side character), death of friend(s), murder of parents, discussion of human trafficking, graphic on-page murder, extreme torture, gore, funeral home/mortuary, alcohol and drug use, grief, survivor's guilt, car accidents, and explicit sexual content (a full list is posted to my website.)

If you have any questions about this list, please don't hesitate to reach out to me directly.

HELL'S HEATHENS MOTORCYCLE CLUB

Camden Young "Chaos," President

Rhys Hudson "Sin," Vice President

Crew Lawson "Malice," Sergeant at Arms

Axel James "Wrath," Secretary

Reid Knight "Rogue," Road Sergeant

Aaron Miller "Noose," Road Sergeant

Jesse Davis "Rolo," Treasurer

Sean Jackson "Stitch," Doctor

Here are some club terms and their definitions you may hear in the story.

Church: The official meeting place for club members where club business is handled and discussed. A deeply important and sacred place.

Old Lady: A committed, voted-in partner in an exclusive relationship with a patched member

Prospect: a potential member in their probationary period

Patch Bunny: a woman who is free and independent and hangs around the club and often hooks up with patched members

Cut: a sleeveless leather vest that members wear as a symbol of their affiliation, loyalty, and identity within a club

Colors: patches on the cut that reflect a member's road name, rank, and achievements

This one is for everyone out there who is wandering through life feeling lost and stuck. The world deserves to feel your impact on it. You belong here, keep pushing until you're not just living, you're thriving.

And to all my book lovers who fall for a morally gray man who really just needs someone to love all their sharp and pointed sides. Malice is for you.

Malice
/ˈmaləs/

noun

the intention or desire to do evil; ill will.

CHAPTER ONE

MALICE

The bass of the music is drowned out by the sounds coming from Elliot and Harper's mouths. Elliot? Eli? Elija? No, it's Ellis. I'm about 95 percent sure it's Ellis. They're loud ones. Just the way I like it.

Ellis twists the dildo as he presses it inward, my ass clenching tightly around the thick silicone.

Fuck that feels good.

"Ohhhhhhmygodddd," Harper moans again around my cock, the vibrations ricocheting up my length. The noises are obscene; moans and unintelligible words mixed with wet slapping and lapping of skin and toys. It's like a symphony, and I'm the conductor, but I need the grand finale, when everyone is finally screaming until their throats are hoarse from overuse.

Harper pulls against the restraints at her wrists, her eyes shedding tears. Ellis grunts behind me, his cock slamming into Harper so hard she jerks upward.

Can't say I've done this position before, but it's gotta be a new favorite. My legs are spread across Harper's chest, my cock down her throat, while Ellis fucks me with a dildo, his cock filling her messy pussy. It's rare I get to be the one on all fours, and I'm more than happy to comply.

Good idea, Ellis.

Today was a long day, working at the mechanic shop and dealing with club business. I didn't get a single minute of quiet, and when that happens, the adrenaline and energy that I have to work to keep locked up starts to bubble forward.

This is the perfect release of that energy. It's this or finding someone to slowly kill.

Harper moans again, the vibrations traveling up my length and settling within my heavy sack. Her wet tongue curls against me as she sucks, just as the dildo pegs my prostate. Euphoric pleasure unfurls, my body breaking out in a sweat as goose-bumps scatter over my skin.

"Fuck, yeah, fuck, fuck, fuck, yeah!" I chant as I start to press deeper into her welcoming mouth, the thick silicone stretching my asshole, combining into deep-seated pleasure.

I look down to meet Harper's face, the way her lips look wrapped around my dick. She's spread-eagled on her back, her wrists and ankles cuffed to the bed, her holes stuffed with cock. She looks so good this way.

Ellis grunts behind me, his free hand bracing himself on my hip as I fuck myself into her mouth and back onto the dildo. Hell, it feels good. I haven't been fucked there since Saige's best friend, Seb, locked us down here in the dungeon for three days of explosive, kinky fun. Too bad I don't seem to have any limits,

I could use my brain being shut off for longer than it takes to fuck.

That's how it's always been with me. The anger, the malice, the rage, and the desire for destruction create adrenaline inside me, and I either need to kill or fuck to release it. My mind is idle while doing those two things, but the moment it's over, those feelings start to creep back in, slowly filling me up until I blow.

I look down at Harper, the tears that streak down her temples from the corner of her eyes, blown and starry-eyed as she starts to unravel, her plush lips a deep red and puffy. She looks thoroughly wrecked, and I fucking love it.

"Fucking hell, gonna come," Ellis moans as he slips from Harper's wet cunt. I'm right behind him, pleasure scattering through my body as she sucks hard around my head, the dildo gliding against my prostate, once, twice. I rip my cock from her mouth, grabbing the base and stroking it hard just as I feel the first splash of Ellis' cum coating my lower back.

Harper snaps her eyes shut, opening her mouth wide as she waits for me to paint her with my mess. Her chest heaves, breasts pressing against my inner thighs, while Ellis rubs his palms over my ass cheeks, spreading them wide and pulling the toy free. It's quickly replaced with his tongue, and that sends me into outer space. Ellis licks my used hole like he's starving. Wet, warm licks that take me right over the edge. I grip my dick harder, spraying white pearly seed over Harper's lips, chin, and cheeks. My head swims with the force of my orgasm, but then it's over, my body tightening, my mind foggy. I've heard my patch brothers talk about post-nut clarity, and I've never experienced it. It's the opposite for me. That calm, centered feeling only lasts as long as I'm fucking. But I'm sated for now, and that's what matters.

The three of us clean up with warm wash cloths I keep ready in the bathroom. They both seem to be in their post orgasm haze, which makes getting them out the door easier. I don't ever let anyone stay over. We can spend days fucking and playing, but if we're sleeping, it's not in my bed and not next to me.

I lead the way up the stairs, the two of them trailing behind me. Even though the lockdown has been lifted for months, our club president, Chaos, has strict rules for guests. Which are my job to enforce as the sergeant at arms here. Chaos' trust only extends to those he knows personally, and even then, it depends on the day and the person. I don't mind walking my guests out, though; it's the polite thing to do. After all, they did just let me fuck them to within an inch of their lives. Not to mention, given my position within the club, I take the security here seriously. We've been hit at home before, and I don't want a repeat of it.

The three of us reach the large main double doors of the clubhouse that frame the front of our common area. A large room with couches, TVs, two pool tables, dart boards, and a large-ass bar members tend to congregate to.

"It was a good time, thanks for, uh, having me—us—over," he says as he pulls the door open, the hot and balmy summer air assaulting me.

"No problem. Until next time, Ellis."

He rubs his hand behind his neck, his deep-set brown eyes crinkling at the sides. "Uh, it's Elias." *Damnit.*

I slap my palm against my forehead. "Could have sworn it was Elliot, my dude. *Elias*, be safe getting home. Harper, it was fun!" The two of them leave the clubhouse with a wave and walk to their respective vehicles. I watch as they each retreat into the darkness down the long dirt driveway that leads to the outside world beyond our compound.

The Hell's Heathens clubhouse sits on ten acres of mostly dense forest, with a small field off to one side, and a section where some spare houses sit. The entire compound is surrounded by a high chain-link fence, armed sentries at the front and back gates, and twenty-four-seven patrols, up until recently.

Even though the Hell's Heathens home base is surrounded by security measures, it's never felt like a cage to me. The opposite is true, actually. I had never felt true freedom and liberation until I was accepted here. I know the oppression of a cage, and this isn't it.

The door shuts behind me as I turn and walk naked back toward the stairs that lead to my basement bedroom. By living down there, I get more space than anyone here, even our president, which doesn't sound like it should be a big deal, but it is. He's the big dog at Hell's Heathens. In fact, now that I'm thinking about it, Chaos doesn't even have the second-largest room; Sin does. Or did, until he and his old lady moved out a few weeks ago. Hmm. Maybe he likes small places?

"Mal! Pants! We've talked about this, man," a loud boom of a voice bellows through the quiet stillness, scaring the living shit out of me. My hands flail, my knee rising to protect my precious, delicate bits. My club brother sits shrouded in the darkness like a ghost from his place at the bar. A really large, scary, angry ghost that I don't want to piss off.

"Make yourself known, good sir!" I reply as my body relaxes, knowing there isn't a threat I need to face.

Rolo raises his eyebrow at me, tipping the top of his beer bottle in the direction of my body. I look down at myself, my tattoos a hodgepodge of random metaphorical puzzle pieces of my life, patched randomly all over my body. My limp dick hangs off to the side, the metal from the piercings glittering slightly in the low light above me. "Why do you look like you've never seen your own dick before? Cover it up and come have a drink, for fuck's sake."

I roll my eyes, jogging downstairs to pull on a pair of sweats, then bounding back up again to take a seat at the bar. Our club treasurer, Rolo, has a beer in his hand, and the scent hits me right away. I hate the smell of it. Everything else is fine, but beer makes me crack my neck side to side while I push away the intrusive memories.

The glass sweats in droplets of condensation down the amber bottle. He's been here a while. At the bar. I guess he's been a member of Hell's Heathens for a while, too, but I digress.

"Have a good time?" he asks as I grab a Shirley Temple 7UP from behind the counter and pop the tab of the can. It hisses as I bring it to my lips for a sip, the cool, bubbly carbonation slipping down my throat.

"Yep," I reply, popping the *p*. "Told you guys my hair would bring in more playthings. I've been busy!"

Rolo looks up at my wild blond hair. Last year, I dyed it on a whim and like it better than my naturally dark brown locks. I nervously run my hands through it, trying to get it to lie flat, but it just pops back up again.

I have an aversion to letting anyone but myself cut my hair, so it's always a bit . . . wild. *Kind of like me*. But I think that just gives me an edge. The sergeant at arms for a badass motorcycle club should be slightly unhinged. I want to fit the part. Sue me.

"Glad you enjoyed yourself, Mal, just try to pull on some pants next time you walk your company to the door, yeah?"

My face scrunches together. "Wrath gets to have his dick out, why can't I?"

"Cause Wrath doesn't walk around with his dick flopping around like you were. He's using it with someone else when it's out."

"Ahh. I see the difference there. No one wants to see a flaccid penis."

Rolo chuckles, so what I said must be funny. "Only our own, Mal, only our own."

"Noted. No public flaccid penises. What's got you so messed up? It's like two in the morning," I ask after a beat of silence that starts to make my skin itch. Rolo shrugs, taking a long pull of his beer. "You're usually snuggled up with your wifey before now."

"Couldn't sleep. I don't know, it's been . . . peaceful? It's been almost a year since all the constant bullshit with the Widowmakers, and then the fallout with what they were connected to."

"Yeah, but that's a good thing. We had a decade of peace before all that shit went down. It's time to relax and live how we used to, without having to constantly look over our shoulders."

"You don't feel it? Like something's on the horizon? Something bad?"

I open my mouth to say the first thing that comes to my head but decide against it. Instead, I cock my head to the side and study his face. Maybe it's a midlife crisis? Maybe he's feeling his morality catching up with him? Deciding I need some backup, I pull out my phone from the loose pocket of my sweats.

Me: SOS Biker Besties!

Wrath: Are you fucking with me right now?

Me: Don't pretend you're asleep, we all know you don't have such a habit

Sin: This had better be important, Mal. Bristol and I are trying to sleep

Me: It is! Rolo seems off?

Wrath: Is that a question or is it a fact?

Me: I dunno. He's drinking by himself at the bar. I don't know how to explain it. I don't know what to do.

Rolo eyes me suspiciously, glancing down at my phone. I squint at him, turning my body in the opposite direction so he can't see what I'm doing. Nosey fucker. I bounce my knee, looking down at the group chat between Chaos, Sin, Wrath, and me. I created it after things started to go to shit with the Widowmakers last year. Figured it was time we had one place to get all the information out.

Chaos: Tell him I said to go back to Morgan and get some sleep

Sin: Same

I turn back to face Rolo, his head hung low, his fingers swiping the wet droplets off the beer bottle before they can reach the bar top.

"You think maybe you should go talk with Morgan? I'm sure she'll make you feel better."

"Yeah, Mal, you're right. Morgan makes everything better."

Relieved, I relax slightly, taking a big gulp of my sweet soda. We sit in silence for a few passing moments, my eyes darting around the room, wondering why this big oof isn't getting up to go be with his old lady.

"I really think everything is gonna be fine, Rolo," I say, unsure how to really comfort him. I grew up in a house with abusive drug addicts. Can't even call them parents, because they never did any actual parenting. Sperm donor and incubator, I guess I could call them. I was abused all of my childhood, until one day, it stopped.

But the neglect, the lack of human contact, touch, and communication, I know it did a number on me. Even if I struggle to see how much.

It's times like these where it makes my skin crawl; my mind is telling me my patch brother needs something from me, but I don't know what that is. Comfort? Advice? I don't know how to do any of that. So, I give him my company. Like he's done so many times for me before.

Hell's Heathens Motorcycle Club is filled with a bunch of outcasts, men who've had the world turn its back on them, the abused, the broken. But we all have one thing in common, we put our family—our club—above all else.

Footsteps gently clap against the concrete floor from behind us. Rolo seems lost in his thoughts, so I turn around to greet her. I learned at a young age to pay attention to footfalls. Everyone has their own unique way of walking, their strides, their gait, the force with which they land each step. I know it's Morgan before I meet her concerned eyes.

She's been at the clubhouse longer than I have. Story goes, she showed up one day for a party with some friends, met Rolo, and never left. She was the first old lady who wanted to be at the clubhouse full time and not in one of the houses on the property. By the time I came here, she was already the mother hen to all the patch bunnies, on top of taking care of the house and helping our cook and doctor with things they needed. She has a heart of pure gold.

Morgan narrows her eyes at me, nodding toward Rolo, silently asking a question I don't have the answer to. I shrug, dropping my elbow into Rolo's side to get his attention. He sits up straighter, turning in his seat, his face lighting up as he sees Morgan.

I want that.

Within the last two years, one of our road sergeants, Rogue, our club president, Chaos, and our vice president, Sin, have all found their queens. Now I want one. I don't even care if it's a woman or a man. My sexuality has never had limits or constraints, and I've never really defined myself with a label.

Mostly because I don't understand them. All I know is I like it all, and my head and my dick are in agreement.

My insides churn at the thought of finding someone for myself. As much as I envy what they have, I know in my core it won't happen. I'm too fucked up in the head for anyone to accept that. Who wants a deranged, sexual deviant, murderer for their man?

Rolo opens his arms, Morgan walking between his legs and wrapping her arms around his neck. Knowing he's in good hands, I polish off my Shirley Temple and toss the can into the bin.

They don't seem to notice as I creep over to the door that leads back downstairs, having learned a long time ago to keep my footfalls silent and stealthy.

CHAPTER TWO

MALICE

"Who's coming to ransack Daily Rise with me?" I announce into the large common room full of bikers. Everyone is mingling around, having cups of coffee, or smoking their cigarettes to wake up. I light one up, pulling a long drag into my lungs.

"Mal, when you say ransack, you make it sound like you're going to rob the joint."

I gasp. "I'd never do such a thing! Mrs. Odette would beat my ass, and then she'd come for all of yours!"

"No one is pissing off Mrs. Odette!" Sin declares, his eyes leaving no room for argument, as if any of us would. Daily Rise is our small town of Amberwood, Washington's bakery and coffee shop, and we all revere it.

"If she bans us again, I'm coming for Mr. Bun-Buns!" I tease, pointing at Sin's pet bunny in the crook of his arm. His old lady, Bristol, sits next to him and covers her smile with her hand, looking away. She knows my secret—that I'd never actually eat his bunny—but Sin doesn't need to know that.

"Mr. Bun-Buns is not fuckin' food, Mal!"

"Well then, who's coming with me? I need muffins!"

"I'll go," Saige says as she moves to stand. Chaos' hands grip either side of her hips, forcing her into his lap.

"Like hell you will, vixen, you're keeping your pretty little ass right fucking here where you belong."

Oh, she's not going to like that one bit. I take another drag of my cigarette, ready to watch this one play out.

"Fuck you, Camden. You can't tell me what to do." *Knew it.* Saige has been with Chaos for almost a year now, and she gives our president a run for his money every step of the way. She came to the clubhouse against her will because she was trying to kill him, and the two of them fell in love. She fits right in as one of us now, and it's almost like she's been here all along. She and I bonded quickly over our infatuation with blood and slitting throats.

Saige drives her elbow hard into Chaos' ribs, his arms going limp just long enough for her to stand and get out of his reach. With her eyes on me, she nods to the door.

"Sorry, Prez, the queen has chosen!" I bellow maniacally.

Saige and I walk together into the humid summer heat, the rare Washington sun beating down on us. It'll feel good to get on my bike and get the wind on my skin. I run my fingers across the body of my baby, the pink chrome glistening in the sunlight. She's a beauty, and it took me forever to fix her up to what she is today. Turns out, I love working on motorcycles as much as I love riding them.

The engine purrs to life under me, rumbling and filling the air with the scent of gasoline and exhaust. I revel in it. I glance over at Saige, who's already pulled out on her sleek, all-black bike. She extends her arm upright at the shoulder with her palm facing forward, the signal for me to follow her. She and I both know Chaos would want me to flank her and not lead, needing to keep my eye on the safety of the president's queen, even if she can probably handle herself in the face of danger better than I can.

Saige is a force to be reckoned with.

She is not someone I would intentionally fuck with. I visibly shiver at the thought. No thank you.

Together we ride up the gravel driveway, picking up dust in our wake. The ride to Amberwood is slow and peaceful. I love the wind in my hair and on my skin, the world zipping past me in a blur. It's easy to let myself go while I'm riding.

Our territory stretches the entirety of Amberwood and slightly beyond. It's a quaint, small town that I didn't know existed until I was dragged into it. In my defense, with how sheltered I was, I didn't know much of anything.

I was serving time for breaking and entering. Granted, the house was fucking *abandoned*, and I was just looking for someplace to sleep that wasn't a park bench, when I met Rolo, who I knew as Jesse at the time. He was serving twelve months for simple assault when he saved my ass from doing twenty to life. A gnarly fucker with a shaved, tattooed head and rotting teeth took one look at me and thought I was easy prey. I'm a tall guy at six foot four, but I'm lanky as fuck at one hundred sixty-five pounds, and you can't see what muscle I do have under the prison party suit.

It started with little verbal jabs, which escalated quickly one day when he physically attacked me. I quickly outmaneuvered him, lying on top of his body with my thumbs pressing into his eye sockets. I would have gladly pressed until I gouged them out, but Jesse came out of nowhere and pulled me off. His large arms bound around my chest, hauling me back. *"No, kid, no! You've got six months, and then we're out. You are not throwing your life away for this piece of shit. Trust me, he's not worth it."*

He had my back the rest of the time we were in. Jesse was released a week before me and promised he'd be there to pick me up. I chalked it up to talking a big game, that once I was out, I'd be back on the streets at square one with no one in my corner. Which was fine, I didn't know any different at the time.

In my head, free shelter, a warm bed, and daily meals while being locked up was a pretty good gig compared to the alternative. Especially during winter. The thought of having to go back to searching for food and shelter wasn't really appealing. Even my cage at the jail was bigger than the cage I grew up in.

To my shock, Rolo was parked outside the jail in a beat-up truck with another man I didn't recognize. They were both wearing black leather vests with patches all over them. Jesse nodded his head at me as I took the stairs from the building. With my shoulders back, I walked up to them, stopping a few feet away, unsure what was going down.

The stranger in front of me crossed his beefy arms across his broad chest and looked at me from my holey shoes to the top of my wild head. I remember Jesse looking at the beast like he was waiting for approval. When he nodded slightly, Jesse reached through the open window of the truck and pulled out some black leather, throwing it at me. I snatched it out of the air and held it up. It was similar to the vest they each had on, except this one only had one patch.

PROSPECT.

"Get in. We'll explain everything."

Then I was brought to my new home and never left.

Saige and I park our bikes right in front of Daily Rise, the scent of warm bread already hitting my nose over the gasoline.

"Heard you had quite the party last night."

My head snaps to Saige, her dark black hair framing her face, her bangs hovering right above her eyes. "Heard from who?"

"Rolo."

"What a big mouth! I didn't peg him for being a little gossip. I hope you're happy, you just earned him a dick punch."

"Well, I'm just glad you're not hooking up with Seb anymore; he tells me way too many details."

Seb is Saige's best friend, whom I've hooked up with a few times. He's a hotshot lawyer who helped us take down a massive human trafficking ring. We did all the heavy lifting and legwork, but once it gets to a certain level, we need to hand it over to the Feds. Seb's a good plaything and is always down for some kinky fun.

"He's a good time. You know he really likes food play? I wouldn't have guessed that from looking at him, but man, he's really into it. He had me put a—"

"Nope! Shhh! No, no, we don't need to speak of the extracurricular activities, just know I'm glad you both had fun."

"Fine," I groan. Saige pulls open the door to Daily Rise, and we're greeted by the smell of butter and sugar. Mrs. Odette has been running this place for as long as I can remember, and she makes the best pastries I've ever had. She's truly a marvel at her craft.

While we wait, I count the pastries in the glass case, tapping each number out on my thigh. When it's our turn to order, Mrs. Odette's face lights up, her grey curly hair wispy around her face, eyes crinkling as her lips turn upward in a toothy smile. She's always so happy to see any of the Hell's Heathens. God knows why. We're a bunch of hellions, and she's banned us from her shop more times than I can count. Which usually starts issues at the club for the guilty party. None of us wants to be restricted from getting her coffee and pastries.

"Crew, Saige, good morning! I've got boxes already! Let me grab them."

Saige raises a brow at me, and I shrug like it's no big deal.

"If you haven't noticed, I come here every Thursday and return with a little bit of everything."

"Even on lockdowns," she says, knowing that when Chaos first brought her to the clubhouse—against her will, but that's a different story—we were under lockdown and I still snuck out to get Daily Rise.

"Even on lockdowns. Been doing it for years at this point."

"I get it, her stuff is good. I had never had half these things until Camden put them in front of me and had me try them all." Saige smiles, a rare sight since she's typically more reserved and resolute in her disposition.

"You look like you're someplace else," I say, nudging her with my elbow.

"I was. Just remembering when Camden was trying to figure out all my favorite things."

"He really loves you. We all thought he was only ever going to love the club," I tell her honestly. Our president has been dealt a rough hand in life that led him and his brother, Lucas, to Hell's Heathens. After Lucas was murdered, he just wasn't the same. Until Saige.

All the women my club brothers have found have changed them for the better. The one common factor between every Heathen is that we're all lost boys. We made our family with each other, but we're all broken inside. But the four that have their queens? They've been healed.

I want that. Even if I know it's not in the cards. There's no healing someone who doesn't just live and walk in the darkness. I am the darkness. There's no escaping it. Chaos and Rogue were wandering through it, looking for their light to bring them out. That's not me. There's no leaving it. I'm not looking for redemption or a savior; those things aren't attainable for someone who craves what I crave.

"Now *you* look like you're somewhere else," she says, throwing my words back at me.

"Just lost in my head."

"That's a scary place to be."

"If you only knew, Saigey. If you only knew."

Mrs. Odette returns with several pastry boxes a moment later and charges my card. We say our goodbyes and head outside.

After strapping everything down on the back of my bike, we head back to the clubhouse. I keep my head on a swivel, never wanting to take our extended peace for granted. If I've learned anything from watching my brothers, it's that the moment you become complacent and comfortable, all hell will break loose. I can't afford to let anyone down, so I'm always on edge, always ready. Even if it doesn't seem like I am.

Some of our club ranked members, Wrath, Rolo, and Noose, are all outside on the large porch when Saige and I pull up. It's barely nine in the morning, and the heat is already brutal, so I don't understand how they're standing out here smoking in jeans, T-shirts, and layers. I hate clothes and rarely wear a T-shirt. The only reason I put one on today was that I knew Mrs. Odette would throw me out of Daily Rise if I wasn't dressed.

I unstrap the boxes, holding them up above my head as I walk up the stairs of the clubhouse, knowing everyone will descend on me like a pack of starving, feral wolves.

"You get those donut croissant things?" Wrath asks as he releases a puff of earthy smoke.

"I got whatever Mrs. Odette put in these boxes. You know I don't get to choose unless it's my birthday," I reply.

"You don't even know when your birthday is, Mal," he quips.

"Which is why I reserve the right to tell her it's my birthday once or twice a year when I get a craving for something special."

"That's bullshit," he argues.

"You're bullshit, sir. At least you have a birthday."

"You have a birthday, Mal, you just don't know when it is."

"Then do I really have one, Wrath? Do I?"

"You do know what a birthday is, right?" Sin asks as he flicks open a box to snag a banana muffin for Bristol. I've learned they're her favorite and he hand-feeds them to her like she's a baby bird. I've never seen him chew it up first, though. I make a mental note to ask him. I bet they do that in private.

I wonder if all women like that. To be hand-fed. Not to have their food chewed up and spit into their mouth. Then I look over at Saige and bristle. I would bet my right nut she isn't one of them. She'd likely bite someone's fingers off.

"Prez, Saige let you feed her?"

"What?" he says, pulling his long dark hair out of his face and tying it in a bun.

"Does. Saige. Let. You. Feed. Her?" I say, enunciating my words very slowly.

Wrath and Sin both chuckle through their bites of food. "She'll do whatever the fuck I tell her to do."

Saige's head whips in his direction, her bangs swishing above her eyes. "Like hell I will, Camden. You want to test that theory and see how that works for you? I dare you."

Mission accomplished. I laugh, turning my focus back to the open boxes spread out on the bar, quickly snatching up a chocolate chip muffin. I like everything Mrs. Odette bakes and would have taken the scraps of anything left behind, but I'm glad it's a chocolate chip muffin today.

"So, what was last night about?" Sin asks between bites of food.

"I had a threesome. Was pretty decent, too. I bottomed for this dude who wanted to fuck me and her at the same time."

Chaos chokes on his bite of food, and Sin pats his back hard as he coughs through it.

"I meant with Rolo, Mal, not your sex life," Sin says with an eye roll.

I bark out a rough laugh. "Ahh. What, you guys don't want to hear about my blended orgasm?" Sin and Wrath both chuckle, and I smile, amused with myself. Most of the shit out of my mouth is just to get them to laugh, and I like pushing their buttons. Chaos looks at me with sharp eyes that could cut glass.

"No," Chaos replies roughly.

"I do, what the fuck is that?" Wrath asks.

"It's an orgasm through blended stimulation. Last night it was my prostate and my cock. Overfilled her mouth until she was gurgling on it, and it seeped out the corners."

"For fuck's sake, Malice," Chaos says under his breath.

"Didn't take you for such a prude, Prez. Pretty sure you're fucking Saige until her violent little brain goes empty." Chaos moves fast, pulling his knife and holding it to Sin's neck, his other hand grasping a fistful of his hair and yanking his head backward. A drop of blood beads at the blade, and I watch as it grows in size.

One. I mentally count.

Blood has always fascinated me. The color, how quickly it can leave your body. The different ways it can leak, seep, or spray.

Sin puts up his hands in defense, palms facing outward, with a big cheesy-ass grin on his face. He loves pushing Chaos to his limit just as much as I do, and talking about Saige will get him there quickly.

"What'd I tell you about talking about my woman like that?"

Sin just chuckles, the bead now trickling slowly down his neck just as another one forms.

Two.

I lean into his space, putting my face right in Sin's ear. "He said not to," I whisper.

"That's right. Listen to Mal, Sin, or I'll slit your throat from ear to ear just like my woman does. Got it?"

Three. Tap.

"Yeah, Prez, you angry fucker, I get it." Chaos releases Sin and sits back down to finish his food while Sin smiles and cleans up the streak of blood down his neck. I grin at all of them like a fool, my eyes darting around.

We're all crazy, but this is home.

The rest of the day passes in a blur of mindlessness, and as night falls, the party kicks up. I get dressed in a pair of tight leather pants that hang low on my hips, the bones of my pelvis protruding from the top. I drag a thick layer of black eyeliner under my eyes, then I slip into my leather cut. My eyes clock the Sgt. at Arms patch on the front. Hard to believe someone with my start in life is a ranked member of a respected motorcycle club. I've never had an opportunity to want for anything, always just trying to survive, but I've got a place here. A home. A family. And this position? The club's enforcer and security officer? It's exactly right for me.

The bass hits me square in the chest before I even open the door from my bedroom. The kind of thumping bass that you feel behind your ribs and not in your ears, the beat taking over the rhythm of your heart, controlling your breathing. My head bobs to the sound as my bare feet lead me to the bar.

The clubhouse smells like a hearty mix of beer, cigarette smoke, and engine oil. Won't be long before the scent of sex mingles with it. It's familiar and gets my blood pumping. Minus the beer, that scent alone will tap into the demon I keep locked up.

The massive bay doors are propped open wide, large fans trying to pull in some cool air from outside. Inside the clubhouse is all sticky heat and noise, so I grab one of the Shirley Temple 7UPs from behind the bar and head outside to light up a smoke.

Bikes are lined up like guard dogs, the chrome catching on the floodlights. My eyes scan them, tapping each one out against my thigh with my middle finger. The earthy, smoky scent of marijuana hits my nose, and I clock Wrath at the end of the porch, a patch bunny bent over as he drills his hard dick inside her, a joint resting between his lips. Cora grips the banister, her back arched, ass jutted out. My eyes trace down the fine line of her spine. She's one I haven't fucked yet, and now I'm wondering why.

I relax against the side of the building, crossing my feet at my ankles to get comfortable for the show. Smoke swirls around my head as I exhale, the cherry glowing bright between my fingers.

Wrath likes to be watched, and he doesn't give a shit whose eyes are on them. Fuck knows the patch bunny doesn't either. They're all here willingly, and we provide a bunkhouse for them to have privacy and space from the club members. But they know why they're here. Free shelter, free food, and fucking. Lots and lots of fucking.

Voyeurism doesn't really do it for me, but I'm happy to help one of my patch brothers out. One of Wrath's hands grips her hip, his fingers pressing deep into her flesh, the other hand wrapped around her long blonde ponytail, forcing her head backward. The long line of her neck is exposed, and I have to push away my sinister thoughts. I bet she'd look so pretty painted in crimson. Her moans float on the air, accompanied by the harsh grunts coming from my patch brother.

"That's it, Cora, fucking take it," he grinds through clenched teeth. And she does. Holding on for dear life as he tunnels into her used-up pussy until he's pulling out, filling the condom outside of her cunt. It's something I've noticed he always does, even with his dick wrapped up, and knowing all the girls are on birth control, because Morgan makes sure of it, he never comes inside them. A problem I don't have to worry about. I snipped any possibility that there could be a baby Malice running around the clubhouse.

I'm enough death and destruction for one club.

Buckling his jeans back up, he smacks Cora's ass in thanks and walks over to me, resting his forearms on the porch rail.

I take a long pull of the bubbly soda, the fizz hitting my tongue and sliding down my throat, sharp and sweet.

"Enjoy the show?"

"Yep. Already getting your dick wet, huh? Party just started," I ask.

"I'm addicted to it. Warm, wet heat enveloping my cock. Soft curves and long lines, pretty, pouty lips. Who doesn't want that shit as often as possible? The day I stop fucking is the day the devil comes to bring me home." Wrath replies with a tilt of his lips. He's not wrong there. I fucking love sex. It's an outlet. An adrenaline purge. That's all it's ever been for me. A means to a release. I don't get that shit nearly as often as he does. But I'm into darker shit than Wrath is. He's an exhibitionist, and I'm one kinky fucker who won't say no to anything. Men, women, all sizes, all colors. I've got an appetite for it all, any way I can have it. I bet if the planet were invaded by blue aliens, I'd find my way into an orgy on day one.

The floor vibrates under our boots as the music is turned up, laughter and voices tangling together until it's impossible to tell where one ends and the other begins. Leather cuts are everywhere, girls half naked, everyone with drinks in their hands. Rolo stumbles out onto the porch, his tree trunk of an arm slung over Morgan's shoulders.

"Hey, fuckers, pool time. Come get your asses kicked," he barks. Wrath and I share a look, knowing we're both better than him at the game. Following him into the house, we leave the cooler night air behind us and return to the sticky heat of the clubhouse.

The party has fully tipped past the point of no return, and I know even the heavy scent of cigarette smoke and alcohol will cling to me until tomorrow, thick and pungent. The noise is thundering, and I have to constantly fight to stay firmly rooted in the present, with the clubhouse roaring with life around me, because it's the only place I'm supposed to be.

The metal of the cage rattles from the force of the kick. I press myself to the far corner as much as I can, wrapping my arms around my shins, burying my head into my knees as I rock.

Back and forth.

Back and forth.

Back and forth.

The blanket draped over the top keeps me shrouded in darkness, but I blink anyway, trying to focus. It's always dark. Never any light. Never any sunshine. Never any warmth. I pull my bare legs closer to my chest. It's always cold. Why isn't there any heat? Why can't I get warm? I stopped wondering a long time ago what it would feel like to be held, to be comforted and safe. All I know is pain. Cold. Fear.

Why doesn't anyone come for me? Why doesn't anyone care?

Back and forth.

Back and forth.

Back and forth.

The scent of smoke fills my nose, acrid and ashy, making my head swim and feel fuzzy. Another kick to the cage, the piercing shatter of glass, the click of a lighter, the pop of a can. Liquid trickles from the top, and my dry, cracked lips open wide enough for my parched tongue to lap at the fluid pooling in front of me. Bitter tang seeps in, and I dry heave.

Back and forth.

Back and forth.

Back and forth.

I wonder if freedom will ever come for me, or if I'll be locked away forever.

"Mal! Mal! Malice, wake up, brother."

I lurch forward, gripping the neck of the body in front of me and flipping him onto his back, my legs straddling his torso, my forearm pressing down on his windpipe.

"Crew! It's Jesse!" he chokes, holding his hands out in front of him and not fighting me back. "Crew!"

My vision clears, looking down at the familiar face of my patch brother. Shit. I pull my arm off his airway; his coughs immediate.

"Man, get your fuckin' dick off my chest, for fuck's sake!" I look down at my body, and yep, sure as shit, I'm nude. "With how often you have nightmares, it'd be cool if you wore underwear from time to time. I've been telling you for over a decade."

I climb off of Jesse, quickly pulling on a pair of boxer briefs. "Sorry," I say, running my hands through my hair, only for it to stick right back up again.

"Don't worry about it. You okay? I was having a drink when I heard you screaming."

"Just another one. I'll be fine."

"You wanna talk about it?"

"Nah. Go back to Morgan. I'm good."

Rolo nods, knowing better than to push.

Fuck these nightmares. Even after all these years, they're still finding ways to torture me. My torment will never truly end.

CHAPTER THREE

MALICE

"You're up early," Wrath says as he takes a seat next to me in the Adirondack chair with a steamy mug of coffee in one hand, a cigarette in the other. I pull out my own, lighting it up and taking a deep inhale, the smoke mingling with the woodsy scent of summer—pine needles, Sitka spruce trees, and wild lupines.

"Only slept a few hours, been up since three."

"Nightmare?"

I nod. "What do we got going on today?"

"There's some issue at the build site of the new club, gotta go down there and get shit sorted."

Last fall, our nightclub, Hell's Asylum, was burned to the ground because of some shit that went down with Sin and Bristol. She was engaged to one of the men directly involved with the human trafficking ring we took down, and he wanted to send a message that he didn't like Sin getting near Bristol.

The club had been a prominent business for Hell's Heathens long before my ass came in, and hurt a lot of the old timers here. Hell, it hurt me. We've all got an attachment to that place.

Seeing it reduced to brick and ash broke something inside Chaos and Sin that day, and they've both been hell-bent on getting it rebuilt ever since.

"What's the issue?"

Wrath shrugs, taking a long drag of his cigarette. "Dunno, Rolo's taking care of it."

"I'll go with him."

"Nope, Prez needs you here today. Some shit with the prospects. He wants ranked members in church in an hour."

I nod. "You think he's pushing a vote?"

"Nah, I think he wants to postpone it. Do you think any of them are ready? I sure as hell don't, and that's not a reflection on you. They're all running from something, but that doesn't mean they'll have our backs when the fight comes knocking again."

He's not wrong. One of the biggest foundations Chaos has put in place since he became president when Queenie died was trust. He doesn't rule as our leader; he's one of us. He doesn't force anyone to be here or to become a member. There's no coercion or blackmail, just loyalty and family. We have to know that the men who become patched members will have our backs without thinking. You can't buy a man's loyalty with force or fear, and Chaos knows that.

So, I'm with Wrath on this one. I don't think these men are ready yet.

"You're not wrong. It hasn't even been that long since all that shit went down with the Widowmakers, we've got time. There's no rush. We've gotta play this right."

"Agreed. I'm heading to shower. See you in there."

I nod, standing and deciding to do the same. Wrath steps into the building and moves off to the side just as Rolo steps out, two prospects in tow: Garrett and Luca. Luca has been with us about a year and is the only current prospect who would get my backing if it went for a vote today. He's got a good head on his shoulders and is focused. Jury is still out on Garrett.

"You heading out already? Prez wants us in church."

"Yeah, better to get shit done this morning. Chaos is letting me skip since the stuff at the club is pressing. We'll head up to the shop when I get back. Cool?" Hell's Heathens has several businesses we own and run in Amberwood, and I split my time between working at the auto shop and working at the clubhouse with Chaos. Rolo brought me there and taught me everything I know.

"Yeah, works for me. See you when you get back," I reply, giving him a salute just to be a jackass. Then I evil eye the fuck out of the prospects standing at his back. Luca is calm and collected. He's wearing a pair of denim jeans with boots, a plain white T-shirt, and his cut that says PROSPECT. His dark brown hair hangs around his shoulders, a deep, healed scar running from just under his right eye to the corner of his lip. His hands are stuffed in his pockets while he rocks on the soles of his boots. He's about twenty-five, if I remember correctly, and has answered the call without hesitation over the last year and a half he's been with us.

Then I look at the ugly fucker next to him. Garrett looks like he was scraped from the bottom of a dumpster. And I can judge because I've been in just as rough shape. He's got a shaved head that's covered in tattoos, thick biceps that are crossed over his chest like he's bracing for a fight, and isn't intimidated by me in the slightest. He's wearing a pair of jeans and a tight white tank with his cut. His eyes are too far apart, and his teeth are black as soot.

Rolo nods at me before walking down the porch steps, Luca following him. I snarl as Garrett passes me, my eyes catching a faded snake tattoo on the side of his skull. There's a familiarity there, but I can't place it.

I catch the grind of his molars, the squint of his eyes, and the way his back stiffens further. He must think I'm stupid, or he just doesn't give a shit if I notice his reaction to me. I may be aloof and come off a little empty-headed sometimes, but that's just because I'm eternally caged in my own goddamn mind. I'm always thinking. Constantly. Even when I sleep. Nothing shuts the shit off. I may be physically out of my cage, but the one in my head holds me hostage.

Wrath is right, some of these motherfuckers aren't ready. I need to step it up with them. Especially this dumb fucker.

I watch them leave before heading inside, taking my shower, and dressing in a pair of jeans, boots, and my cut. Fuck the T-shirt. The only reason I'm wearing pants is that Chaos has a pants-on rule now.

Church is sacred to us. The room sits at the back of the clubhouse off our main living space, and the two heavy wooden doors keep it closed at all times. All of our important club meetings, votes, and conversations happen behind these closed doors. Doors I never thought I'd see behind when I first got here and was learning the ropes from Rolo.

We all take our seats—Chaos at the head of the table, me to his side, Sin on his other, Wrath, and Noose filling in, with Rolo and Rogue's left empty. I get comfortable in my seat, ripping open my bag of Famous Amos, and popping a crisp cookie into my mouth.

The crunch is loud, and everyone pauses to look at me with expressions that irritate me. My eyes dart around to each of them. "Problem you want to share?"

"No," Chaos snaps. "Otto wants in."

Every single one of us has the same reaction, our mouths dropping open like assholes too stupid to speak up. Crumbs fall from my mouth and onto my lap. He's not fucking serious.

"Fuck no," Sin demands. "Are you outta your mind? He's a kid! It's bad enough that you brought him on all that shit with the finances."

Last fall, we needed help to unscramble a trove of bullshit financial accounts that ultimately helped us find who was the head asshole running the human trafficking ring. Otto is Mrs. Odette's grandson. Chaos has been helping keep him on the straight and narrow for a while now. His being a hang-around is one thing, but a prospect? Fuck being banned from Daily Rise, Mrs. Odette will kill us.

"His parents are dead. All he has left is his grandmother. He needs us."

"No offense, he needs anything but us, Prez."

"I disagree," Chaos says firmly, his eyes tracing the carved pattern of the Hell's Heathens symbol in the center of our table.

"If you're sticking us in here for a fucking vote, mine is no. That kid needs mentorship, I'll give you that, but not club life." Sin speaks the words viciously, no sign of the man behind his alter ego to be found.

We spend the next thirty minutes arguing back and forth. Otto is barely nineteen and has his whole life ahead of him. A good life. We've all seen him grow up outside of the club, and to take him now just feels wrong. Like we'd be doing a disservice to him. Failing him.

"We're not voting without Rolo and Rogue here. Not on this," I add, tapping my middle finger against my leg, mentally counting the scratches in the tabletop. "Wrath?"

"Sorry, Prez, it's a no. We aren't voting without them. It's against the laws of the club." Everyone but Chaos relaxes in their seats, relieved our club secretary has a pair of balls, because no one tells our president no. He's a ruthless sonofabitch, and no one wants to be on his bad side.

My phone buzzes in my pocket a split second later. I pull it out, not recognizing the number, and click accept. All eyes are on me in the room, and it makes my fucking skin crawl.

I don't say anything, waiting for whoever is on the other line to speak first.

"It's Luca! It was a trap! We're shot! We need backup!" the voice yells and stutters into the phone, and I stand quickly, pure rage flowing through my veins.

"Where's Rolo?" I demand, my vision clouding over. "Where are you?"

"The-ah-the Asylum . . . he's hit. I-I don't know. I'm hit. I can't get to him."

"We're coming." I hang up the phone without another word.

There's a moment of shock, of pure terror, and then Chaos yells his demand, and we all spring into action, moving on autopilot.

"Round 'em up! On bikes in two! Malice, give it to us."

I relay the short details, jogging to our armory and pulling out guns and ammo, unsure what the fuck we're about to head into, but needing to be prepared regardless. Wrath gets all the girls in the house to a safe room, leaving Saige, Noose, and some other trusted members behind to keep them safe. The majority of us are outside, revving up our bikes in a minute. We ride in a staggered formation the moment we hit the pavement, pushing our bikes to the limit but staying together.

We've been through shit and back since I became a Heathen. I've seen my patch brothers hold their murdered siblings, I've seen them get stabbed, shot, beaten, and bruised. I have more blood on my hands than most of the men here. But I've never been scared. I've never felt fear.

Not until now.

We come to a fast stop outside Hell's Asylum, and we all make the same movements, pulling our guns free and holding them in front of us. Sin and I flank Chaos, looking around the construction site. There are no bikes here besides ours, no people milling about. It's a fucking dead zone, and confusion swirls in my head. But I'm on edge.

Something's not right.

I'm a split second from thinking the entire area is going to blow until I hear a moan followed by a cough. We jog over to find Luca leaning against the back of a dumpster, his shirt soaked in blood, his hands clutching his middle. Blood oozes from his side, the ground below him a wet mess.

Chaos crouches down just as Stitch drops to his knees, ripping Luca's shirt down the center. Sin and I stand guard, our guns ready, looking around us for any danger. Where the fuck is Rolo?

Sin gives me a look, raising his eyebrows. He's just as nervous as I am.

"Talk!" Chaos demands. *Fucking finally.* Before he bleeds out all over the ground, and we don't get the info we need.

"He-he shot at us. I got in front of him, but I went down, and he kept shooting," Luca says between wheezing coughs. Stitch starts to work on him, and I look down to find two bullet holes on the side of his stomach. Luca groans, and I roll my eyes. What a baby. I've had worse.

"Who shot at you?"

"Garrett."

"Fuck," Sin hisses. I should have fucking known. Goddamnit!

"Where the fuck is Rolo? You said he was shot. Where?" I spit, looking all around. Luca lifts a weak arm, pointing at the construction site. I don't waste any more time, running into the framework of the new building, my eyes scanning the area.

Then I see him. Limp and lifeless. Lying in a pool of his own blood, the crimson color darkened against the freshly laid concrete. The world gets hazy around me, the edge of my vision darkening. Blood rushes between my ears as I stare down at the man who saved my life.

I drop to my knees at his side, checking his pulse, even though his eyes are open and the light is gone. This can't be fucking happening. There's no fucking way I'm looking at Rolo's dead body.

I slap my hand against my head repeatedly. "Fuck!" I scream. Pain laces through my chest, my shoulders curving forward, my stomach contracting as it cramps, the bile churning. I hear men behind me, footsteps, voices, breathing. But this time, I don't register who they are. I don't care.

"Fuck, man."

"Goddamn it, not fucking Rolo."

"Mal?"

I don't look away from his body, the leather vest. I count out the patches, tapping my middle finger against the top of my thigh, trying to breathe.

Rolo. One.

Washington. Two.

Original. Three.

Treasurer. Four.

My voice is eerily calm when I speak. "He knew something was coming, he fucking felt it, and I didn't listen."

"What do you mean, he knew?"

"That night at the bar when I texted. He was drinking alone and felt like something big was on the horizon. He fucking felt his death coming. He knew."

"Malice, even if that's so, there's nothing we could have done. We're going to find that sonofabitch who took him from us. We will get our revenge."

"Fuck that. Why the fuck was he allowed to come here alone? I should have gone with him! Fuck you, Chaos, for letting him go! Fuck you!"

"Mal, there's nothing any of us could have done!" Sin says, trying to de-escalate the situation.

"There is! I could have gone with him! I could have tracked him! No one misses fucking church except Rogue! No one! Why the fuck was he out with only two prospects? After everything we've been through! I know better. I do!"

"Buddy, we do it all the time, even when there was the constant threat of danger, I was leaving, you know I was," Sin replies. "We're all hurting. We're all going to get through this together, and we're going to find Garrett. Make him pay."

"Fuck you! Jesse didn't deserve this! He saved ME! *Me*! When I had no one, when I had never known an ounce of kindness, Jesse fuckin' gave it to me! And look at him!" I spin on Chaos, needing a place to unload my feelings. "He was the fucking best of us. And he's fucking dead!"

Chaos meets my anger, rising to the challenge like I knew he would. "You think I don't know that, Mal? You think I don't see it? You think I don't carry that fucking guilt with me every single goddamn day? It's like a fucking shadow, hovering over me every goddamn minute. The devil himself walks with me, and I never know when he's going to claim one of my brothers. He already took Ace from me." Chaos pounds on his chest with his fist as he enunciates each word. "I! Fucking! Know!"

"This shouldn't have happened. I won't sleep until we find this motherfucker. No one had better touch him but me."

"Get him out of here," Chaos says, looking at Sin, then turns to face Wrath to bark out more orders. "This is too public, and we have Morgan to think about. We can't handle this one on our own. Call Deputy Evans, explain the situation, and let's get this cleaned up."

Everyone moves as I fall back down at Jesse's side. I move his body, working hard to get his cut removed before someone takes it as evidence or it ends up lost. Sin squats down on the other side of him, working to help me in my task. Neither of us speaks. We don't need to. I catch the shake of his hands in his movements, the way he grinds his molars together.

Someone from inside our home turned on us, took one of our club officers, took one of our brothers. That won't stand.

Anger floods me fast and violent, licking up my spine and setting my nerves aflame. I try to breathe in, to stay rooted to the present, to stay in control, but there's no containing it. It builds and builds. Heat blooms behind my ribs, a steady thrum under my skin, coursing through my veins. I can feel my pulse everywhere—between my ears, my throat, my fingertips, a roaring thunder drowning out all else. My muscles coil tightly on their own, my jaw locked so tight my teeth grind against each other. The world around me starts to narrow, the edges blurring, the only color the blood red covering my palms, the floor, the man in front of me.

My blood boils within my veins, pain replaced with pure *malice*. I've never wanted vengeance more. I crack my neck side to side, my mind taking me to a place that isn't here. A place that's just as dark. A place that haunts me. A place where I first felt the sweet cosmic relief and freedom that came with taking vengeance. The first time I got blood on my hands.

CHAPTER FOUR

MALICE

The aftermath of Rolo's murder isn't pretty. Watching Morgan fall to her knees in Saige's arms, her screams, her tears, they'll be stuck with me until the day I die. I haven't slept or eaten, my only focus finding that piece of shit who turned on us and making him pay.

I'm a madman. I've always had a screw loose, but I've been able to control it. Somewhat. The twenty-four hours after I stared at Rolo, riddled with bullets, are madness. The fire that I fight to control every day rages as an inferno now, hungry, ravenous, and unstoppable. It burns away any hesitations, restraints, or doubt, leaving only fury and death in its wake.

While everyone was at the clubhouse taking care of Morgan, getting plans together, and figuring out how the fuck to move on, I embraced the devil at my back and went on a killing spree. Saige's best friend, Seb, is a silent reporter of pieces of shit who don't deserve to continue walking the earth. Men who've skirted the law for whatever reason and needed a reckoning. And I was happy to give it to them.

The blood that spilled at my hands didn't snuff out the fire. I would have taken some of it out on a patch bunny or two in the form of some rough fucking, but even though I'm a monster, I know they deserve their time to mourn and take care of Morgan without me dragging them away to be bound against my bed or cross while I fuck them into oblivion.

I'm sitting in church, the air thick with a volatile mix of rage and sadness. It's palpable, and I soak it in, letting it meld with my own, letting the fire inside me build and build until I'm ready to blow again.

"Rolo had a life insurance policy we didn't know about. So, his death is public record. Instead of Deputy Evans bringing his body here, he's at the Amberwood Mortuary. They're going to handle stuff for us, and then we'll do our final ride, bringing him down to the cemetery for a burial. We need to handle the funeral arrangements. Morgan said she can't bear to do it, so one of us needs to." That's not common for us. The majority of members who have passed are buried right here on Heathen property. Things can get messy when you involve others, especially when you've got bodies with bullet holes and stab wounds.

"I'll do it," I reply, knowing I need to be the one to do this. For Jesse, the club, and for Morgan.

Sin taps his fingers against the table. I count each one. "No offense, Mal, I don't think you're in the right space to handle all that. Bristol and I can take care of it."

"I said I'll fucking do it, and that's the end of the conversation. I know how to reel myself in, Sin, so fuck off. Now, where do we start looking for Garrett? Any leads on why the fuck he turned on us? Turned on Rolo?"

All eyes are on me, and for a moment, silence stretches in the large meeting room, until finally, Chaos breaks it.

"None yet. Wrath and Noose, clear out his shit at the bunkhouse, don't leave an inch untouched."

"You think he was working for someone?"

"I don't trust a fuckin' soul, you all know that. But I dunno. This seems personal, almost."

"But why Rolo?"

"Did he have beef with anyone that we didn't know of? Wasn't he the one who sponsored Garrett? There's too many fuckin' prospects right now."

"We had to! We took too many hits after the Widowmakers attacked us here," Sin adds.

"We need a deep dive, pull all the prospects in. Time to test their knowledge. We aren't a herd of sheep, we're fucking Heathens. And it's time to remind them all what that means."

We all leave church and filter into the common area of the clubhouse. I bounce on the soles of my boots, cracking my neck side to side and shaking out my hands, like an MMA fighter getting ready for a match. This is where I shine. Sin may be the club's go-to for being willing to get anything done, but I excel at torture.

All the club members file into the room, the prospects lined up in front of us, including Luca, who's still healing from his gunshot wounds. I take my time, eyeing each and every one of them. I may not be good at reading people, or knowing between right and wrong, or anything about what's socially accepted, but I'm the epitome of feral, and I can pull answers from them without breaking a sweat.

"One of our men was murdered in cold blood. A prospect—one of you—was shot and almost died. Who knows Garrett?"

A younger kid, not much older than eighteen, is the first to speak up. He's got a head full of ashy brown hair and deeply set eyes. He's scrawny as fuck, but he holds himself well.

"He kept to himself. Didn't talk to us much, just grunts and head nods."

Chaos doesn't look amused. "That doesn't tell us anything we need to know in order to find him."

Sin stands next to me, his fists clenching at his sides as he looks over each man, looking for something I'm missing.

"You," Sin says, his voice deep and angry. He points to one of the larger dudes, standing in a pair of black joggers and a charcoal grey hoodie. His lips are pursed, and he doesn't seem shocked that Sin is calling on him. Wrath drags a chair to the middle of the room, the wood scraping on wood piercing my ears. Noises have always bothered me. It's the silence that I crave most. "Take a seat, buddy. Let's have a chat, yeah?"

Sin grips the man's shoulder, guiding him and pressing him firmly into the seat. I watch the other prospects, but can't get a read on them until Wrath nods his head in the direction of another one. Similar build, slightly shorter, hair growing back from being recently shaved in the last few months. I cock my head to the side, looking at the one sitting in the chair. Same hair. Clearly growing in. I lean into Wrath's space, whispering. "Get me a razor."

Wrath's eyes bulge for a moment before he looks at the ground of the clubhouse. "We'll need to take him down into the basement if you're gonna skin anyone else. No one wants to clean up that shit from the clubhouse."

"I've never skinned anyone."

"Yeah, you did. That night you and Rogue took care of those few Widowmakers at the drug den."

I think back to that moment that shouldn't feel so long ago.

"What the fuck happened?"

"Apparently he wanted to make a coat," Rogue tells Wrath as their eyes look at me from my boots to my head. I admit, I'm looking a little gruesome. The man was a squirter and covered me in blood. Pretty sure there are brain matter chunks on my vest and for sure on my neck.

"A coat? Like a human one?" Wrath asks, looking queasy.

"Unfortunately."

Wrath gives Rogue a look that I can't quite read, and I suddenly feel itchy all over. Rogue grabs a towel and some bandages and helps to get the wound on my arm taken care of. Luckily, it's just a flesh wound, and I didn't even notice it until I started oozing. Blood leaks all over Rogue, both from me and the fucker I killed. He doesn't look too happy about that, and I can't help but smile.

"You're a crazy sonofabitch; you know that, right?" Wrath says, making me laugh. I throw my head backward, cackling into the night. If they only truly knew just how fucking crazy I actually am. It's why I was kept locked up. To contain me. To protect themselves and others. That didn't end like they thought it would.

"What the hell's wrong with you, dude?"

"You two idiots think I would actually skin someone?" I ask, curious about their answer.

They share a private look, and my eyes narrow in their direction. "You do know what your road name means, yeah? And how you got it?" I'm very much aware. I crave evil. I am evil.

"Yeah, but I wouldn't skin anyone," I lie. I think about it for a moment, the process, what it would be like to actually skin a human. Would I wait for them to be dead, or would I attempt it while they were still alive? I bet the screams would be pretty. Messy, though, and a lot of work. I'd probably get hungry and need to take breaks. And if I needed to take a break, I'd probably want to fuck. Then he'd just start to rot and decompose, half-skinned. Probably not worth the effort when there are plenty of other ways to make someone hurt. "Yeah, no. I couldn't. I stabbed him in the neck and hit an artery. Or two. Shit erupts like a geyser." I motion an explosion with both of my hands as I talk. "There's no stopping it once it starts. Did you know hearts are slippery?"

"I remember. And I thought about it, but I've never skinned someone, and I couldn't do it. Not worth my time. I want to shave his head."

"You want to shave his head?"

"I. Want. To. Shave. His. Head."

Wrath punches me in the arm, earning us a few stares from onlookers. "For fuck's sake. Why?"

"Just a hunch."

Wrath rolls his eyes, but he walks away in search of a razor.

"What's your name?" Sin asks the man sitting in the chair.

"Jason."

"Alright, Jason, what do you know about Garrett?"

"Not much. Like he said, he was quiet, didn't talk much." He shrugs, and I don't fucking like it. Why isn't he taking this more seriously?

"You see, Jason, I don't believe you. Men who have something to hide, they behave a certain way, overly confident that they won't get caught, won't be questioned, and, if they are, that they're good enough at lying and deceiving that it'll go unchecked." Sin squats down to look Jason eye to eye. "You know why they call me Sin, Jason?"

"No. But I don't—" The punch to his face comes hard and fast. I wince, my eyes squinting and my face screwing up. Jason's head snaps to the side as blood flies from his mouth, and there's an audible click on the floor from where a tooth lands.

Sin is a gigantic motherfucker, and his haymakers will rattle even the toughest man's skull. I'd need to bring a knife to a fist fight to get on even ground with him, just to make it fair. "You answered the question, now shut the fuck up!"

Wrath returns with hair clippers and hands them to me.

"What'd I miss?"

"Sin just knocked his tooth out."

"Damn. That didn't take long."

"Nope, but this is already taking too long for me," I tell him, cracking my neck again.

"I got my road name because there is no law, divine or otherwise, that I won't break to get what I need, to protect what I love. I will do anything, but it's not me you should be afraid of today." Sin looks over at me and nods, and I step forward, a slow grin spreading across my face. "Do you know why we call him Malice, Jason? Because he *wants* to inflict pain, *wants* to induce suffering. He doesn't just do it because he has to, like me; he *craves* it."

A shiver runs up my spine, and I bristle, even though he's talking about me. I step up to the plate, wanting to get to the bottom of this, wanting to uncover the truth about what happened to my friend. My patch brother.

"Jason, is it? That's a stupid fucking name, Jason." I don't know if it is, really, but it sounded cool to insult him before I physically hurt him. I click on the clippers, the battery vibrating to life in my palm. I jerk his head to the side, shaving him down to the skin. Bits of hair fall to our feet, dusting the floor. Then I step back and admire my handiwork. Slightly patchy, but it got the job done. I find what I was looking for, and I look over the snake tattoo, a coiled snake poised to strike. I flick the tattoo at the side of his head. "What's the snake tat, Jason?"

"It's a random tattoo, man. What's the big deal?"

I jerk my head to the other ugly fucker Sin was looking at. Wrath grabs him, forcing him down onto his knees next to Jason. This one puts up a little more of a fight, but we easily get him down, and I repeat the process, shaving his head down to the skin and finding the same tattoo.

I get back in Jason's face, gripping his cheeks and forcing his mouth to hollow out as I squeeze them together.

"What's the big deal? The big fucking deal, *Jason*, is that you two assholes wear the same tattoo I saw on Garrett. I don't know about you, but I'd say that's a big fucking deal. Pretty sure the men standing behind me think it's a big fucking deal, too." I stand up straighter, releasing his mouth and shoving his head backward. "What's the tattoo mean, boys?"

The two men in front of us look at each other, Jason making a subtle shake of his head. Rage overflows my bloodstream. Images of Rolo lying on the ground, shot in cold blood, Morgan falling to her knees and screaming in emotional pain I could never fathom.

"Well, if it doesn't mean anything to you lads, then I'll just remove it, yeah?" I love the look that fills their eyes, and I throw my head back in a laugh. "Does that scare you? This will be nothing compared to what I'll do if you don't start talking."

I start with the first fucker, Jason, and flick out my knife. His fight or flight must finally kick in because he stands quickly, throwing a piss-poor attempt at a punch in my direction. Asshole number two takes that as his sign to run, so much more pathetic than asshole number one, at least that one's trying to fight.

Neither matters. They'll both die here today.

We quickly subdue them, tying them to chairs, and then I get to work, slicing into poor Jason's head and cutting off a piece of his scalp. Blood pours out of him, and I jump back, tossing the piece of flesh to the side. It falls to the ground with a wet slap.

"Damn!" I yell, looking back for Saige. "Did you know head wounds bleed that much? Like a river!" Saige rolls her eyes, mouthing "show off" to me. His screams are brain-rattling. I'm sure it doesn't feel good, and he's getting one hell of a headache right about now. But the slicing of the skin was cool. Maybe I should rethink the skinning thing after all. Very messy, though. I'm sure Chaos is pissed we're doing this unexpectedly here.

I move to dumbass number two and lift my blade. Blood flows down my hand as I make my first slice. I decide to go slower this time, sawing at him rather than slicing, trying a new technique to see if his screams are any more or less than Jason's.

Once I've finished, I toss the bloody chunk of skin to the floor to pair up with the other one, their ugly-ass tattoos facing upward. Then I take a step back, letting Chaos step forward.

"You ready to tell us what the fuck those tats mean and who the fuck you all are?"

"Kingsnakes MC," the second ugly fucker mutters as blood trickles down his face.

"And what the fuck are you doing in my club?"

"Orders."

"To infiltrate the Hell's Heathens? Why was one of our men targeted?"

"Fuck you. That's all you're getting from him," the first one yells.

"Ohhh, Jason, you are not a smart man. That's okay. Your buddy here can watch while I have my play time," I taunt as I step forward again.

I take my time torturing him. Slowly, methodically, but then I get messy as the rage builds, the images flashing behind my eyelids again until Jason's entrails are hanging out of his stomach and stretching down to the floor, and his face is a hollow sphere. Minus his brain. I let him keep that.

When I turn to the next man, he's pissed himself, puke lining the front of the leather cut he doesn't deserve, shaking in his chair, his teeth clattering together like he's cold.

"You will die tonight, no matter what. But how you leave this plane is going to depend on what you know and if you're willing to divulge that information," Sin tells him. I huff my annoyance because I'm not fucking done yet.

"Rolo's brother is the new president of the Kingsnakes. He wanted him dead. Our job was to get in and get out."

"So why the fuck did you stick around?"

"'Cause you fucking feed us."

"You don't get food where you came from? You thought you'd just come in here, kill our brother, and you could just stay so you didn't have to go hungry? Fuck you. Where are they?"

"Clubhouse is a few hours west, on the coast, but I don't remember where. I was a new recruit."

"Sure you don't. That all?"

He nods, and then Chaos turns his back on him, his eyes meeting Saige's, giving her a subtle nod. My shoulders deflate.

"Rude," I say under my breath.

Saige walks up to him and runs her knife across his neck from ear to ear. Blood gushes from the wound, opening it up further and spilling down his chest. He gurgles and shakes, his eyes wide and scared.

"Always the same," Saige mutters, rolling her eyes.

"Show-off," I whisper to her as she passes me by.

"Shave all their heads. Every single one of them is going to be bald by nightfall. I don't care if you have to tie them down; check them all. We don't sleep until we know everyone under this roof isn't affiliated with the fucking Kingsnakes," Chaos shouts as he grabs Saige around the waist and hauls her out of the room.

We nod, ready to get to work on the rest of the prospects. Then it's hunting season.

CHAPTER FIVE

MALICE

The crunch of my combat boots on gravel hits my ears as I step off my bike in front of the funeral home. The sun is out, and I squint my eyes against the bright onslaught. I'd much rather it be cloudy and overcast. Hell, I'll take rain over this bright sunshine bullshit. I'll never understand the people who prefer the sun to moody clouds. The sun makes too many things visible in the light when I'd prefer they stay hidden in the darkness.

This is the last thing I want to be doing today. Wrath and Sin both offered to come with me, but I know it's something I need to do alone. Being a member of Hell's Heathens Motorcycle Club comes with its risks. We've lost patch brothers, siblings, parents, and it's one of those things that just comes with the territory . . . *literally*. I've seen the people around me in pain, I've seen them lose themselves completely to the dark side that is always simmering right under our skin, but I've never truly felt it until now.

Losing Rolo has left a chasm I don't know what to do with. I shove my hands into my pockets, cracking my neck side to side as I walk up the front steps to the Amberwood Mortuary. Not sure what the difference between a mortuary and a funeral home is, but here we are.

A gaunt, elderly man meets me at the front of the building. My head rears back slightly at the look of him, and if I wasn't easily spooked, he'd have done it. His eyes are sunken in, his cheeks hollowed out, with dark spots mottling his face. What's left of his hair is white and wispy, with bushy, unkept eyebrows that look like fat, fluffy caterpillars. He looks more suited to be *in* a casket than selling one.

I make a mental note to start eating more green vegetables and fruits. I've never cared about my physical appearance, but I'd like to age better than this. He's got one foot in the ground already, the poor guy. I wonder if anyone's told him he doesn't have much time left. I open my mouth to let him know he should start making his arrangements, but then I remember I'm actually here for a reason.

A fucked-up reason that never should have happened.

"I'm here to meet with George," I say, hoping like hell this isn't George and his name is Chester, or Clarence, even a Barney would suit him. But, no, luck doesn't ever seem to be on my side, and the skeleton man in front of me is George.

"I'm George. You must be here on behalf of Hell's Heathens. We're happy to take care of you all." Happy? That our brother was murdered and we've lost one of our own? I arch a brow at him, giving him an opportunity to try again before I nail him to the cross in front of us and burn his establishment to the ground. "I misspoke. We're very sorry for your loss, and we will make sure we do our very best for you and your loved one."

Better. Still not great.

I follow Ebenezer through the small lobby, the potent scent of floral arrangements assaulting my nose. I sneeze once, then another time, my eyes filling with tears.

"God bless you."

"Oh, for fuck's sake," I mutter under my breath as I roll my eyes into the back of my head.

The lobby opens up to a large showroom, with several rooms off of it. We walk farther into the space, passing by what looks to be a chapel and an office. The room has vaulted ceilings with natural light spilling in from the skylights above us. We're surrounded by caskets. Or are they coffins?

"As you can see, you have many different options. Are you wanting him buried or crem—"

"Are these boxes caskets or coffins?" I ask as I knock the back of my knuckles against the closest one, staring at my reflection in the shiny wood.

"Uhh, well, it, uh, depends entirely on the shape. Caskets have hinges and are what's common in the US, where coffins are found in other parts of the world. I'm sorry, do you want a *coffin*?"

Would Rolo want a coffin? I probably should have asked Morgan. She'd know. But she asked us to handle it, which is customary anyway for him being a ranked member. Granted, we just do normal boxes, and they go six feet under on our property. I close my eyes for a brief moment, the pain lancing right through my chest. Fuck, I can't believe he's gone. Everything I have is because he gave me my second chance at life. He's the reason I'm here.

I scan the room, counting the doors and *caskets*, tapping each count with my middle finger against my leg. Old Man Winter continues to talk, but his voice is drowned out when I see a flash of baby pink from the room off in the distance behind him. I lean to the side, trying to track what I saw. Was that a woman? The pain fades, replaced with morbid curiosity and something stronger than I've ever felt before. A pull. Like something inside me just snapped taut.

"All of that sounds great, Georgie. Let's make it happen. Send the final bill to the Hell's Heathens MC. I trust you can find the address?" I cut him off mid-sentence, wanting to be done with this conversation.

"Ye-yes, Mr. Lawson. Tell Mr. Young we're sorry for his loss and grateful for his trust and business. We'll take care of everything expertly as we've been doing for many years."

When he hobbles toward his office, mumbling something under his breath, I know he's expecting me to leave. Our business has concluded, but what he doesn't know won't hurt him.

Keeping my steps silent, I walk to the back of the building, passing the rows of caskets, flower arrangements, and easels, feeling a pull from the center of my chest leading me. The carpet ends at the edge of a large, open, heavy door, turning into sealed concrete that seems to slope toward a drain in the center of the room. Very similar to the one we have in a hidden basement under one of our garages. This must be where they drain the bodies.

My eyes turn up from the floor, only to have the breath stolen from my lungs. Lit up under the bright lights of the room is the most ethereal creature I've ever seen. I'm bewitched. Mesmerized. A tiny wisp of a woman floats around the room, utterly clueless that a predator lurks just outside her doorway, that danger is hovering, entranced, captivated by the bright energy radiating off of her. It's nearly blinding.

She's light.

Hair the color of rose gold sits above her shoulders. She's wearing a flowy, dark green dress with daisies all over it. My eyes squint at the rain boots on her feet, and I wonder if that's intentional because of her job or a style choice. She leans forward, dusting something over the eyelids of a dead body laid out on the table below her.

I'm no stranger to death; it's been my constant companion since I was a child. A dark cloud shrouds me, follows me everywhere I go. But her? This mystical little pixie, fluttering around the dead like a butterfly, she's no stranger to death either, yet sunshine hovers over her like it's an honor to bathe her in its rays.

I watch hidden from the doorway, my head cocked to the side as I admire her while she works. She must have headphones in her ears or a song playing in her head as she slowly dances to a beat only she can hear. I wonder what it is.

I wait, hoping for a glimpse of this pixie's face. My fingers dig into my palms, wanting to go to her, wanting to spin her around to finally get the vision I need to tame the demanding beast inside me. She works silently, peacefully, completely homed in on decorating this man's face.

I've never given thought to why a dead body would need makeup, but then an image of the dead bodies I've seen flashes before my eyes, and it makes sense. No one wants to say goodbye to the ones I've seen. But usually, they're quite mangled everywhere by the time the light burns out behind their eyes.

The pixie in front of me continues to sway her hips side to side, bobbing her head slightly as she dips a small brush into some powder, and goes back to work. My cock hardens rapidly behind my tight denim jeans, the zipper digging painfully into my length. Downside of never wearing underwear. A hazard of the decision, for sure.

Unable to control the urge a moment longer, I take a step forward into the room just as she's reaching for a new tool, her eyes catching me out of the corner.

"Cheese and crackers! You scared me!" Well, shit, that wasn't my intention. I walk further into her space, my head cocked to the side, enraptured. She doesn't run, or balk, or scream, or cry. Someone like her seems like she would run in the face of danger, of a predator. I know what I look like, and I know I don't look friendly. I would run if I saw myself, too.

She's all bright colors, sunshine, and happiness. As if all the good in the world has been bundled up in this tiny little human. I catch a glimpse of our reflection in the stainless-steel appliances around us. We're starkly opposite. I'm darkness and death. She's light and life.

My eyes roam over her face, quickly trying to count all the freckles that dust the tops of her cheeks and the bridge of her nose. Her eyes are the color of the sky, blue and endless, her pink hair framing her petite face around her chin.

"Stunning," I breathe roughly as I take her in, trying to commit every one of her features to memory. Her cheeks bloom a pretty pink that matches her hair. She's adorable. I lift my tattooed finger, the black nail polish chipped and peeling, reaching out slowly to run it down the length of her nose, feeling the slight bump in the center, before running my finger across my own and then dropping it back to my side.

Malice lurches forward, and an overwhelming emotion takes over that I can't hold back. It's more than protectiveness; it's obsession, complete and utter loss of control.

Her eyes squint, her delicate lips turning up in a half-smile that jump-starts my heart. It's . . . *beating.*

"Who hurt you?" I demand, my voice coming out harsher than I mean to.

Her eyes flash with something I can't read, too quick for me to study it. "Hurt me? No one hurt me."

"The bump, it's from a break?"

"I was born with it, silly."

Her voice is silk, wrapping around my heart and squeezing as gently as a freshly spun spider's web. Could this be the one? My queen? A weird sensation blooms inside my stomach, swirling and mixing, my heartbeat starting to race behind my ribs. There's a knot lodged in my throat, and I'm suddenly overwhelmed with . . . nerves? I don't get nervous. Not since . . . *then.* Back when I was scared. Back when I was alone and cold.

I shake my head. This is different. She isn't them. She is all that's good.

"You're the most beautiful creature I've ever seen. What's your name?"

She smiles so brightly I feel it in the marrow of my bones. So soft, and kind, and genuine. So *warm*.

"Monroe. What's yours?"

"*Monroe*." The prettiest name for the prettiest girl I've ever seen.

"That's my name, what's yours?" she laughs. A melody that I want to hear over and over again for the rest of my life.

"Crew."

"Hi, Crew."

"Hi, Monroe."

We stare at each other for moments, minutes, maybe longer. Until my phone vibrates in my pocket, pulling me back down to Earth. It's a call I can't ignore.

"Until next time, *Monroe*."

Without another word, I turn and leave. I'm not a man who restrains or denies himself. Of anything. If I want something, I find a way to get it. Walking away from Monroe feels like I'm being gagged and beaten, shoved in the cage from my childhood, and kept from what I need most. Before today, that was food, shelter, sex, and blood. Now, all that exists is Monroe.

I will make her mine. I need to.

CHAPTER SIX

MONROE

My cheeks burn from the smile that refuses to leave my face. What an absolutely bizarre interaction. Who was he? With his ripped-up denim jeans, plain black T-shirt, and leather vest covered in patches, his wild blond hair, and eyes so dark they almost appeared black, he looked every bit as dangerous as he was going for. I recognized the leather vest covered in patches, and I know exactly what it means. He has a motorcycle club affiliation. I've heard of them. Everyone in Amberwood knows who the Hell's Heathens are.

Both my parents are high school teachers in Amberwood and know most of the families who live here; they've seen their fair share of former students be recruited or end up in the club. They don't have a bad reputation in Amberwood; in fact, they do a lot of good for our community. But they are still a violent club, and I've heard the rumors.

Even still, not an ounce of fear traveled through me as we

stood toe-to-toe, just two strangers curiously looking at each other. What an incredibly odd greeting.

The thoughts follow me the entire walk home. After he left, I couldn't seem to focus and packed up for an early evening. It was late enough in the day, and Mr. George doesn't mind me choosing my own hours as long as I'm getting everything done when we need it to be done by.

I've never been under such scrutiny before, but despite his rough physical edges, he had a childlike wonder about him that is so rare in adults who have typically been beaten down by the world around them. I've seen that happen more times than I'd care to admit. It's refreshing to see the opposite. Especially in a man who's a Hell's Heathen.

The walk to my house takes twenty minutes, and once I open the small gate that surrounds our little front yard, I can already hear the noise from inside. A smile stretches across my face as I skip up the steps, the paint whitewashed and aging from the ever-changing weather of the Pacific Northwest.

I've lived here my entire life, in the small town of Amberwood, Washington. It's quaint, sitting at the base of the Olympic National Forest, less than a day's drive to the Pacific Ocean, and blanketed by a near constant cloud cover. I don't mind the lack of sun so much, but on days like today when it peeks through the clouds, I soak up its rays until it goes back into hiding. I love the feeling of the sunshine on my skin.

My hand reaches out to the aging bronze doorknob, giving it a twist, pulling it upward slightly at the same time as I throw my hip into the center to give it just a little pressure. The door opens with a whine, the boisterous noise escaping outward and ringing in my ears.

From upstairs, my twelve-year-old sister, Lucy, attempts to play her trombone, the noise traveling through the small, multigenerational home I share with my grandparents, my parents, my seven siblings, two cats, Eros and Psyche, and a guinea pig named Goose. You can credit my mother's love of Greek Mythology for the pet names, and my sweet sister for Goose.

My fourteen-year-old twin brothers run past me as I kick off my boots, tackling each other into the ground, Wyatt attempting to steal the football from Miles. I respond on instinct, my hands reaching out to grab Wyatt's shirt and pulling him off.

"Hey! Hey, you two! No football in the house, remember? Why don't you take it outside? That's the whole perk of having a huge backyard."

"Oh! Hi, Monroe! When did you get home?" Miles asks as he stands up and wraps his arms around my shoulders. Hard to believe these two are bigger than me, and they're only fourteen.

"Just now. How is everyone?"

Wyatt shrugs while Miles shoves him. "Everyone's good. How was painting dead people?"

"I don't paint dead people, dingus. I apply makeup to make them feel beautiful one last time. And I do a lot more as a mortician than just put makeup on them."

"Yeah, but they're dead, why's it matter?" Wyatt jokes. Typical fourteen-year-old boy.

"We've been through this before. You need to clean out your ears. Because it's respectful," I tell him as I rub my hands over his brown locks, further messing up his purposefully messy hair. "Even if their souls have passed on, we should honor their bodies before they're taken to their final resting place. Our bodies are good to us and make living possible. It's a good send-off, don't you think?"

"I think you're doing really cool things, Roe," Miles says with a proud smile.

"Yeah, but it's still weird to have a sister who's a mortician," Wyatt adds. These two may be twins, but they are complete and utter opposites. I roll my eyes, setting off toward the kitchen and the scent of olive oil, garlic, and onions.

My grandparents sit side by side in a loveseat in our living room as I walk through, my nana's glasses perched precariously on the edge of her nose as she looks down at the new e-reader she got for her birthday last week. She's always been an avid reader, and we thought having control over the font size would help her. Turns out we were right, and she's read more books in seven days than she had in the previous month.

My grandpa relaxes next to her, dozing off to another episode of *The Office*. They've been married for an eternity, and I'm hopeful to find that kind of love someday.

"Hey, Grandma, I hope you're ready for Saturday!"

"You know I am, my girl!"

Before continuing on, I drop a kiss on each of their heads, my grandpa reaching up and giving my hand a gentle squeeze without opening his eyes. My heart swells.

I find my mom in the kitchen, peeling roasted Roma tomatoes.

"Hey, Mom. Spaghetti for dinner?"

"Your favorite, my darling girl. How was work?"

My mind immediately drifts to Crew, the mysterious, curious man with the darkest eyes I've ever seen. The feeling of his finger as it trailed down the bridge of my nose. It's not typical that a stranger would feel comfortable enough to reach out and touch another, but he didn't seem to be doing it to breach any potential physical boundaries I may have; it was almost as though he genuinely didn't know it would be frowned upon. It was endearing. Sweet, even.

"It was a good day. Did you get to spend any time outside? It was beautiful out there."

"I did, went for a walk this morning, and ate my lunch outside."

"Good, Mom, I'm glad you could soak it up. Summer will be over before you know it, and you'll be back in a stuffy classroom. Need any help?"

"Always. Wash those mushrooms for me?"

"You got it."

Together, my mom and I finish preparing her red sauce, letting it simmer on the stove while she gets the pasta ready. I wash and chop some veggies, tossing together a quick summer salad to pair with it.

The deafening chime of the dinner bell rings out loudly from where my mom shakes the rope attached to the bell near my head. Then the stampede erupts from above us. I smirk over at my mom, knowing how much she loves having us all under one roof.

I'm the oldest, and at twenty-eight, there's quite an age gap between me and the rest of my siblings. I'm their only biological child, and my seven sisters and brothers were adopted. After so many years being an only child, by the time my sister, Aurora, was brought home, I was ten and so happy to share life with someone else that the gap didn't ever matter. My parents kept adding after that, and we've been so lucky to have such a huge family.

My mom and I finish setting everything out on the bar top just as everyone lines up. The easiest way to feed the masses here is an assembly line, first-come, first-served style. There's definitely no hierarchy in this house.

"Oh, hi, Roe, you're home!" my little brother, Cooper, yells excitedly. "Did you know that sloths can hold their breath for up to forty whole minutes?"

"Ooo, you got me with this one! I didn't know that, Cooper!"

"Yep! And octopuses have three hearts and blue blood!" he states. Cooper was nonverbal until about a year ago, and it was like a switch went off for him, because now he's a little chatterbox. Sometimes it's still a little challenging to understand his words, especially when he's excited about his animals, but he's been making such incredible progress in speech therapy.

"I did know this one! I think I'd like to see an octopus someday, what about you?"

"Yes!" he squeals, almost dropping his plate.

I help him put noodles on his plate, adding the sauce to the side, and the salad next, making sure the items aren't touching, just the way he prefers. With a smile on his face, Cooper takes his food and finds his spot at our extra-large dining room table.

The rest of us follow, and in no time, we're all gathered around with plates full of food. Growing up, it was customary that we always had family dinner together in the evenings. It became especially important as our family expanded. It was so easy for someone to fall into the background, and my mom and dad wanted to make sure there was a set time, every single day, that we all checked in with each other.

Cue our nightly—and mandatory—pit and peak.

"Monroe, I believe it's your turn to start tonight," my dad says, his voice jovial and so full of love. You'd think the man would be exhausted after raising all these kids at his age, but he says we keep him young.

I think for a moment, my mind flicking to Crew and deciding that interaction was the peak of my day. It was so out of the ordinary, and for some reason, I can't shake the impression he left on me. However, I decide to keep that little bit of information to myself. A little secret that's just for me.

"The pit of my day was that someone's loved one was brought into the mortuary, and he was very young. It's always hard when young people come in. But the peak of my day was that the sun came out; it made everything better. Your turn, Atticus," I say to my fifteen-year-old brother to the left of me.

Together, we eat our dinner, and one by one share the pits and peaks of our days. Sometimes going off on a little side conversation around someone, like my sister, Hazel, whose pit was that Tommy from across the street told her no one would come to her birthday party next week. It's so hard for me to grasp bullying behavior. Especially amongst kids.

After dinner, I help my dad clean up, doing the dishes and watching the sun set behind the mountains from their large kitchen window. The sky stretches with blues, pinks, and yellows. I love living in this small, peaceful part of the world.

"Thanks for helping out, kiddo," my dad says as he finishes drying the last pot.

"Happy to. I think I'm going to head home early; tomorrow will come quickly."

"Don't I know it. We're proud of you, you know that?"

I dry my hands off and turn to face my dad directly. Having gone grey younger, he has a full head of silvery strands, ice-blue eyes that match my own, and a bump on the bridge of his nose. My finger trails along the bridge of mine as if feeling the phantom touch of Crew. Why am I still thinking about this man? What was it about him that my mind keeps returning to? His eyes flash behind my own, the way they lingered and held mine a second longer than polite, as if he was lost weighing possibilities. And then the way he left me standing there, moving with such controlled ease, like he's gone through life and learned to conserve his energy, learned to purposefully be quiet. I didn't hear him when he approached, and had my back been turned to him again, I wouldn't have heard or felt him leave.

"Monroe? You okay, honey?"

I return back to reality, realizing I just completely checked out.

"Of course I am. Just lost in thought."

"Okay, we're always here if you need to talk about anything."

"I appreciate that, Dad. I promise, I'm okay. Everything is good. Great, even." Which is the truth. My dad wraps me in a hug that warms my soul, and I breathe in his comforting, woodsy scent.

“Good night, kiddo.”

“Night, Dad.”

After saying goodnight to everyone else, I grab my rainboots and bag, slipping out the side door barefoot. I lock the door behind me, jogging down the steps and crossing the yard to my tiny home, the grass cool on the soles of my feet.

After I turned twenty-one, my dad helped me turn the large storage shed at the back of the property into a mini home just for me. My parents refuse to let me pay rent, but I help out in other ways, saving my income instead. As much as I love living with my family, it is nice to have my own space, while still being close to share everyday things.

I unlock my front door, stepping into my space and flicking on the lamp to my right. It's one large studio, with a bathroom off by itself, and a kitchenette. The walls are painted, with twinkling fairy lights trailing along the edge of the space. Plants sit on most surfaces and a few wall shelves. My daybed functions as both my bed and my couch, and since I'm too busy to occupy friends or boyfriends, it works perfectly just for me.

I take a seat at my piano, a beautiful keyboard that I saved far too long to be able to afford, and stretch out my fingers. Then I play, letting myself get lost in “Fur Elise” by Beethoven, its soft melody transcending me to someplace else. There, I'm not Monroe, I'm not a daughter, or sister, or worker bee, not the girl everyone in town looks at with pity in their eyes. Here, within this music, I just get to exist and feel.

I play for what seems like hours, easily flowing from one song to the next, until my fingers are tired and my eyes grow heavy.

After getting ready for bed, I slip into a satin nightgown with thin straps and lace that lines the hem at my thigh. I don't have anyone to wear it for, but it makes me feel good and sexy, so I wear it anyway. I grab my journal from my small end table, my nightly ritual, and write about my day. To no surprise, the only thing I want to write about is *him*.

Dear Diary,

Today I met a man. He was mysterious, dark, and dangerous but he was also curious and intriguing. There's something about him that held me hostage. I don't know why I decided against telling my family about him, but something inside me wanted to keep it to myself. Like he was a secret. Nothing overly exciting or interesting happens in my life, which is good, safe. But this was something new and it was refreshing. The man was so expressive but also so shrouded in secrets. He had the kind of presence that quiets everything around him without trying. He wasn't loud or flashy, or vibrant, he was just there, like a shadow, dark, observant, and stealthy. I didn't hear him or feel him until I saw him. That should frighten me. The fact that it didn't should scare me even more. And the fact that I'm intrigued? I'm not sure what to do about that fact or what that says about me.

I hope I see him again.

CHAPTER SEVEN

MALICE

“Why are you looking at Maya like that?”

“Like what?” I reply to Wrath, his perfectly coiffed hair slicked and stupidly perfect. I wonder how he gets his hair to stay put like that. Mine’s always wild and crazy, no matter what I do. Wrath’s is always perfect. Such a pretty boy.

“Like you’re disgusted. You’ve hooked up with her a dozen times.”

I look back over at the patch bunny, the bottom of her ass peeking out of her tight denim shorts as she bends over the pool table. Wrath is right, I’ve hooked up with Maya tons of times over the years, same with Savannah and Delilah. Wrath has, too. Patch bunnies are here for all of us, and most of my patch brothers have openly passed them around depending on the night and if they’re willing—which they usually are.

Any time I’ve needed to clear my head, someone’s been readily available, eager, and more than willing to spend a few hours in my dungeon being my plaything. Except lately, all I've wanted to do since Rolo died is spill blood.

But looking at them now, there's no desire coursing through me. The opposite, actually. Maybe I am disgusted. Not by them, per se, they're great and haven't done anything wrong, but the idea of being with them. All I want now is my little pink-haired pixie. Just the thought of her alone makes me harder than steel.

I hope she's not already taken. Sin was way too easy on Bristol. That goddamn pet bunny made our VP soft. He was patient and kind, even though she was engaged to someone else, waiting until Bristol came to him. There's no way I'd be okay with that. Knowing my little one was sleeping next to another man night after night?

Fuck that shit.

The thought alone makes anger surge to the surface.

"I didn't know I was."

"Since when don't you have complete control over your facial features and body language?"

"The hell if I know," I snap, standing quickly, pulling out my knife, and flipping it around in my hand.

Wrath jerks back in his seat and puts his hands up. "Whoa. Whoa. Okay, buddy. Calm down."

"What's with the million fucking questions?"

"I get that you're angry, brother, but I am not the bad guy here. We'll find them."

I sit back down in my seat, flipping the knife over in my hand.

One.

Two.

Three.

Four.

I close my eyes and let myself picture Monroe. The sun beating down on her flawless, freckled skin, the way the rose gold of her hair shimmers in the light. My temper gradually decreases, and when I open my eyes and look at everyone around me, for the first time since Rolo brought me to the clubhouse, I don't want to be here.

I stand up, pocketing my knife in its sheath, and turning to leave.

"Where are you going?" Wrath yells.

"I've got shit to do."

The nippy summer air cools my heated skin, and as I swing my leg over my bike, starting it up, I'm eager to feel the wind at a much higher speed. I peel out of my spot, the back of my bike spinning off to the side. I correct her quickly, straightening up and taking off down the long gravel driveway of the clubhouse.

The gates open as the sentries see me coming. I half expect to see Rolo standing out here and am startled to see Noose instead. Then I remember, it's because Rolo is fucking gone. As our club treasurer, he was never needed out here working with the sentries, but he always was, anyway. Wanting to mentor, wanting to shape and heal. Rolo was the fucking best of us. He truly believed he could save us all. Give us lost boys some place to go and have a home.

The sun has long set, the road only visible by the light of the high moon and my headlights. I know these mountain roads like the back of my hand, and I push my bike hard as I ride into town, leaning into every curve, feeling the wind ripple over my skin, my hair whipping around wildly.

I park my bike just on the edge of town by the old diner. My stomach grumbles, reminding me that I haven't eaten since yesterday. Maggie's has got some of the best sandwiches I've ever had. Wrath and I both are addicted. We frequently hit it up, and Wrath flirts with one of the waitresses who usually gives him extra shit on his. *Asshole.*

Not wanting to be seen, I slink through town, staying in the alleys between the brick buildings and away from the cobblestone sidewalks and streetlights. It's always been easy for me to go undetected, having learned from a very young age to never be seen or heard. Especially if I wanted to survive.

My destination looms in front of me like a beacon, sitting tall on the rounded corner of Main Street. The all-brick building looks more like a small cathedral than it does a mortuary. But I suppose the two can't truly be differentiated, both serving as the bridge between life and death.

I stuff my hands into my front pockets as I make my way to the back of the building. The forest stretches endlessly behind me, a mix of massive trees and flowers, wildlife probably tucked away for the evening. Unless they're nocturnal. Like me. The most dangerous creatures hunt at night.

It's easy enough to break into Amberwood Mortuary, the back door easily unlocking. I roll my eyes at the lack of security. Even though our small town is pretty safe, all things considered, petty theft and breaking and entering happen. I guess not that many people want to break into a fucking mortuary where they've got dead bodies in the freezer.

After closing the door behind me, I take in my surroundings, seeing just enough with the moon shining in through the large windows that line the chapel and the skylights above us.

The words 'Memento Mori' are carved into a stone archway above the sanctuary, a lectern in the center. I roll my eyes. *Idiots*. There's no preparing for mortality. It's going to drag you away, and you'll never be ready to go. Death is a shroud, a force that pulls you into eternal darkness, and no amount of reminders that it's coming will force people to live a brighter life.

After running my fingers over the stainless-steel table in the room I found Monroe in, disappointed to find her scent doesn't linger anywhere in the sterile environment, I navigate through the maze at the back. Finally finding what I'm looking for, I waltz into the office. File cabinets line one wall, and something tells me Georgie-boy isn't up with the technology of things and keeps his paperwork trail hidden away in the filing cabinet instead of a computer.

I use my key to pick the lock, opening the top drawer. I know nothing about Monroe, and that needs to change. I flick through the manila folders, when my phone vibrates in the tight pocket of my jeans. I pull it out, the screen lighting up.

Biker Besties

Chaos: Your fucking tracker is off. Where are you?

I roll my eyes, ignoring him and pocketing my phone. For someone who hates group chats, Chaos sure as shit uses it more than any of us. What a dingus. He's probably worried that I'm out hunting the Kingsnakes by myself again, which he strictly forbade me to do. Not that I listen. Most of the time I do, but sometimes not so much.

"Ah ha!" I finally find what I'm looking for and pull out the thin manilla folder and take a seat in the worn-leather chair at the desk, propping my combat boots up on the top and crossing my ankles.

I pull off the wallet photo of her and hold it between my thumb and forefinger. She's wearing a pretty baby-blue blouse that ties in a bow at her delicate collarbone. The freckles on her nose and cheeks aren't as noticeable, and I curse the old geezer for not taking a high-resolution photo of her. Monroe's rose gold hair is slightly longer in this photo, dusting her shoulders instead of framing her chin like it is now. I place it in my pocket, deciding it's mine now, and scan the information I came for.

Monroe St. James, twenty-eight, graduated from an online college in mortuary science, did a fifteen-month internship at Amberwood Mortuary with crypt keeper George, and is now their full-time employee. I wonder why a beautiful, smart, young woman went to school online for something she's passionate about instead of going in person. Isn't that the dream for most? Leave home as soon as possible and live it up at college? Not that I ever had an opportunity to know what college even was until much later, but I do know what it's like to want to leave someplace.

I snap a photo of the information, including her home address. After putting the folder away, I ease my way back into the sterile room, looking over the walls and stainless-steel cabinets and freezers. I know Rolo is in one of these, and I can't help but feel like maybe he brought me to her. Seems like something the bastard would do—give me one last gift, even in death.

I find a perfect spot at the very edge of an open shelf and place my discreet security camera where she'll never notice it. I pull out my phone to make sure it's working when it dings again. Needy today, hell.

Chaos: Where the fuck are you? Your tracker is off and it shouldn't be. Your rules, remember?

Me: Hey bike bestie. You sure use this group chat a lot for someone who hates group chats

Chaos: Where are you Mal?

Sin: Malice, word to the wise, I wouldn't push him right now if I were you

Me: You're all a bunch of whiny assholes

Chaos: Malice

Me: I'm shopping

Chaos: Shopping for what?

Me: Information

Wrath: What kind of information

Sin: And where?

Chaos: No one is supposed to be out alone

Me: Yeah but I'm stealthy, no one ever knows I'm there

Chaos: Your bike gives you away

Me: Okay that's a solid point

Me: But I'm careful. Just needed to get some things

Me: Heading back in a few.

Chaos: Turn your tracker back on

Me: No can do Prez

Chaos: Malice. Tracker. Now

Me: I can't hear you

Chaos: But you can read

Me: Never learned how to do that either

Chaos: for fuck's sake just get home

Sin: I'm gonna be pissed if we have to scrape you off the road with a shovel. Take it easy Mal and get home

Me: Aye-aye Captain!

After seeing the room light up on my phone through the security app, I close everything out and head back outside. For the first time in a long time, I'm eager for morning to come so I can get a glimpse of my little pixie.

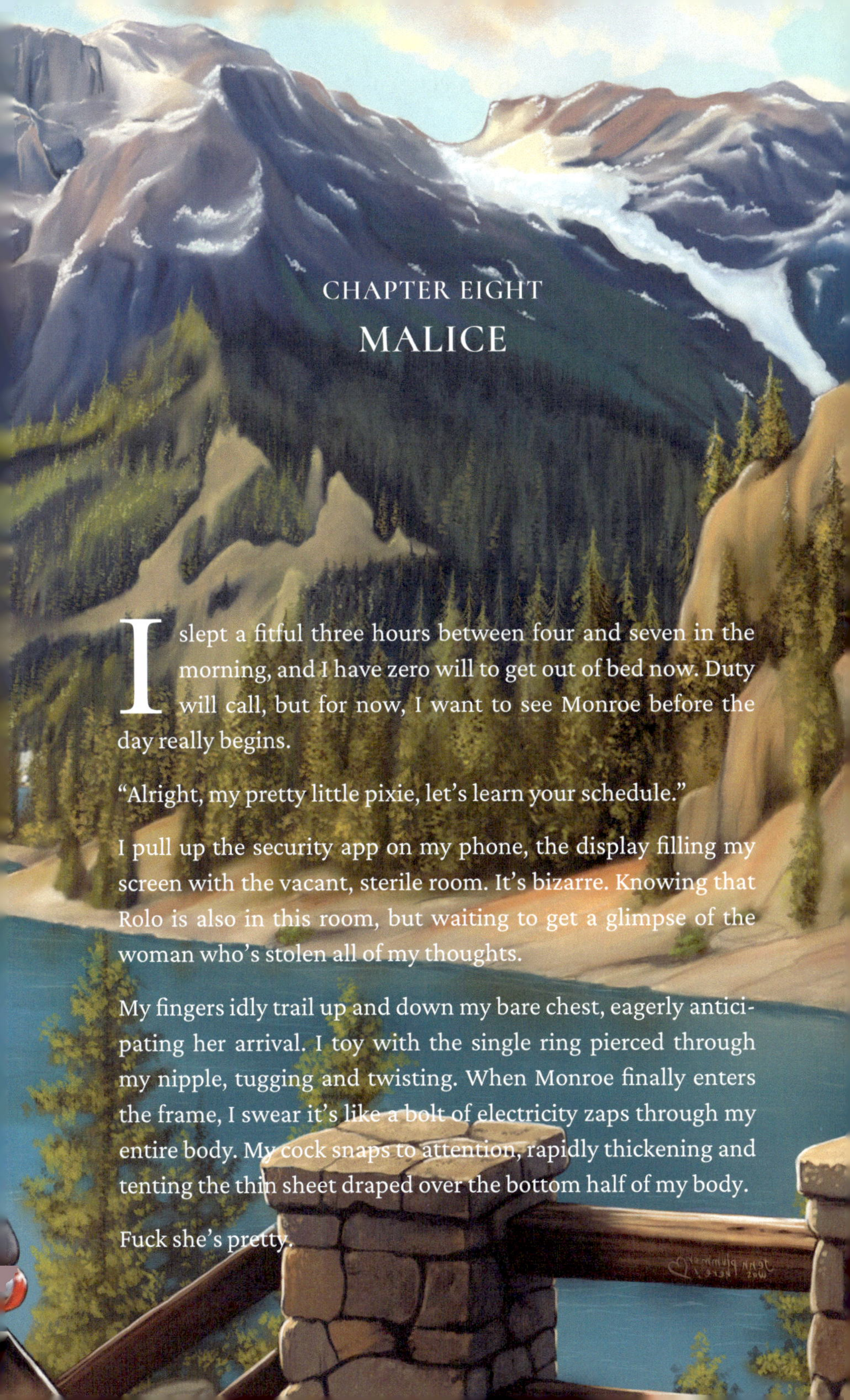

CHAPTER EIGHT

MALICE

I slept a fitful three hours between four and seven in the morning, and I have zero will to get out of bed now. Duty will call, but for now, I want to see Monroe before the day really begins.

"Alright, my pretty little pixie, let's learn your schedule."

I pull up the security app on my phone, the display filling my screen with the vacant, sterile room. It's bizarre. Knowing that Rolo is also in this room, but waiting to get a glimpse of the woman who's stolen all of my thoughts.

My fingers idly trail up and down my bare chest, eagerly anticipating her arrival. I toy with the single ring pierced through my nipple, tugging and twisting. When Monroe finally enters the frame, I swear it's like a bolt of electricity zaps through my entire body. My cock snaps to attention, rapidly thickening and tenting the thin sheet draped over the bottom half of my body.

Fuck she's pretty.

She's wearing a long, baby-blue dress with dots scattered across the fabric. The top scrunches around her small breasts with what looks to be a delicate little tie. Disappointedly, sleeves cover her shoulders, but the entire outfit is so pretty, so her. Rose gold hair frames her sweet face, and I wish I could see the blue of her eyes from here.

She moves around the room with grace and elegance, almost as stealthily as I do. She's bright and airy, and it suddenly hits me that she looks and dresses nothing like how I imagined a mortician dressing. Isn't there a rule for wearing black while in mourning? Are morticians ever in mourning with all the death that surrounds them?

I make a mental note to ask her.

Monroe looks unaffected as she sets up her room. My fingers play with the short hair at my pelvis before diving deeper, until I'm grasping the hard steel rod between my legs. My thumb brushes over my pierced, engorged head, sending shivers down my spine.

I watch as she opens one of the freezers, pulling out a long, empty tray. At least there's no human lying on it. I can't promise I would have stopped touching myself while she worked on one. She's too addictive.

My hand squeezes the base of my cock hard before I bring it up to my mouth, spitting several times into my palm. Then I'm stroking from root to tip, watching as my pixie girl works around the room.

Pleasure spreads throughout my body, lighting me up. I groan as I start to cant my hips, bucking into my hand, my palm squeezing just to the edge of pain, while my thumb swipes over my head at every upstroke.

My eyes roam the petite frame of her body, her tiny little tits that are begging for my mouth. I imagine how rosy her nipples are, how she'd arch into my mouth, what her fingers would feel like as they thread through my hair.

I stroke myself faster, my orgasm building quicker than ever before. I have the endurance and stamina of a fucking god, and I've never come this fast.

I don't take my eyes off her, the shape of her pretty face, how pretty her pink lips will look when they're wrapped around my thick cock. I imagine myself on my knees, her dress shoved up around her waist, my head suffocating between her lithe legs. I want her pussy all over me. I want her scent to coat me.

And fuck, to sink into her tight heat? I have no doubt her tight pussy would strangle the shit out of my dick, milking the cum right out of me until she was overflowing with it.

When Monroe drops a pen on the floor, her body turning and bending over at the waist, I groan out loud. The fabric of her dress is thin, and I can see the perfect peach shape of her ass. Firm, tight, and begging for my mouth to ravish. There will be no place left untouched that my mouth, tongue, hands, and cock haven't been once I'm done with her.

My orgasm erupts, ropes of pearly white cum spurting from my slit like a fucking geyser. I coat my lower abdomen and chest with it, moaning out her name as the euphoric waves crash over me.

I never take my eyes off of her, wishing she knew exactly what she just did to me. She's so perfect. So good. Self-loathing starts to creep in, reminding me how unworthy I am of having something so pure, untainted, and good.

With one last longing look at my pink-haired pixie, I close out of the app and head to the shower.

After cleaning myself up, I pull on a pair of low-slung denim jeans and slide into my cut. Fuck the T-shirt, socks, and shoes. My phone pings as I'm trying to do something with my hair, alerting me that I should probably come out of the dungeon at some point today. Especially with all the shit we need to do to find Rolo's murderer now that we know who the Kingsnakes are.

Luckily, we didn't find any more treasonous bastards among us, and the two that we did are no longer breathing.

Wrath: Who wants Maggie's for lunch?

Sin: I'm down

Me: Can you two read minds?

Wrath: What?

Me: I've been craving subs

Me: It was meant to be

Sin: I guess so buddy

Wrath: I'll have my usual

Sin: You aren't coming? You're the one who asked us if we wanted it

Me: Rude, sir!

Wrath: You know damn well that evil woman has banned me from entering

Sin: That's because you fucked her and her sister, man

Wrath: I didn't know they were sisters!

Sin: They're identical!

Wrath: Just go get the damn sandwiches before I chew off my arm

Sin: We have food here

Wrath: And I want Maggie's sub sandwiches

Me: I'll go. Haven't been in there in months

Sin: Wait up, I'll go too. I need to pick up lunch for Bristol to bring to the shelter anyway

Sin: You're a pussy Wrath

Wrath: Fuck off and get the subs

Me: Chaos?

Me: Prez?

Me: Pookie bear?

Chaos: Fuck off

After grabbing my boots, I meet Sin outside the clubhouse doors, his big ass already straddling his bike, ready to go. We ride into downtown Amberwood side by side, parking damn near the same place I parked last night.

Maggie is working the front counter, just like she always is, her chocolate brown hair hanging around her face in tight, natural ringlet curls.

“Hey, boys, aren’t you looking like trouble,” she flirts.

“Maggie, haven’t you heard? I’m a taken man now!” Sin says, and I don’t miss the pride laced in his voice. I bounce on my toes, looking at the menu in front of me, even though I always get the same thing.

“Who’s the lucky lady, Rhys? She must be pretty special.”

“Bristol. She’s a veterinarian in Bloomfield, and the prettiest, smartest, kindest woman I’ve ever met. No offense, Maggie.”

“None taken. I’m happy for you, Rhys. She sounds perfect for you. What about you, Crew? You tie someone down, too?”

I immediately think of Monroe and what she’d look like tied to my bedposts. Fuck, that’s a pretty sight. “We’ll see! Only time will tell! Now, time to eat?”

Maggie laughs. “What can I get you two?”

Sin orders first. “I’ll have two club sandwiches and a side of fries.”

“Two? Quite the appetite today.”

“As good as your clubs are, I gotta bring my old lady her lunch.”

“Well, that makes more sense. Crew? What about you?”

“I’ll have the BLT, no side, and an Italian sub with extra tomatoes and pickles.”

Maggie shoots her eyes up at me and squints. Fuck. Wrath always orders the same goddamn thing, and she’s gotta know it’s for him. Maggie’s demeanor changes quickly, plastering on a large smile and tilting her head off to the side.

"Coming right up."

I bristle. Rhys leans into my space as we move to the side to take a seat and wait for our food. "She scares the shit out of me."

"Same. Did you see that look she gave me?"

"She knows it's for Wrath."

"Just stay cool."

"When am I not cool? Am I not cool?"

"Of course you're cool. Just stay that way."

"Then why tell me if I already am?"

"Just because you're at risk of not keeping cool."

"Whatever." I brush Sin off, instead pulling out my phone, my body itching to get eyes on Monroe again. Turning to the side, I bring up the feed, only to find her working on Rolo. I should close out of it. I should turn away. But I can't. I'm enthralled. Entranced.

My brother lies on the stainless-steel table, dead, cold, nothing but a shell of the man he once was. But Monroe is such a light. She washes his body carefully, meticulously, as if she reveres him. She gives Rolo such care and attention that I can't help but watch. How is she so pure? So good?

"Order up, you two," Maggie calls out. Sin and I both stand, straightening our cuts. I like that Maggie never tells me to put a shirt on before coming in here like Mrs. Odette does. She's got a cool "come as you are" mentality that I dig. Even if I've never been interested in her that way.

"Thanks, Maggie, we appreciate it," Sin says with a smile.

"No problem. But do me a favor, yeah? Tell that sleazy fuckwad of a brother of yours I said to try not to choke on his food. And that I hope he enjoys my secret ingredient."

I shake in my boots. "Jesus, Maggie, you're terrifying," I tell her.

"Good. Remember that. Don't ever try to cross me."

"You got it, there are no worries there, won't happen," I say as I take the bag of mine and Wrath's food. I lean in toward the counter and whisper my next words. "Is my food good, though?"

Maggie pops her hip out, placing her hand on it as she raises her eyebrows. I wait for her to confirm or deny, but she never does, just flicks her hair off her shoulder and turns and walks away. I spin on my heels, turning around and finding Sin already gone.

"What the fuck?" I huff. I round the corner just as Sin is revving up his bike.

"Thanks for leaving me high and dry, fucker."

"You're a big boy. See you tonight."

I toe the gremlin bell dangling from the bottom of his bike and feel good knowing there's a tracker sitting in it. Sin drives off as I take a few steps over to mine, my eyes flicking down to my own gremlin bell, the memory washing over me, followed strongly by grief.

Mine is silver, the Hell's Heathens insignia etched into it. Rolo gave it to me the night the vote happened and I was initiated as a full member of Hell's Heathens. Gremlin bells are gifts of guardianship and protection against road spirits. At least I can carry a piece of Jesse with me now wherever I go.

Back at the clubhouse, I toss the sandwiches down on the bar in the common area to eat. Wrath opens his greedily, laying the white paper out flat and picking up the first half of his sandwich.

"So, is there any reason I got a call today from George at the mortuary asking questions regarding Rolo? 'Cause last I checked, you were there to take care of it all," Wrath says after swallowing a bite of his food.

"I did take care of it." *I think.*

"Did you, though, Mal? Cause the old man was sweating bullets, I could hear him panting on the line, scared shitless to fuck something up."

"Yup. I said it all sounds good."

"He asked if we wanted him to import a coffin, Mal. Any idea why?"

"Hmm. Nope. Did you get it all sorted?"

"I did. You were distracted. Why?"

I don't like his questions, so I quickly flip the discussion. "When's the last ride?"

"Saturday. Rogue is coming in Friday night and staying through the weekend. He's not taking it well, and he's been holed up with Kinsey." One of our road sergeants, Rogue, lives in Aspen Ridge, a few towns over, closer to the mountains, with his old lady. After the murder of his sister and Chaos' brother, he was never the same. Once you become a Hell's Heathen, there's no way out besides death, and even then, we're bound in the afterlife by the devil himself.

Chaos allows Rogue to live apart from the club and report back two weekends a month and whenever duty calls. He's still a member of this family even though we don't get to see him every day. He's a ruthless, gigantic fucker, who works as a tattoo artist in their tiny little town. He kept his identity hidden from everyone there until it caught up with him.

I was with Rogue and Wrath the night we went after the Widowmakers. And because of our actions that night, it spurred a vendetta against us that ended with his woman's kidnapping. We fuckin' love Kinsey, and just like we love Morgan, Saige, and Bristol, we'd protect any of them until our last breath.

"Any updates on where we can find the goddamn Kingsnakes?"

"None. Chaos has Otto helping me."

"Lovely. That kid needs to stay a hang-around and not a prospect."

"However we get our answers, I don't give a shit anymore."

"Let's get through tomorrow, and then we'll move forward."

The last ride is going to hurt like a motherfucker. It's where we'll ride Rolo's casket—not coffin—through town, the entire club in a tight formation, until we reach the cemetery where his final resting place will be. It's emotional and deeply important to all of us.

That night, I don't sleep, like usual. Instead, I park my bike down the road from 7 Wildflower Lane and stand across the street from the aging white picket fence, the dusty-blue house that's worn and well-loved.

The shutters and trim are white, and as I stare at it, I realize it's a quintessential home to raise a family in. Almost exactly the one I imagined when I would close my eyes and dream of a family that loved me, that wanted me, while I was locked in that cage.

I wait for a glimpse of pretty rose gold hair in the window, but she never comes. I wonder what her life must be like inside those walls. I bet it's beautiful, just like she is. Full of love and joy. I could never give her that. I'm destruction. Death. There's no light here, and I don't deserve hers.

I shove my hand into my pockets and rock on the heels of my feet.

Back and forth.

Back and forth.

Back and forth.

I'm not alone anymore. I'm not in a cage anymore. But for the first time in my life, I want more than just being free.

CHAPTER NINE

MONROE

Dear Diary,

The atmosphere felt different today. Charged. I've been a mortician for the last five years and not once have I been freaked out. But today I felt like I was being watched. There aren't any windows or cameras in the preparation room, so it was just me, the freezers, and the deceased. But all day, I couldn't shake the feeling that someone was there with me, watching. The worst part? It wasn't unease that I felt, but excitement. What does that say about me? I have to be losing my grip.

Sunlight starts to pour into the room of my little house. There's no real need for me to close the curtains since I live behind my parents' house, and the forest is all around us. I love waking up with the natural light shining in.

After pulling myself from bed and stretching out my muscles, I strip the soft fabric of my nightgown and jump in the shower. I move through my morning routine, showering, shaving, and blow-drying my hair. I decide on a pretty, pure-white eyelet summer dress that hangs just below my knees and is appropriate for work. It's kind of ballsy to wear white to work, but today I'm doing cosmetics and dressing, and I'll wear my PPE anyway.

The feeling of having eyes on me that I felt throughout the day yesterday hasn't been with me today, which is comforting. It must truly be my mind at play while at work. Even so, I'm eager to get in today.

I brew myself a cup of coffee, pouring it over ice and adding my favorite caramel syrup and whipped cream. My coffee habits change with the seasons, and through summer, I'm all about the homemade caramel iced coffees.

Before heading into the mortuary, I jog up the back steps of my family home and let myself in with my key. Like usual, it's a madhouse. We're a family of early morning risers, and today is no exception.

The scent of sizzling ham and eggs wafts through the house as I make my way to the kitchen. Miles and Wyatt are already arguing over who gets to play the new sports game on the VR, and Lucy and Hazel are fighting over a hairbrush, even though they each have their own. I look for my two other brothers,

Atticus and Cooper, and find them sitting at the bar with a plate of food.

My dad works to sling breakfast, and I walk up to him with a cheesy grin. This man loves being a father, and I swear, I think he'd add more if they could afford it. I lean in and give him a half-hug while he flips over several fried eggs.

"Morning, Dad, where's Mom and Aurora?"

"Upstairs. Aurora wants her room rearranged today, and Mom needed her to go through her closet before we agreed."

I laugh. "Fair is fair. I'm sure Lucy will appreciate some hand-me-downs." I take a seat at the bar next to Atticus, looking over his shoulder at the book he's currently reading.

"*Naruto*?" I ask.

"Yeah, ever read it?"

"Nope. You really love Manga, huh? We should see if Ink and Ivy can order some more. I'm sure you've already cleared out the library?"

"Yep."

"Any plans for the day?"

"You see it. Reading, then I'm gonna watch the show."

"Well, I'll see you later, bud. I'm heading to work."

"Yeah, to take care of deeeead people!" Wyatt yells from behind us. I roll my eyes, and my dad does the same. I move over toward Cooper, who's stuffing his face full of eggs.

"Can I have a hug before I leave, Coop?" Cooper leans into me, dropping his head on my shoulder and letting me wrap my arms around him. After he swallows, he looks up at me with his big, beautiful, dark brown eyes. "Did you know that koalas have fingerprints like humans?"

His eyes go wide, and I feel triumphant. I lift on my toes and do a little dance, making him laugh. I never stump him.

"Did you know that owls can't move their eyeballs? They're just stuck like this." Cooper opens his eyes wide and freezes, moving his head slowly to the side while keeping his eyes focused on me. I can't help but laugh.

"I did know that one, sweet boy. Try to stump me again later?"

"Okay. Bye, Roe!"

After saying a quick bye to my family, I head out the front door and start my twenty-minute walk into town. The sun is out, it's a beautiful day, and I can't help but hold my arms out wide and look up at the sky for a moment. It's rarely cloudless here, and I soak up the pretty blue that stretches endlessly above me.

I've lived in Amberwood my entire life, and even though it's a small town, I've loved living here. Once upon a time, I had dreams of getting out, of going to college out of state, a desire to see new places and meet new people. I craved culture and languages, food, and people, and had such a thirst for adventure. But in the span of one night, all of that disappeared.

Before I hit town, I walk by the field and look out past it at the lake off in the distance that almost claimed my life at its shore. I mindlessly rub the scar at the back of my head, the tight, raised portion of skin that's hidden beneath my hair.

. . .

"You two made it! Didn't think you had it in you to sneak out, especially you, Roe."

"Shut up, Tyler, she's not the goodie two-shoes you all think she is," my best friend, Nora, snaps at the two boys sitting in the front seat of their busted-up Honda Civic. My hands shake as I slide into the back seat with Nora. I've never done anything like this before, but she's been going out with Tyler for a few months now, and he just got his license. I don't know how I let her convince me to sneak out of her parents' house this late at night to go for a ride with them, but here we are, trying to live a little.

The tires screech as Tyler presses down on the gas. The car jerks as it lurches forward onto the road outside of Nora's neighborhood. My hand finds hers between us, squeezing it lightly. I snap the top part of my seatbelt, telling her to put hers on, but she just waves me off and laughs.

"Damn, girl, you're looking so fine in that skirt," Tyler says as he turns in his seat to look back at Nora. "You know, Roe, Javier has been checking you out all school year. We just heard rumors you don't put out, so he hasn't tried anything yet. Maybe you could convince him to give you a shot before he moves back to Spain, huh? A little last hurrah."

My insides churn, but Nora squeezes my hand, nodding her head and encouraging me to say yes. It's no secret that I'm still a virgin going into my senior year of high school while everyone around me lost theirs way before now. I just haven't met anyone worth giving it to yet. No one has excited me to the point where I want them to stick their appendage inside me.

I cringe in my seat at the thought. How is everyone just doing this so openly, like it isn't a huge-ass deal?

But here we are, heading to Lookout Lake, and I just know Nora and Tyler are going to want the back seat to screw, or maybe he'll just bend her over the hood like he apparently did last week.

Nothing screams losing my virginity like being folded like a pretzel in the back seat of a car on its last leg, by a guy I don't even really like, who's moving in a few weeks, while my best friend and her boyfriend get it on feet away from us. Sounds riveting. A girl's dream.

I kind of thought it would be, I don't know, call me crazy, but in a bed? With someone who I loved and who loved me, who took their time with me and actually cared about my well-being. Letting Javier stick it in me right now would be a mistake. But damn if the peer pressure doesn't suck.

"Seriously, Roe, I'm down if you are. I could even give you a mustache ride first if you want that."

My face must show my reaction because even through the dark light, Nora squeezes my hand so hard I wince. Do guys really think girls want to be talked to like that? Ew.

"I think I'll pass on the mustache ride and impalement tonight, Javier. Thanks for the offer, though."

"Aww, why you gotta be such a prude, Roe? Would you rather join me and Nora? Maybe she's more your type." Because of course I must be a lesbian just because I'm not putting out for men. I hate high school. Things had better start looking up once I'm in college, or I'll be a virgin forever.

"How about we just head home? I'm no longer feeling great," I say. But Nora shoots me a glare so lethal I swear the pupils of her eyes glow in the moonlight.

Tyler flies down the road, and I lean forward to check the dashboard. I know the road leading up to Lookout Lake is thirty-five. I've been up here a million times. But the roads are still hard to navigate, and he's going seventy.

Adrenaline surges forward, my palms starting to sweat as he barrels around another sharp corner. I'm forced to lean into Nora while her laugh echoes through the car. My stomach turns, my head starting to swim.

"Slow down, Tyler, you're going way too fast," I tell him, pulling my seatbelt tighter.

"Chill, Roe, I'v—" his words are cut off as the front of his car slams into an elk, the car spinning quickly and hitting the gravel on the side of the road.

My seatbelt cinches so hard the wind is pulled from my lungs, and then I'm upside down, and right again, then upside down. We flip several times down the side of the embankment before we come to a stop at the edge of the lake, and everything goes dark.

The morning goes by quickly, but the moment I step into the preparation room, that spine-prickling feeling of being watched returns. I've never been one to believe in ghosts or hauntings, but I'm starting to question my sanity. It seems to only be in this room, which is fitting since that's where the bodies are resting until they're moved into their caskets or we take them to be cremated.

I slip into my personal protective equipment, laying the water-resistant gown over my dress, then my plastic apron, gloves, goggles, and rain boots. Things can get messy during embalming, and I'm not one to take any chances.

Since the mortuary has a full-time funeral director, I just get to focus on preparing the bodies for their final rest. We were taught through school to expect the possibility of having to juggle multiple roles while working in a funeral home or mortuary, but I've been really lucky here in Amberwood with George.

I line up my instruments with a care that borders on reverence. I love my job, and I try to make that shine through in everything I do. Just as I move to stand in front of the embalming table, the air changes, like a held breath or a broken clock, and everything freezes for a moment.

Every molecule in my body seems to stand at attention, and that sense of being watched slides over me, slow and deliberate, settling into the marrow of my bones. It's not sharp or unpleasant, it's more like . . . *anticipation.* Like when you know your name is about to be called at school and you have the answer on the tip of your tongue.

Instead of shaking it off, I move more carefully, every step measured and intentional. I'm deeply aware of every minute detail, the way I stand, how my spine straightens, and I catch myself smoothing my apron repeatedly, adjusting my stance, and schooling my features. I feel like I'm naked and on center stage, the overhead lights beaming down and making me the star while darkness surrounds everything else.

I'm absolutely losing my mind. Absurd, really. I'm putting on a show for an empty room. For the sterile tile walls. For the dead. For nothing I can see or name. Yeah. I'm losing my grasp on reality.

I do my best to push it out of my mind as I work through my tasks, but as the day goes on, that itch spreads deeper, a quiet insistence demanding my attention. The feeling never follows me out into the hallways or the breakroom where I have my lunch, but I felt an emptiness as I left the room.

I take a bite of my strawberry and goat cheese salad, but its typically bright and summery flavors are lost today. I don't realize I've completely checked out until a voice breaks my thought process.

"Feeling alright, Monroe?"

I look up to find George taking a seat at the other end of the table. He's about seventy-five, a widow, and has the biggest heart. I think he's truly biding his time for when death claims him, like it eventually claims us all, so that he can reunite with his wife again.

I've had a run-in with death, and I'm unsure if I believe in an afterlife. It's a nice thought, though, something to dream about when life is hard. That there's more to all of this after we leave. I'd like to think Nora is someplace else, someplace good.

"I'm okay, just feeling a bit off today. How are you?"

George and I share a bit of small talk, but in the back of my mind, I feel a pull to the preparation room, an invisible string yanking ever so slightly for me to return, that something is there, waiting for me.

The strangest part of all of this is that I don't feel afraid. The presence is familiar, close, and intimate without touching, and instead of shrinking or running away, I want to rise to meet it, to uncover it.

When I finally leave for the day, the feeling loosens its grip, and my body relaxes, no longer feeling an innate need to be on display, but it feels empty somehow, like there's something there that I need.

No matter how many times I ask myself what's wrong with me and if I'm truly losing my mind, I know that I'm eager for tomorrow to see if I feel it again.

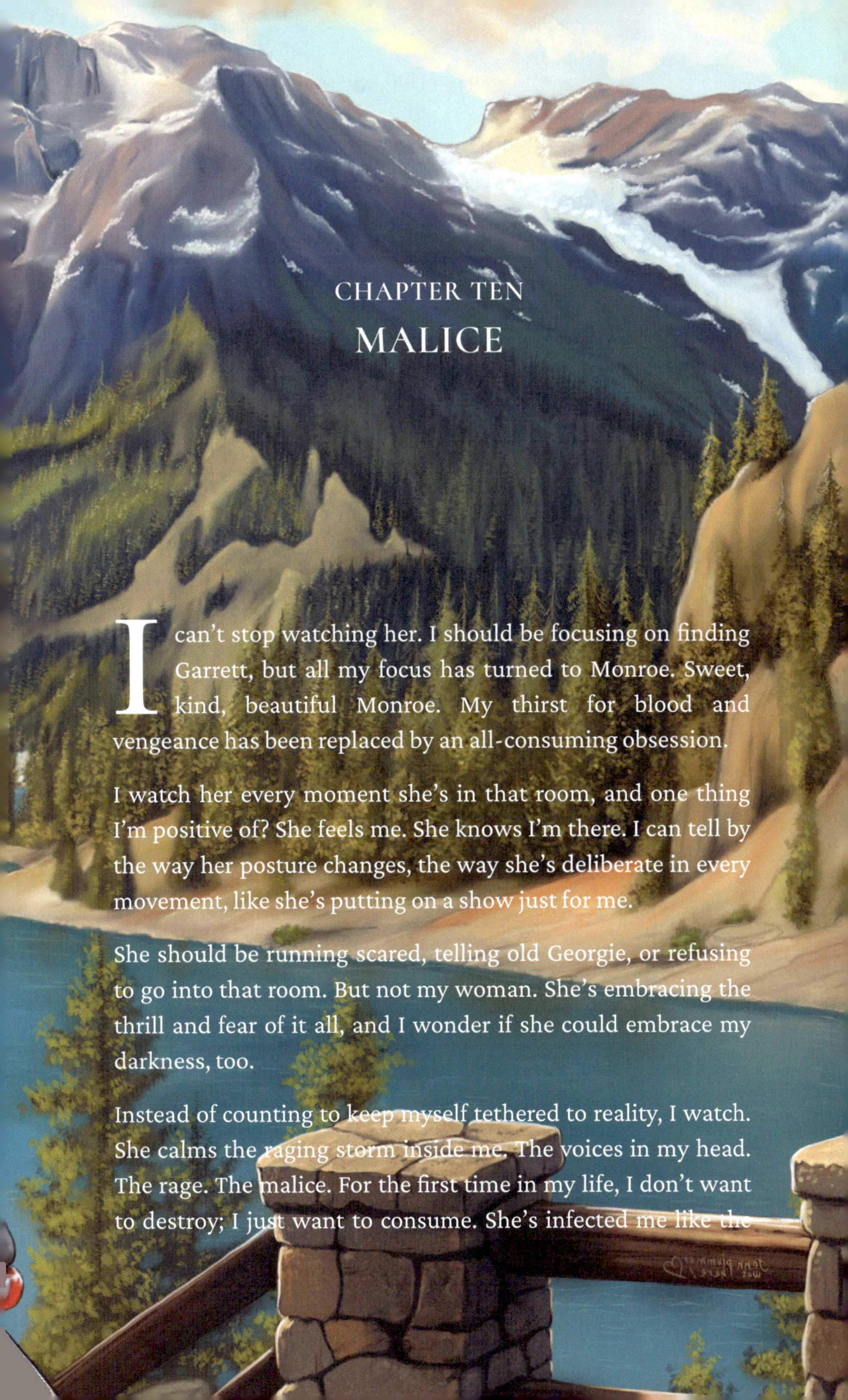

CHAPTER TEN

MALICE

I can't stop watching her. I should be focusing on finding Garrett, but all my focus has turned to Monroe. Sweet, kind, beautiful Monroe. My thirst for blood and vengeance has been replaced by an all-consuming obsession.

I watch her every moment she's in that room, and one thing I'm positive of? She feels me. She knows I'm there. I can tell by the way her posture changes, the way she's deliberate in every movement, like she's putting on a show just for me.

She should be running scared, telling old Georgie, or refusing to go into that room. But not my woman. She's embracing the thrill and fear of it all, and I wonder if she could embrace my darkness, too.

Instead of counting to keep myself tethered to reality, I watch. She calms the raging storm inside me. The voices in my head. The rage. The malice. For the first time in my life, I don't want to destroy; I just want to consume. She's infected me like the most potent drug, filled my veins with a chemical that only thrives for her.

My brothers have noticed my distraction and rapid change in focus, and while I'd like to keep Monroe my secret, I need to tell them. We're all sitting in the common room together, discussing the final ride for tomorrow, and now seems like as good a time as any.

"I found her," I announce. All eyes go to me, their words frozen.

"Garrett had a dick, I'm pretty sure, Mal."

"No, not Rolo's murderer. I found *her*. My queen."

"You what?"

"I. Found. My. Queen," I repeat slowly for Chaos, pissing him off.

"I heard that part, dickhead. What do you mean you found her?"

"She just appeared. Like someone sent her to me. She's angelic like that."

"And you're the devil's son. That tracks," Sin chuckles.

"Does she feel the same way?" Wrath asks.

"She doesn't know *I* feel this way. We've only met once. I've been . . . watching her."

Sin rubs the thick hair of his beard, shaking his head. "Fuck, Mal. Okay, buddy, you can't stalk people. We've talked about this." Well, had I stalked Rolo, he'd still be alive.

"It's not stalking. Not really. It's just watching. From a

distance." And through the camera I set up in one of the rooms at her work. But they don't need to know that.

"Mal, that's literally the definition of stalking."

"Is it, though? Is it?"

"Yes!" they all yell in unison.

"Rude. There's no need to shout, I'm sitting right here. Plus, I think she likes that I watch her."

"And how do you know that?"

"I can tell. How'd you know Saige really wanted you even though she kept making your nose bleed?" I say, giving Chaos a pointed look. "Or how Bristol did when she was engaged to that assface? Or you, you big fucker who's never around anymore," I say, pointing my finger at Rogue. "How'd you know Kinsey was into you when she was your best friend's sister and completely off-limits?"

"Not his best friend's sister," Chaos says through gritted teeth.

"Ohh, someone's jealous!" I squeal.

"Fuck off, Malice, I don't get jealous. But we get your point. You found your person."

"My queen," I correct.

"What do you need from us?"

"Well, I've had more sex than most of you combined, but never dated anyone. I can make her come until she's in subspace, but I don't know shit about the rest. How do I woo her like you wooed your queens?"

"First of all, you gotta stop calling them our queens," Chaos says matter-of-factly. He's wrong.

"You're wrong, that's exactly what they are," Sin interjects, speaking my thoughts out loud. I give Chaos a look, arching my brow.

"How do I make her fall in love with me?"

My brothers share a look I can't quite discern. My eyes pinch together, a sick feeling churning in my gut. The sperm donor and incubator didn't love me. No one I've ever been with sexually has loved me. I've never had a girlfriend or boyfriend. Why would Monroe love me? I don't like this feeling, the unease, the insecurity creeping its way in. It makes me want to claw out of my own skin. I crack my neck from side to side and wipe my clammy hands on the ripped surface of my jeans.

I want to pull out my phone and look at Monroe's face, but I can't do that here. So, I look down at the bar top, counting the grains in the wood, tapping my middle finger against my leg.

One.

Two.

Three.

Four.

"No one's ever loved me before," I whisper under my breath, feeling like shit, trying to hold back the feelings I don't want to face.

Five.

Six.

Seven.

Until a hard punch hits my shoulder, followed by a smack to the back of my skull. I wince, rubbing the back of my head and looking up to find four pissed-off bikers, their eyes narrowed at me.

"We love you, you idiot," Wrath says with conviction that makes my heart squeeze.

"We're a family here, Mal, and it's not just because of the oath. We're all misfits. Born, abused, and forgotten by the cruelness of the world, but we found our home here, our family, here," Chaos says as he presses his pointer finger into the bar top.

"Don't you dare think we don't love you," Sin adds, making me blush. I feel like the Grinch, my heart swelling and doubling in size. I know I have my home here, but I guess it was easy to feel like our little fucked-up family of bandits took care of each other out of obligation to our club. Feels good to hear otherwise.

"They like flowers," Wrath says, pulling a long drag of his joint. "Women."

Rogue nods, running his hand through his long hair. "And honesty."

"Since you've got the fucking part down, make sure you're communicating with her, talking. Hell, even while you're having sex, check in with her, make sure everything you're doing is okay."

"They also like to feel supported and encouraged," Chaos adds, Sin shaking his head in agreement.

"Just be yourself, buddy, you're a cool guy, and your heart may be black, but it still beats. If Chaos can get someone to fall in love with him, I don't think you're gonna have issues," Sin says, ducking from the punch that comes from Chaos.

Just be myself. Be honest. Check in. And flowers. I can do that.

Later that night, I head into town, stopping by a field of wildflowers and looking at the different types with the flashlight on my phone. Wild lupines grow everywhere you look, the scent making me sneeze several times. Not those ones, then. I keep walking, passing by sunflowers and some pink things, until I find a pretty white daisy that reminds me of the ones on her dress the day I met her. Plucking it from the ground, I smile as I admire it. A pretty daisy for my pretty pixie girl.

Following the same path I previously took, I stick to the darkened alleys and head toward the mortuary. Once again, it's easy to break in. It seems no one has noticed the lock is broken on this door now, either, which is also a concern. Not that I'll let anything happen to her.

Once I'm inside, I waste no time going right to the sterile stainless-steel room, leaving the daisy on the long table that sits in the center, directly in line with the camera. I don't want to miss her reaction.

I hope she loves it.

Instead of going right home, I continue my walk, navigating to 7 Wildflower Lane easily, and standing outside of the house that holds the woman who consumes my every thought, my every breath. Who knew love would be so consuming? It's the best feeling I've ever felt.

I may not deserve her, but I'm going to take her anyway.

Hours later, I'm lying in bed as the sun rises, peeking from behind the overcast clouds. The weather is appropriate for the day, as in just a few hours, our entire club will be taking the last ride for Rolo's funeral procession.

I flick my tongue piercing between my teeth and play with it while I watch the empty space of the white tiled room, waiting for Monroe to appear. The daisy has wilted slightly since I plucked it from where it was thriving in the ground, and if that isn't a metaphor for me in general, I don't know what is. I killed it. It's what I do.

My feet rub together back and forth, my fingers trailing up and down my bare chest as I try to quiet the energy rising in my veins, my blood simmering just below the surface. Then she walks in, and everything is silenced.

Monroe freezes in the doorway of the room, her eyes glued to the long green stem and the white petals of the daisy. Her fingers move to rest flat against her stomach like she's trying to calm the feelings beneath her skin. *Me, too, pixie.*

I sit up straighter in my bed, my fingers trailing across the small version of her on my screen. Her hair is half-up, half-down today, the top half pulled up high and giving an unobstructed view of her pretty, freckled face.

Her lips fall open ever so slightly, and I so badly want to wipe my thumb across them before sticking it inside. I bet she'd respond right away.

She looks like a goddess of the underworld in an all-black dress with lace sleeves. It's the darkest thing I've seen her in yet, and while part of me misses the pinks, yellows, and baby blues, this reminds me of a Gothic queen.

My heart pounds against my rib cage, desperate and feral, wanting to claim what's ours.

She walks up to the table, picking up the flower and examining it, spinning it around in her fingers before lifting it to her nose and inhaling. A faint smile toys at the corner of her lips, which makes me grin like a fool. I did that. I made this perfect, gorgeous creature smile.

Me. A harbinger of evil and death. I did something *good.*

I've never felt real pride before, but this is it. I want to make her smile every day.

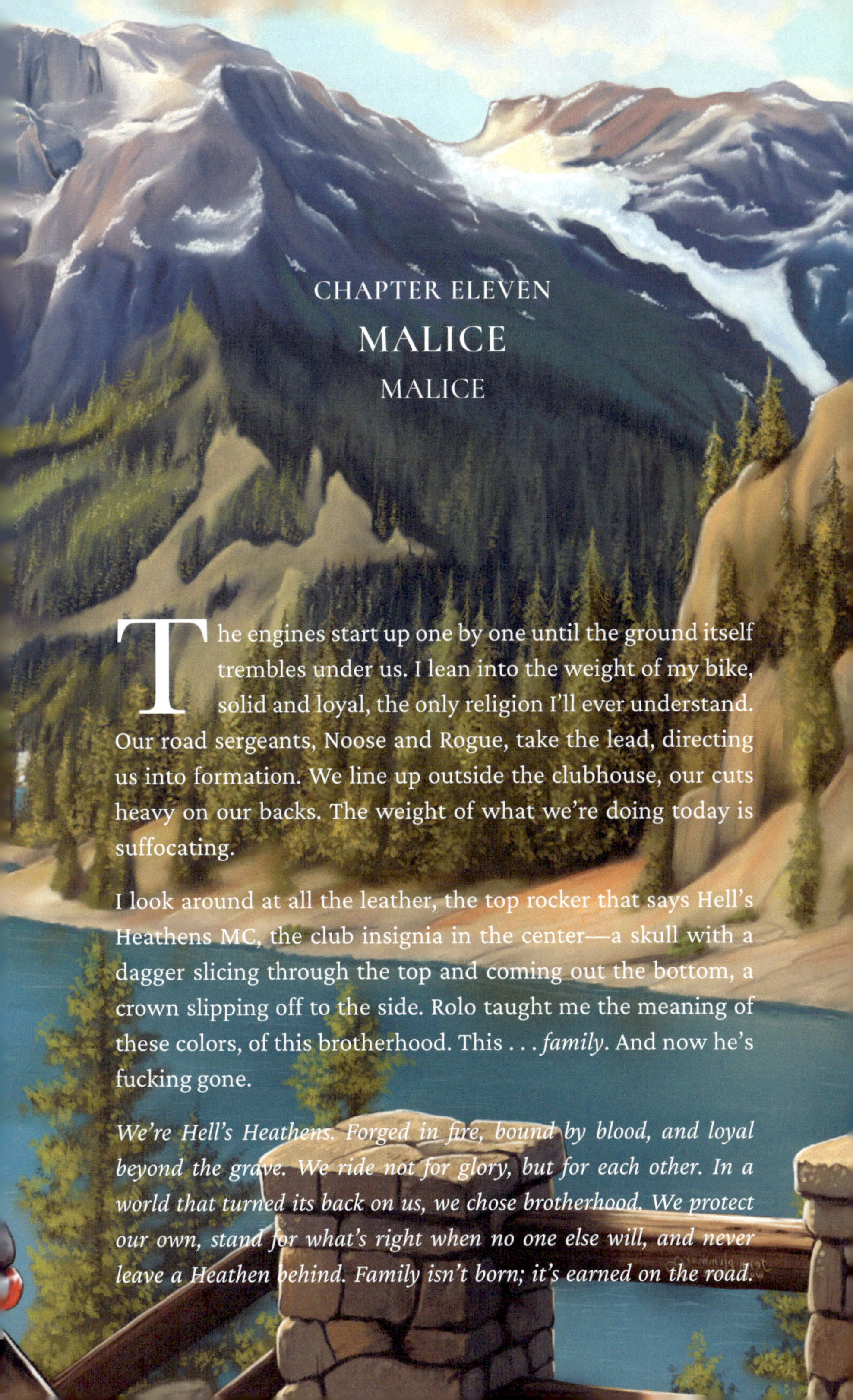

CHAPTER ELEVEN

MALICE

MALICE

The engines start up one by one until the ground itself trembles under us. I lean into the weight of my bike, solid and loyal, the only religion I'll ever understand. Our road sergeants, Noose and Rogue, take the lead, directing us into formation. We line up outside the clubhouse, our cuts heavy on our backs. The weight of what we're doing today is suffocating.

I look around at all the leather, the top rocker that says Hell's Heathens MC, the club insignia in the center—a skull with a dagger slicing through the top and coming out the bottom, a crown slipping off to the side. Rolo taught me the meaning of these colors, of this brotherhood. This . . . *family*. And now he's fucking gone.

We're Hell's Heathens. Forged in fire, bound by blood, and loyal beyond the grave. We ride not for glory, but for each other. In a world that turned its back on us, we chose brotherhood. We protect our own, stand for what's right when no one else will, and never leave a Heathen behind. Family isn't born; it's earned on the road.

Home is the clubhouse; family is the cut. We live and die for each other. The only way out is back through hell's gates.

Noose and Rogue slowly roll forward at the front of the lines, the rest of us falling in, the hearse carrying Rolo right behind us. The air fills with motor oil and leather, but there's no denying the thick weight of grief and rage. Especially coming from me. There's a sharp, hollow ache that sits right under my ribs, and I have to crack my neck side to side to ease some of the pressure.

Morgan rides with Saige on the back of her bike, and the respect I have for both of those women just grew tenfold. Rogue gives the signal, and I ease off my clutch, starting to roll forward with a knot in my throat.

Our formation is tight, four bikes side by side when the road allows it, tightening up to staggered pairs as it narrows around bends. The sound of us coming rattles the trees around us, a living heartbeat made of steel and gasoline, a thunderclap that echoes into the open space around us.

As we reach the edge of downtown Amberwood, people pull over, letting us take our final ride through, and showing us respect we don't deserve. I keep my eyes forward, my vision blurring at the edges as I try to maintain control. This isn't our first time having to do this, and it won't be our last, but it sure as fuck is the first one that hurts like this.

The procession slows as we reach the mortuary, rounding the corner to head toward the cemetery gates. Monroe stands at the edge of the street, a beacon of light in a pretty yellow dress that takes away some of my pain. I watch her for as long as possible, soaking up some of her light, wishing I could bathe in it like she does.

The rumble drops to a low growl as we line the road to the cemetery on both sides, letting the hearse pass through the center. We bow our heads in respect to our fallen brother, the ugly, raw truth of losing him passing right by me. I'm no stranger to death, but right now, I've never hated it more.

As the hearse passes the front of our formation and into the cemetery, Chaos revs his engine three times, and we answer the call right back. It's a final salute, the last rev, our goodbye to our fallen brother. The man who saved me.

That night, when I find myself standing outside of 7 Wildflower Lane, I don't stay across the street. Using the shadows to my advantage, I walk around the house, looking for any sign of my pretty girl.

It's late, much too late for anyone to be awake, but as I walk to the back of the house, I'm shocked to find her. Behind the large house sits a smaller one, no bigger than a large shed. It looks like it was renovated into a tiny house, perfect for my little pixie. She has a garden out front that lines the entirety of the perimeter, filled with yellow flowers with orange centers. The building is painted a light blue with white trim and flower boxes.

Monroe stands in front of a large window in a thinly strapped nightgown, showing so much skin I almost drop to my knees and crawl across the lawn. She's ethereal. Her beauty unmatched.

She looks out into the abyss for mere moments before turning and retreating further into the room. My feet are moving before I realize it, leading me directly to her. A low growl rumbles through my chest at the sight of her sitting at the edge of a bed.

The nightgown lifts up her thighs, just barely hiding the paradise between her legs. She takes turns lifting each leg and rubbing lotion down every inch. What I woudn't give to be those hands. To be able to touch every inch of her soft skin.

My cock strains in my pants, and I grip it hard, pinching the tip to stave off some of the pleasure pulsing through me. But then Monroe stops, setting her feet back down on the plush carpet and turning her head to look out the window. To look at me.

Our eyes connect, and even though I know she can't see me, I know she senses me. We hold each other hostage for a passing moment, maybe longer; time seems to lose all sense and meaning when she's around. She bites her bottom lip, and instead of getting under the blankets like she should, my little minx lies on top of them. Her bed faces the window, and it's like I'm standing directly in front of her.

Monroe's dainty fingers slide up her inner thigh, and just before she reaches her panties, she pulls back. Ever so slowly, she works herself up, teasing, running her hands over her smooth skin. Her hips start to move, her knees falling open slightly.

When her free hand comes up and dips into the thin, silky fabric of her nightgown over her breast, I lose it. Quickly, I unbuckle my belt, spreading open my jeans enough to pull my cock free. My fist wraps around it, stroking from root to tip, sending pleasure scattering over my body with a shudder.

The hair on the back of my neck stands up, a chill working through me. I've never been so turned on before. Monroe is so close, all it would take is me opening the front door, and I could sink between those sweet thighs and bring us both to the stars.

How would she like it? I'm rough. I fuck like the demon that I am. Monroe seems like she'd want it soft and slow, passionate, and sensual. I want to try to be that for her. I want to give her everything she needs.

The only thing better than going in there and touching her is this. Watching her touch herself, knowing she feels me close, but not having proof. My dirty girl is putting on a show for the big bad hunter lurking just outside her window.

My eyes rake up long legs, from the pretty pink toenail polish all the way to where her hand has finally settled between her thighs. My view is blocked from seeing anything more, but I can imagine it.

Monroe arches into her palm like such a good girl, her back bowing, and I imagine what it would feel like to have her on all fours for me, head down, spine arched, ass out. I know she's going to squeeze my cock so good when I finally take her.

Monroe's eyes don't leave the window as she squeezes her tit and fucks her fingers. I jerk my hand over my cock in time with each of her movements, working myself over. It feels so fucking good to watch my pixie girl play with herself for me. She's going to make an amazing plaything. An even better queen.

Monroe's eyes squeeze shut, and I let myself go, thinking that she's about to orgasm, but then she rips her hand away from her pussy and drops it to her side in frustration.

My cock pulses as my orgasm barrels through me. I brace myself against the trim of the window while I unload my cum all over the pretty yellow daffodils that line the front of her house.

When I'm spent, I find her on her side, the blankets covering her body like nothing happened at all. Seems like my woman needs a helping hand to get off.

"Don't worry, pixie, your Heathen is coming for you."

I've never wanted anything for myself, but I want Monroe St. James.

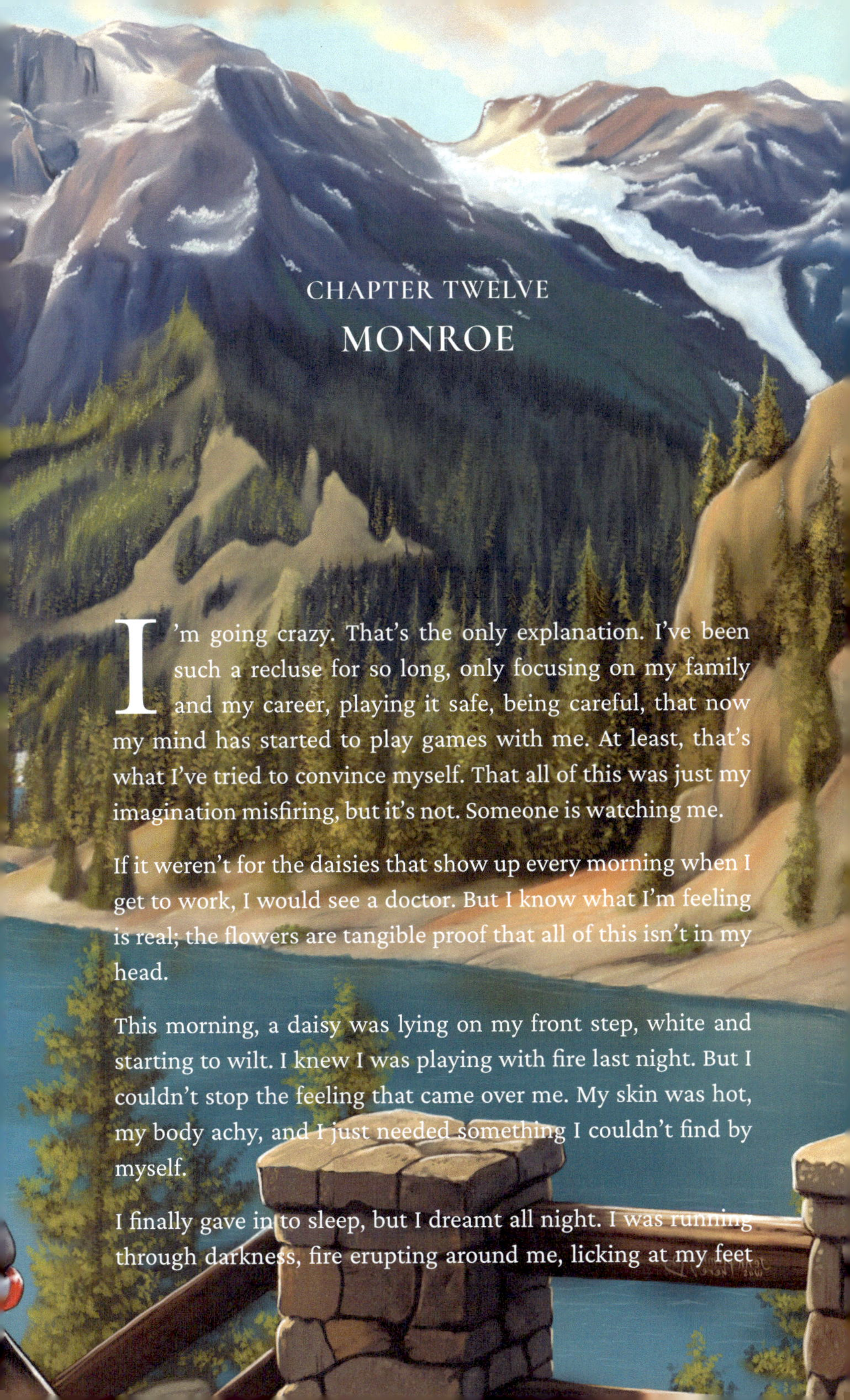

CHAPTER TWELVE

MONROE

I'm going crazy. That's the only explanation. I've been such a recluse for so long, only focusing on my family and my career, playing it safe, being careful, that now my mind has started to play games with me. At least, that's what I've tried to convince myself. That all of this was just my imagination misfiring, but it's not. Someone is watching me.

If it weren't for the daisies that show up every morning when I get to work, I would see a doctor. But I know what I'm feeling is real; the flowers are tangible proof that all of this isn't in my head.

This morning, a daisy was lying on my front step, white and starting to wilt. I knew I was playing with fire last night. But I couldn't stop the feeling that came over me. My skin was hot, my body achy, and I just needed something I couldn't find by myself.

I finally gave in to sleep, but I dreamt all night. I was running through darkness, fire erupting around me, licking at my feet but never burning me. I was terrified, my heart pounding so loud in my chest, I could hear it between my ears. I pumped my arms so hard, trying to get away from it, but it was all around me, consuming and threatening. Darkness shrouded everything, the flames not even strong enough against it to bring much light. Until I slammed against a hard, bare chest, arms closing around me, a warm cheek pressing to the top of my head as they held me reverently. The fire dimmed to ash, taking my fear with it.

I woke up as the sun was starting to rise and spent too long trying to understand the meaning behind it by writing it out in my journal. Ever since my accident, I've played it safe. The one time I was reckless, the one time I went along with being a typical teenager, I regretted it. I'll regret it for the rest of my life.

Life is precious.

So, I live it safely. Even if sometimes I crave more. More experiences. More connections. Just . . . more. Being the only survivor of that accident has made me live with guilt that weighs me into the ground. I'm happy and grateful, but I always feel guilty for every step I take. Like the world is watching to see exactly what I do and judging me for it. Why is it fair that I get to continue on when they didn't? Why do I get to have these life milestones when Nora, Tyler, and Javier will forever be seventeen?

I think that's why I prefer to surround myself with the dead. There's no judgment. I understand them more than I do anyone else. Maybe it's also because I envy them. They're free. Free of constraints, of expectations, of guilt and pressure.

After pulling myself together for the day, I head out, stopping at my family home to see everyone. I find my grandparents sitting side by side on the couch, curled up together, with mugs of steamy coffee in their hands. My mom sits across from them in the love seat, all of their faces conspiring and deep in concentration. My mom pats the spot next to her as I walk into the room.

I plop down, curling my legs underneath me.

"You three look like you're plotting your revenge against someone. Let me guess, Wyatt pranking you all again?"

My brother has been mischievous and has made himself quite the wild child of our family. A title he wears proudly. He's especially serious about pranking us when we least expect it.

"Of course we're conspiring against Wyatt. He needs to be removed from his position as family trickster. He's going to give your grandmother a heart attack."

"Oh, please with that crap," my grandma says, waving her hand at my mom. "My heart is healthier than that boy's! I just want to get him back and get him back good." We all laugh.

"That boy needs to be brought down a few pegs. We'll think of something good," my mom adds.

"Yes, he does! Little monster thinks he's going to get away with it, too. But we're going to get him when he least expects it."

My little brother, Cooper, walks into the room a moment later, his eyes brightening when he sees me. It makes me so happy when he looks at me like that.

"Roe! You're here!"

"I am! And guess what?"

"What?" he says as he takes a seat in front of me on the ottoman.

"I think I'm gonna stump you today. Are you ready?"

"I'm ready!"

"Did you know that reindeer's eyes turn blue in the winter to help them see better?"

Cooper's eyes widen and his mouth drops open, pure shock written on his face. I feel a moment of triumph before he laughs. "Got ya! I knew that one, Roe!"

"Oh my gosh, you little devil! You need to stop spending so much time with Wyatt!"

"My turn! Did you know a Cuttlefish has bluuuuue blood?"

I laugh. "I did not know that one, Coop!"

My little brother runs off triumphantly.

"We're having your grandpa's favorite dinner tonight, Roe. Anyone you'd like to invite?" my grandmother asks. My face blushes even though I try my hardest not to think of Crew. "Nope!" Knowing I need to get going, I pop up from my seat and adjust my dress. "I'm heading into town. If anyone needs anything, just let me know."

"Roe . . ." my mom says, stopping me in my tracks with that concerned tone of hers. "It's been eleven years, you don't have to keep going."

I give her my best smile. "I do, though. I don't mind."

. . .

For being such a small town, the Amberwood Cemetery is big. Thirty-three acres house the final resting place for generations of people who've lived and died here. A large iron gateway serves as the entrance, its paved sidewalks weaving through the headstones. I pass by markers that are decades old, moss climbing up the edges, the etching faded and difficult to read, family and friends long gone, and no one's left to keep it clean.

My heart hurts when I think about it. How we only have a few generations after our death to keep our memory alive, and then we're dust. How long has it been since someone has uttered their names?

I make my way toward the end, the headstones getting cleaner, shinier, and brighter, the writing crisper. My white sneakers hit the grass as I step off the pavement, walking past several plots until I see her face. Forever frozen at seventeen. I almost wish Nora's family hadn't chosen a headstone where her photo was etched into it, but it's not like I could ever forget what she looked like if they hadn't. How am I going to feel looking at my best friend when I'm old and grey, and she's forever this way?

Her pretty blond hair cascades over her shoulders, her palm holding up her chin. Her smile is so bright and happy, and she loved this photo the most. She had chosen it for her senior photo, the senior photo that turned into an "In Memory Of" page in the school yearbook. My mom had purchased me a copy, even though I didn't attend that year and wasn't in it. A dark laugh bubbles out of me. The girl who survived the crash that killed three Amberwood High School teenagers wasn't even in the yearbook, as if I needed a reminder as to what everyone was already thinking.

"Something funny?" The voice startles me, and I turn around quickly, coming face-to-face with a ghost. My eyes fall closed for a moment as I catch my bearings. "Why do you still come here, Roe?"

"Because she was my best friend, who else is going to come here? Her parents are gone, Zach."

"I wish you'd stop."

"That's too bad. I have every right to visit them, just like you do."

"Except I wasn't there when they died."

"I'm not guilty of that accident, Zach. When will you stop blaming me?"

"For as long as my brother is dead and you get to keep living."

My head snaps back like he physically hit me, tears springing to my eyes. It's one thing to think it, another thing entirely to hear the words spoken out loud.

"I know that's harsh, but it's not fair. I'll never get over losing him."

"Would you rather we all died?"

"No." But the rest is unspoken. He'd rather Tyler had lived than me.

"I'm sorry," is all I can think of to say. I wipe away the tears that fall across my cheek, refusing to cry anymore. I turn back to Nora's headstone, running my fingers across her face. "I miss you."

Then, without looking at Zach, I leave, knowing next week, I'll just come right back again.

. . .

That night, I can't sleep. So, I give in to the restlessness of the night and sit at my piano, letting all my feelings out to Debussy's "Clair de lune." It's melancholic, but there's so much hope, and my heart soars as I close my eyes and let my fingers move over the keys, imagining myself dancing under the moonlight with a stranger masked by the shadows.

We twirl round and round, and although I can't see his face, I feel more whole than I ever have before. He holds me close, like I'm the most precious thing in the world. If I try hard, I can smell his woodsy scent, all fire and rain. When my fingers stop, my eyes snap open, a chill running down my spine.

I look around the room, my eyes scanning the darkness. Nothing has changed, but my skin prickles with alertness, nonetheless. I move to my front window, looking out at the pitch-black of the night. My eyes squint, trying to see something that isn't there.

My shoulders stiffen, suddenly aware of how exposed I am, how visible I must be through the window, even though my brain is telling me there's no one in front of me. It's just my body doing its best to convince me otherwise. My pulse has already picked up, beating faster, louder, like it's trying to warn me before my mind finally catches up.

The silence thickens around me, stretches and molds to every dark corner of my small house, deliberate and suffocating.

I should run. I should move away from the window, close the curtains, and hide away in my bed.

But I don't.

The worst part of all of this insanity is that it isn't fear that's thrumming through me, it's the creeping certainty that whatever is watching me right now feels familiar, and it's not unwanted.

Dear Diary,

I don't think I truly realized how lonely I was until I started looking for my stalker everywhere I go. I only feel him when I'm in the preparation room at the mortuary or late at night in my house. I don't understand what's happening to me or why I haven't told my parents, or hell, even the police. Which I guess is a lie. I do know why. It's because it brings me comfort that's different from the comfort I get from my family. This feels warm and makes my heartbeat pound erratically in my chest. I want to open my door and welcome them inside so I don't have to be alone anymore. Which is insanely fucked up. Here's my written reminder to Google if ghosts can move things around in the real world, because I haven't ruled that out yet.

CHAPTER THIRTEEN

MALICE

The day doesn't go as planned. I'm only able to check in on Monroe twice, and even then, I only had seconds before I had to focus. The road stretches out in front of us as Wrath, Noose, and a few trusted prospects and I drive to scope out a location where the Kingsnakes MC may be hiding out. Wrath reached out to other clubs in Washington for more info on them, but we only got one hit. Either everyone is too scared to speak up and negatively impact their relationships for snitching, or the Kingsnakes really are sneaky sons of bitches.

After a two-hour ride, we pull over to grab a bite at a small diner in a town I've never heard of—Autumn Bay. I take a seat at the closest table to the windows in front of our bikes so I can keep an eye on them. You never know. Sometimes people see a group of bikers and suddenly get ballsy. I much prefer it when they cower and stay clear of us. It's quieter that way.

A waitress drops a few menus, and I pick up the sticky plastic, making a face before dropping it back to the table. I haven't had much of an appetite since Rolo died, so I order a water and relax in the booth, pulling out my phone to check on Monroe. To my disappointment, she's not in the preparation room, and I wrack my brain with how to get more cameras to follow her everywhere she goes. I definitely need one in her bedroom. Especially after the other night when I got to watch her touch her pussy. Even if she didn't climax. My poor, sweet girl. I'll take care of her soon enough, and I plan on making up for all her missed orgasms.

"What do you keep doing on your phone? You're never on your phone," Wrath asks. I quickly pocket it.

"Where do we go next? They're not hiding in an actual snake den; someone has to know where they are or who the fuck the Kingsnakes are," I say, changing the topic. I'm not going to answer to anyone. Not about Monroe.

A soft, timid voice breaks our conversation. "Sorry for intruding, but did you say Kingsnakes, like the motorcycle club?" I look up as the waitress sets our drinks down on the table, her eyes looking at our cuts. I hadn't noticed her before now, but she looks scared shitless. The side of her neck is covered in deep scars, and when she sees me looking, she adjusts her collar, looking like she'd rather the floor open up right now so she could disappear. She has the most unique, near-white, blonde hair I've ever seen, and I recognize the look in her eyes. Fear.

"You know 'em?" Noose asks her. The girl's eyes dart around the long room of the diner. "We won't hurt you, but we need to find them."

"I-I, I don't know. I shouldn't have said anything. I'm sorry, I don't know anything."

Wrath reaches out and touches the top of her shaking hand that's crossed at her front. "Why don't you take a break, huh? Head to the restroom. I'll knock twice, and then you'll let me in, okay? I won't hurt you, have never hurt a woman in my life, but you know something, and I can tell you're scared. They hurt someone close to us. Our brother. I *need* you to tell me what you know. Nod once if you understand, sweetheart." I roll my eyes as much as I'm impressed. Wrath is a smooth asshole. His calm demeanor has always made women relax around him. Probably helps that he's pretty to look at, too. Especially sitting here with me and Noose. Noose is an ugly fucker. I glance over at him and bristle. Yeah, he's an ugly fucker.

The woman holds Wrath's stare for a few silent moments, and my eyes dart around, before she finally nods her head once and then quickly returns behind the counter.

Wrath raps his fingers on the tabletop several times. "I'll be right back, boys," he tells us. Noose snorts.

"How about I go?" I suggest. I'll get the information out of her. Wrath may be smooth with women, but I know how to get what we need.

Wrath and Noose both laugh. "Absolutely the fuck not. No offense, Mal, but you're probably one of the reasons she looks terrified. You look like Death himself."

I run my fingers through my hair and screw my face up. "I do not." Even if I know he's right. "Whatever. Just get the information. I want to get the fuck out of here if we aren't bringing bodies back with us today."

Wrath nods and then stands, adjusting his leather cut as he heads toward the restroom, while I stay rooted to my spot, sipping on my water. The diner is nice for being on the outskirts of town. The coast isn't far from here, and I could smell the salt air as we rode in. It's no Amberwood, but I can see the appeal.

Wrath is back within ten minutes, giving me a subtle head nod that tells me it's time to leave. Wrath drops a few hundred onto the table, and Noose and I both widen our eyes.

"She needs it more than we do. Let's go."

We follow him outside to our bikes, the prospects flanking the three of us.

"What'd you find out?"

"The Kingsnakes MC used to be respected. She said they took care of the town and its people, loved everyone. Rolo's brother had just gotten out of jail, was just a member, then he killed the former president in his sleep, took over the position by force with a few other assholes that had his back, and has been slowly dismantling and destroying everything the club had built."

"Fucking shit," Noose mutters.

"Any info on Rolo's brother?"

"He's a real piece of shit. But get this, his road name? Cain."

Noose snorts, and my eyes narrow. Kind of a weird fucking road name.

"Cane? Like he needs one to walk? How the fuck old is this guy?"

"It's biblical, Mal. He's considered the world's first murderer.

He killed his own brother." How very poetic of him to take that name and then commit the same act.

"How does she know all this?"

"Her brother is a member."

"What's her brother's name? Is he our in?"

"Saint. He's gonna help us."

After gathering our information from the waitress, we went back to Amberwood to get a plan together. Wrath left the waitress, Sienna, with the number to his burner phone. We just have to hope like hell she doesn't get too spooked to talk to us any further. We need to connect with her brother if he can get us information on where the fuck Garrett is. Finding out the hit came from a club president—Rolo's own brother, no less—changes things and makes them a bit trickier than just going in guns blazing.

After checking in at the clubhouse, I snuck back out, needing to get my eyes on Monroe. My heart pounds in my chest as I wait for her to leave the mortuary. I'm angsty, anticipating getting my eyes on her. I thought about her all day, wishing like hell she knew who I was.

Monroe leaves the building, a smile on her face as the sun shines down on her like it's been waiting all day to touch her with its rays.

I watch her from my spot in the alleyway, her petite, pale legs, lithe and so thin. She's wearing one of those dresses again, and I realize I've never seen her in jeans. Which is fine, I like the dresses, and she must like them, too. This one is black from the waist up with a pretty satin-looking bow tied around her dainty throat and buttons that descend down the front. The skirt poofs out slightly at her waist, the hem stopping just past her knees. It blooms in nude tulle, scattered with black butterfly appliqués that seem to dance in flight as she sways.

If only I could get her to strap my gift to the outside of her thigh, she'd complete the entire look flawlessly.

Me: She looks so pretty right now

Wrath: Who does?

Sin: Where are you?

Me: In the alley between the library and Daily Rise

Chaos: For fuck's sake, what do I gotta do to get control over you all?

Chaos: Mal stop following her

Sin: Where was that rule when he was stalking me?

Chaos: You're a big boy

Me: And she's a queen. She can handle herself

Wrath: Against you?

Me: Yeah if need be. I got her a present

Chaos: Mal. What kind of fucking present?

Me: The fun kind!

Wrath: Shit. That could be anything from a butt plug to a flower

Sin: Hopefully it's the latter?

Wrath: Why are you phrasing that as a question?

Sin: Some women like butt plugs?

Wrath: Again, make a definitive statement

Sin: Nah

Chaos: Shut the fuck up

Chaos: Malice what did you get her?

Me: ....

Chaos: Malice

Me: ....

Chaos: Crew I swear to fucking God

Sin: You don't believe in God

Chaos: I'm about to put a bullet in all three of your heads to find out

Sin: But how would you know if we're all dead? We'd be the only ones to know

Chaos: I hate you all

Chaos has left the chat

Wrath: Mal buddy, is it safe?

Me: Yeah it's safe

Wrath: Good man. Let me know if you need anything

Me: You think she'll like it?

Sin: We don't know what it is buddy, but if you put your heart into it, I'm sure she'll love it. Women like sweet gestures

Me: K. I shall keep you updated my brothers from other mothers!

Monroe crosses the street, her low-heeled sandals tapping against the pavement as she lightly jogs to quickly get out of the way of an oncoming car. I can't rip my eyes away. Look at her, so innocent and sweet, all goodness and light. Her pink hair shines in the sunlight, her skin glowing ethereally.

My hands itch at my sides, wanting to run my fingers through her silky hair, over her soft skin. I want to count her freckles. Bask in her warmth.

Monroe stops, squatting down to look at some pretty yellow flowers similar to the ones in front of her house, and I can't take it a moment longer. I have to have her. I have to take her as my own. I know a man like me doesn't deserve a woman like her. But I can't fight the call to her. Maybe her light and love can snuff out some of my darkness and hate.

I snort at the thought. There's no saving me. But that's not going to stop me from being with her. I flick out my cigarette, then I rev up my bike, letting the engine purr under me, the smell of gasoline filling the air. I pull out of the alley and drive slowly up the road. Monroe pauses as I pull over, turning to look at me. All the air is sucked from my lungs, the world itself blurring except for this ethereal goddess standing in front of me. From my seat on my bike, we're eye to eye. She really is a tiny little thing. So fragile.

The sun glows behind her, turning her into my own personal beacon. She's perfect. She's everything. Her face lights up when she sees me, the blues of her eyes shining just a little brighter as they meet my own. Her delicate little fingers tuck her hair behind her ears, and she has the nerve to look sheepish. In front of me. A demon. A reaper. A murderer.

"Crew." My name on her lips is the sweetest sound. I never had a name while growing up, never gave much thought to why or that I needed one. I was John Doe up until Jesse brought me to the clubhouse.

"What's your name, kid?" the president, Queenie, asks. I go to open my mouth, but Jesse claps me on the back as we step up to the truck to climb in. I clench the leather vest tight in my grip. It's the first thing someone's ever given me, and I don't know what to do with that.

"Crew. His name is Crew." I look at Jesse and narrow my eyes. My name is John. At least, that's what the police started calling me. "Everyone needs a name that suits them. No offense, but you're not a John. You're part of our crew here. You're a part of something now. Something bigger than you, bigger than me. You've got a family now, Crew."

"Why are you walking? Don't you have a car?"

Monroe's smile grows, filling her face. "It's a beautiful day, why would I drive when I can walk?" She didn't answer my question, though. I turn my bike off, toeing the kickstand down, and climb off. I tower over her now, and I wish I didn't. I feel bad she has to arch her neck to look up at me, but when she does, I nearly melt at her feet. "Going to walk with me, Crew?"

I shove my hands into my pockets, so I don't do something like reach out and touch her.

"If that's okay with you. Where are you headed?"

"Between the Notes."

My eyebrows raise. "The music store?"

"That is what Between the Notes is," she laughs. "Have you ever been?"

"Can't stay that I've ever needed to. Do you play something?"

"The piano. I fell in love with it a long time ago and taught myself to play." Of course she does. I bet she has so many more incredible hidden talents that I've yet to discover. Unlike me, whose only talents are the different ways I can kill someone or dismember a body.

"You really play the piano?"

"Why do you seem so shocked by that admission, Crew?"

"You've got it wrong, pixie, it's amazement, not shock."

Monroe stops walking and turns to look up at me, her pretty sky-blue eyes sparkling in the sunlight. "Pixie?" *Shit.* I've already gone and fucked this up. I trace the freckles that dust the bridge of her nose with my eyes, tapping against my thigh with my left hand. Then, without thinking, I run the back of my pointer finger down the bridge of her nose.

Sparks fly between us, an electrical current surging. My heart rate speeds up, and my eyes flick to the pulse point at her neck. The way it rapidly pumps the blood flowing through her body makes my dick wake up.

"Yeah, pixie. You remind me of a fairy. Like you were carved out of light instead of darkness. You're radiant and so full of life. Beautiful and charming. Something not of this world. Plus, you're a tiny sprite of a thing, especially compared to me."

Her eyes seem to twinkle, her teeth capturing her bottom lip between them. "Well, that's a smooth answer. But you do know that pixies are notorious for being mischievous trouble-makers, right?"

"If you only knew the trouble you started, *pixie*, then you would understand how much it suits you."

Monroe's cheeks flame with pink, and if even possible, the freckles on her cheeks bloom and brighten. I'm itching to trace over each of them. This girl is so pretty it hurts. She bumps me playfully with her shoulder before turning and continuing her walk up the cobblestone sidewalk of Main Street. We walk in silence, the hustle and bustle of the town moving around us, until reaching Between the Notes, and I don't understand why I'm not itching to crawl out of my skin. I hate the noise of downtown. But with Monroe? Every cell in my body seems to breathe for her, and the noise is comfortable.

A bell chimes overhead as I open the door for us, and as Monroe walks in front of me and into the cool air-conditioned building, I don't hold back from getting my fill of her backside. Fuck, she's hot. And smart. And talented. And witty. And way too fucking nice to willingly accept my company.

I follow her inside like a lost puppy, and I wonder how she'd feel if I dropped to my knees and asked her to parade me around on a leash. She owns me, anyway. I'll beg for anything she'll give me.

The cool air is a welcome reprieve from the outside heat, and Monroe rubs the back of her neck like she's also grateful for it. I stay a few feet back, just watching as she walks up an aisle and flips through books of sheet music.

She truly is stunning. I lean my shoulder against a large beam and pull out my phone, pretending to look at something on it, but I'm really snapping photos of her. She doesn't seem to notice, lost in the little world she's created right now. I could watch her forever.

Her nails are painted pearly white, short and square, and I focus on them as she flips through the different plastic books. I'm lost in the image of her until I hear footsteps coming closer. My spine straightens, but I don't step forward.

A man not much older than Monroe steps into her space, a little too close for my liking. Hell, I don't want anyone near her at all. His jeans are cuffed at the bottom, his shirt tucked into a pair of dark pants, with suspenders. *Suspenders.* His hair is styled in some complicated slicked-back bullshit I wouldn't be able to do with mine with a pound of product, if I wanted to look like a total douchebag.

I stay silent, ever the ghost, and watch as he speaks to her. Monroe takes a step back from him, but he matches it. My head cocks to the side as I watch her demeanor change.

I can feel the tension radiating off her in waves. He doesn't seem to notice that she keeps shifting her weight, or that her shoulders are tight, but I do. He leans into her space, his voice not loud enough for me to make out what he's saying. She takes another step back, but he mirrors her, closing the space between them again. My molars grind, and I quickly snap a photo of him just as Monroe glances around the room, a quick flick of her eyes that says she's looking for something. For me. My chest tightens. I pocket my phone and take several steps toward them, done watching him make her uncomfortable. I'm the only one who has the right to do that, and only because she likes it when I do it. *Even if she doesn't know it's me yet.*

When dipshit finally notices me, his eyes widen, his arm slowly reaching out for Monroe. As if he could protect her from me. As if I could even fathom harming her. I walk right up behind her, and I swear to the devil himself, her body relaxes. We aren't touching, but we're close enough that I can feel the body heat radiating off her on my chest.

I wonder how she'd feel if I flipped up her dress, bent her over the shelf, and ate out her pussy right here. Then maybe he'd understand that she's mine. My cock gives a good kick behind my jeans. It's been hard since the moment I saw her, and with how she affects me, there's no chance of it going down anytime soon.

"Roe?" he says her name like he has any right to. Monroe looks up at me, her pretty blue eyes my only focus. When she breaks our eye contact and turns back to him, he seems to get the hint. "Be careful, Roe. I don't know what you've gotten yourself into, but be careful." Ballsy little asshole, isn't he? He retreats, probably understanding that he wasn't going to survive facing off with me, especially when it comes to her.

"Who was that?" I ask, taking a deep inhale of her delicate

scent. She smells like pure sunshine, coconuts, and citrus, bright and perfectly her.

"Hmm?"

"Who was that man? He seemed very familiar with you."

"Oh, he, yeah, I guess. That's Zach." Zach has a death wish.

"Just Zach?"

"It's a long story. We used to know each other."

"I've got all night if you want to talk about it."

"That's sweet of you, but I should probably head home. My family will be waiting for me." *Family*. She must read whatever facial expression I had because she places her hand on my forearm. It's like being lit up by a firework from the inside. No pleasure has ever compared to this woman's touch. "Not my family. Well, they are my family, but not like that. I'm not married or a mom. I actually don't even want kids, to be honest. Which is also very strange since I wanted siblings so badly while I was growing up, until my parents adopted so many, I lost track. I'm sorry, I'm totally rambling. You make me nervous, Crew." She sighs, but she's smiling up at me, so I guess it's not a bad thing to make her nervous.

I reach out, tucking a rogue strand of hair behind her ear, loving the way it slips through my fingers. "I make *you* nervous? I feel like I can't breathe around you. You're so good, so perfect, and I'm . . . me," I say, gesturing to myself.

"And what's wrong with you, Crew? We're clearly seeing different things." Monroe bites her bottom lip and looks away. Is she . . . flirting with me? I've never flirted before, not really. If someone wants to hook up with me or vice versa, it's always been straightforward. There was never any need for wooing. But Monroe is different. So, I need to be different.

I gently move my hand to her chin, gently clasping it between my thumb and pointer finger. Her breathing hitches at my touch, her pulse fluttering wildly in her neck. I want to kiss that spot, feel it beat against my lips as I get it to climb higher and higher.

"I'm okay with you seeing something different, pixie, as long as you see something at all."

"You're hard to ignore," she says to the man who's spent his entire life being a ghost. I lift my thumb from her chin, swiping it slowly across her bottom lip before dragging it down. Her pupils are blown wide, her chest rising and falling harder. I don't give a shit that we're standing in the middle of a music store, I'm completely enraptured by this gorgeous creature standing in front of me, letting a monster touch her like I have any fucking right to have this privilege. I'm not good enough for Monroe, but I'm going to have her anyway.

"Why did he call you Roe?"

"It's a nickname. Everyone calls me that except one person." Anger starts to push forward right under my skin.

"Who?"

"You," she whispers with a smile, and my heart does this weird tumble in my chest before squeezing. It's not painful, it's good, but it's new. "I should get home, I always have dinner with my parents, grandparents, and siblings. It's important to them. To us."

"I wouldn't want to keep you from something like that. I'll see you soon, *Monroe*."

"I hope so, Crew."

I shove my hands back into my pockets and rock once on my heels before turning and leaving the store. Fuckface Zach already left, so I'm not worried, plus, the tracker that I slipped into her purse will help me keep my eyes on her whereabouts.

CHAPTER FOURTEEN

MONROE

I run my fingers across my bottom lip the entire walk home. I'm buzzing with energy. Crew is . . . all-consuming. The moment I saw him on his bike, my heart went into overdrive. There's something so alluring, so different about him that I can't get enough of. He's so much more complex than meets the eye.

His striking physical appearance would scare the wrong person, but to me, he's gorgeous. Tall and muscular in all the right places, with a strong, chiseled jaw, and deep, mysterious eyes. He's covered in tattoos, and when he stepped off his bike without a T-shirt on, I swear I could feel my pulse between my legs.

Ripped, toned muscles span across his abdomen, a splatter of random tattoos covering his flesh. His nipple is pierced with a hoop, and I had to use all of my control not to ask to touch *all of him*. Crew is gorgeous. One of the sexiest men I've ever met. And he seems to be interested in me.

If it weren't for having plans this evening, I could have spent the entire rest of the day walking around and talking with him. I don't care if the entire town whispers and watches. Let them. They do anyway.

Before I realize it, I'm standing in the front entryway of my parents' house, kicking off my sandals. My mom rounds the corner, her light blonde hair styled in a chic side braid. She comes to a stop in front of me, grabbing my biceps, her smile widening as her blue eyes dart all over me. God, her mom instincts are always so spot on. She's like a bloodhound on the chase. I never could keep anything from her.

"I know that face. Did you meet a man?" I can feel my cheeks flaming with heat.

"I did," I squeal, jumping from foot to foot as I shake my head in excitement.

"Ah! Tell me everything!" My mom drags me to the couch where my sister Aurora is already lounging. She perks up, clearly ready to hear any possible tea I may have.

"He's tall, muscular, and handsome. He's a little rough around the edges, but he's endearing and sweet," I confess. It's clear Crew is layered, so multifaceted that it's going to take me a while to peel back each one and get to know him, but I'm up for that challenge. I hope he comes around again so that I get the chance.

"He's different from every guy I've ever met before, but the biggest thing is that we've only met twice, and each time I felt the same. Comfortable, but also excited? The rest of the world just disappears when he's around, and I can't help but want to get lost in him and the world he lives in."

My mom smiles at me like she couldn't be happier. I hit the jackpot when it comes to the parent lottery. They've always been the most supportive people in all our lives, but especially me. After my accident, they could have locked me up, put me in a bubble after coming so close to almost losing me. But they've always pushed me to keep going, to not let nearly dying and being the only survivor of that car accident stop me from living.

They've only ever wanted to see me thrive. Something I'm still figuring out how to do.

It's easy to let fear take the reins, and trust me, more than a few times, I almost gave up control. Mostly because it seemed easier to give up than to keep going. The real courage is living. But with my family behind me, I was able to come out of the depression that lasted for the first few years after the accident.

Was the plan to always become a mortician? No. I wanted to be a nurse. But after almost dying, well, dying and coming back to life, taking care of the dead just seemed more natural to me than taking care of the living. I still don't understand why I was the only one who survived that day. Why all of our lives were claimed, but I was the only one who came back. I struggled for years with the grief, the guilt, the lack of understanding and comprehension. I still do.

It would have been so much easier to just stay gone with Nora, Tyler, and Javier than be forced to live without them. Today is a reminder of those feelings. The trouble with living in a small town like Amberwood is that you run into everyone from time to time. And coming face-to-face with Tyler's twin brother is like looking at a ghost. An angry ghost who wants to haunt you and remind you that you should have been the one who's gone and his brother the one who lived.

Trust me, Zach, I've thought the same thing more than once. Even if Tyler was an arrogant asshole all those years ago, my best friend loved him, and he didn't deserve to die. None of them did.

So, I live for all of us. I'm grateful for every day, but I still haven't found a way to live life to its fullest.

Maybe this is why I gravitate toward Crew. He's not like the rest of the town; he's different and doesn't seem like he cares about anything anyone thinks or says. I guess you'd have to feel that way if you're a Hell's Heathen.

There's an awareness inside me that knows I should be fearful of him, but my mind refuses to go there. I've never once felt like he was dangerous, despite exuding a savage viciousness that he's so clearly capable of.

"Where did you meet?"

"We first met when he came into the mortuary. His friend passed away too young. I didn't see him again until today. He saw me walking on the side of the road downtown, and he stopped to say hi. We ended up walking together to Between the Notes while I picked out new music."

"He just dropped everything he was doing to walk with you?" Aurora asks. She yawns like she's bored, but I know she loves to hear this kind of stuff. She's been wanting me to date for a while now.

"He did." I omit the part where he got off his motorcycle and how hot he looks riding it.

"That's sweet, Roe," my mom adds. "You think you'll see more of him?"

"I hope so." Butterflies take flight in the pit of my stomach at the thought of him popping up again. If anything, I could use a new friend around here. Someone who doesn't look at me like the girl who survived the accident that killed three teenagers in such a small community. Who doesn't look at me like the girl who came back from the dead. The girl everyone looks at with pity, even though I'm doing my best to *live*.

The rest of the night goes by in a blur of dinner with my family, gossip around the table, a game of animal gotcha with Cooper, and then I finally head home to my little sanctuary.

I completely forget about my stalker until later that night, when I feel like eyes are undressing me through the window. It's subtle at first, an inky caress that travels down my spine. The air thickens in the small space of my little home, and I pause, listening for a sound that never comes. Sensations slide over me, slow and deliberate, my body breaking out in goosebumps.

This time, I don't let myself get lost in the fantasy of it; I face it head-on. I'm probably breaking every major no-no from every slasher movie ever made, but I don't care. I need to know.

Walking to the front door, I quickly flick the outdoor light on and open it, stepping out onto my little porch and looking from side to side, scanning the landscape as far as my eyes can see. Nothing but flowers and darkness greet me, but when I look down, I've trampled all over a freshly picked daisy. A shiver runs down my neck, my blood rushing between my ears, my pulse a rapid drum against every major blood vessel in my body. I stare at it for a moment, the crushed petals detached from the center. Someone was here. Someone has been here. I knew it, had the proof of it, but this feels different. This feels more real than ever before.

I don't feel fear, not really. I know fear, that sharp blade that comes from out of nowhere, the panic that tries to claw its way out of your body. This isn't that. This is softer, intimate, *attentive.* As if someone is trying to learn me by heart.

My pulse drums under my skin. Somewhere out there, someone is very aware of me. Waiting. Watching. And the most alluring part is how personal it feels, as if whoever is there already knows me and is taking their time. Hunting me. Taunting me.

I pick up what's left of the flower, stepping back inside and locking my front door. I flick the lights off and bathe myself in darkness, quickly climbing into bed, feeling more exposed than ever before.

That night, I toss and turn again, dreaming of being in the back seat of Tyler's car right before the accident. I feel it all again and again, the fear, the adrenaline, the horror, the split-second rush of emotions before my heart shatters into a million pieces. The only difference is this time, instead of being pulled out by EMTs, I'm pulled out by a tattooed stranger who smells like fire and dew, so warm and safe. He pulls me into his chest, where he breathes life back into me, my heart beating once again. And then I'm whole again. Chosen to live on. Claimed by some other entity that didn't find me ready to pass with my friends.

When I wake up the next morning, I swear I can smell the faint scent of smoke and rain, like the aftermath of a storm, lingering in my room.

. . .

"Good morning, lovely daughter. You're looking a little under the weather. Are you alright?" my dad asks as I steal a piece of bacon from the plate at the bar.

"I think so? I had some weird dreams last night. I ran into Zach Martin yesterday, and it's always unnerving."

"It is for everyone. Imagine how Zach feels when he looks in the mirror."

"I can't imagine, Dad. It's hard to think about, and when I do, even after all these years, it's difficult not to spiral. I know he resents me. I know he's pissed I survived and Tyler didn't. But it's been eleven years! I shouldn't feel guilty for living!"

My dad clicks off the stove where he's flipping pancakes and walks around to the other side of the bar, wrapping his big arms around me and pulling me into a bear hug. I rest my head against his broad chest, inhaling the fatherly comfort he's always given freely.

"I know it's not fair, honey, but you cannot feel guilty for surviving. You are here, breathing, blinking, thinking, walking, living. We just need to get you to the thriving part."

Maybe what I need is a change in scenery.

CHAPTER FIFTEEN

MALICE

We wait to hear from the waitress, but the text never comes.

"We need to take the fight to them. You didn't hear how terrified she was, Chaos. And she's just one person. Autumn Bay is a small town, just like Amberwood, and they're running it into the ground, controlling everyone by terrorizing the people who live there. You heard that prospect, they aren't feeding their men! What do you think they're doing to the women? We can't just stand by knowing what we know now."

"No offense, Wrath, you're a good man, but I've never seen you feel so strongly before. You know what you're asking goes deeper than just retribution for Rolo's murder. Going after another club, whether they deserve it or not, is a big deal. And we've taken hit after hit for too long now."

"You didn't see the fear in her eyes."

Chaos' eyes flick to Saige, and we all know he's imagining the fear of someone getting ahold of her and doing the unthinkable. Not that she wouldn't probably take out a dozen or so men before it ever got that far, but most women aren't like Saige. She's the exception, not the rule. Which is why I want to teach Monroe how to use her new knife. *As soon as I give it to her.*

"We don't have anything solid to go off of, Wrath. Get me more concrete information. Where's their compound? How many men? Weapons? Who are they aligned with? You and Sin work on getting it together, and then we'll talk. We all want vengeance for Rolo's murder, but not at the risk of your lives. Not like this. We do it smart, just like we always have." With those final parting words, Chaos storms off in the direction of his room, Saige hot on his heels.

Wrath looks down at his burner phone, and I can see his frustration. Hell, I feel it, too. The desire for vengeance is a living, breathing thing that isn't easily sated. I know that just as much as anyone here.

"Good news is that we've at least got a solid lead," I tell him, giving him a pat on the back. He shrugs me off.

"And if we don't hear from her brother? Saint?"

"We find a different way, just as we always do. You get a legal name?"

"Just her first name. She wouldn't tell me more than she did, and I didn't want to press. How can anyone hurt an innocent woman?" Wrath asks, running his hands uncharacteristically through his dark hair. I play with my barbell between my teeth, trying to think of how to answer his question. I crave death. I enjoy inflicting pain on others. But I've never felt the desire to harm someone innocent. Call me a psycho. Call me unhinged. But I have a moral code. Just like every man here. I know what it takes to do what I do, how I feel, and I can't imagine the type of person who is able to inflict pain on someone innocent, especially a woman.

"I don't know how to answer that, but I do know I look forward to the day I can teach them a lesson."

"You and me both, brother."

My phone vibrates in my pocket, and I pull it out, seeing the little pink pixie bubble moving around. Looks like it's time for me to go pluck my goddess from her garden.

"I'm heading out, you good here?" I ask Wrath.

"Yeah. I'm gonna tap into some contacts I've got, work with Sin on getting this shit figured out. Tracker on?"

"Tracker off."

"Mal. You can't stalk her."

"I can and I will. Now, good day, sir."

I head out the door before Chaos can catch me and order me back inside. Not that I'd listen. I've been juggling my duties as the club's sergeant at arms plus Monroe just fine. Better than fine.

The summer sun was blazing today, but as it begins to set, it's slowly starting to cool off. If I can get to Monroe on time, I know exactly where I want to take her. My bike rumbles to life under me, the heavy weight of it in my grip grounding me as I take off down the long strip of gravel road. The sentries open the gates, and then I'm gone, my tires spinning on the pavement as I peel out. I race to get to her, going faster than I should, but wanting to chase the sunset with her.

Once I'm in downtown Amberwood, I find Monroe walking up the road in the direction of her house. I've yet to see her drive to work. She can't possibly like walking that much. Can she? I slow my bike to a crawl, sidling up next to her, my heart pounding mercilessly behind my ribs.

She stops for a moment, turning to face me, her entire face lit up like I hung the fucking moon. No one's ever looked at me like this before. My heart squeezes behind my ribs, my body practically melting. Fuck, she's so beautiful. Like the sun and the stars, everything that is bright and good. I don't deserve her.

Her hair is down, framing a delicate face, and she's wearing a plain dark blue summer dress with thin straps. Her bare legs are on full display, looking so lean and gorgeous in the wedged sandals she has on. My mouth waters as my eyes roam every inch.

"Crew."

"Pixie," I reply as I meet her crystal-blue eyes. "You look beautiful today."

"Did I not yesterday?" she says as she starts to walk away.

My mouth falls open slightly, shocked by her quip. She's witty. "You look beautiful every day, but I didn't have the balls to tell you yesterday. I'm a coward when it comes to you; now you know my secret." I stay seated on my bike, walking it forward to stay next to her.

To an onlooker, it must look alarming, a tattooed biker following the pretty, unsuspecting girl up the road. I wonder what they'd think if they knew I watched her while she works and sleeps.

"And you suddenly have the balls today, huh?" She playfully turns around to walk backward, her hands clasped behind her, looking so innocent and sweet. If she were only aware of the havoc she wreaks on my heart and mind, she'd understand just how not-so innocent she is.

"Have you ever been on a motorcycle, Monroe?" She looks over the bike, her eyes sparkling.

"Never."

"Let me take you for a ride."

"A ride?"

"Let me be your first." I hold out my hand in offering, nerves filling my stomach. I don't get nervous. Not until Monroe. My eyes meet hers, and I wonder what she sees.

A Monster. A Criminal. An Outlaw.

But when her soft skin meets mine, my eyes shutter closed. I've felt pleasure before. In all different forms. Nothing has ever felt as good as Monroe's skin on my own.

I gently guide her forward, realizing I've never done this before. Never had a woman on the back of my bike. Never been on a date. Never tried to get anyone to fall in love with me.

I remind myself I've ridden this bike a million times, it's the same machine I built myself, same steady heartbeat I've trusted for years, just with the added pressure of carrying something so fragile. So precious and important.

"I promise I won't let anything happen to you."

She looks hesitant, unsure, and I wish I knew what I could say to make her feel comfortable. I'm not good with words. Touch, I can do. Words, not so much.

Be yourself.

Sliding my free hand around her waist, I pull her until she's mere inches away from my bike, my fingers rubbing soft circles at her back. We're eye to eye at this level, and I love being able to look at her pretty, freckled face.

"I promise I'll keep you safe. Swing your leg over behind me, don't touch this exhaust. We'll go slow." Especially because I don't have a helmet for her, and that scares the shit out of me.

To my surprise, Monroe squeezes my hand, stepping out of my hold and pulling up her dress high on her thighs. My cock responds immediately, thickening behind my jeans. Yep. She's ours, buddy. Hopefully soon.

Monroe's legs frame mine hesitantly, like she isn't sure if she's allowed to touch me or be this close. *Fuck that shit.* I steady the bike easily with my legs and feet on the ground while I grab Monroe's thighs, pulling her flush against my back, the warmth of her bare skin seeping into me through the fabric of my jeans. Fuck clothes. Fuck these barriers keeping me from feeling more of her skin on mine.

Then I wrap her arms around my waist over my leather cut. Like usual, I don't have on a T-shirt, so her delicate fingers splay out across my bare stomach.

My muscles contract, my eyes rolling to the back of my head at the contact. She feels so fucking good. "Feet on the pegs, hang on tight, and lean with me. I've got you," I tell her, trying to keep my voice easy to mask how fucking nervous I am, like I'm not hyper-aware of every inch of her touching me, or the magnitude of having her on the back of my bike. This spot is sacred. Reserved only for a biker's old lady. I wish she understood how much this means to me, but I guess I'll just have to show her.

Monroe nods her head.

"Words, pixie."

Her face beams with a smile before she bites her bottom lip. "Got it. I'm ready." She squeezes me around the waist, and then I'm giving the throttle a little juice, pushing us forward. Monroe gasps as we take off, her nails biting into my skin, body tightening around me. Her cheek rests against my cut between my shoulder blades, and the heavy pants of her breath can be felt through the leather.

I pull us out onto Main Street with one location in mind, the best place to watch the sunset in Amberwood. Lookout Lake.

I keep it slow, slower than I've ever ridden before, leaning easy into each turn, guiding her movements with mine. She responds naturally, her arms locked around me like she's afraid to let go and trusts me enough to keep her safe. The wind slices past us, humming in my ears as the town fades behind us, replaced by the wide-open road, large trees, and mountains.

I can feel the moment her breathing changes, steadier and even, relaxed. I feel the panic ebb every foot we travel farther into the miles of solitude stretching in front of us. I fucking love being on my bike like this, and I love it even more with her on the back of it.

We're in perfect sync as we lean into every tight bend, and on the first straightaway, I sense her movements before I feel them. My curious little pixie. Monroe's grip loosens, her chest lifting away from my back, as she sits up a little straighter. Then, so fucking slowly, her arms slide off me.

I have a split second where every basic instinct I have roars forward, screaming at me to slow down, to reach back and pull her close again, but despite my body fighting me, I let her go. I keep the throttle steady and focus on driving the bike I know like an extension of myself. She's trusting me to keep her safe to explore, to feel the world around her like this, and I'll be damned if I let my newfound fear keep her from doing just that. I internally laugh. *Fear.* I don't feel fucking fear.

Not until Monroe.

My heart bottoms out as she stretches her arms out wide, reaching for the sky, the way it reaches for her every day. Her laugh travels on the wind, and it hits me square in the chest, a jolt right through my heart. She's perfect. This is perfect. I never want it to end.

Monroe's thighs tighten around me, grounding herself in her own way, trusting me. She's trusting *me.* A monster. A demon. Just that knowledge alone, that of all the places she could be, of all the people she could be with, she's choosing and trusting *me*, clinging to *me.*

I've carried a lot of things on this bike since Rolo brought me to Hell's Heathens.

Rage.

Pain.

Death.

Grief.

Darkness.

Blood I couldn't wash off my hands, no matter how hard I tried. But this? This is light. This is hope wrapped in leather and lace. I never want to give this feeling up.

The change happens quickly, and I almost panic, unsure what unseen danger I've missed while wrapped up in the moment. Monroe's arms bound around my waist, squeezing me hard repeatedly, her thighs clenching around me. I'm not great at reading people, but I feel her panic. I slow to a stop and pull over at a small lookout point, the gravel crunching under my tires.

I turn around slightly to check on her, only to find her eyes blown wide. I recognize this one. It's fear. All of the feelings that filled me a moment ago shatter. Is she scared of me? My heart sinks.

"Are you okay?"

"No. Please don't go up there. Please don't take us to Lookout Lake." I look up the road at the windy incline. Is she afraid of heights? I cut the engine, turning around just enough to grab her by the waist and spin her around so she's sitting in front of me, her legs lying across mine, her ass in my lap. Her dress has ridden up in the process, but I stay focused on her face, as much as I want a peek at her bare thighs.

"Okay, we'll stay right here. I wanted to take you to see the sunset. Are you okay?"

Monroe visibly relaxes and nods. I reach out, brushing the backs of my fingers over her cheek before tucking a strand of windblown hair behind her ear. Electricity sparks at the contact, and based on the way her eyes seem to glow, I'm guessing she feels it, too.

Please feel it, too. I don't know what the fuck I'm doing.

"Fuck, pixie, you're so beautiful to look at." Her face heats with crimson, making her freckles pop. The sun continues to descend, the rich reds and oranges spanning across the horizon. Its beauty has nothing on the woman in front of me.

"I don't know about that."

"It's true. A monster like me shouldn't get the privilege to even look at you."

She reaches out and runs her fingers through my hair, my eyes involuntarily shuttering closed at the contact. It feels so good. It's not sexual or arousing, it's something I'm not used to. Tender and sweet.

"I don't see a monster anywhere." Hell, she's perfect. How can this goddess look at me and think anything else? "Tell me about you, Crew. Where are you from? How'd you end up a Hell's Heathen?"

Unease starts to settle into my bones. "Those are very sad stories."

"Then we'll start with the basics. Tell me your favorite color." That, I can do.

"Black. What's yours?"

"Pink." I reach for her hair, studying the light pink shade between my two fingers, the chipped black nail polish that coats my nails such a stark contrast. Her fingers delicately swipe across the bare skin of my waist, like she doesn't even realize she's exploring me. I feel every single point of contact down to a cellular level.

"Why don't you ever wear a shirt?"

I laugh at this one. "I hate clothes. Too restrictive. I wouldn't wear any if it were socially acceptable. But my president said it's a mandatory rule when out in the open unless you're fucking." I realize I've said it a moment too late. But I get the privilege of watching Monroe's face heat slowly, a pretty pink blush that creeps across her cheeks.

"Fair enough. Is that . . . is that something that happens?" Oh, my curious little pixie. She's full of surprises.

"Fucking out in the open?" I ask, my voice dropping slightly deeper as my chest rises and falls a little harder. Monroe bites her bottom lip again, and it's so sexy.

"Sometimes. Some men like it, like our secretary, Wrath. He gets off knowing people are watching him and his partner."

"Oh."

"I like privacy for the stuff I'm into." Her fingers twitch around me in response, her eyes downcast until she slowly looks up at me through her long, pretty eyelashes.

"And whh-what's that?" My eyes flick to her lips—so soft, pink, and pouty. I can't look away, my head dipping closer and closer to hers, until we're sharing air. Our breaths mingle, our chests rising and falling harder now.

"You'd have to experience it to understand," I whisper. My hands slide into Monroe's hair, angling her head from side to side as I run my nose up the length of hers and back down the other side. Pretty blue eyes flutter closed as my lips brush hers, swiping back and forth several times, inhaling her rich scent. Then I'm kissing her.

This is what I'm good at. Touch. Physical connection. Fuck words. Words are meaningless. Action is everything. And right now, I want to kiss this woman until I erase every trace of everyone who came before me. Until she lives and breathes *me*. Until there's no question how I feel about her and where she stands.

My tongue swipes across her seam, demanding entrance. She opens up willingly, meeting my tongue in the middle. Sparks fly between us, an energy flowing at a cosmic level. I've never experienced anything so intense. But now I'm even more convinced. She was made for me, and Rolo put her right in front of me.

She may look delicate, but there's nothing fragile about her. She's a queen. Even if she just rules over me. Monroe quiets the dark desires, my thirst for blood and vengeance, and that alone isn't an easy feat. She's light and goodness, and instead of trying to fix me, she's embracing my darkness and sharing her light.

This woman makes me feel like there's hope for me, a chance to be different and better. She deserves everything, and I'm determined to be the man who gives it all to her.

My hands grip her thighs, my fingers slipping under the thin fabric of her dress and slowly sliding upward. Her bare skin is so soft and smooth, and despite the chilly night air, she's burning up.

Monroe moans into my mouth, and I greedily swallow it down. I reach the outside of her thighs where her legs meet her hip and dip around, gripping the top of her ass and jerking her forward. Her core meets the hard outline of my dick through my jeans, and she shudders in my arms, a gasp on her lips. I rock her against me as her hands explore my chest, her fingers taking a moment to toy with the hoop pierced through my nipple.

Her touch ignites a wildfire within me. I'm burning up, my emotions firing on all cylinders. It's all too much and not enough at the same time. It's an awakening. Like a veil has been lifted, and I'm suddenly living for the first time.

Monroe tastes like sweetness, delicious and rare, and I can't get enough. I suck her tongue into my mouth, wanting more of her, wanting all of it. Her fingers continue to sweep across my chest, a touch that's somehow soft but also confident.

When we break apart, we do it slowly, my fingers gripping her hair one last time, my lips gently placing delicate kisses to each corner of her mouth before sitting back to look at her. I keep my hands on her, not wanting to sever the connection.

"I never do this," she confesses, running two of her fingers over her puffy lips. Her eyes are heavily lidded and hazy, and I so badly want to see what she looks like after I've made her come so many times she's taken to the stars. But I'm determined to take my time with her. She deserves that. She's nothing like the patch bunnies or playthings I've brought to my dungeon to fuck into oblivion, so I'm not going to treat her that way. I've got to make this different.

"Kiss?"

"Kiss near-strangers."

"Do I feel like a stranger, Monroe?"

She looks up at me, meeting my eyes, the blue getting lost in the darkness of my own.

"No, no, you've never felt like a stranger."

She doesn't to me, either. We're two halves of a whole and have finally found our missing piece.

"Let me take you home," I tell her, even if it's taking all my strength. I want to pluck her from her life and have her join me in mine, but I need it to be her choice. I'm smart enough to know that much.

The ride back into town goes by too quickly, as I drive to 7 Wildflower Lane. Monroe climbs off the back of my bike, taking all her light with her. She doesn't seem to notice that I know where she lives, but I'm sure it'll hit her later.

"Thank you, Crew. That was . . ." she starts, then trails off. I reach for her face, running the back of my knuckles across her cheeks.

"Yeah," I say, because I know exactly what she means.

"I'll see you soon?"

Sooner than you realize, pixie.

CHAPTER SIXTEEN
MONROE

The next day, I throw myself into work, despite the lingering feeling of Crew on my lips and the stalker's eyes constantly on me. I've started to feel the heat of them everywhere I go. It's become my constant shadow, a part of me now.

I pull on my PPE and start the washing and disinfecting process of Mr. Acers. Once he's thoroughly clean, I get to work on massaging his body to relieve the rigor mortis, and setting his facial features, needing to use sutures for this one to keep his lips closed and mouth in the correct form.

Taking care of the dead has never bothered me or made me squeamish. I've never thought it was any different than taking care of the living. Except, it's easier to make up a narrative in my head about the type of person they were and the life they led, while I pay my respects to the body that made that living possible.

I often think about how my friends were taken care of and if the mortician struggled to prep their bodies. I was in a medically induced coma for eight weeks to give my body time to heal from my injuries. I do know they all had closed-casket celebrations of life instead of viewings, and I can only imagine why. The image of Nora's hand slipping from mine in less than a heartbeat as she was thrown through the middle of the car and out the windshield will never leave me.

After I've finished with my tasks, I make a small incision and start the arterial embalming process. I finish with Mr. Acers right before lunch, and instead of going to the breakroom, I decide to eat out, craving a sandwich from Maggie's and needing some fresh air.

Just as I'm about to cross the street, a firm hand grips my forearm, pulling me back. I stumble with a gasp, but quickly right myself and come face-to-face with Tyler's twin brother, Zach. My heart sinks into the pit of my stomach.

"Glad I caught you."

"Hi, Zach." I don't know where to look, so I shift from foot to foot, nervously playing with the hem of my dress. Every time I look at his face, I see Tyler's eyes through the rearview mirror. A year after the accident, Nora's family moved out of Washington, claiming they needed a fresh start. As much as I'd never want to really leave Amberwood, I get the appeal. Everyone knows everyone here, and there's no hiding your secrets. Why would my best friend's parents want a constant reminder that I got to live when their daughter didn't? Javier was a foreign exchange student who was living with Zach and Tyler's family that year, so that just leaves me. Alone. Here in Amberwood. A constant walking reminder of the tragedy that rocked every single one of the residents to their core.

"How are you, Roe?"

"I'm good. Is there something you need? I only have so long, and I need to go grab my lunch before getting back to work."

"I just wanted to warn you about that man you were with the other day. That's Crew Lawson, but he's known as Malice. He's the Hell's Heathens bloodhound, their resident psychopath. You need to stay away from him, Roe. He's dangerous," Zach mansplains like I live under a rock and haven't heard the rumors or read the name tag on Crew's leather vest with my own eyes.

Crew may look dangerous, and he very well may be dangerous if the rumors are true, but he'd never hurt me. I don't actually have any reason to know that, but it's a feeling, something deep and raw that I'm confident about.

"I appreciate the warning, Zach, but I promise you, I'm fine." I take a step forward, ready to leave, when Zach's hand grabs around my forearm, making me wince.

"You don't understand. He's killed people, Roe. The rumors are as bad as it gets. Why are you hanging out with him anyway? Trying to stir up some trouble?"

"Excuse me?" I say, ripping my arm out of his hold. "I don't know what you're insinuating, but you really should mind your own business."

Zach chuckles under his breath, surprising me. "You know, I've heard about this: people who cheat death either become reckless or put themselves in a bubble. Here we all were thinking it was the latter, but clearly, we were wrong."

"I didn't cheat death, Zach, I was brought back to life against my own will. You all should mind your own business and not be so worried about what I'm doing." I make another attempt to step away from him, but Zach's eyes squint, his arm reaching out and grabbing me again, jerking me into his front. My hands connect with his chest as I try to push him off me. "What are you doing? Let me go!"

"If you're looking to be a reckless slut, I'd be happy to let you work it out with me. Consider it payment for surviving when my other half didn't. I'd like to know what makes you so special."

What happens next is a blur. One moment, Zach has a brutal hold on my biceps, and the next, I'm standing behind Crew, his arm reaching behind him to hold me there and out of the way. I blink away the haze and find Zach pressed against the brick building we're standing in front of, Crew's hand around his throat, holding him in place and restricting his airway. Zach grapples with Crew's arm, but it doesn't do any good.

"She doesn't owe you or anyone a fucking thing. You so much as look in her direction, and I will gut you like a fish while you're still alive. And if you ever touch her, I'll make sure you and the rest of your family join your brother in the afterlife. Nod if you understand me."

Zach nods, and Crew squeezes one last time, like he's having to restrain himself before letting him go. Zach falls to his knees, coughing and heaving air into his lungs.

Zach's warning replays in my head. That Crew is dangerous. But just like I've felt all along, he's not a danger to me, and watching him defend me, watching him hold Zach like that, a warmth spreads low in my belly, my panties dampening with arousal.

I'm so fucked up.

Crew turns to face me, clearly not worried about Zach behind us as he struggles to get his lungs what he needs to survive. Crew's hands gently cradle my face, the hands that just held Zach by his throat and promised him a slow, painful death. He touches me with reverence, so gentle and sweet.

"Are you alright? Did he hurt you?" His voice is soft, so at odds with how he sounded while threatening Zach.

I shake my head, looking into the inky darkness of his eyes. They swallow all the light instead of reflecting it, unreadable but expressive at the same time.

"Words, pixie."

"My arms are sore, but he didn't hurt me. I'm okay." Crew's eyes bounce all over my face like he's working hard to read my expression. He doesn't seem convinced. I don't know what comes over me, and I couldn't explain it if I tried. But in this moment, I want—I need—to put him at ease. I can't bear the tortured look on his face.

I lift up on my toes, gripping his forearms for leverage as I pull him down to me. My hands wrap around his neck, and my lips meet his. He takes a moment to respond, but then his arms curl around my waist, easily lifting me off the ground and standing tall. My feet dangle as I'm held in his arms, as he holds me close. He tastes like mint gum and something so wholly him. His tongue tangles with mine, kissing me like he's desperate for it, like he's waited all day to be able to do it. I tease the barbell pierced through his tongue, and I love the way it feels against mine. I can't help but imagine what it would feel like on other parts of my body.

Crew sets me back down on the ground, his hands moving up

to clasp my cheeks before he drops several more chaste kisses to my lips, like he can't get enough.

"Oh! I have a present for you!"

"A present?"

"Yeah, and it's the perfect time!"

Crew pulls a sleek black case from his pocket and hands it to me. At first look, it passes for a jewelry box, but when I open it, I'm staring down at a quite beautiful knife. It folds closed, and the pommel is a stunning mother of pearl. I run my finger delicately across the smooth, white surface.

"It's beautiful, Crew, thank you." Of all the things I thought a man would gift me someday, this wasn't even in the top one hundred. But somehow, I like this more than any of those other options.

"I wanted you to have something to protect yourself with." I glance behind him at Zach, who's still struggling to breathe.

"It's perfect," I tell him as I put it in my purse.

"Hungry?" he asks.

"I'm starving." Crew steps away from the building and onto the cobblestone sidewalk. I follow him, but as I get closer, I reach for his hand, lacing our fingers together. He flinches, and I'm suddenly unsure if holding it in public was the right move.

"Is this okay?"

"You want to hold my hand? Out here?"

I look around at downtown Amberwood, at the people I've known my entire life, wandering around town, living their lives. I look at the businesses that have been here longer than I have and then back up at Crew. My head cranes backward to look at him. He's so much taller than me, and I secretly love that. I hate that he looks so confused, so concerned, like he's spent his life hiding and has become so accustomed to the dark, he doesn't dare step into the light.

"Why wouldn't I?"

Crew gestures to himself with his hands, giving me a look that says, "hello?" He's wearing a pair of tight, ripped denim jeans that hang low on his hips, a tight black T-shirt, his leather vest, and combat boots that are laced up past his ankles. He looks bad-boy hot, and I'm obsessed with the stark difference between the two of us. He's rebellion and anti-conformism, and I'm playing it safe.

Dark eyeliner lines his eyes, his septum pierced with a hoop, his hair is wild and unnaturally blond, and a dangling knife earring hangs from one of his ears. He's authentically himself, and it's everything I wish I had the guts to be.

"I like you, Crew. A lot. People have been whispering about me for years; it doesn't bother me. Let them stare, let them talk. I don't care. I want to have lunch with you. Will you keep me company?" Crew adjusts his tongue ring between his teeth, and the action has me rubbing my thighs together slightly. I want him.

"Let's go get you fed, then." Crew clasps my hand, rethreading our fingers back together as we walk up Main Street toward the bright red building that says *Maggie's* on a glowing neon sign. The door chimes as we walk in together, and based on the silence that stretches and the eyes that fall on us, you'd think we just walked in completely naked.

Maggie stands with her hip popped out to the side, hands braced on the counter, with her eyebrows raised.

"Corrupting the innocent, Crew?" she says as we approach.

"Only if she'll let me."

And that warmth between my thighs just turned into molten lava.

"Run while you still can, Roe. Take it from me, those Heathens are nothing but trouble."

Crew gasps from next to me, putting his hand over his heart. "Maggie! You've wounded me, ma'am. I've never done a thing to you."

"But your patch brother sure did, didn't he? Did he like my surprise, by the way?"

"I don't know, let me ask him."

"Go ahead and do that. How are you, Roe? You look good, happy."

Maggie and I went to school together. Granted, she was two years older than me, and we never ran in the same circles, but you know, small town and all. Crew pulls out his phone, typing something out. My eyes roam the solid structure of his face, the bump on the bridge of his nose. He's so handsome. So forbidden and mysterious.

"Looks like it's too late for you," Maggie says with a smirk.

"What do you mean?"

Her eyes flash over to Crew, and my heart stutters in my chest. She may be right.

Crew shakes his phone, laughing at whatever he's about to share. "Wrath says, and I quote, 'that devil woman poisoned me.' I fucking knew it wasn't a coincidence."

"Serves him right. Roe, if you ever need my secret sauce to get back at one of these fuckers, you know where to find me. Now, what can I get you two?"

I have no idea what any of that means, but Crew and I order our sandwiches and walk over to one of the booths in the back, away from prying eyes. He slides into the seat across from me, looking every bit the dangerously handsome bad boy that he is.

"What was all that about?" I ask him.

"Oh, Maggie? Wrath fucked her, then fucked her sister, and claims he didn't know it wasn't her. Maggie got pissed."

My mouth falls open slightly. "Were they dating?"

"Nah, Wrath doesn't date. Just fucks."

I shrug. But when Crew says that last word, I can't help but squeeze my thighs together. My core clenches at the thought of what Crew's like when he *fucks*. I run my fingers across my lips as I remember what it felt like to have him kiss me, just moments ago, and the other day. I've been dreaming about that since it happened. The way he held my ass in his palms kept my core pressed against him. He was so hard, and I could feel exactly how I affected him.

Crew watches me, his lips turning up on one side, his eyes squinting like he knows exactly what I'm thinking about and how he affects me.

"What are you thinking about in that pretty, curious little brain of yours, pixie?"

"Oh, uhm. Just thoughts."

"Mmm. Just thoughts? Are you thinking about what it was like to sit in my lap with your pussy pressed against my cock while I kissed you?"

Oh, God. My face heats, and my core pulses. I shift in my seat, my panties dampening.

"You're so pretty when you blush, Monroe."

"You're very skilled at making me blush, *Crew*."

"Tell me about your family. There's a lot of you?"

Good. A change in topic is very, very good. Because I'm two seconds away from crawling over the table to kiss him again.

"They're the best. We're all really close. My grandparents on my dad's side live with us, and my parents have eight kids total. I'm the oldest, and their only biological kid, not that it matters. Then the other seven were adopted. After me comes my sister Aurora, who's eighteen, then my brother Atticus, who's fifteen, then the twins—Wyatt and Miles—who are fourteen. Lucy is twelve, Hazel ten, and the youngest, Cooper, is six. We're all really close." Crew just looks at me like I hung the stars, like he's clinging to every single word. "Do you have any family?"

His eyes take on a more serious emotion, and I anticipate the worst. "Just the club. The man you took care of, Jesse? He saved my life. I didn't have anything before he came along."

"I'm so sorry for your loss, Crew. He was way too young."

Crew taps his middle finger against the tabletop. "I haven't thanked you for taking care of him, for getting him ready and all that."

"It's what I do. Honestly, it's my honor. I lost someone close to me, too. She was my best friend and taken way too young. I wonder about how her body was taken care of, and it's important to me that I'm respectful with everyone who comes in. They're someone special to someone."

"I wish you'd never felt that kind of loss, Monroe." Me too. "How'd you end up being a mortician?"

"I thought I wanted to be a nurse, and then I realized the dead are easier to be around than the living."

Crew nods, as if he understands that completely. For the first time in a really long time, I feel seen, and it feels so good, I never want it to end.

CHAPTER SEVENTEEN

MONROE

I wake from my sleep slowly, but my body feels alert. I feel it before I can explain it. The back of my neck tingles, the air itself leaning closer, as if it, too, is holding its breath. That same feeling that's been haunting me for weeks, so strong it steals the breath from my lungs.

I don't dare open my eyes, my ears listening for footsteps, breathing, anything. But it's the same room, the same quiet that comforts me every night, even if it feels different.

The silence thickens around me, and I open my eyes, letting them adjust to the heavy darkness that blankets the room. My swallow is as loud as a drum beat, but I still don't hear anything out of the ordinary, even if my body is convinced otherwise. I don't know how to explain it. Intuition? My conscience? I know I'm not alone.

My eyes dart around the room, looking for shadows in the dark corners. With shaky hands, I quickly push myself up to sit, facing forward, my eyes tracing over every inch of my studio.

The house is the same, nothing out of place, and no one here but me and my plants.

I can't explain it, but I could swear I'm not alone. Even now, I can see that I am, but my body and mind refuse to submit to the facts. I *feel* it. Feel a presence.

I flick on my end table lamp, the dim light illuminating the space around me in a warm glow. My eyes focus on the chair sitting in the corner of the room, and I gasp, scurrying back against my headboard. I blink away the blurriness, my eyes adjusting further, making out the bright blond of his hair, the way the light reflects off his skin, and my heart sinks into my stomach. Crew is in my bedroom, sitting there like it's the most natural, normal thing in the world. My heart pounds in my chest, blood rushing between my ears as I sway slightly.

"Crew?"

"Monroe."

Understanding washes over me. Oh my God. It's been Crew all along. Of course it's him. The familiarity, the scent, the way I welcomed it like an old friend. It all started after I met Crew that day at the mortuary. How did I not put that together on my own? He's been watching me, leaving me flowers. Anyone else would have felt wrong, terrifying. But from the moment I met him, I've been enamored.

"What are you doing?" I ask when he doesn't look up from his lap.

"Reading." I scoot forward, looking at what he could possibly be doing in my room, reading, when it hits me.

"Crew . . . is that my *journal*?"

"It is."

"That's an invasion of privacy."

"So is me being in your room every night to watch you sleep."

My mouth falls open. "You-you do that?"

He just hums his agreement, and I don't know what to do with that fact. How can he think this is normal and acceptable behavior, and why does the idea of it turn me on? But then he starts reading out loud, and my face heats with fire.

"'Crew brings out a different side of me I've never experienced before. I always play it safe, careful, but when I look at him, I start to unravel. Heat pools low in my belly, my heart rate skyrocketing, my hands shaky. He affects me in a way I've never felt before. I wonder what it would feel like to be touched by him. To feel him moving above, to feel him inside me. I want him. All his dangerously dark, sharp edges. So instead of going after what I want, because I don't know how to ask for it, I resort to touching myself. Touching myself to thoughts of him doing it for me, of him pleasuring me. But I can never seem to get myself there. It's frustrating, and I don't know what to do about it.' Dirty pixie. Is that what you do when you're all alone here at night? Touch your pussy to thoughts of me? I've only ever seen you do it once, and it looked like you didn't get what you wanted."

My face is burning, a flaming heat I've never felt before. I want to hide my face in my hands, but every fiber of my being is telling me not to. My heart is racing, and I can't get enough air into my lungs.

"Tell me. I really want to know."

I nod my head without looking away from him.

"Words, pixie."

I look down at my hands twisting in the fabric of my sheets. "Yes."

"Yes, what?"

"Yes, I touch myself to thoughts of you."

"Mmm. Show me."

My eyes snap to his. "Wh-what?"

"Take off your panties, Monroe. Show me how you touch yourself when you're dreaming of me."

"Crew . . ." I plead. But even as I say his name, I'm not sure if I'm begging for him to stop this before it starts, or never let it end. I can feel how wet my panties are already. I know I want this, want everything he has to offer me.

"Show me. Let me see." His eyes are dark orbs staring at me with all the focus in the world. He toys with his tongue ring between his teeth as he relaxes back in the chair, his long legs spread apart casually, his arms draped over the back like he has all the time in the world to wait for me to give him what he so desperately desires.

I don't know where the courage comes from, but ever so slowly, I lift my nightgown above my hips and hook my fingers into the string of my panties. Crew freezes his ministrations, his tongue retreating back into his mouth, instead leaning forward and bracing his forearms on his knees, waiting, watching. I drag them down my thighs and over my knees before they fall to my ankles. Once the first foot is free, I kick the fabric off, where it lands on the floor.

Crew reaches forward, picking up my black lace panties and holding them to his face. My mouth parts, watching in shock as he takes a long inhale, breathing in my scent, his eyes rolling to the back of his head. Jesus Christ, he's breathing in my dirty panties. Why is that so hot?

"Fuck, you smell so good. So sweet. So perfect." Crew pockets my panties before leaning back down against his thighs. "Show me. Make yourself feel good."

I take a slow, stuttering breath and open my legs. The room is shrouded in darkness, my light spilling in just enough around me to illuminate things. I know he can see all of me, and there's something about it that gives me a boost of confidence, that makes me feel powerful. This dangerous, strong man is begging to watch me touch myself for him. *Me.* Of all the places he could be, of all the women he could be with, he's here with me.

The moment my legs fall completely open, a deep, primal growl fills the room. It's more animalistic than human and should have me screaming for help. But I feel my core clench in response, my pussy dripping with need.

"Damn, that's a pretty pussy," he growls.

I slip my fingers through my lips, finding myself just as wet as I knew I was. I press a single finger inside me, rubbing the heel of my palm against my aching clit.

"Look at my pretty little pixie girl being so dirty for the big bad Heathen."

"Oh, god."

"There's no such thing as God. There's only a Heathen here.

Make yourself come, show me what you look like when you let go."

I squeeze in a second finger, but it's tight, pumping into myself several times before dragging my wetness up to swirl around my aching clit. Crew doesn't say anything, and the only noise filling the room is our heavy breathing.

I want him to come touch me, to use his fingers or his mouth. I almost beg him, tell him that I need him. But I don't want to break the moment.

Pleasure spirals out from my core, spreading through my body. My knees start to shake slightly, but just as I start to feel that climb, it starts to ebb.

"Come for me, Monroe."

"I-I can't," I whine in frustration.

"Yes, you can. Relax and let go. Don't think, just feel. That pretty pussy wants to come for me so bad. I can see you dripping from here."

I bite down on my bottom lip, capturing it between my teeth while I focus on Crew. His eyes are the darkest I've ever seen them, practically black and soulless as they watch me. His fingertips stroke up and down his bare chest mindlessly, and I wonder if he's hard right now under those jeans. He's cocooned among the shadows like a ghost, sitting in the corner, stretched out like the king of the underworld.

I press down on my swollen clit, swirling my fingers in a circle around it. Pleasure starts to climb again, and I grip the sheets with my free hand, a small moan escaping my lips.

"That's it. Just like that. Now dip a finger back inside and go back up to that needy clit."

His mouth. I didn't know men actually spoke like this to their women. *Their women.* Is that what I am to him? It sure has felt like it since the very first moment I met him. Crew is all-consuming.

Tension coils tighter and tighter, and knowing Crew is right there, his dark obsidian eyes watching me, knowing that those eyes are the same eyes that have stalked me, who have been with me for weeks now, threatens to snap that tension into oblivion.

My hips start to move of their own accord, and I keep my eyes focused on him, watching how he plays with his tongue ring, how his fists clench and unclench at his sides. He watches me touch myself like an addict staring at his next hit, like he's desperate for it, like he'd do anything to have it.

"That's my good pixie. You're so close. Come for your Heathen."

And then, just like that, I'm coming. I scream out as my back arches, my legs shake uncontrollably, and my stomach clenches. Wave after wave thrashes me with pleasure I've never felt before. My core clenches as my fingers slip through my wetness. I'm completely gone to the sensations, and even though I don't want to, even though I fight against it, my eyes flutter closed as my body heats and vibrations roll through me.

When the last wave ebbs, I let my hand fall away to the side, my knees falling shut as I try to regain my ability to breathe normally. Just as I open my eyes, I realize Crew is gone, and my heart plummets. I can't help but wonder if it was all a figment of my imagination, or if Crew was really here with me at all. If it weren't for the lingering scent of fire and rain, I'd almost believe he wasn't.

CHAPTER EIGHTEEN

CREW

I barely make it outside and to the side of Monroe's house before shoving my jeans down my thighs and stroking my hard cock with her lace panties. I brace myself with my hand on the wall, rubbing from root to tip in a firm grip, my thumb passing over my pierced crown. Precum spills from my slit like a greedy fucker, and it only takes a few strokes before I'm erupting with her name spilling from my lips.

Rope after rope coats the delicate little flowers below me, my knees nearly buckling into the mulch. Monroe is more than I ever could have bargained for. I didn't intend for tonight to go the way it did. I just wanted to slip into her room and watch her sleep again and finally place the cameras I had ordered. But when I found her journal and opened it to the page I did . . . my cock woke up, and so did Monroe.

Fuck, she's so hot. So responsive and needy. She struggles to get herself off on her own, and it makes me wonder how experienced she is. It took everything I had not to bury my face between her legs and get her there myself, but I wanted to watch. Needed to watch.

My phone buzzes in my pocket, and I yank up my jeans, not bothering to button them, and pull out my phone.

Chaos: Tracker is off again. Mal really?

Me: You're a needy fucker

Me: You really do like this group chat, huh? I knew you would! You just wanted to play hard to get

Chaos: You had better not be stalking her

Me: I don't stalk people

Wrath: Are you watching her and following her?

Me: Yes

Sin: Does she know about it?

Me: She does now

Sin: What?

Me: She woke up while I was watching her sleep

Chaos: Are you shitting me right now?

Me: Sir! We don't talk about bathroom habits in the group chat!

Sin: That's not what that means buddy

Wrath: Tell us you didn't break into her house

Me: I didn't break into her house

Chaos: Turn your fucking tracker on and get back to the clubhouse. I can't lose any more brothers

Wrath: We heard from Sienna's brother. There's info and movement.

Me: Who's Sienna?

Wrath: The fucking waitress in Autumn Bay

Me: Fuck I knew that. Post nut clarity isn't coming

Chaos: Jesus christ what did you do?

Me: Not her if that's what you're worried about

Sin: Get your ass back here

Me: On my way

Tension is radiating off every surface the moment I walk into the clubhouse. Wrath takes one look at me and rolls his eyes.

"Put yourself together, fucker. At least button and zip up the damn pants after you've fucked," Wrath snaps.

"I didn't fuck. At least, I didn't fuck *her*. Like I said. I fucked my hand. Have you ever come on flowers? I wonder if it'll help them grow or if it'll kill them." Wrath blinks slowly at me, and I wonder if it was something I said. "What?"

"Do I even want to ask?"

"Ask what?"

He takes a deep breath, looking up at the ceiling before staring at me straight on. "I know I'm gonna regret this. Why are you blowing your load on flowers, Mal?"

"Where else was I going to let it go? I was jerking off on the side of her house."

"Mal, what the fuck, dude? Did she know?"

"I'm not going to kiss and tell, good sir. I am a gentleman!"

"For fuck's sake. You're a twisted fuck."

"That's rich coming from you. Everyone here has seen that beast you're packing. Have you thought about decorating it?" I tease, loving giving these guys shit.

"What?"

"Piercings." I start to pull open my pants. "Like these."

"Put your cock away, Malice!" Chaos yells as he storms into the room. "Church!" Wrath slaps me in the stomach, and I button and zip my pants back up, following them into our sanctuary.

The six of us take our places around the table, my eyes settling on Rolo's empty seat before looking away. It's hard to believe he's actually gone. I've been avoiding Morgan, and guilt starts to creep in. I would rather it had been me that day instead of him. I'm out here craving death and destruction, and Rolo was working hard to save anyone who needed saving.

"The waitress got the burner phone number to her brother. He contacted us tonight. So, she turned out to be trustworthy, at least so far. He's willing to meet halfway tonight. He doesn't want to do phones," Chaos reports. I look down at my phone that's in my lap to check the time. It's fucking two in the morning. I guess I don't sleep, anyway.

"I'll go. Wrath, you up for a ride?"

"Yeah. When is he free?"

"Right fucking now, so get on the road. Trackers on, Malice, I don't want to tell you again. Bring your guns, and be ready for anything. I don't like this. But if we want to get our hands on Garrett, this is the way in. See what he wants, stay on guard, and don't make any decisions without bringing it here first."

Tension rolls through me, deep and thick. I crack my neck to the side, standing and straightening my cut. I want that fucker to beg for death, and I'll do just about anything to get him.

A car flashes its lights at us from the side of the road as we reach the coordinates. Wrath and I pull off to the side a few yards in front of him, and as we're getting out of the truck, I check my gun and knife one last time. The man waiting for us steps into the light, holding both of his arms out wide, showing us he's unarmed. At least in his hands.

I nod at Wrath, and together, we walk toward him, stopping short of just a few feet distance between us. I size up the man in front of us. Pretty fucking wild he came alone, but I know firsthand that desperate men do desperate things. He's wearing a pair of dark denim jeans, Converse sneakers, a plain T-shirt, and street clothes. His head is shaved damn near to the skin, but his full beard and eyebrow ring kind of round it out.

"Saint," he says.

"Malice. This is Wrath."

"I come with a gift, but first, I want to plead my case."

My eyes narrow at him, unsure where the hell this could be going.

"We didn't drive an hour to negotiate. We need the information. Garrett or whatever fucking name he's currently going by killed one of our own. Infiltrated our clubhouse with two other men. We're lucky he didn't do more damage. They could have slaughtered us all." Well, they could have tried.

"Yeah, I got that from what my sister told me. Figure it's safe to assume the other two men were dealt with, so in a show of good faith, I brought him to you. He's in the trunk of my car. However this next part goes, you can still take him with you. He deserves whatever slow and painful death he has coming, and I won't stand in your way."

Adrenaline pumps through my veins at an alarming rate, and I crack my neck from side to side. He's just going to give him up to us?

"He's here?" Wrath asks.

"Have a look for yourself if you don't believe me. But then we're talking. You owe me that much," Saint demands, and my respect for him grows a little more.

I'm not going to argue with him if fucknuts is actually in the trunk. We follow Saint around his car, and I put my hand on my knife, staying alert and focused, even if my vision is closing in at the sides, my mouth salivating like a fucking hound on the hunt. Saint pops the trunk and sure as shit, the ugly fucker himself is gagged and hog-tied, looking awfully uncomfortable squished in the small trunk. How unfortunate for him.

I nod my head, turning to face Saint, tapping my middle finger against the outside of my thigh. "Alright, we're listening. What do you want?"

"My club back."

I snort, but Wrath's eyes narrow at him.

"And how are we supposed to help you with that?"

"Just like that. Your club helps me take it back."

"How many do you have backing you?" Wrath asks, and my head snaps in his direction. We agreed to listen, not negotiate. What the hell is he doing?

"Not enough to make a difference, but enough to count. Don't forget this affects you, too. The new president of my club was your guy's brother. He put out that hit. We'll help you get vengeance; you help me get the club back. I brought this dipshit to you as an olive branch. We can work together, and all get what we want."

I look him over, trying to size him up. Wrath already seems to have made up his mind as he nods. Too bad we need to take it to Chaos and Sin for a vote. Looking for Garrett is one thing, attacking another club—whether we have the right to retaliation or not—needs a vote and preparation.

"We'll take him back with us and relay your message to our president and club. We'll contact you through the burner."

"His name is Cain. And he's a ruthless sonofabitch. He needs to be dealt with. I—look, I've got personal reasons I need this done, other than the obvious. He's got his eyes on my sister. I can't get close enough to kill him myself, and even if I did, he's got his dogs that are just waiting to bite. I'm man enough to know when to be humble and ask for help. I don't think you fully understand the severity of the trouble we're in here, so here I am. Tell your president that he can have whatever he wants; we'll owe him, and he can cash in whenever he needs. You all can have Cain. We just need this dismantled, and we need your help to do it."

Damn. From my short amount of time on Earth, I know it takes a lot for a man to practically beg. But if someone he loves is in jeopardy, I get it. I'd burn the world down for my little pixie, and I know my brothers would do the same for their old ladies.

"I get it. I'll make it a priority. Keep the phone close."

"My sister has it. I can't take the chance. But she knows how to get word to me, so relay everything through her. She's grown up in this life. She'll be discreet."

"Alright, then. We'll be in touch." I take a step closer to dear Garrett and slap his face twice. He's still unconscious, so whatever Saint gave him is doing the trick. I can't wait to see his face when he wakes up and finds out his life is going to end.

He's about to learn what happens when you deceive a Heathen.

CHAPTER NINETEEN

MONROE

Dear Diary,

Last night was unexpected to say the least. Even as I lay here in my bed, I can't stop staring at the chair in the corner of my little house. I slept the rest of the night off and on, tossing and turning and going back and forth with whether or not it happened at all or if I really was dreaming. But I know what I felt, and I'll never be able to erase the feeling of Crew's eyes on me. The same eyes that have followed me for weeks now. The ones that I crave, the ones that I look for everywhere I go. It was Crew all along. Crew is my stalker. It's like the two pieces have finally come together and knowing it now makes perfect sense.

I've felt stuck for so long, stuck in my quiet, safe routine, stuck in my mundane existence where I'm walking a tight rope between the living and the dead.

Crew makes me want to live. He makes me want to chase the feelings he brings out in me and explore every possibility. I've never been in love before, and I don't know enough about him to understand why I feel the way I do. But I recognize it. I think I'm in love with the dangerous ghost that is Crew Lawson.

For the first time in my career, I called out of work for a sick day. George was more than understanding since I've been such a dependable employee, and part of me felt guilty for not going in. But I needed to get my head on straight, and I wasn't going to do that at work with the feeling of my stalker—Crew—on me all day long.

But being in my house all day didn't change anything. Somehow, that feeling is with me constantly now, even in my home in the light of day.

Despite the lingering feeling that takes my breath away, I spent the day pampering myself. I took a long bubble bath, shaved my legs, and painted my toes a pretty new shade of bubblegum pink. Then I pulled out all the ingredients to bake chocolate chip cookies, but that feeling nagging at the back of my neck prevented me from making them right away. Instead, I decided to sit down at my piano and let myself be taken away with the music.

Each song flows easily into the next, my eyes closing as I play songs that come out with muscle memory. My body starts to feel lighter, and even though that feeling doesn't ever go away,

I embrace it, putting on a show even though there's no proof anyone is here but me.

A knock at the door startles me as my fingers flow over the keys, and I drop my hands to my lap, wondering if I heard it correctly. Turning to face the door, I stand, looking down at my short dress, something I wouldn't really wear out of the house, but is comfortable for just being at home all day. I tug at the hem and walk to the door, expecting one of my siblings or even my parents.

The sun pours into my room as I open the door wide, coming face-to-face with my stalker himself. God, he is gorgeous.

"Crew," I say on a rushed breath, my heart seizing in my chest. He's wearing a pair of tight jeans that hug his hips, no T-shirt, and his club vest. My hands itch to reach out and trace each of his tattoos. When I meet his eyes, he's looking at me like he's seeing the light of day for the first time.

Then, his arm pops out from behind his back, holding a bouquet of freshly picked daisies, and hands them to me. God, it really is him. I knew it, but my mind was still struggling to accept what my heart and body already knew. But now here's the proof.

The daisies.

I accept them, bringing them to my nose to inhale their fresh, clean scent.

"Thank you, Crew."

"You were wearing a dress with daisies the first time I ever saw you. They remind me of you." And there go the last shreds of my heart.

"Thank you. That's sweet. Do you want to come in? I'd really like for you to come inside. With an invite this time."

Crew laughs, and it sounds so foreign, so good, and makes butterflies take flight in my stomach. "Yeah, pixie, I want to come inside." My cheeks burn from the smile that just won't go away around him.

"Didn't want to hide in the shadows anymore?" I joke.

"Oh, trust me, pixie, I'll forever be in the shadows, watching you." My heart stutters, a rapid pitter-patter, feeling like it's suddenly sprouted wings. He seems to notice my abrupt change but misreads it.

"Do I scare you?" he asks as he steps inside my tiny house, pulling the door closed behind him. It used to feel just right for me, spacious and just what I needed. But with Crew standing in the center of it, everything suddenly feels like it's closing in on me, suffocating in the best way. Consuming.

"No," I answer honestly. I've never once been scared of either side of him.

"You should be." He says the words as he combs his hand through his wild hair, the muscles of his bicep flexing with the movement. I track it with my eyes, the tattoos stretching slightly, the muscle bulging.

"I know," I manage to whisper.

"But you're not."

I shake my head in response, pulling my bottom lip between my teeth.

"Words, pixie."

"No. I'm not scared of you, Crew. Despite finding out you've been stalking me."

He takes a step forward, and I take one back, his head cocking to the side, watching me, eyes roaming over every inch of my face. How can I feel so exposed and seen just from his eyes on my face?

"Is that what I've been doing? Stalking you?"

"Yes. You've been watching me, leaving me flowers, sneaking into my bedroom at night."

"Stalking sounds so malicious. I was just watching. Tell me, do you feel my eyes on you?"

My breath starts to come faster as he approaches. "Yes. From the very first moment, I felt it."

When he's backed me up against my counter, only inches separate us. His gentle hand reaches up, running the back of his pointer finger down the bridge of my nose before threading his fingers through my hair, tilting my head backward.

Crew looks down at me with reverence, with awe, and if he doesn't kiss me right this second, I think my heart will explode out of my chest. Luckily, he doesn't make me wait long. Crew bends his knees, dropping down several inches before his lips are on mine. My eyes fall closed as my hands grip his forearms, bracing myself, holding him there.

Just like everything about Crew, his lips consume me. He kisses me like it's the best part of his day, like he can't get enough. His lips move over mine, his tongue slipping into my mouth and tangling with my own. He swallows down the mewl that escapes as his fingers squeeze a handful of my hair. He's a man teetering on the edge of control, and there's something so powerful about knowing I'm affecting him like this.

He breaks the kiss too soon, dropping his forehead to mine, his hands cupping my cheeks.

"I've been thinking about kissing you all day, pixie."

"Me too," I admit as he drags his thumb lightly over my puffy bottom lip, his eyes tracking the movement.

"I can't believe a monster like me gets to kiss a queen like you."

"I don't see any monsters here. Just a man I can't get enough of."

"I don't deserve you."

"You're wrong," I whisper, as I pull him back into a kiss. There's no tongue, no rush, just a hard press of our lips so he can feel how much I mean my words. It kills me how undeserving he thinks he is. I'm determined to show this man how worthy he is of love.

When we break apart, his hands clasp my face, holding me still as he kisses the center of my forehead, breathing me for mere moments.

"Did I hear you playing the piano before I interrupted?"

"You did."

"Will you play for me?" He takes a large step backward, and I miss his proximity immediately. I turn to fill up a vase with water, placing my daisies in it on the counter.

"You want to hear me play?"

"I do. I've never heard someone play in person before."

Nerves suddenly catch up with me, my hands slightly shaky, but how could I ever say no?

"That's a tragedy we have to fix." I grab Crew's hand, leading him over to the chair he sat in last night when he snuck into my house. But instead of taking a seat, he grabs me around the waist, easily picking me up and taking two strides to my piano bench. He sits down in front of my piano and positions me in his lap.

"Is this okay?" he asks as his hands travel down my waist, over my hips, and settle on my thighs. My back leans against his chest, the top of my head coming to right under his chin. Yes. Yes, this is very much okay. I nod, lifting my hands to hover them over the keys.

"Words, pixie."

"This is more than okay. Are you ready?"

"Play for me, my pretty girl." My heart freaks out at his words, and I have to hold back a slight laugh. Can women have heart attacks at my age? It feels like they can.

I take a deep, centering breath, then my fingers are moving across the piano, flowing into the first song that comes to mind. Its melancholic melody has brought me comfort so many times, the tune bringing me hope as I navigate my life. Now it reminds me of Crew. It's dark, but there's light, too. Just like Crew and me together. The more time I spend with him, the more I'm convinced we're each other's missing pieces.

My fingers stutter over the keys as Crew's fingertips start to rub small, soft circles on the bare skin of my thighs. I quickly adapt, flowing into another song just as his lips press against the top of my shoulder. Then another. It's just a featherlight touch that lights up every single cell in my body. I'm aware of every touch, and it's becoming harder and harder to focus on anything else.

Crew's fingers move up higher, the bottom lace of my dress inching up as he resumes light circles on my skin. Goosebumps break out as his lips brush across the back of my neck and reach my other shoulder, where he repeats peppering kisses.

"Is this okay, pixie?"

"Yes." My breathing has picked up, my chest rising and crashing harder with every stroke of his fingers, every whisper of a kiss across my bare skin. It's all-consuming.

Crew gently grips my thighs, pulling them to rest on either side of his legs as he slowly spreads them open. Then his fingers are gently sliding up my inner thighs, just skating the flesh like blades on ice, up and down, up and down. I'm so turned on, I feel like I'm going to combust. My panties are soaked, and if he goes up any higher, he's going to find out just how he affects me.

His kisses turn deeper, his tongue peeking out and dragging up the length of my neck to my ear before biting it so softly. My head falls back against his chest as my fingers fall flat against the keys, resulting in a loud smash of noise.

"Keep playing, pixie."

"Oh, god." My fingers return to the piano, playing softly, sloppily as he continues to tease me.

"That's it," he says as he nips me again. Then he's kissing the area, pulling my earlobe gently between his lips.

My pussy throbs with need, and I know my wetness has probably seeped onto the inside of my thighs at this point. I've never wanted to be touched more than I do right now. Just as I'm about to beg for it, Crew slides his fingers up higher, running a featherlight touch over my seam.

A deep, primal growl rumbles from his chest, the vibrations rattling through my back.

"You're so wet for me, pixie. Can I touch you? Is this okay? Will you let me make you feel good?" he whispers against the curve between my neck and shoulder. Shivers run down my spine, and I shudder in his arms.

I nod as my eyes close, my heart racing behind my ribs, my fingers clumsy on the keys as I struggle to focus on the feelings Crew is bringing out in me and the music. His fingers hook into my panties, pulling them off to the side with his left hand as his other finally comes in contact with my flesh. My entire body practically convulses in his lap as pleasure jolts through me. And just as I move, I feel the hard, rigid outline of his cock.

Crew is going to wreck me.

And I've never welcomed anything more.

CHAPTER TWENTY

CREW

My fingers slip through Monroe's silky center like a blade through butter. She's so soft and so warm that I'm barely keeping it together. There's so much building inside me, that voice in my head telling me to pillage, to control, to dominate, but I'm determined to be different for this girl, take things slower, and that surprises the hell out of me. I don't want to fuck Monroe like I'd fuck a plaything. She's nothing like them, and I'm realizing I want something completely different with her. It has to be different because she's different, special. Even if I don't understand any of this, even if I don't know what the fuck I'm doing, and I'm probably going to fuck it up, I have to try. She's worth it.

My hands tremble as I gently slip my finger down to her pussy, dipping through her wetness and dragging it up to her needy clit. I can't explain why I'm nervous as hell, other than fear of fucking it all up. I just want to make her feel good, I know I'm good at that, but I don't know how to be anything other than a fucking Heathen. To be anything other than Malice.

She continues to play the piano, her fingers gliding over the keys, in an uncoordinated and distracted fashion. Fucking hell, she's so goddamn perfect. I love the feel of her in my arms like this. Her back against my chest settles my breathing, and I relax slightly, focusing on bringing her right to the edge.

I tease her slowly, delicately slipping my finger through her arousal, painting my finger with her cum, my other arm gently stroking up and down her thigh. She drops her head backward, lifting her hips slightly as I tease and play with her swollen little clit. I bury my head in her hair, breathing in her sweet scent, filling my lungs with everything that's her.

I shift us slightly, spreading her legs wider to give me better access. Then I'm lining my middle finger up with her hole. Wetness drips from her center as I gently rim my finger around her silky opening, before sliding it home. Monroe immediately squeezes around me, her walls fluttering and flexing. She's warm velvet, a softness I don't deserve.

"Fuck, you're so tight, squeezing around my fingers so good, pixie." My mouth finds her neck, kissing and nipping lightly as I slowly start to fuck her with my finger. I've never felt something so goddamn tight before, my finger barely fitting inside her.

"Is this okay?"

"Crew," she whines. "I'm—" I nuzzle further into her neck, holding myself back from taking a bite right out of her.

"You're what? Words, pixie. I need them." I may not be good with words myself, but I'm even worse at guessing how someone feels, guessing the truth. I need to hear them.

"I'm a virgin. I've never done anything like this before."

My fingers stop in their tracks. She's a *virgin*?

That fact does something to me. Something carnal. Tapping into something deep and forbidden. I can teach her so many things about pleasure and her body. Things she has no idea are even possible. And to be the only person who's ever had her like this? But why the hell would she choose to give herself to a monster like me? That's sacred, right? Girls like to hold onto that for men who are deserving of it. I'm not deserving of this privilege. Fuck, is it different with a virgin? Do I have to do anything different? I'm half-tempted to pull out my phone and ask my biker besties for some tips, but then Monroe snuggles back against me, pulling my attention out of my head and back on her. I get to fuck her, and no one else has? A smile toys at my lips.

"Fuck." My heart hammers in my chest, my cock throbbing against my zipper at her words. "No one's ever touched you like this before?" I ask as I resume my strokes, staying shallow, before pulling out completely and sliding back up to her clit. Her back bows the moment I caress it, and I know she's close.

"Only you, Crew. Only you," she moans as her fingers stutter over the keys of the piano.

"I wish you knew what that does to my head. I don't deserve you. You're too perfect, and kind, and bright."

"You-oh, god," she moans as I press a circle on the tender, needy spot between her legs. "You deserve everything you want."

"All I want is you, pixie."

I press down on her clit, giving her just enough pressure as my lips kiss their way up her neck to her ear again.

"Come for me, pretty girl. I want you to let go and see the stars." Monroe comes as if she were waiting for my request. Her legs shake as her back arches, her ass pressing further onto my aching, hard cock. Her hands fall from the piano, gripping both my wrists, her nails biting into my flesh. It's a sight to behold, and I'll replay it over and over again.

When she comes down, she sags against me, and I wrap my arms around her stomach, not wanting to let her go.

"You play beautifully, pixie, especially when you're coming on my fingers."

"Mmm," she hums.

"You really are incredible."

"So are you."

"I'm glad you think so, that's all that matters to me." I turn her around in my lap, letting her legs fall together so she's sitting sideways. My hand around her back holds her close to me, my free hand pushing the hair from her face and tucking it behind her ear. "You're really a virgin?"

"I know that probably sounds crazy and unbelievable. Time just kind of went on without me, and I became stagnant."

I know from her file that I took from George's office that Monroe is twenty-eight. It's unexpected that she's never had an intimate experience before, but I'm not mad about it. I love being the only man who's ever had the privilege of touching her. I only hope I can live up to her expectations.

I pull her close, cradling her head, my fingers gently running through her hair. Monroe's eyes flutter closed as I massage her scalp, but they pop open the moment my fingers brush over a raised, tight portion of her head. Rage bubbles up quickly, and I have to crack my neck from side to side to try to keep it at bay and keep my voice steady.

"Monroe, what is this? Who hurt you?" I practically growl. She bites her bottom lip, her eyes glassy as she looks up at me through her eyelashes.

"You remember that guy who was talking to me at Between the Notes?"

"Did he hurt you? I'll fucking kill him. When?"

Her hand falls to my bare chest, fingers lightly scratching up and down, slowing my heart rate with just her touch. "No, no, no, he didn't hurt me, he's never touched me. Well, except for that day you caught him grabbing me." I relax some, but not much. This scar is huge, long and deep, and on her fucking skull. This was no little thing.

"Will you talk to me? My brain is doing really fucked-up things right now."

Monroe shifts in my lap, putting her legs on either side of my thighs so she's straddling me. Knowing this can't be comfortable for her on this small bench, I stand with her in my arms and move us to her bed. She doesn't have a couch in her tiny house, so this will have to do. I lean against the headboard, dropping her little ass in my lap. My hands stay low on her waist, my eyes on her pretty, freckled face.

"Is this okay?" I ask her, wanting her to be comfortable, trying my damndest to be a better man for this woman.

"It's perfect, Crew."

"Tell me what that scar is, pixie? Please."

Monroe takes a deep breath and then starts opening up to me. "Right before my senior year of high school, my best friend, Nora, and I snuck out of her house to go meet with her boyfriend and his friend. Her boyfriend's name was Tyler. Zach, the guy being an asshole, that's his identical twin brother. It's hard to look at him without seeing Tyler's face, without wondering what he would look like now. Tyler had just gotten his license, and his parents got him this shitty-ass Honda Civic he was so proud of, and Nora was excited to have someone to drive us around. She was so full of life. We'd been best friends since kindergarten, and I was convinced she was going to do huge things with her life." Tears start to fall from her eyes, and my chest starts to hurt, a painful stab behind my breastbone.

"Anyway, we snuck out one night and got in Tyler's car with his friend Javier and headed to Lookout Lake. I put my seatbelt on, but no one else wore theirs. I tried to tell Nora a few times to buckle up, but she was so happy to be out that she just wasn't paying attention, or just didn't care. We were teenagers, being stupid and careless. It wasn't her fault, and I should have tried harder to make sure she was safe. Tyler was speeding, and I grabbed Nora's hand in the middle of the seat. None of it felt right, from the very beginning. I just had this feeling in the pit of my stomach like something was wrong, Crew. I told Tyler to slow down, and the next thing I knew, we hit this massive elk and then started to flip down the side of the mountain."

Fucking fuck. My fingers tap my leg, trying to process what she's saying. I don't know what to say. I don't know how to fucking comfort someone. I've never known how to do this shit. But then my eyes start to burn, and I realize they've welled up with tears. I've never cried a day in my life. Not through the childhood I spent in a cage, not when I was locked up in prison, not when Queenie or Rolo died. But just knowing that this perfect bright light in front of me felt that kind of fear, that she was hurt from it, I can't fucking imagine, and I definitely can't bear it.

"I'm so fucking sorry, Monroe."

"We all died that day, Crew. All of us. I was brought back, and I've never . . ." Her voice cracks as the tears breach the dam and cascade over her cheeks. "I've never understood why I was chosen to live when they all had to die. It's not fair."

The breath leaves my lungs.

"You *died*?"

"Yeah. I was pronounced dead at the scene, but a paramedic refused to stop working on me and got my pulse going again. I was in a medically induced coma for a while to let my body heal from all the injuries, especially the one on my head."

I pull Monroe impossibly close, holding her to my chest and kissing the top of her head repeatedly.

"I can't imagine a world where you're not in it, pixie. The world deserves your light, and you deserve to feel everything it has to offer."

Monroe pulls back slightly, looking up at me through tear-beaded eyelashes, her hand reaching up and stroking my cheek. It feels so good, and my heart starts to race.

"Is it offering me *you*, Crew? Because for the first time since my accident, I actually feel like I'm living and not just existing." Her words stun me for a moment. I've never felt like I've given anything good to anyone, and this woman is lying here in my arms, proving me otherwise. What the fuck did I do to deserve this, Rolo? I'll never give this gift up. If it's the one good thing I get out of this life, I'm going to greedily accept and not fuck a minute of it up.

"I'm already yours, and I'm not going anywhere."

Her delicate little fingers slide into my hair, my eyes falling closed for a moment, then she's pulling me down to meet her mouth. Kissing Monroe is unlike anything I've ever experienced before. It's touch on fire, electric, and euphoric. I've never touched drugs a day in my life, but I imagine she'd be the hit of the century, the dose that makes you an addict.

I capture her lips with mine and wrap my arms around her, pulling her body flush against mine. Our tongues tangle and caress, slowly and unhurried. I could kiss her like this all night and not go any further, but when her hands start to push at my cut, I know she wants more. I'll give her everything she wants and then some.

Breaking the kiss, I shrug out of my leather cut, folding it in half and tossing it to lie on the bench in front of the piano. Monroe's hands don't waste any time exploring my abs as she sits up on her knees, pushing me to lie on my back. I go more than willingly, letting her explore my abdomen, my chest, and my arms. Her fingers trace over various tattoos, the hodgepodge of splattered ink I've decorated it with over the years.

She looks so pretty, her thin dress hiked up high on her thighs, her blush-pink hair framing her face as her eyes follow her hands. She maps all of me, taking her time and memorizing every inch. Fuck, do I want to do the same to her?

Then she starts to gain more confidence, fingers dipping lower until the tips slide beneath my waistband. My cock is hard as steel, bulging and throbbing against the fabric, and I know she can see it. My breaths are coming harder now, and I've never felt excitement like this before, wondering what my curious little pixie will do next.

Her fingers work the button of my jeans, sliding down the zipper, successfully putting my heart in my goddamn throat. Why does this little creature make me so damn nervous? I don't get nervous. Before she can pull my jeans open any further, knowing I don't wear any underwear, I lightly circle her wrists with my hands, stopping her in her tracks. I need to do right by her. It's the only damn thing that matters.

"We don't have to go any further. I'm happy to just kiss you and hold you all night."

"I may be a virgin, Crew, but that doesn't mean I don't want to explore with you. In fact, you're the first person in my life I've ever wanted to. Do you want to stop?"

"Fuck no, pixie. I just want to make sure you're comfortable."

"I promise to tell you if I'm not." That's all I ask.

"Then go ahead and explore me, my curious little thing." The smile that appears on her face could light the way to fucking heaven, and goddamn am I lucky sonofabitch that I get to see it.

Monroe pulls open my jeans, my hard, thick cock springing free and falling with a slap against my abdomen. Her eyes go wide as she takes it in, her bottom lip sucked right between those teeth of hers.

I run my hand up the length, giving it a squeeze, watching her face as precum spills from my tip. I know right now her mind is racing that there's a cock in front of her; hell, I don't know if she's ever even seen one before, but I know mine isn't the norm. I've got an apadravya through the center of my head and a frenum barbell pierced at the underside.

I swipe my thumb over the top, spreading the precum down over the silver decorating it.

"You like what you see, pixie girl?"

"Crew . . ." she breathes roughly.

"You can touch it, you know. It won't bite."

"God, it looks like it could."

"Trust me, pixie, nothing but pleasure will come for both of us. I could come right now just from you looking at me with that expression on your face."

With her bottom lip held hostage between her teeth, she finally puts me out of my misery, running the pads of her fingers up my length. My cock jerks at the contact, and I love the cute little look of surprise on her face. She runs her fingers softly over every inch, doing a damn good job at teasing the hell out of me.

Then I grab her hand, wrapping her fingers around me and squeezing just how I like it. Her fingers can't close all the way around me, and something about that makes me feel fucking good. I keep her hand under mine as I slide us up my dick. I moan, deep and low, loving the feel of her soft hands on me.

"That feels good?"

"Fuck, yeah. Yeah, it feels so fucking good," I huff as my hips buck into her fist. I show her how I like it, and after a few more strokes, I let her go, letting her jerk me on her own. She sits between my spread legs, her free hand braced on one of my thighs as she strokes me. Her face has bloomed with crimson, her freckles popping bright as her pupils are blown nice and big.

Pleasure flows through me at such a high dose, I have to really focus to not blow my load right here like this. It feels so fucking good. I don't remember the last time I had a hand job, and I've definitely never had one quite like this. My orgasm starts low and deep, and I quickly pull her hand off. I flip her over onto her back, her little yelp making me smile.

"It's my turn now."

Monroe lies on her back in front of me, and I know I need her naked. I need to see her laid bare. I start to work her dress up her thighs, revealing inch by inch of her beautiful skin. My hands caress over her hip and follow the path up her sides.

"Is this okay?"

She nods and sits up for me, letting me pull the fabric from her body and toss it to the floor.

My hands fall to her thighs as she lies back down, my eyes tracing over every inch of her perfect body. She's wearing a matching lace bra and panty set, in pure fucking black. It's so thin I can see the rosy buds of her nipples peeking through the lace, and my mouth waters. Her beauty takes my breath away.

"Fucking hell, pixie, you always wear this kind of stuff under your dresses?

"Yeah, it makes me feel sexy. Powerful, even."

"Fuck me," I breathe under my breath. "Do you have any idea how beautiful you are?"

Her face reddens further, and it's such a pretty color on her. The crimson spreads down her neck and across her chest, which is rising and falling harder now. I could gaze at her the rest of the night, but I need to get my hands on her.

"Can I touch you?"

"Please touch me, Crew. I need you." *She needs me.* I've never been needed before, and fuck if I'm about to let her down. The devil himself will have to come pull me away from her, and even then, I wouldn't leave without a fight.

I lean over her body, capturing her mouth in a kiss before peppering her jaw, and down her neck, and over her collarbone. My tongue licks a light path over the bone, down to her sternum, loving the goosebumps that break out on her skin behind my touch.

Her hands run up and down my sides as I kiss and lick her perfect body. Monroe arches into me, the tip of my leaking cock tapping at her stomach. My eyes flick up to meet hers, her eyes heavily lidded and needy, just as desperate as I am.

I brace myself up on my forearm, and with my free hand, I pull down one of the cups of her bra, her tit spilling free. She's got the most petite breasts, a perfect palmful, with rosy pink nipples that are begging for my mouth. I can't deny them.

"Is this okay?"

"Yes, Crew. It's all okay."

Leaning forward, I suck the pert nipple into my mouth, drawing out a moan from her sweet lips. I pop off, kissing my way down her breastbone, over her navel, to her panty line. Then I'm licking a line from hip to hip and back again, her fingers threading through my hair.

When I sit up on my knees, she's panting. "You doing okay with all of this?"

She grabs my face gently, looking me in the eyes. "I meant what I said, Crew. I don't want to stop."

"I'm supposed to check in with you."

"What?"

"Never mind. I just want to do this right. This is new for me, too."

"Crew, this is perfect. Being here with you is perfect. This is all I could ever ask for."

"Just promise to tell me if you want to stop at any time."

"I will, I promise."

I trail my fingers up her thighs, settling on her bent knees. "Spread your legs for me, let me see you."

She pulls her bottom lip between her teeth, but she listens, spreading her legs nice and wide for me. My heart rate kicks up behind my ribs, my heart in my throat. I run the pads of my fingers over the damp fabric of the delicate lace covering her center, hooking my fingers into the hem and pulling them off to the side.

Then I'm finally getting a good look at her perfect center. My fingers dance through the light swatch of hair over her pubic area, a deep, appreciative moan rumbling through my chest. Hair on women is so fucking sexy, and my cock bucks in response. This woman is doing things to me I never thought possible, and she doesn't even realize it.

I slowly peel her underwear down her legs, pressing the wet spot to my nose and inhaling before stuffing them in my pocket for later. I've been wanting to get my mouth on her from the moment I first saw her, and I'm not going to waste any more time denying myself her sweet taste. I love oral sex, and I can't wait for her to feel my tongue ring on her wet pussy.

I have to talk myself down multiple times, reminding myself to go slow, to not rush anything, and be gentle. So instead of diving right into my meal like a man starved, I pick up her right foot, bending her leg at the knee and pressing a soft kiss to the inside of her sole, then her ankle. I work my way up her leg, dragging my tongue and lips over every inch of her. When I get to her center, I blow lightly against her core, loving how her body trembles for me. Then I repeat the same thing on the other side.

When I reach her center again, I lie down on my stomach to get comfortable, setting her legs over my shoulders. Then I use my thumbs to spread her open wide. Her scent hits me like a drug as I drag my nose through her center, taking a deep inhale of her sweet musk. I look up her body to meet her eyes so full of arousal, and I about bust right here from the expression on her face. God, I can't wait to make her come again.

"I'm going to kiss you now, pixie. Right here, where no one's ever been before."

"Please. I need you to," she whines.

Her thighs are already shaking, and I smile into her flesh as I take my first long, languid lick of her pussy. Her taste coats my tongue, and something snaps inside me. The restraint that was pulling tighter and tighter is slowly breaking at the seams. I'm crazed, infatuated, completely lost to her pleasure, to making her feel good.

I keep her lips spread open for me, and then I bury my face into her pussy. I lap at her from ass to clit, making sure there isn't an inch of her that hasn't had my tongue. Monroe moans as her hands grip the sheets below us. I hope she loves this as much as I do, because I don't plan to ever come up for air.

CHAPTER TWENTY-ONE

MONROE

Of all the times I imagined what having a man go down on me would feel like, it never came close to the real thing. Crew's tongue is warm and wet, and his piercing adds a cooling, strange feeling that makes it that much better. He alternates between deep French kisses, licking up my slit, and sucking. The sucking about does me in every single time. My orgasm builds and builds, and then he pulls back, switching it up again.

"How does it feel?"

"I've never felt so good in my life. I never want this to end."

"Mmm. My dirty pixie likes to have her pussy eaten?" God, his mouth when he talks like that makes my heart skip a beat.

"Please, please don't ever stop," I beg. My hands thread into his hair as my hips take on a life of their own, rising and falling, chasing the orgasm he's drawing out of me.

"You taste so good, so fucking good." He flicks his tongue against my clit repeatedly, the barbell making it feel so much more taboo. My thighs shake over his shoulders as the pleasure finally snaps, the dam breaking.

"Oh, god, Crew! I'm coming! I'm coming!" The world blurs at the edges of my vision as tears spring to my eyes. I squeeze them closed, gasping for air, as wave after wave takes me under.

Crew pulls back just as the sensations become too much, gently kissing my tender flesh in short, chaste kisses.

"Crew, that was . . . I don't have words, actually."

"For me, too. I'm obsessed with your taste, your scent, the feel of you against my tongue and lips. You're perfect, so perfect for me."

"Come here, I want you up here with me." I watch as Crew reluctantly leaves his new favorite place and stands at the end of the bed, kicking off his boots and pulling his jeans all the way off. I take the time to admire him, eyes roaming over his tattoos, his taut, muscled stomach, his strong thighs and thick length. Crew is a sight to behold.

"We don't have to do anything more, but I really want to lie naked with you. I've never done that before."

Where did this man come from?

He crawls up my body until he's bracing himself above me, his thick cock resting against my thigh. An ache spreads through my lower abdomen, deep and throbbing. My arms wrap around his shoulders as his forehead rests against mine. We share air as his eyes meet mine, desperate and longing.

"Take me, Crew." His eyebrows pinch inward, his dark obsidian eyes practically glowing from their depths. He looks pained, like he's struggling with something monumental.

"I don't deserve you, pixie."

"I want you to have me. I've never believed in fate or things happening for a reason; I've never been able to find meaning in anything that's happened to me. Until I met you. So, take me, please. I want you so bad I feel like I can barely breathe."

"Monroe . . ." he pleads, his voice breaking. My hands move to either side of his face, my lips pressing against his.

"You deserve good things. Take it." His lips meet mine again as he settles between my legs, his hand reaching between us to line up the tip of his dick with my center. He puts just a bit of pressure on my opening, eyes boring into mine as he cradles my face with his other hand.

"Are you sure?"

I nod my head fervently.

"Words, pixie."

"Yes."

Crew claims my lips before pressing inward ever so slowly. The burn is instant, my core stretching around his girth, but my arousal makes him slip in easier. I dig my nails into his shoulders, holding on as he presses in further. It's torturously slow, and I gasp against his lips.

"You feel so good, Monroe. You're so damn tight."

I can't respond as the air leaves my lungs, and I clench up everywhere, my muscles tight, my head spiraling, focusing on the burn and tiny pricks that are spreading at my center. Crew notices immediately and stops, pausing inside me where he is. His hand brushes the hair from my face, kissing my cheeks and nose.

"I need you to breathe for me, relax, and let me in. The pain will pass, and then it'll feel so good."

I take a deep, settling breath as he smiles down at me. "That's it, my pretty girl. You're stretching around me so good. Just a bit more." He pushes in another half inch and stops again. "This is going to hurt, but only for a minute. Breathe, pixie."

I try to relax, but then he's breaking through my barrier, and I arch my back with a loud gasp. His tender hands are right there, cupping my neck and jaw, kissing me everywhere his lips can reach. "Shh, you're okay, you took all of me, Monroe. Fuck, I can't believe I'm inside you."

"Crew, it burns."

"Just breathe, I won't move until you're ready. Relax and just feel me." His hands are everywhere as he kisses me, grabbing my breasts through the thin fabric of my lacy bra, twisting my nipples. My core pulses around his length, my arousal dripping between us. I never imagined how full this would feel, how complete it would make me.

"Are you alright? I hate that I'm hurting you."

"I'm okay, I want you to move now. Show me what this is like."

"I've never done this before, pixie."

"Done what? Have sex?"

He looks down at me with his dark eyes, giving me an expression I can't quite read, but it makes my heart ache, nonetheless. "Make love to someone."

The breath whooshes from my lungs as my mouth falls open slightly. Of all the times I imagined what losing my virginity would be like, who the man would be, never in a million years did I think it would be a biker with a craving for violence, who makes me feel more loved than I ever have in my life.

I wrap my legs around his waist, pulling him deeper as he starts to move inside me. Crew pulls out, a slow drag of his cock that I feel everywhere. The pain starts to fade, and pleasure starts to push through.

Crew's body works over mine, our foreheads resting together as our breaths mingle, our chests rising and falling in a cadence that matches each other. Every thrust feels better and better, and soon, I'm meeting him in the middle, my clit grinding against his lower abdomen with every stroke, his hand running down my side and over my hip, gripping my ass to pull me closer to him.

"You feel incredible. Monroe, I've never, this is . . . *fuck, pixie.* This is too good. I'm not gonna last . . ."

"It's okay, it's okay."

"Can I come inside you? I was just tested, and there's no chance I can get you pregnant."

I barely hear his words through the blood rushing between my ears as his pace picks up.

"Yes. Yes, Crew," I moan. Then he's taking one last final thrust and staying so deep, I can't help but wince. I can feel every inch of him inside me as his cock pulses and jerks, filling me with his cum.

For the first time since I was seventeen, I feel like I'm finally living. And nothing has felt better.

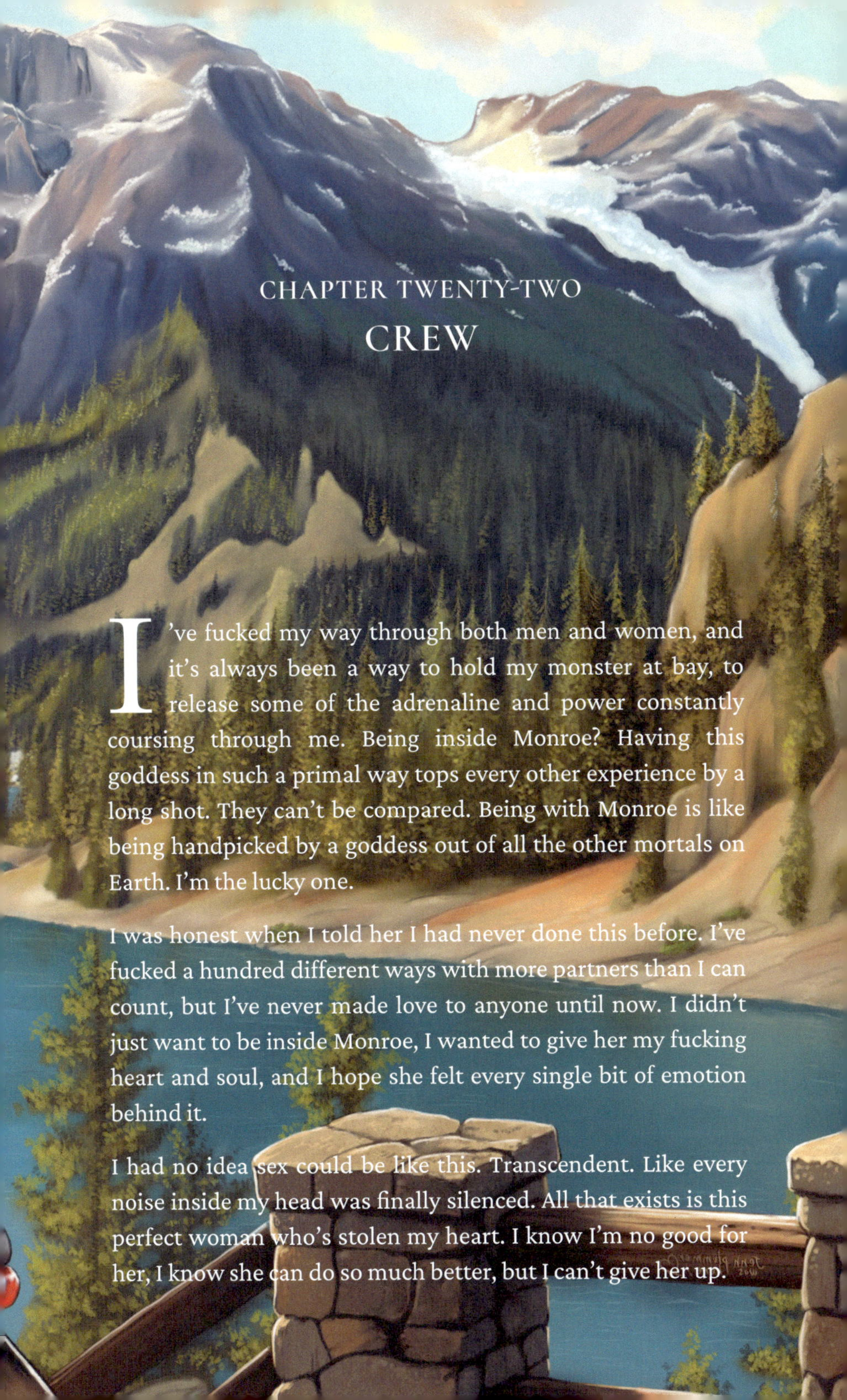

CHAPTER TWENTY-TWO

CREW

I've fucked my way through both men and women, and it's always been a way to hold my monster at bay, to release some of the adrenaline and power constantly coursing through me. Being inside Monroe? Having this goddess in such a primal way tops every other experience by a long shot. They can't be compared. Being with Monroe is like being handpicked by a goddess out of all the other mortals on Earth. I'm the lucky one.

I was honest when I told her I had never done this before. I've fucked a hundred different ways with more partners than I can count, but I've never made love to anyone until now. I didn't just want to be inside Monroe, I wanted to give her my fucking heart and soul, and I hope she felt every single bit of emotion behind it.

I had no idea sex could be like this. Transcendent. Like every noise inside my head was finally silenced. All that exists is this perfect woman who's stolen my heart. I know I'm no good for her, I know she can do so much better, but I can't give her up.

What is this woman doing to me?

I gently kiss her lips, dragging my tongue back and forth across the seam. “Nothing has ever felt this good. This pussy was made for me. *You* were made for me.”

I slowly pull myself from her body, sitting back on my knees between her legs to watch her swollen little pussy leak my cum. I can’t believe I’m the only person to ever get her body this way. I wonder if I’m the only one to get her heart, too.

I lay down on my stomach between her legs, pressing a kiss to her center. Monroe gasps, trying to scooch away from me, but I grip her hips, dragging her ass back down to meet my face.

“What are you doing?”

“You didn’t come with me inside you, so I’m going to make you come again with my mouth.”

“I—Crew, there’s blood, and you came inside me.”

I chuckle against her wet, puffy flesh. “Pixie, you think a little blood and cum are going to stop me from devouring you? Never. I’m obsessed with this pretty pussy, obsessed with you. Now, lie back and let me take you to the stars, where you belong. You’re too good for this place.”

I don’t waste any more time, my tongue spearing inside her wet pussy. The taste of our cum combined with the coppery tang of her blood hits my tongue, and I lose myself all over again. I eat her pussy like I’m starving, like she’s my only source of sustenance. And maybe she is. Maybe wading through hell brought me to her. I’ve seen my brothers find the light at the end of their darkness, I just never thought I was deserving enough to have it.

When Monroe comes, her entire body shakes and trembles, and I don't let up until I've pulled every bit of pleasure I can from her.

"Crew, holy shit," she says through little gasps and pants. I sit up between her legs, wiping my hand over my mouth to discard some of the mess covering me. She looks thoroughly fucked, sated, and relaxed.

I lay down next to her, pulling her half on top of me so I can hold her naked body against mine. If I could spend the rest of my life just like this, listening to her breath and feeling the steady pulse of her heart, I would give up everything.

"Are you okay?"

"Yes. Better than okay. I'm just sore."

The next moment, she looks down at us, getting a glimpse of my still semi-hard cock. "I can't believe that was inside me."

I look down, grabbing it with my palm and slowly stroking it. It's sensitive, but not overly so. I could fuck her ten more times tonight if she could handle it.

"You took every inch."

"You're huge . . . and *pierced*."

I smile, fully and unrestrained. What man doesn't want to hear that he has a huge cock? It's not as big as Wrath's, and if she's amazed by mine, I had better make sure she doesn't see the goods he's packing. He's prettier, both his face and his stupid cock. Yeah, I really need to keep her away from Wrath.

"I'm clean, too. Obviously. I've never been with anyone but you."

"I get tested once a month at our clubhouse and haven't been with anyone since I laid eyes on you. I knew you were it for me."

"Thank you. What about . . . you . . ."

"Filled you up with my cum? You can say it, in fact, I'd love to hear those words come out of your pretty little mouth." Her face blushes like the words embarrass her, even after everything we just did. It's so cute.

"You . . . *filled me up with your cum.* I'm not on birth control. What did you mean when you said you can't get me pregnant? Or did I imagine that?"

"Such a good pixie," I praise her as I run my hands up her back, just wanting to touch her now that I can. "You heard me right. I'm sterile. Had to make sure my line ended with me, so I got snipped. You don't have to worry about getting pregnant." Her shoulders relax, and I hope like hell it's relief she's feeling. She mentioned before that she doesn't want to be a mother, so I hope she isn't upset. There's nothing I can do to change that now. I can't be a dad, won't.

My fingers thread through her hair, angling her face upward.

"I've always been an addict, Monroe. For blood, for violence, for death. But never for anything as good and pure as you. I can't give you up." I won't.

Monroe falls asleep within a few moments, her body draped over mine, my hand lightly trailing up and down her spine. I breathe in her scent, filling my lungs with everything that's her. I don't dare fall asleep, not wanting to lose a moment.

My heart aches as I lie here and relive the last few hours. The fact that she's a virgin at her age makes much more sense, knowing her story. This sweet, perfect woman lived through something so traumatic. Monroe isn't fragile at all. Her strength rivals any of the men at the club, and I know she'll fit right in with the rest of our queens. Saige is a little rough around the edges, but Bristol, Kinsey, and Morgan will welcome her with open arms.

Knowing what I know now, though, makes that fucker face, needle dick cornering her every chance he gets that much worse. He needs to leave her alone, give her space to breathe and live without the pressure of a ghost's brother haunting her every time she turns the corner. Hopefully he understood that she's under my protection now, and he won't fuck with her again. If he does, I won't be so kind. It took all my strength not to collapse his windpipe where we stood.

I make a mental note to talk to her about Lookout Lake. It makes sense why she doesn't go up there, but I want to help her overcome that fear.

When she wakes up sometime later, her stomach growls, making her laugh through her fog. She's so fucking cute. "I'm starving. Are you hungry?"

I run the back of my finger over the bridge of her nose, smiling down at her sweet, freckled face. "I could eat."

"How about we bake? Have you ever done that?"

"Bake? Like cookies or some shit?"

Monroe laughs as she sits up, pulling the sheets to cover her breasts, suddenly being modest. "Yeah, like cookies or some shit."

"Didn't you know? We bake all the time at the clubhouse."

Her eyes pinch inward, her face scrunching up. “Wait, do you really?”

I bark out a laugh that surprises both of us. “No. Do I look like I bake, pixie?”

“You look like you could do whatever you want,” she says with a flirty little voice, eyes roaming all over my naked body. Fuck, she’s a dangerous little thing when she wants to be.

“Yeah, and what if I want to eat your pussy again so I can swallow down all your sweet cum?” Her face brightens, that deep crimson blooming across her skin. “There’s that blush I love so much. Fuck, you’re cute.”

“And you’re a distraction. Let’s clean up, and then we’re baking.”

Monroe stands from her bed, pushing open the pocket door of her closet. I get an unobstructed view of her entire backside, and it takes every fiber of my being not to launch forward and take a bite right out of her ass. My eyes travel down the length of her spine, the curve as it dips in right before her ass and the little dimple it creates there. This woman is so sexy.

To my disappointment, she pulls out a soft-looking dress that looks like it has to be a nightdress. It has thin straps, lace around the hem, and fits her like a glove.

When she turns around and sees me staring, that blush reappears.

Monroe moves to her kitchen on the other side of her house, opening the fridge and pulling out a bowl of purple grapes and two sticks of butter. I pull on my pants and tuck my cock away, painful as it is, but I don’t bother buttoning or zipping them.

The sun has set, and the moonlight pours in from her kitchen window, illuminating her like the ethereal creature she is. I move up behind her just as she pops a grape into her mouth. One of my hands finds her waist, the other reaching around to snag a grape.

"Alright, first we're going to cream the butter with white and brown sugar. We need three quarter cups of each." She sets a large bowl on the counter in front of me and hands me a measuring cup and two different containers of sugar. "You measure those out, I'm going to soften this butter."

Figuring this is easy enough, I scoop out the sugars and drop them into the bowl, just as she returns with the sticks of butter. She adds them to the sugar and uses a wooden spoon to mix it all up until it's light and fluffy. I'm impressed, and watching her work, hell, watching her do anything, is my favorite thing to do.

"I'll keep mixing. Can you crack two eggs?" Positive that I can, I pick up one of the eggs she set out and look at it in my hand. Then I smack it against the counter, the inside goop splattering outward.

"Crew!" she laughs. "Have you ever cracked an egg before?"

"Never needed to. We have a cook at the clubhouse, and we eat out if he isn't cooking," I shrug as I grab a paper towel to clean up the mess. "Okay, let's try again, then." Monroe moves in front of me, her body flush against mine as she grabs an egg. "Hand over mine, feel how I do it." I do as she says, holding the outside of her hand with mine, and then she gently taps the egg against the bowl twice, using her other hand to separate the shell. The inside shit falls into the bowl easily, and then we drop the shell into her trash. "See? Easy. Your turn."

Feeling like a fool, I pick up the other egg and copy exactly what she did, successfully getting the egg into the bowl, even if pieces of the shell fall in as well. Monroe doesn't seem to mind, though, and that makes me feel good.

She adds vanilla extract, then stirs it all up. This is all so domesticated, and it makes my heart pound against my rib cage, but I also feel something I've never felt before, something soothing and light, like the pressure all over has eased some, and I can breathe a little easier.

"Now two and a quarter cups flour. The measuring cups are right there," she tells me as she points to a stack of cups nestled inside of one another on her counter. I grab them, getting the right scoop and diving into the flour. I've never touched this shit before, and when I dump it from way too high above the bowl, I immediately recognize my mistake.

"Oh my gosh, Crew!" she squeals as a plume of flour erupts in front of us. "You're terrible at this." Hell, I love this woman's laugh. I quickly snatch her around the waist, hauling her up and wrapping her legs around me. I love that she's not wearing anything under her dress because her pussy rubs against my bare abdomen like this.

I nuzzle into her neck, kissing and nipping the area right above her shoulder. "Mmm. But I think you know what I am good at."

"Hmm. Do I? I'm not sure I remember," she teases.

"Is that right?" I slip my hand between us, easily sliding through her tuft of hair until I'm pressing against her needy clit. I love how she feels. But I love it even more when she's wrapped around my thick cock.

Monroe's head falls back against a cabinet as I play with her, rubbing tight little circles over her flesh. I nip at her chin and jaw until her mouth comes down to meet mine. This kiss is different, heated, more of a race as her mouth opens to accept my tongue. Instead, I suck hers into mine, swallowing down her moans. My cock throbs, hardening, the tip sticking out of the top of my jeans, already leaking, already desperate.

"Can you take me again, pixie?" I whisper against her mouth.

"Fuck me, Crew." *Thank, fuck.*

"Yes, my queen."

I'm quick to shove my jeans down my thighs and line up my cock, pressing in slowly so she has time to adjust. I'm sure she's sore as fuck, and I don't want to hurt her. I fill her easier this time, her body more open and relaxed now that she knows what to expect. I thrust deep and slow, holding back with restraint I barely have.

But when she starts to lift herself up and down on my length, that restraint snaps. My hands sink into the flesh of her ass, holding her while my hips piston into her faster. I sink in deep on every thrust, her tight pussy spasming around me.

"Look down, pixie. Watch how your little pussy takes me, look at you stretching around my cock. You feel so good."

She listens, my curious girl, and her mouth falls open in a sexy little "O."

"Holy shit, Crew, oh god."

"That's it, feel it, you're going to come all over me this time with my cock inside you, aren't you, pixie?"

"Crew!" she moans. I stick my thumb into my mouth, getting it nice and wet before slipping it between us, finding her swollen clit, and rubbing it. Monroe's eyes practically roll to the back of her head, and I wish I were recording us right now. What I wouldn't give to be able to replay this entire evening on repeat whenever I wanted.

I feel her pussy walls start to flutter around me, her body tensing as her orgasm builds and builds. Mine is right there with her, tingling at the base of my spine, my balls drawing up close and tight.

"Come for your Heathen, pixie, and take me with you when you do."

She combusts, her nails digging into my shoulder so hard I know they've broken the skin, her walls tightening like a vise around my length, locking me in as she comes. She does exactly what I needed her to, practically milking the cum right out of my cock.

There's nothing in the world that can compare to this. She's changed something deep inside me, something buried and broken. I feel like her sunshine is starting to fill my veins, pushing out some of that darkness.

CHAPTER TWENTY-THREE

MONROE

The next morning comes with light streaming in from the large windows at the front of my house and a warm body wrapped up behind me. Last night was intense and mind-blowing. I'm reminded of the reality of what we did by the throbbing ache between my legs.

Not losing my virginity until now wasn't exactly the plan, but after the accident, I spent so long healing, then focusing on school, and now working, that dating never became a reality. Let's not forget that the dating pool in Amberwood is slim, especially when everyone knows me as the girl who survived when three other kids didn't.

I don't want anyone's pity, and I certainly didn't want to give away my virginity just because it was a box to check off. I've wanted to have sex before now, I just haven't had the opportunity. I never gave much stock to holding onto it, mostly because I wasn't saving it for some special occasion or the right person. But after last night? I've never been more glad that I didn't experience that with anyone but Crew.

I slip out of bed, his body not even stirring, and head to the bathroom to clean up, washing off in a quick shower. Once I'm out, my hair is easy to fix since it just naturally hangs straight around my face anyway, but I spend a minute wiping away the mascara that bled through my tears.

After I leave the bathroom, I get started on some pancakes for us. I hope he likes them. The fact that he had never cracked an egg before was so endearing. I love that I got to teach him something and show him something new. I can't imagine what his life has been like or how he ended up in a motorcycle club to begin with. The last time I asked him about his past, he said it was a sad story, and that breaks my heart. I'm eager for him to meet my family, and I know they'll accept him for who he is.

After getting the batter whipped up, I pour cupfuls on the pan, the sizzling louder than I'd like. I get through two rounds on my little frying pan before Crew stirs behind me.

"Good morning. I was wondering if you were going to sleep all morning. I was so scared my cooking would wake you." I take the last of the pancakes off the skillet and turn off the burner before spinning to face him. Crew snatches me around the waist, hauling me on top of him as he falls back onto the bed. He turns us so we're lying on our sides, his hand finding its home cupping the side of my neck and jaw. "You sleep like the dead. Has anyone ever told you that?"

"No, because I don't sleep."

"With people?"

"No, period. I don't sleep. I'm lucky if I get two hours a night."

"That sounds terrible. Why?"

"Nightmares, pixie."

"But you slept here, we slept together."

"I can't explain it any more than you can. You calm me. Settle me. Bring me a peace I've never had before."

"Crew, I don't know what to say."

"There's nothing to say, pixie girl. I'm glad I met you." I smile up at him, my hands roaming through his wild blond hair.

"Me too. I made us pancakes. Do you like those? I wasn't sure and thought it was a safe bet."

"I love anything, I'm not picky."

"Perfect. I'll make us plates. There are towels in that closet right there. You can use that bathroom if you need."

"And wash you off me? I'm not ready for that."

I don't know what to say to that, but I smile anyway. He's truly insane. And I'm falling fast and hard for him. Crew sits up in my bed, resting his back against the headboard as I make our plates, loading his up with the majority of the pancakes and some blueberries I had in the fridge.

I climb back into bed next to him, and we both dig in, eating in a comfortable silence. I could get used to this.

"What do you have going on today? I'm not ready to give you up."

"Promise not to laugh?"

"I'd never laugh at you."

"My grandma is part of a bowling league, and she kind of weaseled me into joining when the Amberwood librarian, Mrs. Payne, broke her hip a few months ago."

"What's bowling?"

My face falls, unsure if I heard him correctly.

"What?"

"What's. Bowling?"

"Crew. You don't know what bowling is?"

"Why would I know what bowling is?"

"Oh my god. Okay, hold on. It's so fun." I pull out my phone and bring up some videos online of people bowling and show Crew. He watches with sweet curiosity, and it's the most endearing thing to witness.

"You're a member of a bowling team like this? That's cute."

"You think that's cute? Wait until you hear their name. Ball-busters."

Crew laughs, and it's a sound that seems so private, so rare, that I soak up every beat of it. "Yikes, that sounds ominous. I'm surprisingly not into that," he says as he cups his crotch. "You're something special, pixie. I bet she loves having you there."

"She does, actually. We have a lot of fun, and those old ladies, man, they're competitive and know how to talk some serious shit."

"I need to see this to believe it."

"Well, would you want to come?"

"To your ball-busting bowling game?"

"Yeah?"

"Hell yeah, pixie. I'm going. As long as my junk gets to stay intact."

I put on my baby-blue jersey with "Ballbusters" written in elegant script on the back and hop onto Crew's bike behind him. Excitement flows through me at having him join me in this. I love bowling with my grandma and her league, and the fact that Crew's never been, heck, the fact that he didn't even know what it is, makes me eager to give him a new experience.

We pull up outside of The Strike Zone, and I climb off his bike, Crew kicking down the stand and joining me. He gives the tip of my nose a chaste kiss before I grab his wrist and pull him inside.

After checking in to get our shoes, we walk to the end of the long building to where my grandma and her friends are congregating, probably gossiping and teasing each other.

My grandma sees us coming, and a smile lights up her face. My heart lodges itself right in my throat. I've never brought a man home. Ever.

"I was wondering if you forgot about us," she teases. "You have stars in your eyes, my girl."

I lean in to kiss her cheek. "Never in a million years. This is Crew. He's going to bowl with us today, if that's okay."

"The more the merrier! It's nice to meet you, Crew. I'm Roe's grandma, Dee-Dee."

"Nice to meet you, Dee-Dee."

I turn to face the other women, who are looking at us with curiosity and intrigue.

"And these lovely spitfires are Rose and Iris."

They eye him from head to toe, clearly checking him out. I think I even see Rose throw a wink our way.

"Do you three have no shame?" I tease. "Leave this poor man alone."

They all laugh as my grandma shoos them away. "We're going to get started while you two get set up."

"Sounds good, Grandma."

Crew and I move to the back chairs to switch out our shoes, and I use that time to check in with him.

"You doing okay?"

"I felt like they were undressing me with their eyes," he says with a full-body shiver. I throw my head back in a laugh.

"You're fine. Just stick with me."

Once we're laced up and find our balls, we move forward and set them in the ball return.

"I've never bowled before, so hopefully I can learn a thing or two from you ladies," Crew announces innocently. I open my mouth to give him some reassurance when Iris speaks up first.

"Don't worry, honey, we'll teach you how to use your fingers the right way."

Crew chokes, and I can't hold back my laugh, so I slap a hand over my mouth. The moment the women turn their backs, he leans in, whispering in my ear.

"That funny, pixie? Pretty sure you're well aware that I know how to use my fingers." My face brightens, and I can feel the heat radiating off my cheeks. I'm not going to survive this.

All three ladies bowl before us, then it's Crew's turn. My stomach swoops with nerves for him, but he seems completely unbothered. Always so in control. Except when he isn't.

"Just like they did—walk up, pull back, bring it forward, and let it go," I encourage him.

"And don't forget to bend your knees, sweet stuff," Iris adds, and I shoot her a look of pure mortification.

Crew steps forward, and I hold my breath.

"Look at those arms, so strong and firm, shame if he rolls a gutter," Rose says, and I bury my face in my hands.

My grandma chimes in with, "Girls, leave the poor boy alone. It's not his fault he's so tall, muscular, and handsome."

"Grandma!" I whisper-shout. Though I can't say that I blame them. I can't stop looking, either.

"Ladies, you flatter me. But I've only got eyes for one girl," Crew says as he winks at me before hustling to the line, pulling back, and releasing the ball. It sails into the air and lands with a hard bounce, careening into the gutter. I wince.

Iris walks up to Crew and squeezes his bicep. "It's okay, happens to a lot of men. Performance anxiety."

Oh dear god, it won't be Crew that's the death of me, it'll be these old biddies.

"See? You get it! I was nervous, it was my first time!" he jokes, and my mouth falls open in shock. It's quickly followed by a huge smile.

His second throw thuds halfway down the lane and then drifts into the gutter with no pins being knocked down. When he turns to face us, the women give him tips. They all seem to love him immediately, just like I knew they would.

By Crew's fourth frame, he finally knocks down five pins, and you'd think he just cured world hunger with the way these women fawn over him. I jump up, wrapping my arms around his neck. He's quick to return my hug, spinning me around. It's such a small, innocent thing, but he's having fun, and it feels like I've given him something good, something genuine that he can keep with him forever.

When he sets me down, he turns to face his new fan club, bowing with a flourish. "Thank you, thank you. I'd first like to thank the Ballbusters for teaching me how to ease into my first time, and to not be afraid to really go for it, you know?" They all laugh and clap for him—Rose even wolf-whistles, the hussy—and it's truly a wild spectacle of ridiculousness. But he's having fun. He's lighter, more carefree.

He takes a seat next to me and drops an arm around my shoulders. "Your grandma's friends are ruthless. I think I'm in love."

"Like hell you are, Crew!" I go to push against his chest, but he grips my hands instead, kissing the inside of each wrist. I fall just a bit harder.

By the end of practice, I overhear them all discussing whether or not I'm going to be replaced by Crew, and I have to slap my hand against my chest in mock shock.

"You know we love you here, Roe, but this man and his tight jeans are mighty fine to look at."

I know they'd never replace me, but the amused look on Crew's face is totally worth all the shit they gave him tonight.

CHAPTER TWENTY-FOUR

MONROE

"Alright, I think it's time to get you home."

I nod in agreement, knowing it's getting late. I reach for his hand as we head toward his bike, pulling him close and resting my head against his arm. My head is telling me how fast everything is moving between us, but my heart is singing a different tune.

I loved watching him with those women today. They're a group of feisty old biddies, and they surely gave him a run for his money. But Crew took everything in stride, giving it right back to them. And seeing him flirt? God, I know it made their year. I wish he could see himself how I do, how others clearly do.

Crew thinks he's all darkness and doom and gloom, but I'm convinced he just needed the right person to come into his life and accept him and open his eyes to how sweet and caring he truly is.

The bike rumbles under us, a deep, hungry vibration that travels from the steel between my thighs and into the marrow of my bones. My core is overly sensitive from last night, and I can't help the whine that breaks through my lips. Crew walks the bike slowly out of his spot before turning the opposite way from the direction toward my house.

"Where are you taking me?" I yell over the purr of the engine.

"I told you, pixie, I'm not giving you up. I'm taking you home. It's time you see the clubhouse." He says the words like the weight of them isn't huge, as if he's taking me out for coffee instead of directly into the center of his world. My eyes go wide, my heart pounding in my chest as Crew takes off down the road.

I rest my cheek against the leather at his back and brace myself for what's coming next. My fingers splay flat against his bare chest, holding on tight. I could pretend it's for safety and balance, but I'd be lying. I hold him tight because I want to be close to him.

The wind whips around us, tugging at our hair, pushing at his leather vest. I press my cheek further into the center of his back, the scent of fire, fresh rain, and leather filling my nose even through the rush of air around me. It's intoxicating. *Crew* is intoxicating.

We ride through the long stretch of mountain highway that leads to the deserted side of Amberwood. Everyone knows what's over here, and I've never had an interest to go looking. Until now.

The ride is silent, the wild wind and the purr of the engine drowning everything else out, everything except my thoughts. I wait for some sensible voice in my head to show up, to tell me not to get more involved with a man like Crew, but she never comes. I've already made up my mind.

Crew may be dangerous, he may do terrible things, but he's capable of kindness, even tenderness. I've seen it with me. The way he handled me last night, he's so sweet and loving. He's just so tightly controlled, and it's offered in such small doses that I bet he doesn't even realize there's goodness inside him. A fact I want to rectify. He's so deserving of love and to have all the good and bright things come to him. I'm convinced he's been wading through the darkness with his demons too long that he's become blind to it.

The road stretches long and empty ahead of us, the only thing visible the few feet in front of us where his lights guide the way. He takes the roads like he's done it a million times before, which I'm sure he has, turning into every tight curve with the confidence of someone who has no fear.

Crew's hand slides back, curling around my calf and giving it a squeeze. It's reassuring, possessive, and makes my heart fall harder. I run the flat of my hand up and down his chest, over his abdomen and pecs, loving how his skin feels.

Tall gates are lit up in the distance by floodlights, and a guard station at the entrance is manned by several armed guards. I tighten my arms around Crew's waist, a natural instinct for approaching the Hell's Heathens compound. I've lived in Amberwood all my life, and I've grown up hearing stories about this place. Some good, some bad. But never in a million years would I have imagined myself riding into it on the back of one of their high-ranking members' bikes.

The guards open the gate, several of them nodding to Crew, either in respect or acknowledgment, but it makes butterflies take flight in my stomach, nonetheless. He means something here and to these people.

We turn onto a long driveway, and Crew slows the bike down further, the crunch of the gravel under his tires loud after miles of smooth pavement. The massive dark building looms at the end of the road as it comes into view, intimidating and untouchable.

He squeezes my calf again, and I squeeze him back, silently letting him know that I'm good. I'm more than good, actually. I feel alive in a way that I haven't before, in a way that's almost frightening. I've spent so long trying to live that I haven't actually been living. And being with Crew has reminded me of that.

He brings the bike to a stop outside the clubhouse, and I take a deep breath. The large barn-style building has a massive wraparound deck where a couple of bikers linger. They're all wearing vests, boots, and their attention is on us.

My heartbeat stutters in my chest, and I grip Crew's hand tightly as he helps me climb off the bike, adjusting my dress. Crew's fingers pinch my chin, directing my attention back to him. His eyes are a dark onyx that seem to glimmer in the floodlights, and I can't help but smile up at him, despite the heavy, persistent feeling of eyes on us.

He cups my cheeks in his large palms, thumbs brushing slow, absentminded swipes back and forth against my skin. He just stands there for a moment, so close that I can feel the heat radiating off his body. A charged awareness hums between us, loud and incessant, and impossible to ignore. I could get completely lost in this man, and there's not a single fiber of my being that is scared to face that prospect.

His face morphs slowly, his eyebrows pinching, his lips pursing like he has something to say, but doesn't know how to express it. I reach my hands up and circle his wrists, silently urging him to open up.

"My home is your home, Monroe, and I want you to meet everyone, to see it," he says, dropping his voice even lower, nerves lacing his voice. "But if you get uncomfortable, we'll leave. No questions."

A choice.

He's giving me an out, and that's my undoing. There's no pressure, or force, or coercion. Just a simple choice. But the nerves written all over his normally confident, controlled face are worse than anything, my feelings be damned.

"I'm not going anywhere. Introduce me to your people. I want to see your home." Something shifts in his expression and lights my heart on fire, the last shreds of it breaking away for him. He looks relieved, and something close to pride fills his features.

His fingers lace with mine, strong and certain, so at odds with the first time I reached for him. He steadies me as we walk toward the stairs that lead to the deck. My pulse kicks up again, but it's not fear, it's anticipation. I want to learn more about him and where he's from, and if showing me things is how he communicates best, then I'm along for the ride.

The scent of gasoline and smoke hit my nose as we reach the top of the steps, three bikers' eyes looking me over. Not so much in an unwelcoming way, but more morbid curiosity. The man leaning against the frame of the door speaks first. He's beautiful. There's no other way to describe him. Flawless skin, straight, perfectly white teeth, meticulously sculpted hair. He's dazzling, and I bet he has ladies falling and begging at his feet.

"Couldn't be bothered to put your tracker back on?"

"Don't need you all tracking me. I'm the one who handles security, I know where I am, and that's all that matters," Crew replies, and the man rolls his pretty eyes. "This is Monroe."

The man steps forward, holding out his hand to shake mine, only for Crew to slap it away. "No touching."

My mouth falls open, slightly shocked but also amused.

"These fuckers call me Wrath, but my name's Axel. I'm the club secretary. It's good to finally meet you, but blink twice if you're here against your will."

Crew reaches out and slaps Axel in the back of the head, which makes him laugh. There's an ease between them that makes my heart swell.

"I promise, I have all my free will. I want to be where Crew is."

"Damn, brother, you actually got her to fall for you."

"Yep," Crew says proudly. "And I didn't have to use a shit board to do it."

"A what?" I laugh.

"I swear he's calling it that just to fuck with us; he's a dink. He means a charcuterie board. It's a long story for another day. You can ask our vice prez or his old lady, Bristol, about it when you meet them. They've already headed back to their house for the night."

The double front doors open, and a small group of people

pours out. Four men and a woman slide to a stop as they see us.

"New plaything, Mal? She's a pretty one. Might need to see if she's down for a ride on my cock when you're done with her." Malice moves quickly, pushing me behind him. Another hand grips my arm, not tightly, but enough to turn me. I come face-to-face with a woman with sleek black hair, bangs that I wish I could pull off, and gorgeous almond eyes.

"You may want to look away, sweetie," she says, her voice a playful warning. Of course, in my confusion, I don't listen and look back at Crew just as he drives a knife into the man's hand, nailing him to the wood railing. The man howls as Crew grabs his jaw with force. I slap my hand over my mouth in shock, my eyes wide and wild.

"She's mine. You look at her again, and I will gouge out your eyes. You speak to her, I'll cut out your tongue. And if you dare to touch her, I'll take my time and rip you apart piece by piece. Understood?"

"Yeah, Malice, understood."

Malice pulls his knife free, wiping the blood from either side on the man's shirt before putting it away and turning to me.

"He'll be fine, non-life-threatening puncture wound. He's not the first person to be stabbed by Malice, and he sure as shit won't be the last," the woman whispers.

Crew returns to my side, wrapping an arm around my waist. I'm frozen to my spot, blinking, my hands shaking. Did that just happen? The man behind us wraps a rag around his hand and lights up a cigarette like nothing happened.

Did Crew really just stab someone for making a lewd comment toward me?

“I see you met Saige,” Crew says. “She’s with our president, Chaos. Or he’s with her. Chaos is in charge of us, but she’s in charge of him. She wears the pants. We’re all scared of her, so just don’t get on her bad side. We’re too much alike, and I don’t want to fight her.”

“Do you stab people too?” I ask, surprising her. Her lips turn up in a little grin, eyes sparkling.

“No, I like to slit their throats.” A man wraps his arms around her waist, pulling her back flush against his front.

“She’s a violent little thing, but I wouldn’t have it any other way. Who are you?” This man is also beautiful. With a head of thick, dark hair that’s shaved close to the sides, the top long and tied back in a high bun. I should have been paying more attention to these club members over the years because they’ve been hiding the town’s stock of hot men. Even if none of these men hold a flame to Crew.

“Monroe. I’m here with Crew.” The man raises his eyebrows at Crew, and I have to crane my neck to look up at Crew’s face.

“Are you here willingly?” the man asks.

“Why does everyone keep asking that? Is bringing women here against their will a common occurrence?” The man, who I assume is their president, based on who he’s got his arms around, smiles at me, nodding his head.

“Welcome to the clubhouse.”

“Thanks?”

Crew guides me inside with his palm on the small of my back. Sticky heat warms my skin quickly with the loss of fresh air from outside, and now I understand why so many people were congregating there.

The front room opens up into a large living space, with heavy wood beams creating a vaulted ceiling. There are couches and chairs lined up against most walls, pool tables, dart boards, and a full bar. Leather vests are everywhere I look, people hanging out and talking. A man is standing between a woman's legs, her ponytail wrapped around his hand as he arches her neck. The scent of motor oil and cigarettes follows us into the house, and I don't see how anyone could get used to it.

"This is where we all end up usually. There's a kitchen through there." He motions to the side behind the bar. "And a bedroom off of that. Most of the bedrooms are upstairs, but mine is downstairs. I get the basement, but it's been nicknamed the dungeon."

"So you all live here? Together?"

"Most of us. The ranked members do. Except for Rhys. He and Bristol just moved out into one of the houses we have on the property. They've got two animals and want more, so it made sense. Chaos and Saige have a room upstairs. Wrath and Noose live upstairs, too. Rogue lives in Aspen Ridge with his old lady, Kinsey, but you'll meet him soon. They come up here every other weekend or when shit goes down and we need him here. Morgan—Rolo's old lady— lives here, too, and probably won't ever leave. Just because he died doesn't mean she doesn't belong here. The opposite, actually. It's our job now to keep her safe, protect her, and make sure she knows she has a family behind her."

"Rolo was your friend who passed away?"

"Murdered. My friend who was murdered."

"I'm sorry, Crew."

He squeezes my hand but doesn't say anything more. But I can tell there's pain in his eyes, and I assume they were close, more so than just through the club connection. Crew leads me to a side door that opens to a set of stairs. He flicks on a light, guiding me forward to descend.

Once we're at the bottom, there's another door that he opens, and we file through. The lights come on, illuminating the entire basement, and I stumble slightly on my feet.

At first, I don't know what I'm looking at. Then it hits me. I'm not naive or innocent enough to not know what this is, but that doesn't stop the shock from coming. The first part of the basement has been turned into a full-on sex room. I don't even know the exact word for it, but I know what I'm looking at.

A large four-post bed sits in the center of the room with silky black sheets that look like you could just melt into them. To the right is a large leather cross that fills the entire wall. My heart stutters in my chest as I imagine what it's used for. On the other side of the bed is a shelf filled with whips, paddles, handcuffs in different materials, ropes, blindfolds, and a long pole. My eyes roam everywhere, my lungs burning from lack of air. A swing hangs in front of the bed, a small leather chaise off to the other side, a table . . . everywhere I look, there's something new. Heat pools in my center, the inside of my thighs dampening through the fabric of my panties.

"Does everyone use this space?" I finally ask, breaking the silence.

"That's your first question, pixie, really?" he laughs. "No, no one uses this space but me. It's mine. The guys nicknamed it the dungeon."

"So you . . . you're into all of"—I motion around the room with my hand—"this?"

Crew runs his hand through his blond locks, shifting from foot to foot. "Yeah, I'm into all of this. My head is fucked up, Monroe. And I get all this noise, and this buildup of energy, and it needs a release. Only two things calm it. Release it. Well, it used to be two things."

I step into his space, placing a hand over his bare chest. "Sex helps? This kind of sex? But you were so sweet and gentle with me."

"This kind of release. Where the play goes on and on, whether I'm giving or receiving, it's a push of my limits and the many ways to reach it. What happened with you was different, pixie. I've never had sex like that before."

I can't help the insecurities that start to creep in. My sexual experience has been with my own fingers, and now Crew. "So . . . you play down here . . . often?"

"I haven't played with anyone since the moment I met you, Monroe. The idea of being with anyone but you makes me feel sick. But yeah, I used to play down here."

"With those women upstairs?"

"Patch bunnies? There's a few that have frequented, but there's men, too. Sex to me has always been just sex, and I don't discriminate or deny myself that pleasure in any form."

I nod, understanding what he's saying and not needing him to explain further. Insecurities start to creep their way in, though, like a virus poisoning me. I'm so inexperienced, and he's clearly done everything.

"I'm not good at reading people, pixie, but I can see your face, and you look lost in that pretty little head of yours. Talk to me."

"I want you to teach me how to be enough for you."

"Oh, pretty, pretty girl," he says sweetly as he pushes my hair behind my ear. Then he grabs a fistful and pulls my head backward slowly, arching my neck. He leans forward, dragging his nose up the length of my throat, inhaling as he goes.

"You're already more than enough. Everything about you calls to me. When I first saw you, it was just a flash of pink out of the corner of my eye, and I was a goner. I would have followed you to the ends of the earth that day. You're addicting, all-consuming. I don't know how you've done it, but you've bewitched me. You're the brightest star in the night sky I've ever seen. You're the sun on a cloudy day. The light to my darkness. You, Monroe, are more than enough. You are everything. I'm the one who isn't worthy. All I'm asking for is a chance to bask in your warm glow for as long as you'll let me. I'd never hurt you, never cause you pain that you didn't want to feel, never abandon you. Your simple touch feels better than anything we could ever do in this room. I've never needed anything in my entire life. But I *need* you."

Tears spring to my eyes. "Crew," I breathe roughly. "For a man who isn't good with words, you just nailed it. I'm not going anywhere."

"I know, pixie." He says those three words with such confidence, but I know I have the choice to leave whenever I want.

He's trusting me to stay, which means more than anything else ever could.

He grabs my hand, bringing me to the other side of the room that's separated by a long curtain. The walls are painted a deep grey, a king-sized bed sitting off to the side, farthest away from the curtain. A dresser, a door to a second bathroom, and it all dawns on me. He keeps it all separate.

"There may have been many people before you in that room, but no one's ever been here."

I know it's too soon. I know it's insane. But I'm embracing it anyway. I'm falling in love with Crew Lawson.

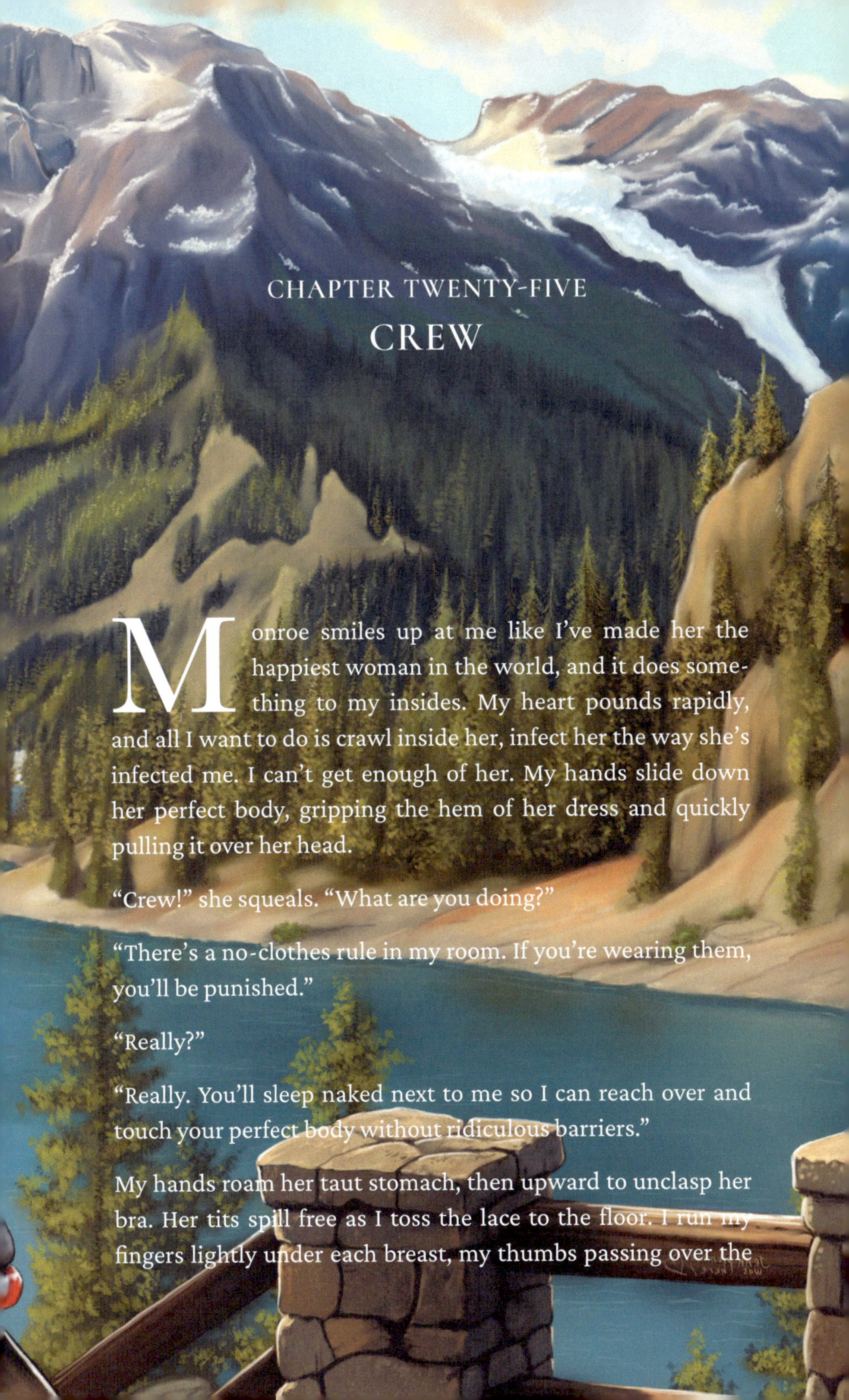

CHAPTER TWENTY-FIVE

CREW

Monroe smiles up at me like I've made her the happiest woman in the world, and it does something to my insides. My heart pounds rapidly, and all I want to do is crawl inside her, infect her the way she's infected me. I can't get enough of her. My hands slide down her perfect body, gripping the hem of her dress and quickly pulling it over her head.

"Crew!" she squeals. "What are you doing?"

"There's a no-clothes rule in my room. If you're wearing them, you'll be punished."

"Really?"

"Really. You'll sleep naked next to me so I can reach over and touch your perfect body without ridiculous barriers."

My hands roam her taut stomach, then upward to unclasp her bra. Her tits spill free as I toss the lace to the floor. I run my fingers lightly under each breast, my thumbs passing over the tight little buds of her nipples before sliding back down her body. I don't stop until I'm threading through the short hair above her pussy. Hell, I fucking love it. So natural, so fucking perfect. She makes me feral. I keep dipping lower until I slip a single finger through her folds, delicately rubbing against her hole. She's already wet for me, and I groan my appreciation.

Monroe's eyes become more heavily lidded as she sways on her feet, pulling her bottom lip between her teeth. "Sore?" She nods, and I tsk.

"Words, pixie."

"I'm sore."

"How about I kiss it better?"

She starts to nod again, but thinks better of it. My lips turn up in a smile as I slip my finger into her, rubbing the heel of my palm against her clit.

"Yes, please."

"So polite, pixie." I pick her up, setting her down on the edge of our bed, and dropping to my knees in front of her. She leans back on her elbows and watches me with lust-filled eyes. My hands run down her right leg, picking up her foot and rubbing my thumbs into the center. My lips meet the top of her toe, dragging them against her flesh to kiss her inside sole, then her delicate little ankle. I kiss up the inside of her calf, her knee, and the inside of her thigh.

Monroe trembles, goosebumps breaking out and spreading against her soft skin. I rest her foot back on the ground and repeat the process to her left leg, kissing, licking, and nibbling as I go. Giving her new sensations as she starts to sag further into the bed.

Her entire body shivers as I rest her feet on the edge of the bed, spreading her open wide for me.

"I'm addicted to how your body responds to me. Even before I touched you, you've always felt me there."

"I wanted you. From the moment I saw you that day, Crew. I craved you. Craved my stalker."

I ghost a kiss over her tender flesh between her legs, my nose nuzzling into the hair there.

"I'm yours." My tongue sticks out and flicks against her lips. "And you're mine." I place a kiss right over her glistening slit. "Your head." I give her a little more pressure with my tongue. "Your heart." I slip it through her folds, her body arching toward my mouth. "This pretty pussy."

"Then make me come, Crew. Show me who I belong to."

Fuck. How can one woman calm the storm inside me and make me crazed all at the same time?

My hands grip her hips as my face finds its home between her legs. I bury myself into her, my tongue seeking out her clit and lapping at it, dragging my piercing along her sensitive flesh. I collect as much of her arousal on my tongue as I can, needing to swallow down her sweet taste.

Monroe's hands thread through my hair, pulling at the strands as she grinds into my mouth. I alternate between long laps and little pulses, my tongue slipping around her soft, velvety texture. I grind against the bed, my hard cock desperate for friction.

"Crew!" Her body stiffens for a brief moment, and then it's all shakes, tremors, and moans while her taste floods my mouth.

Her arms stretch out above her head as she arches and writhes through her orgasm. I lick her through it, sucking her clit between my lips and giving her a little suction. Monroe will never know a day when my head isn't between her thighs, eating this sweet pussy.

Just as she comes down, I stand between her legs, pumping my cock until ropes of cum splash out onto her center. Monroe watches with rapt attention, her breathing labored, her eyes heavy, mouth falling open in a sexy little "O". I squeeze the last drops from my tip, watching it drip down onto her wet cunt.

"Tell me, pixie, have you ever tasted cum before?"

"You know I haven't."

"Good. Mine will be the only cum that ever touches your tongue." With two fingers, I swipe up some of my mess and press it into her mouth. My sweet girl sucks them down, cleaning them off so perfectly for me. I groan, fucking my fingers slowly into her mouth. "So good for me. I can't wait to fuck you here." Her eyes glimmer like she's also thought about it, and that makes me fucking feral. I want to keep going. Want to spend days, weeks down here playing with her, but I know this is all new, and I know she's sore.

Reluctantly, I pull my fingers free and watch as she licks her lips. Fucking tease. I walk to my bathroom, run the hot water, and get a washcloth before returning to her. She hasn't moved from her position at the end of the bed, but her arm is draped over her eyes. It's been a long twenty-four hours, and I bet she's absolutely exhausted.

I take my time with her, cleaning my cum off her pussy and lower abdomen, wiping her down, then tossing the wet cloth into the hamper. I gather her pliant body up in my arms and position us in bed together, a place I've never had another person sleep but me, but I can't be away from her. It's not enough, and I need to be touching her.

She stirs in my arms, wrapping around my waist and resting her head on my chest. "Thank you."

"I should be thanking you, pixie."

"Why don't you sleep? You said you get nightmares?"

I take a deep breath, not wanting to go back to this place but wanting to open up to her.

"I've had a rough life. I had never known a shred of kindness until Rolo—Jesse—came along. The people who had me were drunks and drug addicts. They kept me locked in a cage for as long as I can remember. There's not even a record of me being born anywhere. Jesse said she must have had me at home and didn't tell anyone except whatever man knocked her up and was living there. I didn't go to school, and I never left the house they lived in. Hell, I didn't get to leave the cage often. I was a ghost. The isolation and lack of touch and communication really fucked with me. I was beaten and tortured, but that physical pain heals. The mental," I tell her, tapping my head, "that fucked me up. I used to sit in the cage and rock back and forth; even now, stimulation like that is soothing to me. I tap my thigh, and I count things, all to just keep myself from losing my shit. I own who I am, Monroe. I have a dark side that I work hard to keep locked up. One day, I was beaten and thrown back in my cage, but the door didn't lock. Something snapped in me that day, and I felt like I was someone else."

"Malice," she says, putting the pieces together.

"Yeah. Malice. I craved it. I wanted to make them hurt and suffer. So, I did. I slaughtered them while they fucked on a dirty mattress. I lived in the house with their decaying bodies until I was on the verge of starving to death. I was homeless for a while, sleeping on park benches, until I was arrested for breaking into this abandoned house in the middle of winter. I went to jail and met Jesse. He saved me. Kept me from killing some asshole in prison and told me things would get better. After we were out, he brought me here, gave me my cut, taught me to read, taught me everything I know, and gave me a second chance at life."

Tears stream down Monroe's cheeks, and she climbs over my body to straddle me, cupping my face. "Surviving is the hardest thing any of us will ever do. You're a survivor, Crew."

"I'm a killer, Monroe. A monster. A demon. This is why I'm not worthy of you."

"I don't believe that for a second. I know you've done terrible things, but you're a good man. Look at how you treat me, look at how you took my virginity. You have so much love inside you, you just don't recognize it."

"I wish that were true."

"Have you ever killed someone innocent?"

"Never."

"Then you're doing something good for the rest of us. Don't you see that? Your parents deserved that death after what they did to you. The man who murdered Jesse deserves death. Evil lurks, Crew, and people like you right the scales."

"You and Saige are going to be great friends, pixie girl."

"Yeah? She kind of became my hero with the vibe she's putting out. I wish I were that badass."

"I like you just the way you are. All light and love and warmth."

"Then I'll be your light."

"You already are."

CHAPTER TWENTY-SIX

MALICE

My phone buzzes on the nightstand. For the first time ever, I want to ignore it. I know it's going to pull me away from my sleeping pixie, and I don't want to be anywhere but here. When it goes off a second time, I give in, picking up and opening the chat.

Chaos: It's time to deal with Garrett

Chaos: Wasn't expecting you to have company Mal but we gotta do this tonight

Me: I'll be right up

Sin: Garage?

Chaos: Yep

Wrath: All set up. He's wide awake looking at me like one angry fucker

Wrath: Doesn't seem too happy to be back at the Heathen compound

Chaos: Tough shit for him

Me: Well I'm ready to party then

I peel myself away from Monroe, easily slipping out of the room after getting dressed in a pair of jeans, boots, and my leather cut. I meet my brothers outside, their hard stares all looking at me with the same expression.

"What?"

"Just surprised you brought her here. Last we all knew, you were still stalking her."

"Yeah, well, what can I say? I'm irresistible," I say as I light up a cigarette, something I'm determined to quit doing since meeting Monroe.

"Fuck that shit. How'd you do it?"

"Apparently my little ray of sunshine was charmed by my romantic wiles."

Sin barks out a laugh. "Romantic? You mean stalker-like."

"Whatever. She fell for me. She chose to be here."

"We're happy for you, brother. If anyone deserves to be happy and find their person, it's you."

"You assholes are making me want to crawl out of my skin. Let's go take care of this piece of shit so we can get back to our queens."

"I don't know how long the fucker is going to last. You called dibs on him, but you've been distracted. Wrath had to have Stitch hook him up to an IV to keep him alive."

"That was the point. Well, let's see how much juice he's got then, huh?"

Together we walk into the garage that sits detached from the main clubhouse. Two cars sit in it, unused, making it look like your average, unassuming garage. Little would anyone know, and most don't except our club officers, that below it is a little place I like to call the fun factory.

"When are we going to make a decision about the Kingsnakes?" I ask Chaos and Sin.

"It's hard not to wonder if it's a trap. Send in someone to piss us off, bait us, send in a decoy to seem like our savior, and beg us to go in. If we're working with Saint, they'd have all the details of our attack and would be prepared to counter. We could be walking into a bloodbath."

"We need to get retribution for Rolo's murder. His fucking brother sent out that hit!"

Chaos snaps, his head violently moving in my direction. "That's not his fucking brother. We are his brothers. That's someone who shares DNA, and blood doesn't mean shit. Watch your fuckin' mouth, Malice."

I heed his warning, shutting my mouth even though I've got a shit ton more to say on the topic.

Sin pulls up the hidden door, and we head down the stairs, the scent of dried blood and death eternally permeating the air. The room has been soundproofed, complete with everything you'd need to torture someone in the most creative ways.

The ugly asshole hangs from a hook in the ceiling, his arms stretched wide, his toes dangling just above the concrete ground. Just as I ordered, no one has touched him yet. We've left him down here for a few days, starving him, letting him go insane while he wonders when we'll come to end his life.

"Garrett, glad you're still with us. You fucked up, picked the wrong club to fuck with."

"I was following orders," he groans, his voice sounding like a hundred-year-old smoker. I'm sure with the lack of liquid he's had, it feels like he swallowed shards of glass. Hmm. There's an idea.

"You were following orders. You hear that, brothers? He was following orders!" I yell back to Chaos, Sin, and Wrath. "You killed my brother. Did he know it was coming? Did you tell him why? That his own fucking flesh and blood put out the hit?" My breathing is dangerously slow and controlled, but my veins are burning up, vibrating with fury.

"He knew. His last words were begging me not to kill him. He begged like the pathetic dog he is." Then he spits, the moisture spraying across my face. The room narrows around me, and all I see is him, his body distorting in front of me and turning into Rolo's dead body, lying in a pool of blood. Like a match dropped in gasoline, all I feel is white-hot, blinding rage.

I walk to the table that lines one of the walls of the room, picking up the new fleshing knife I requested. I move in measured steps back to Garrett, spinning the knife in my hand. There are no more words that need to be spoken, just a lesson to be taught. And he's going to feel every single bit of it.

I start with making a shallow cut around his wrist, the blood pooling and starting to trickle down his arm. Then I stick my fingers in, gripping the skin and pulling outward, working my knife into the slot I created to hack away the skin from the muscle, trying my damndest not to nick any of the thin little bastard veins there.

There's no noise but a rushing between my ears, but Garrett thrashes, making my cuts look rushed and sloppy. I work my way around his forearm, taking my time to slowly make a clean separation. He's making it incredibly difficult, but the more skin I'm able to pull back, the easier it gets to continue to cut between his flesh and muscles.

By the time I've reached his elbow, blood cascades down his arm, covering my hands, arms, and chest. I'm drenched in it. Bathed in the blood of my patch brother's murderer. Visions of Rolo stay front and center, but then they morph, the nightmares of the people who put me on Earth. The cage. The hunger. The cold. The noises. The pain.

The fist slams into my cheek, making me stumble, but I don't fall down. Not yet. The pain doesn't register. Having faded so long ago, I don't remember what it felt like. Another punch comes, this time to my stomach. Air wheezes from my chest uncontrollably, and I lurch forward, just as another punch makes contact with my nose. There's a crunch that I hear deep within the marrow of my bones as I fall hard against a large mirror.

The glass shatters around me, and for a moment, I stare down at my distorted reflection, pale skin, eyes dark and empty, the purple-marred skin, my hair a dark matted mess. Blood trickles from my nose onto the glass, splashing and rippling outward.

Then I'm wrenched backward by my hair, dragged across the floor, and shoved inside the cage. The door slams, then rattles and bounces.

I pull my knees close to my chest, rocking back and forth while my eyes stare at the unlocked door of the cage. It's closed, but the lock missed the latch. It's dark, too dark to see much, but the lock clearly missed the hole. My hands shake, my head twitching from side to side in slow jerking movements before my neck finally cracks. The pressure snaps. A release.

Time goes by, but I never know how much, so I sit and rock.

Back and forth.

Back and forth.

Back and forth.

No one comes to fix the lock, but I wait and rock.

Back and forth.

Back and forth.

Back and forth.

Glass shatters. Voices yell somewhere far away, like they're someplace else, or underwater. My body feels as though it's floating, looking down at myself from above. Is this what death feels like? Slowly drifting away, watching yourself in your last moments on Earth.

And still I rock.

But the pressure builds.

I just want it to stop. I want the noise to stop. I want the pain to stop. I want the cold to stop. I want the hunger to stop.

And builds.

It needs to stop.

The cage opens with barely a push, my knees crunching on broken glass and trash as I crawl out. I stop on all fours, looking down at my reflection again in the shards. Eyes the color of darkness stare back at me, and if no light will ever come for me, then it's in the darkness I'll stay.

The shard is slightly bigger than my hand, and I pick it up, the base wide and getting smaller and smaller, coming together in a sharp point at the top.

I grip it tightly in my palm, the rough edges digging into my skin. Blood trickles down my wrist, the edges of my vision blurry and chaotic.

Make it stop.

Then I'm standing to my full height, methodically, controlled, like a demon rising from the depths of hell, with only one thing on my mind. I'm hungry. Starving. But not for food.

It needs to stop.

The edges of the room start to close in on me, a dark haze at the corners of my eyes, blood rushing between my ears. Everything else fades away as I walk into the other room. My eyes make contact with the man and woman who've been my captors, my tormentors. I see their naked bodies moving, hear their grunts and voices, but they don't see me, they don't even hear me. No one does. No one ever will.

My head cocks to the side, taking in their appearances. Dirty bodies, stained with yellow and black marks all over their skin. The man stumbles backward off of her, his eyes going wide as he points at me, his mouth moving as if he's yelling, but I don't hear a single thing. My head cocks to the side. All that exists the rush of blood between my ears, my steady heartbeat.

Thump.

Thump.

Thump.

Make it stop.

My arm moves of its own accord, slashing and stabbing. Deep crimson splashes across the filthy walls, my face, the couch, and the cage. By the time I'm done, I'm covered in blood. Dripping the essence that kept them alive. Kept them alive to instill their hatred against me. But it's silent. And dark. And there's no more cage.

But still I rock.

I hack at his skin with my knife. Counting out the cuts in my head. Out loud. I don't know anymore. All I know is the feeling inside me needs to combust, needs somewhere to go.

Back and forth.

Back and forth.

Back and forth.

I don't stop until I've pulled the skin from his entire arm and separated it from his body, leaving nothing but bloody muscle and veins behind.

When I drop his skin glove to the ground in front of my patch brothers, I finally see Garrett. His head hangs limp, but his chest is still rising and falling. I don't know when his screaming stopped and he passed out from the pain, but hopefully it wasn't too soon. I wanted him to feel all of it.

"Wake him up. We're not done."

I'll never be done.

CHAPTER TWENTY-SEVEN

MONROE

I wake up alone and have no idea what time it is. With no windows in Crew's room, I have no way to judge if it's still the middle of the night or early morning. I reach for my phone that Crew had placed on the end table next to me, seeing it's after two a.m. I have a missed text from my mom, so I open it up.

> Mom: I'm glad you're having a good time. Grandma loves him. Be safe, and I'm here if you need anything

Huh? I sit up in bed, resting my back against the headboard. I look at the above texts, confused.

Me: I'm going on a date tonight and just wanted to let you know so you didn't worry. I probably won't be back home until tomorrow.

Did Crew send my mom a text at some point? I know I didn't send that, so he must have. I don't know how he got my phone unlocked or when, but the thought is touching and not at all creepy. He cared enough about me to check in with my mom. Something I probably should have done, in hindsight.

I put my phone back down on the end table and look around the room. I don't know how long he's been gone, but I don't plan on going to look for him in this place. Everyone seemed nice enough, in a rough-around-the-edges kind of way, but they're still a club of ruthless bikers, and after lewd comments got someone stabbed tonight, I'm not comfortable taking my chances.

So much has happened in the last two days, and I feel like Crew and I are rapidly falling for each other. Or maybe it's a high. Whatever it is, I can't get enough.

Crew's bedroom is simple, with bare walls and no real personal items that could give me further insight into him. Something tells me he's simple, just needing the bare minimum. I suppose after the childhood, or lack thereof, that he had, it would make him a humbler man.

I can't wrap my head around the types of humans his parents had to be to abuse him like that. I'm not sorry they're dead, but I am sorry that Crew had to be the one to do it. That he was pushed so far that he snapped. We can only take so much trauma before we either give up completely or start to fight back. I'd say I don't believe in complacency, but that's exactly how I've been living after my own trauma.

I don't want to live like that anymore.

I want Crew and me both to step out of the shadows we've been living in and enjoy the light. I don't need to release myself of the guilt I have over surviving that accident when my friends didn't. I need to let go of the pressure of living wrong or doing the wrong thing because all eyes are on me. Crew and I just need to live. And I really want to do that together.

He may be unconventional and slightly unhinged at times, but I've embraced it from the first moment he stood in front of me in the preparation room and ran his fingers down the bridge of my nose. Should I be more concerned that he stalked me and broke into my house while I slept? Probably. But he's curious and guarded, and he was exploring me the only way he felt safe to do so. I wouldn't change a thing about how we started, and I'm determined to make this a happy ending for both of us.

I pull the sheet up over my chest and wait for him to return, dozing on and off. I know he doesn't sleep, and I understand why now, but it doesn't seem right that he would leave me the first night he's had me over. Especially after how he slept so soundly next to me in my bed last night. A gnawing warning settles deep in my belly, my pulse beating at a higher rate. Something doesn't feel right, and that worries me. Is this what life would be like with him? I haven't met Jesse's widow yet, but hearing Crew talk about how she'd stay at the clubhouse, how she's all of their responsibility now, was heartbreakingly beautiful. They're a family here. I just wonder how the women handle the fear of something happening to their men, like what happened to Jesse.

My eyes grow heavy, and my head bobs every time my body starts to give back in to sleep, but I don't lie back down. I need to know he's okay before my body and mind can completely settle. It shouldn't be possible after such a short time together, but I miss him. I want to be wrapped up in his arms right now. I'm craving the steady beat of his heart and the slow, controlled cadence of his breathing.

I feel him return before I see him, recognizing his presence as he walks into the room. Silent as a breeze in the night, Crew appears in the doorway of his bedroom. His silhouette is bathed in darkness, a menacing presence looming at the edge of the room. Silent, foreboding. Energy pulses off of him in waves, nearly choking me with something thick and heavy. My veins turn to ice beneath my skin. Is he hurt? Where was he?

I quickly flick the bedside lamp on, the light assaulting my eyes. I squint at the onslaught, blinking to get my vision to clear. Crew stands unmoving in the doorway as I pull the blankets off of me, my bare feet making contact with the cool concrete floor. I yank at the sheet, carrying it with me to keep my naked body covered. I really wish I had clothes on right about now. There's something so incredibly vulnerable about standing in front of him like this with nothing but a sheet to hide behind.

My eyes meet the man in front of me, his head cocked to the side as he looks at me, but he's not seeing me, of that I'm certain. Crew's naturally dark brown eyes are near black, soulless, and empty, and they're looking right through me. I stumble on my feet, my hand moving toward my stomach as my heart sinks into the pit of it.

The man in front of me isn't Crew. This man? This is who he warned me about. This is *Malice.* He's wearing black combat boots, ripped denim jeans, and his leather vest, sans shirt. But there's so much blood. It stains his blond hair, streaking down his face, arms, and his bare abdomen. He's something straight out of a horror movie. I've never seen so much blood covering one person before, and I don't know if it's his or not.

He doesn't move, and while I can't see the rapid rise and fall of his chest in the dim light, I can feel how strung out he is. Whatever happened tonight, it wasn't good.

He needs me.

I take several steps in his direction, coming to the very end of the bed, standing a few feet in front of him. A deep, warning growl releases from his throat, more animalistic than man. I should be scared. I should run. I should scream for help. But I won't do any of those things.

"Crew?" I say hesitantly as I slowly reach my hand out to him in offering.

"Aren't you scared, pixie?" His voice is strained, pained, deeper than normal, like he's using every fiber of his being to stay in control despite the warring emotions and adrenaline pulsing through him.

"I'm only scared of you getting hurt."

"You need to leave. I-I don't want to hurt you." He's worried about *me*?

"You would never hurt me, Crew. I trust you."

"Pixie . . . *please*, go."

Never. I won't abandon him.

"I'm not leaving you, Crew. We're going to get through this."

"I can't hurt you."

"Shh, you won't. I know you won't hurt me. Are you okay?"

Crew's head cocks to the side again, regarding me, his hands clenching and unclenching at his sides as he stands frozen. "I-I don't know."

"Come here."

CHAPTER TWENTY-EIGHT

MALICE

"Come here."

Those two words make me flinch, my eyes hazy with the rush of adrenaline that's running through my veins like knives slicing through silk. I'm vibrating with need, with a desperate pull to unleash the energy trying to rip me open.

She should run. Even though I can't promise I won't chase her.

Monroe pulls her shoulders back, steeling herself as she closes the remaining space between us. I focus on the pretty blue of her eyes, trying to reel myself in. She's not going to hurt me. I can't hurt her. This is Monroe. The love of my life. My queen. My old lady.

Blood rushes between my ears, my heartbeat a heavy thud against my ribs. The crack of my neck is audible through the quiet space of the dungeon as I stretch it side to side. I want to kill. I want to fuck. Pillage. Ravage. Harm. Ruin. That's what I do. Killing Garrett wasn't enough. It just built the pressure inside me, and now it's overflowing with nowhere to go.

I'm destruction. She's creation.

"You should have run, pixie."

I lift my hand, fingers gripping the fabric clenched in front of her, tugging until it releases. The sheet falls to the floor, revealing her pure, untouched, naked body underneath.

Mine. Mine. Mine. **Mine**.

I slide my blood-coated fingers across the fine line of her collarbone, then dip over her sternum, leaving a trail of crimson in my wake. Monroe shudders, tears trickling down her freckled cheeks. My hands clasp her breasts, rolling her pretty, pert nipples between my fingers. Her breathing hitches, that plush bottom lip sitting tight between her pearly white teeth.

Monroe doesn't shy away, and I don't sense any fear radiating off her. In fact, she stands in front of me like the goddess of the underworld, her spine straight, shoulders back, ready to handle the beast she's hitched herself to.

Her hands reach out, running delicate little fingers across my chest. Her touch feels so warm, so soft, and soothing. This is Monroe. I can't hurt her. I can't treat her like everyone else. This is different, and she'll never forgive me.

"Crew, do you trust me, baby? I want to take care of you."

Do I? I don't know anything right now. I can't fucking think straight with this boiling pressure inside me. I'm overflowing with it. The rage palpable, my veins bubbling with the urge to move. I'm just . . . terrified to. I can't hurt my sweet girl. And I refuse to tie her up and spend hours using her body for my own selfish needs. I have to be better than that.

I just don't know if I can.

Her hand reaches for mine, my heart stumbling in my chest at the contact. She lifts my hand and rests it flat on her chest over her heart. My eyes flutter closed involuntarily, her steady pulse beating under my palm.

Thump Thump

Thump Thump

Thump Thump

I sway on my feet as I breathe to the soothing beat of her heart. The heart that belongs to me, that she's willingly handing over.

Thump Thump

Thump Thump

Thump Thump

Her soft fingers run small circles across my skin, and I take a deep inhale, breathing in the sunshine scent. It's faint, mixed with the metallic scent of blood and death permeating the air around us, but I can still smell her. She's so soothing and calm. I swallow down the bitter taste of malice like shards of glass, pushing away the urges that are clawing at my insides like demons trying to escape the underworld.

Thump Thump

Thump Thump

Thump Thump

Monroe takes my other hand and urges me forward a step and then another. I follow blindly.

"Trust me. I've got you. You're safe. It's just you and me here." God, that voice. The only voice that's ever meant something to me. The only one I want to hear. Light and melodic, like a lullaby, her voice guides me forward.

When I open my eyes, we're in my bathroom. She's kept the lights off, a low light peering in from the open bathroom door. Hot water fills the tub, but I don't hear the noise; all I hear is *her*. She whispers softly, reminding me that she's here, that she's not going anywhere, that I'm safe, and it's okay. Reminding me to breathe and to focus on her. On her heartbeat.

She's the light in my darkness, pulling me out.

Monroe turns off the water and starts to strip me of my clothes. She dips a washcloth into the water and begins to clean the blood from my skin, and when the majority of it is gone, she climbs in the tub and settles her back against the edge. She holds out her hand to me, and I join her, squeezing in so I'm lying between her legs.

Monroe wraps her arms around me, holding my head to her chest. Fingers comb through my hair in tender strokes, her chest rising and falling under me. I lay on my side, wrapping my arms around her waist to hold her tight, that precious life of hers beating rhythmically in my ear.

Thump Thump

Thump Thump

Thump Thump

"I've got you, baby. Just relax."

The tight clench in my jaw starts to ebb, my molars aching like I was chewing on gravel, my hands releasing their tight fists. That boiling sensation starts to cool to a simmer, where I can breathe just a little easier.

The world starts to become clearer, as if I'm regaining consciousness after being held underwater for too long.

Monroe's hands move over my body with the washcloth, scrubbing the remaining blood from my skin. I let her, not wanting to move, not wanting this to end.

When she's finished, she holds my head against her chest, her fingers running through my hair. She's tender, and sweet, and so . . . *loving*. I never knew touch could feel this way. So soft and delicate, but so deep and consuming at the same time.

I count her heartbeats, letting the rhythm of her life calm the storm inside me. She's pushing it back by just existing, by just wrapping her powerful arms around me and holding me close. This little pixie of a woman is the strongest thing in the world.

My eyes burn as clarity returns, tears spilling onto her chest. I grip her tighter around the waist, holding on for dear life as everything inside me releases, until I'm empty and spent, and there's nothing left but us.

When the water runs cold, we climb out of the tub silently. She dries us both and then pulls me to our bed, where I lie on my back, and she falls down next to me. Her fingers trace delicate lines over my tattoos, her fingers so purposeful and meaningful.

"Thank you."

"You never have to thank me for being there for you. Especially when you need it most. I won't abandon you, Crew."

"I don't deserve you."

"I disagree, but I'm choosing you anyway." She says the words as she kisses the top of my hand she's holding, then my wrist. She moves slowly, like she's afraid to spook me, scooting down the bed so her head is near my chest.

Her mouth makes contact with my skin, and I shiver in response. Her hair is like silk as it slips through my fingers, her lips trailing across my abdomen with reverence. My cock hardens rapidly, and when she sinks lower, her mouth wrapping around the head, my mind goes completely blank. All there is in the world is this little pixie who just handled the monster inside me like she was made to.

Her tongue tentatively explores my tip, flicking over the piercings that are so sensitive. It feels so good. She doesn't go any further, and I don't urge her to take more. But then she sits up, straddling my waist.

No words are spoken as I grip her hips, lifting her up as she notches the head of my cock at her entrance. So slowly, she sinks down, and inch by glorious inch, my length disappears inside her body. Her pussy envelopes me in wet warmth, her tight, velvety walls fluttering around my length.

I've never given much thought to sex outside of the feeling and the release, but watching a part of me slide into her like a fucking puzzle piece does something to my heart. Just like yesterday, when she gave herself to me for the first time. What I have with Monroe is different.

"Are you sore?"

"Yes. But I'm okay. You feel good inside me, Crew. You make me feel good."

"Yeah?"

"Yeah, baby."

She takes all of me, and I'm so proud. Monroe St. James was made for me. She's the only person who could tame me, and now she's healing me, when I thought I was a lost cause.

She leans down, ghosting her lips over mine as she braces herself on my chest. "I love you, Crew."

Her words momentarily stun me. I've never let myself dream of hearing those words from someone. Even if my club brothers have reminded me they love me once before, this is different. This is *everything*. Monroe loves me?

I cradle her head between my hands, her crystal-blue eyes holding me hostage. "Fuck, pixie, I love you. I've never said those words to anyone."

She starts to rock back and forth, pulling my cock deeper inside her wet channel.

"I know. I feel it."

"I don't deserve you, Monroe. I'm not good for you. I live in the darkness, I'm broken."

She sits up on my dick, looking down at me. She continues to rock slowly back and forth, finding a rhythm that makes her feel good. It's so sexy.

"I'm joining you in it, Crew, and I'll love all your broken pieces for as long as you'll have me."

I sit up quickly, wrapping my arm around her waist and threading my hand through her hair to cup her face. “You’re it for me, there’s no going back from this. I told you before, I can’t let you go. I won’t.”

“Then I better hold on.”

We rock together, our lips brushing as our breathing picks up. I catch a glimpse of us in the mirror, her flawless, freckled skin, pink hair, and the undeniable light she exudes. Then there’s me, my dark obsidian eyes, my tattoos, scars, and marred skin.

An angel and her demon.

CHAPTER TWENTY-NINE

MONROE

It's new to wake up without the light streaming into my window, but I don't mind the darkness or the man who currently has his arm wrapped around my waist. I snuggle back into his chest, breathing in the scent of flames and rain. I hold his hand close to my heart, lifting it and kissing his bruised knuckles.

Whatever happened the other night, wherever he went, it should have terrified me, but not a single part of me wanted to run from him in that moment. Or any moment since I've met him. He's been left to find ways to cope with pain and trauma on his own, and I wasn't about to run away and let him fight his demons alone when he has me by his side now.

I know trauma. I know death. Crew needs love, compassion, and acceptance.

Crew is multilayered, and I'm discovering new things I love about him each day we spend together. There's a constant tension that simmers right under his controlled exterior, like a coiled wire ready to snap at any moment. Violence feels familiar to him, but I don't believe it's exciting; I think it's all he knows. I'm determined to change that.

Crew doesn't need saving, but he does need healing. My phone glows next to my head with an incoming text, and I'm thankful I turned it on silent. Crew and I haven't left his room all weekend, completely consumed with each other and lost to time moving around us.

Guilt starts to creep in that I haven't reached out to my mom, and when I see her text, my heart sinks.

Mom: Just checking in since it's been a few days. Let us know how you're doing. Starting to get slightly worried. Your dad on the other hand is totally losing his shit.

Me: Alive and well. More than well. No need to send out a search and rescue.

I cringe.

Me: Sorry, not a good joke.

Mom: Just wanted to hear from you. We're trying to give you space, you're an adult, but just us being parents, you know?

Me: I know, Mom. I love you guys for it. I promise I'm better than ever.

Mom: That's all we want for you. Thank you for texting me back.

Me: Can I bring someone to dinner tonight?

Mom: Of course you can.

Me: I'm in love Mom. I really want you all to love him

Mom: If you love him, Roe, then we will love him, too. All that matters is your happiness and we trust your judgment.

Me: Be there at 6?

Mom: We'll be here waiting. Maybe you should prep him. It's a zoo over here

Me: Nah, I think a surprise will be better

Mom: You trying to make that poor man run the other way? Because we'll surely chase him

Me: haha. Our family isn't that bad!

Mom: We're just intense and love hard.

Me: Exactly what he needs

I set the phone back on the end table and turn in Crew's arms, just as he starts to slide downward under the sheets. He kisses his way over my pelvis, nuzzling his nose into my pubic hair.

"Crew, what are you doing?"

"Starting our day with my face between your thighs." He parts me then, taking a slow lick between my lips before sucking my clit into his mouth. My back bows as the pleasure spreads outward from my center. I love this man's mouth on me. He's been insatiable the last few days and seems to be addicted to making me come on his tongue.

He pulls away way too soon, tossing the sheets off of us and scooping me into his arms. I squeal, wrapping my arm around his neck, his mouth glistening with my arousal.

"What are you doing?"

"I want to try something. Do you trust me?"

"Of course I do." Crew carries me into the other room, grabbing the swing that hangs from the ceiling in front of the bed. My heart swoops as he sets my ass down into the seat. He sets each of my feet into stirrups, spreading me wide as he drops to his knees, pulling the swing forward to bring my pussy to his mouth.

His lips suction over my pussy, and I grip the straps above me to hang on. He holds me close, using the swing to rock me on his mouth while his tongue lavishes every inch of me. I clench the straps harder, and the feeling is foreign yet thrills me at the same time. It feels so . . . devious.

Crew stands in front of me, his head cocked to the side, his dark eyes crazed and lust-filled. He pumps his big cock with his hand, squeezing the tip on every upstroke. Then he's grabbing the swing and pulling me forward slightly to meet him. When he enters me, it's a completely new sensation. My eyes roll to the back of my head as I moan loudly.

The thick mushroom head of his cock rubs a new place deep inside me, a place that has my vision blurring with tears.

"Oh, my pixie likes that, does she?"

"Crew, I don't know what you're doing, but please don't stop."

"That's your G-spot, pretty girl. Now hang on while I bounce this tight pussy on my dick."

Crew does just that, and I'm barely able to think straight. I can feel every inch of his cock as he thrusts in hard and slowly drags out, his head bumping this spot deep inside of me. My orgasm builds quickly, my legs shaking uncontrollably.

"I can feel how close you are, let go and come all over my cock. I want you to milk the cum out of me," he says, his voice deeper and restrained like his control is barely hanging on by a thread. He bounces me hard, slamming me back down on his length before swinging me back.

"Oh, god, Crew! Don't stop! Don't stop!"

"Fuck, pixie, you feel so damn good. Your pussy is squeezing me so tight. Fucking come!"

When I come, I come harder than ever before, a scream ripping from my body that makes my throat hoarse. My orgasm hits me with the force of a wave breaking on the shore in the middle of a storm. My entire body shakes, everything inside me pulsing and vibrating, my head swimming.

Hands run all over my body, up my legs, and over my stomach, squeezing my breasts and working their way down again. I open my eyes to see Crew looking down at me with so much love and appreciation that it makes my heart stutter in my chest.

"You took that so well. How do you feel?"

"Like I'm on a different planet. I don't know if my legs will work after that, they're shaking so badly."

Crew just laughs as he slowly pulls from my body. He's gentle with me as he gets me out of the swing, scooping me up bridal style and carrying me to the shower. Ever since the night he came back to me covered in blood, it's become our thing to bathe together. I love the connection and closeness of it, and Crew seems to find comfort in being able to safely let all his walls down.

After our shower, we reluctantly get dressed. Not to my surprise, Crew had been stealing my panties and several dresses when he was sneaking into my house at night to have here for when he ultimately brought me home. Once again, it's one of those things that I can either find endearing or be completely freaked out by. But there's just something so innocently sweet and considerate about him that I adore so much, I let it slide and put on one of the dresses, thankful for something clean to wear in front of everyone.

"I want to bring you somewhere tonight, if you're up for it."

"I'll follow you anywhere, pixie. Where'd you have in mind?"

"My parents' house. Dinner is always a really big deal over there, and I want you to meet them all."

Crew looks stunned, his hand running through the wet locks of his hair. Water still beads over his eyelashes as he blinks them away.

"You want me to meet your entire family?"

"Yes, silly. Of course I do. We've already established I'm not going anywhere, and neither are they. Will you come?"

"Monroe, are you sure? I'm the kind of man parents warn their daughters about."

I laugh, dragging his mouth in for a kiss. "My family isn't like that. They are the least judgmental people in the world. My grandma loved you, don't forget that."

"I bet if they knew the blood on my hands, and the things I've done to their daughter, they'd judge."

Okay, so he's not wrong there. "We aren't going to talk about that. You're good, Crew, despite what you may believe about yourself, you are good, and your heart is there."

"My heart only beats for you."

"Well, it's past time it beats for *you*, too."

CHAPTER THIRTY

CREW

Me: Monroe is taking me to her family's house for dinner

Sin: Sounds serious

Me: It is asshole. What do I do?

Wrath: Just be yourself

Me: Have you met me?

Sin: You got that ray of sunshine to fall for you. I'm sure her parents will look past your pointy edges

Wrath: She wouldn't bring you there if she was worried what they'd think

Sin: How'd you get so wise?

Wrath: I pay attention, you should try it

Sin: Oh I pay attention, just ask Bristol

Sin: Actually don't. Stay away from her

Me: On that topic, think you could keep that anaconda hidden while Monroe is around?

Wrath: Why? Scared?

Me: Yep. Everyone here except the patch bunnies are scared of that thing. You'd split me in two

Wrath: Good thing you're not on my menu

Wrath: No promises but I'll see what I can do. You all really should stop worrying so much about my dick size

Me: Whatever

Sin: Mal just be yourself. But maybe keep the thirst for violence locked up tight? And maybe wear a shirt?

Me: Got it. Be myself but not fully myself. Easy.

Talk about nerves. I fucking hate this new emotion that's been plaguing me lately. Monroe gives my hand a reassuring squeeze, the pressure and the warmth seeping into my skin. I run my hand through my wild hair again, wondering what these good people are going to think about me. An outcast. A criminal. A Heathen.

Monroe reads it on my face, tugging on my hand and pulling me down to her level. I bend my knees to look her eye to eye, just as her palms come up to grasp my face.

I'm wearing a pair of jeans with my boots and a plain T-shirt. I feel naked without my cut, but we both knew that probably wasn't the best thing to wear to her family's dinner.

"They are going to love you, baby," she promises, running her thumb over my bottom lip. She lifts up on her toes then, pressing her sweet lips to mine in a chaste kiss, leaving behind the taste of strawberries and sunshine. "Here we go!"

Monroe opens the front door of her family home to a lively circus on the inside. We step through the threshold and kick off our shoes, just as a small child runs past us, chasing an orange tabby cat with half a tail. Monroe must see my question because she answers it before I get the chance to ask.

"We have no idea. She was like that when we adopted her from the Amberwood Animal Shelter. They said it was some type of accident that healed on its own."

"Ahh. Those tend to do that."

"What do?"

"Wounds."

Monroe's pretty face falls for a fraction of a second before she packs it away. "If it's the last thing I do, Crew Lawson, you're going to learn to love yourself."

A woman comes around the corner next, her eyes gleaming, smiling so bright. She looks so much like Monroe that I almost have to do a double take. She wastes no time, walking right up to me and wrapping her arms around me in a tight hug. I have a moment of confusion, then I see Monroe's face smiling up at me with her hand on her heart, and I decide to hug her mom back. It's awkward at first as she rubs my back maternally with her hands before breaking away. She grabs my elbows, looking up at me.

"You are obviously Crew. I'm Monroe's mom, Demi."

"It's nice to meet you."

"I hope she warned you about our family, it's large, loud, and chaotic."

"She did, but I'm ready for it."

"Well, Monroe, make your rounds!"

Two boys yell at each other as they fight over a football, tackling each other into the ground as they tumble into the room.

"That's Miles and Wyatt, they're twins, and this is what they do all day long," Monroe says to me. "Hey, dingbats! Come say hey," she yells at her twin brothers. The boys pull themselves together, walking over to us. They have identical facial features, but completely different hairstyles, and the way they stand couldn't be more opposite.

"Hey. Are you the guy who rides his motorcycle around town?" one of them asks, I'm not sure which.

"Maybe. There's a bunch of us."

"Yeah, but you're the one who doesn't wear a shirt. I recognize your hair."

"Then yeah, that's me."

"Cool. I want to dye my hair, but my mom says not till I get my room clean, and I don't want to do that."

"At least she says you can, dummy. I want a motorcycle, and she said not till I'm eighteen," the other one says.

"Alright, let's move on, or we'll spend all day meeting people. Three down, a bazillion more to go." Monroe grabs my hand and leads me through her family home. It's cozy, with family photos hung on the walls, children's artwork, and family calendars. I've never been inside an actual home, and it's hard not to walk around slowly like I'm in a museum. This is all completely new to me.

We meet her sisters next—Aurora, Lucy, and Hazel—then her brother Atticus, who could barely be bothered to look up from his book. Fine by me, buddy.

Demi was right, their house is loud and chaotic, but so was mine, and this is not the same. This is full of love and laughter. This is what my childhood dream was when I'd get a break from the cage, when I'd sit by the window and watch the other kids outside throw balls around with their parents, when they'd ride their bikes and boards, when they'd get fresh air, and all I got was smoke, beer, and decay.

"Take a seat, I'll go grab us something to drink. You good?" Monroe says as she ushers me onto the couch.

"Yeah, I'm good." Monroe flits off just as another sibling runs into the room, launching himself onto the seat next to me. I can feel the burn of his stare on the side of my face as I sit there, unsure what the hell I'm supposed to do.

"Hi."

I look around side to side, wondering if this little child is talking to me. He's smaller than all the rest, so he must be the youngest.

"Hi?"

"Why do you have metal in your nose like a bull? Did you know bulls are actually colorblind? They can't see the colors red and green."

"I definitely didn't know that. But I'm okay with having matching metal like a bull. Bulls are strong and pretty cool. Did you know nose bleeds can also bleed out of your eyes?" His eyes squint at me like I've challenged him to a duel, and I look around the room briefly, wondering if I should be concerned.

"Did you know the Pirates of the Caribbean ride at Disney World used *real* skeletons?" What the hell is a Pirates of the Caribbean ride at Disney? Where the hell is Disney?

"Did you know you can pull a brain out through a nose?"

"Why would someone pull your brain out through your nose?"

I open my mouth to answer, but Monroe beats me to it, quickly speaking up as she sits down on the armrest next to me. My hand immediately seeks out her thigh, needing her touch.

"For research, and only after they've passed away." My head cocks to the side, her lie settling over me. Ahh. So, he probably shouldn't be told about torture methods. Makes sense. I smack my palm against my forehead. That would have been awkward.

Monroe's mom makes a huge feast of grilled burgers, hot dogs, and pasta salads. Everyone congregates outside on the side of their house, where a massive outdoor picnic table stretches damn near the entire length of it. You can't see Monroe's house from here. I'm glad that she has privacy and a little place on Earth that's just for her.

"So, Crew, tell us about yourself."

I should have prepared for this. *"Just be yourself."* Fuck why does this suck so bad? Monroe squeezes my hand, a reassuring touch that gives me the courage to talk to all these people who mean so much to her.

"Well, I was an orphan and homeless for a little while, but then I met someone who changed my life and gave me a second chance at living. I'm a mechanic, and I mostly work on rebuilds of motorcycles, and I love your daughter. More than anything in the world."

Everyone at the table stops their movements, including Monroe, who is beaming up at me like I'm the greatest thing in the entire world. I grip her thigh under the table, and her hand grabs the back of my neck, possessively, lovingly, her short nails gently scratching the short hair there. Then she leans in, dropping a small kiss to my cheek.

"Uhm, well, that's . . . great! We are so happy to welcome you to our home," her dad awkwardly says. I can't blame the guy; I didn't make it easy on anyone. But I'm here, and showing up is the hardest part. This is Monroe's family, and it's important I try to fit in with them.

"What's it like to be in a motorcycle club? Do you get to have a gun? Are you a bad guy or a good guy?" one of the twins rapid-fires.

"I guess it's just like this. We're a family. We eat meals together, and we take care of each other when bad stuff happens."

"That's cool. But what about the gun?" I laugh nervously, and luckily for me, Monroe speaks up.

"No talking about guns at the dinner table. Eat your food." Okay, bossy Monroe is hot as hell. I wonder if she'd be down to boss me around sometime.

"So you're all close then, Crew?" her mom asks.

"We're brothers. We may not share blood, but we're still a family. I'd do anything for any one of them or their wives."

"Well, we know all about that here. All our children were adopted except Monroe. Family is so much more than the blood that flows through your veins. It's who you choose, who steps up to take care of you when you need it. It's the people who accept you without question and love you through all the ups and downs that life brings."

"I'm not great with words, you said that much better than I could. But I agree."

"I heard you had never been bowling before; you made quite the impression on Grandma," her mom adds. I glance at Monroe's grandmother, who is laughing under her breath.

"You did well, we didn't take it easy on you!"

"No, no, you didn't. And I was terrible at bowling. My life has really been about survival, and there hasn't been much time for playing games like that. It was a good time. Might have to convince my club brothers to make our own league. We can call ourselves the Pinheads."

Monroe's siblings all laugh, and it makes me feel good.

"I think we need to change that," one of Monroe's twin brothers says. "Let's play a game. Everyone looks like they're done eating anyway."

"Shut up, idiot. You just want to flex and show Crew that you're the best at games and always win."

"Thanks for the compliment, I *am* the best at games and always win. Maybe you should try harder, and then you'd actually win something."

Monroe shoulder bumps me. "Ignore them. They've fought like this since day one. It's what they do. Competitive little buttheads. Are you up for a game? I'll warn you, everyone is pretty ruthless here."

"What kinda game are we talking? Like wrestling? Fighting?"

"No," she laughs. "Like capture the flag."

"What the hell is capture the flag?"

"Oh, baby. I hope you're ready. It's about to get real." Monroe turns to the rest of the table, announcing that we're playing the game, and everyone jumps up and heads to their massive backyard between the main house and Monroe's.

We split into two teams; Monroe and I were split up.

"Alright, our backyard capture the flag is simpler because it would be a madhouse if we did it the right way. So, each team's flag is staked behind them. The goal is to work with your team to cross into their side, steal their flag, and then run it back over to our side before they do the same to us. We need runners, blockers, and two guards to watch our flag. Does that make sense, Crew?" her mom explains.

Shit, does it? I guess I could guard the flag because that seems easiest, but it also feels like too much pressure. So I guess I'd be better at being a blocker? Seems easy enough.

"Yeah, I think I got it."

"Great. Let's get ready then."

We spend the next minute strategizing, and then we're turning to face the other team. Monroe, her dad, and some siblings line up in front of their flag, and Monroe looks so fucking cute in her little floral summer dress with bare feet on the grass.

"Did you know bees live everywhere in the whole world except Antarctica?" Monroe's little brother, Cooper, asks me. Is that true? I've never given thought to the whereabouts of bees.

"I didn't. Did you know that the human brain can't feel pain?"

"Whoa! How'd you know that?"

"I don't know, my man. I'll tell you when you're older."

Monroe's dad yells, breaking up our little chitchat. "Ready? Set. Go!"

Everyone breaks out, and I've got my eyes on Monroe; she's cheeky, smiling so big, I'm desperate to get my hands on her. While she holds me hostage, one of her little monster brothers makes a run for it, and at the same time, her sister from my team bolts. I dart forward, wanting to meet him in the middle, and easily tag him out. Her mom cheers from behind me as she guards our flag.

"Crew, get Monroe!" her mom screams, and then my eyes catch on my little pixie, running across the yard, dodging both her sisters and eating up the space between her and our flag.

"I got it! I got it! I got it!" her sister yells, and my eyes catch the bright orange flag she's clutching to her chest as she runs back toward our side. Monroe is able to capture the flag from her mom and starts running back. She's quick, but I'm quicker.

I race toward her, gaining on her rapidly, and wrapping my arms around her waist. She squeals loudly as I pick her up off the ground and flip her in the air into my arms. We fall to the ground just as my team starts cheering from behind me.

"We won, pixie girl. What's my prize?"

"Mmm. I'll give that to you later in private."

Monroe and I stand, brushing off the grass from our clothes as I high-five my team. Her mom pulls me into a huge hug that catches me off guard. I hug her back with one arm, my heart skipping a few beats in the process.

"You're good for my girl, Crew. She's good for you, too."

I've never needed validation, permission, or approval, but this makes me feel like maybe I really am doing something right.

CHAPTER THIRTY-ONE

MONROE

Crew and I leave my parents' house and walk over to his bike. We've been inseparable since the night he showed up at my house, but I don't know if he wants to go home alone.

Crew swings a leg over his bike, the pink and black chrome making me smile.

"Why pink?"

"I don't know." He shrugs. "I guess some part of me was hoping for something bright and good to come rescue me from the darkness." And just like that, I manage to fall even more in love with him. "Do you trust me, pixie?"

"I do," I answer without hesitation.

"Then get on, but you've gotta trust me."

Nerves flutter low in my stomach, but I get on the bike behind him anyway, scooting close and wrapping my arms around him under his T-shirt. I love his bare skin, and I want to feel it under mine now.

The bike rumbles under us as he slowly pulls out of my parents' driveway and takes the turn heading out of town. My heart drops. My breathing picks up. And I know exactly where he's going.

Lookout Lake.

I grip Crew tighter, resting my cheek against his back, letting the wind whip past us. We lean together up the winding roads, heading straight up on the familiar path that I haven't been up since the night we all lost our lives.

Breathing through the impending panic, I squeeze my eyes closed, trying with everything I have to not relive the moment the elk came into view, the squeal of Tyler's tires as we spun and flipped, the crunch of metal, the scent of burning rubber. But then I hear it, the worst part of all of it. It was Nora's screams, it was holding onto her hand with everything I had, and having it ripped from my grip anyway. Her screams that I hear now as Crew takes us up farther and farther to Lookout Lake.

When he makes it to the top, I feel like I can't breathe. Crew must feel my turmoil because he carefully pulls me into his lap, easily picking me up like I'm a doll, and it's no big deal. My legs wrap around him, like the first time he tried to take me up here, unknowing that it was the place of such trauma.

His hands cup my neck and jaw, dwarfing my face. "Breathe for me, pixie. You're safe. You're breathing. I've got you."

He drops his head to mine, our breath mingling. Then he

places his hand over my heart and puts mine over his. "Focus on the beat. Ba-dum, ba-dum, ba-dum."

I close my eyes and breathe in his fire and rain scent, feeling the beat of his heart under my palm. It's calming, steady, and the panic starts to ebb.

"You have no idea how grateful I am that your heart is beating, Monroe. It's the best sound I've heard in my life because it means you're here. You're living. We'll never be able to explain why some people get to live on while others leave, but we can't stay stagnant anymore."

"I know. I want to live, Crew. I want out of this rut."

"Then live. Look around with me, you can't feel guilty for surviving anymore, pretty girl. Release yourself from that. Forgive yourself for that."

Tears stream down my face, and Crew is right there, kissing every single one away.

Crew reluctantly drops me off at work at the mortuary the next day, but I know he's with me through whatever means he's been watching me. When I walk into the preparation room, that familiar caress slides over my body like an old friend. Knowing that it's Crew behind that feeling makes it all that much more heightened.

After George has left for the day, I stay late, deciding that I want to test the waters a bit. The idea came to me before lunch while I was working in here and has made me deliciously giddy all day.

I'm not sure where the cameras are in the preparation room, but I know they're here. I feel them the most when I'm standing at the table, so that's what I go off of and hope for the best. I know I'm playing with fire by tempting the devil, but it's too alluring not to.

I slowly run my fingertips up my arms, pulling my bottom lip between my teeth, as I gently push the thin strap of my dress off my shoulder. Then the other side. With a little help, the dress cascades down my body, falling in a heap at my feet.

I step out of the material, climbing onto the preparation table and lying down on my back. The stainless steel is freezing on my bare skin, and I instantly shiver, breaking out in goosebumps. I can't believe I'm actually doing this: lying on the table where I prep dead bodies every day. My eyes flick to the coolers, and I know four of them are occupied.

All of this should bother me. I'm smart enough to know these things should be alarming. But they aren't. It's the opposite. I feel like Eve in the Garden of Eden, being tempted by the serpent with forbidden fruit. And I greedily accept it, consequences be damned.

I tease myself, running my fingers over my stomach lightly, letting my mind slip into the place where it's Crew's hands instead. I move up to my breasts, grasping both and squeezing, letting my lower back arch slightly as I pull the cups down and twist my nipples.

I can feel the wetness pooling from the heat at my center, my breathing coming faster as I work myself up. Slowly, I slide one hand down my body, slipping it into the tiny lace panties I'm wearing, until I sink between my lips.

I hope he's watching from wherever he is. I hope he's so turned on that he can't think straight. It feels powerful, it feels wrong, but so right at the same time.

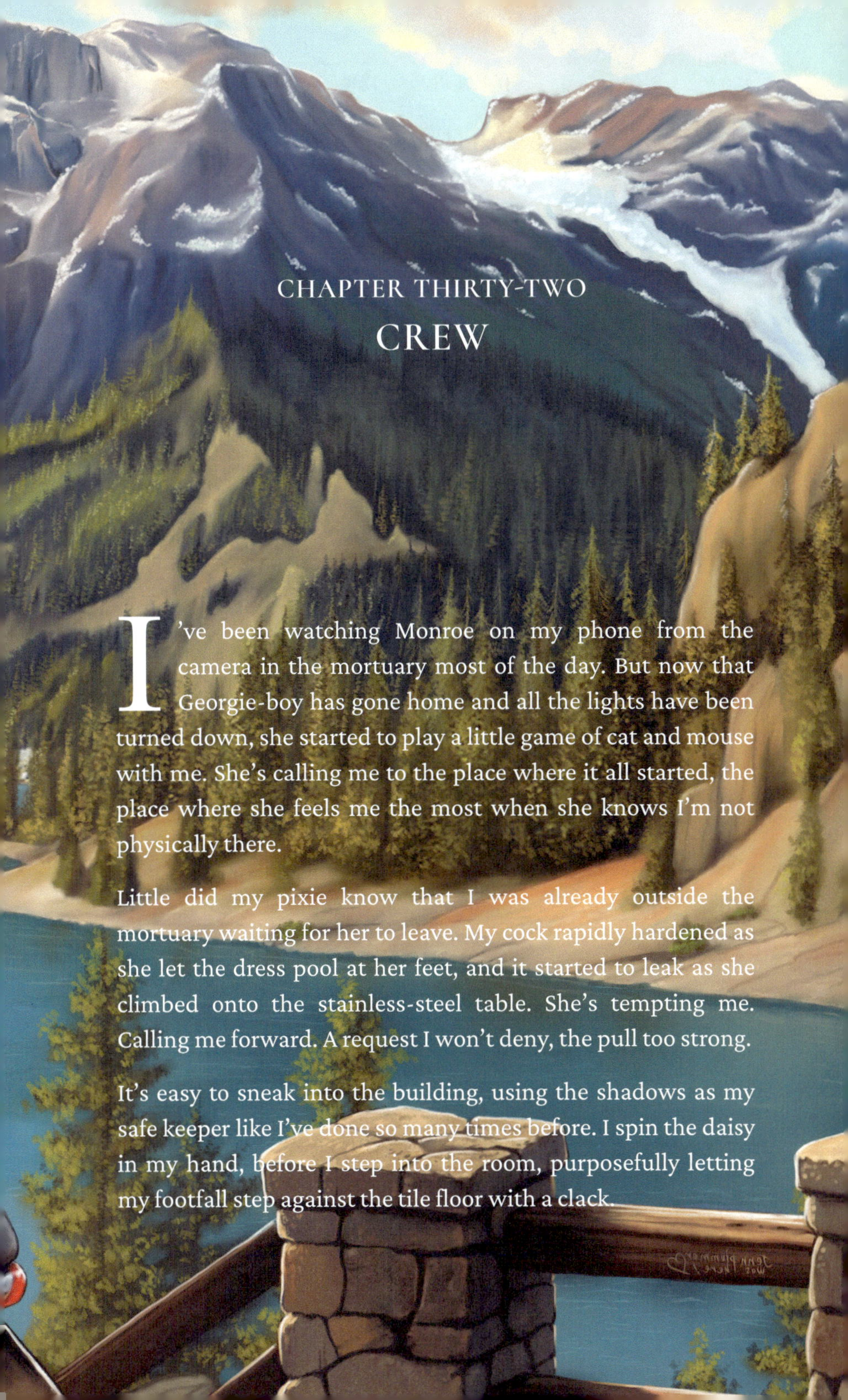

CHAPTER THIRTY-TWO

CREW

I've been watching Monroe on my phone from the camera in the mortuary most of the day. But now that Georgie-boy has gone home and all the lights have been turned down, she started to play a little game of cat and mouse with me. She's calling me to the place where it all started, the place where she feels me the most when she knows I'm not physically there.

Little did my pixie know that I was already outside the mortuary waiting for her to leave. My cock rapidly hardened as she let the dress pool at her feet, and it started to leak as she climbed onto the stainless-steel table. She's tempting me. Calling me forward. A request I won't deny, the pull too strong.

It's easy to sneak into the building, using the shadows as my safe keeper like I've done so many times before. I spin the daisy in my hand, before I step into the room, purposefully letting my footfall step against the tile floor with a clack.

"Crew!" she gasps, her hands flying to her chest, her head turning to face the door.

"My curious little pixie. Did you think it was a good idea to tempt me?"

"You're here, aren't you? Exactly where I wanted you."

"Are you scared?"

"Never of you."

I tsk, shaking my head. I take a step in her direction, her lower lip trapped between her perfect teeth. Monroe grips the edges of the table like she's bracing herself. Her chest rises and falls harder every moment that passes.

I can't take any more space between us.

My hand slowly slides up her bare thigh, as her breathing hitches. I run over her silky-smooth skin until I reach the apex between her legs.

"Scared yet?"

She shakes her head, that damn sexy lip still held hostage between her teeth.

"Words, pixie."

"I'm not scared of you, Crew." Monroe spreads her legs, and I step between them, my hand wrapping around her throat just ever so slightly, the other stroking her velvet-soft thigh.

I look down at her, icy blue eyes blinking up at me with so much lust and desire behind them. I want to give this girl everything and more. All of it. My hand glides up her throat, gripping her jaw with just enough force to get her to open her mouth. My thumb slides right in, her lips closing around it. I groan as her tongue curls around my finger and she sucks, pulling long and hard before releasing and swirling her tongue around it. Her eyes never leave mine, like she knows exactly what she's doing to me.

"Still not scared?" She shakes her head, and this time I don't make her say it. "Fuck, Monroe, you're so fucking sexy."

I pop my thumb from her mouth and replace it with my tongue. Her mouth meets mine like she's just as eager, just as desperate. I suck her tongue into my mouth, and she moans, fingernails digging into my shoulder and the back of my neck as she pulls me closer to her. Fuck, I love her like this. Wanton. Needy. Losing control.

There's something so disturbingly hot about taking her right here. In the room where I first met her, in the room I've watched her take care of countless dead bodies. We're surrounded by death, and a Hell's Heathen is defiling an actual living angel in the center of it all.

She's a fucking queen embracing all of it. She controls the darkness, controls me.

My eyes don't leave hers as I sink to my knees, my thumbs spreading open her lips, giving me a beautiful view of her dripping pussy. Her center is so pink and wet, so fucking inviting.

I eat her pussy until my face is covered with her arousal, until she's a shaking, panting mess, and when I suck her clit into my mouth, I press my finger in deep, curving upward to her stomach. It only takes a moment before she's coming, and it's so fucking pretty when she does.

Monroe shakes and writhes under me, moaning out my name as wave after wave crashes into her. I stand up as she starts to come down, pulling my finger free and dragging her cum across her lips.

"Open."

She sucks my finger into her mouth as my free hand works to unbutton my jeans, pushing them down my legs.

"You taste how good you come for me?" Her pretty, freckled cheeks are flushed, and I love the little gasp as I rub the pierced head of my cock through her folds.

I grip her hips, dragging her to the edge of the table. Monroe always looks beautiful, but like this, laid out in front of me like an offering, I can barely hold myself upright. She deserves to have me at her feet, worshiping her.

I line up my cock with her entrance and push in deep with one hard thrust. Monroe throws her head back and screams out my name in a long moan that has my cock hardening more. Her pussy walls contract around me, sucking me in deeper, holding me there.

I stay deep, giving her a moment to adjust. Even though she hasn't felt any more pain, I know it's still tender. She continues to pulse around me, and I swear to the devil himself, I could come just from that.

I grip her chin with two of my fingers as she pants, guiding her to meet my eyes. "Fuck, you're a tight little thing, aren't you?" I look down as I drag out of her, watching my cock covered in her cum.

"You belong to me and only me, Monroe. I can't let you go, I hope you know that. I love you too fucking much." I thrust back into her wet heat, making her scream again. She sits up, arms wrapping around my neck as she pulls me into a wet, hungry kiss.

"I love you, too. God, I love you, Crew."

Her legs wrap around my waist, and I lift her up, fucking her deep. I'm so lost, so gone for her. She could have chosen anyone, and her life could have been beautiful—soft and sweet, pure and good—like she is. But she chose me. *Me.* I can't guarantee it'll always be easy, but I'm determined to give her the life she deserves.

Monroe takes everything I have and more, giving it right back to me. Her pussy swallows me down, and I'm so greedy for it.

"Crew, don't stop."

"Never, pixie."

Monroe finds my mouth again, kissing me like she's looking for something to hold on to, to ground her. My hands reach beneath us, holding her by her ass as I fuck her, bouncing her up and down on my hard cock. Arousal drips down my length, coating my balls as her velvet walls tighten their grip around me. Her fingernails scratch into my back, my shoulders, my neck; she's just as desperate and wanton as I am.

Her moans fuel me, and when she bites my lip hard enough to break the skin, she backs away, looking at me like she surprised even herself. I stare at the crimson staining her lips, smiling down at the expression on her face.

My curious little pixie. She looks breathtaking, so beautiful and ethereal. I can't look away from her. My goddess of light, embracing her Heathen in the dark, leading my way out.

"Come with me, baby. I need you to come with me, Crew."

For fuck's sake, that'll do it. I come instantly. Pulling her down to take my full length while my cock thickens and jerks, unloading inside her, just as she presses her face into my neck, screaming out her orgasm. We come together, shaking and vibrating with the force of it.

"I love you."

"You'll never know what hearing those words does to me."

My sweet, angelic pixie is healing me.

CHAPTER THIRTY-THREE

CREW

Days pass in a blur of watching Monroe while she's at work and spending every free moment with her. The clubhouse has been in a state of unrest since we tortured and killed Garrett, but we've yet to make a decision on whether or not we're going after the Kingsnakes.

I've been avoiding seeing Morgan, unable to look her in the face with the amount of guilt and loss I feel. The rest of the clubhouse has stepped up to take care of her, Bristol, Kinsey, and the patch bunnies doing most of the work.

I don't know what's different about today, but I feel ready to see her, to talk to her privately. After I drop Monroe off at work, I make a Daily Rise run, picking up my typical weekly order of whatever Mrs. Odette has for me, plus some of the blueberry scones I've seen Morgan eat a handful of times.

"I've got food!" I yell as I enter the clubhouse and drop two large pastry boxes on the bar. I grab the small bag for Morgan before anyone can dig into it and snag a chocolate muffin for myself.

“How are things going with your woman?” Sin asks as he reaches into one of the boxes and pulls out a glazed sunrise brioche.

“Incredible. I don’t deserve her, but I’m keeping her.”

“Story of our lives. They’re way too good for us, but they love us anyway.”

“That’s what makes them queens.”

“You seem different lately,” Sin says, looking at me and running his hand over his jaw. “Softer.”

I flick my knife out quickly and press the pointy end to his throat. “What was that?”

“She made you soft, Mal. Just like you said Bristol and Mr. Bun-Buns did to me. Welcome to the club, brother.”

I press the knife in just enough to nick him, a single bead of blood pooling around the silver, before jerking it away and closing it. “Mhm.”

“You won’t admit it, will ya, buddy?”

“Fuck off, Sin, leave him alone,” Wrath says as he takes a seat on one of the barstools, pulling out the burner phone.

“He doesn’t need to admit it for it to be true.”

“Do you have a death wish? Why push him?”

“Uhm, I’m right fucking here,” I say. “Talk about me when I leave the room.”

"Because our resident unhinged biker has now got a soft side. Same with me, Chaos, and Rogue. Looks like that leaves you, Wrath. No queen for you. Stay focused."

"Oh, fuck off, Sin."

"Aint no way in hell he settles down. His dick likes pussy and ass too much, and he likes the variety," I add, giving him some shit.

Instead of pushing back like he typically would, Wrath stands quickly from his seat and heads out of the room. I roll my eyes dramatically at Sin.

"We'll deal with whatever that was later, I've got someone to go apologize to."

"Whoa! Apologize? Blink twice if Malice is still in there."

I walk away from Sin at the bar, flipping him off and yelling as I go. "She made me soft, remember?"

I take the short walk over to Jesse and Morgan's room on the second floor. Which I guess is just Morgan's room now that Jesse is gone. I knock twice with the back of my knuckles, waiting for her to answer.

The door opens, and Morgan appears, wearing one of Jesse's T-shirts and a pair of sweats. Her hair is pulled up in a messy nest on top of her head, her eyes red-rimmed and heavy.

"Can we talk?" I ask, tapping my middle finger against my thigh.

"Yeah, yeah, come in."

I step into their room, and Morgan follows me, leaving the

door open out of respect for both of us. I hand her the pastry bag with the scones and then run my hand through my hair.

“I’ve been a selfish dick. Emotion is hard for me, but that’s no excuse. I’m sorry I haven’t been around. I’ve been preoccupied, and truthfully, I couldn’t face you. It was too hard.”

“You don’t need to apologize, Crew. Everyone deals with grief in their own way.”

“No, but when a woman becomes an old lady, the club makes a promise to the member to take care of her long after he’s gone, and I failed to do that. I’m sorry. You deserved better from me, and so did Jesse.”

“Well, I appreciate your apology. Never thought I’d see the day Malice apologized or put his heart out there.”

“I’ve recently learned that I have a heart to begin with, so things are changing for me. How are you handling it all?”

Morgan pulls out the pastry and breaks off a piece of her scone, playing with it until it crumbles. “I’m breathing.” She shrugs. “When you fall in love with a biker, you have to accept that there’s this chance, you know? But you never think it’ll be you. Living without him is a pain I can’t describe. It’s emptiness. I keep waiting for him to come home.”

My heart breaks further, this chasm that aches. I want to run from it, but I push it down, cracking my neck from side to side. “He loved you more than life itself, Morgan. He needs you to keep living, and he needs you to eventually thrive.”

“He needs you to do the same. That man loved you so much. You’re all brothers here, but you were special to him. When he got out of jail, and we were reunited, he told me about this punk-ass kid he met in there and couldn’t wait to bring you back to the clubhouse. He saw something in you that you didn't see in yourself. He believed in you. It seems you're finally starting to come around to seeing it, too. He'd be proud of you."

I have to swallow down a hard, painful knot that's formed in my throat before I can speak. "I'm convinced he brought her to me. That he knew she was exactly what I needed."

"I wouldn't put it past him. If his death brought something good out of all of this, then that's something I'll hang onto."

"We'll get through this together."

"That's what families do."

I leave Morgan's room a few minutes later, pulling out my phone to check on Monroe. The itch to go to her is strong, but I push it down, needing to check on a few club tasks before I head downtown to take her to lunch.

The clubhouse is a dead zone right now, everyone working and getting their shit done. I check in with Noose and some other club members on the current prospects and if any have left since we shaved all their heads and threatened to cut out their tongues. The next three hours go by in a blur, and I'm grateful for it. All I want to do is hug my girl.

I park my bike in front of Maggie's since Monroe will want to walk down here for lunch anyway. I wait for her outside the mortuary, watching her on my camera as she cleans up her space and removes the paper gown thing she wears. Then she disappears, and my heart rate ratchets up with anticipation.

The doors open to the mortuary, and then there she is, a smile filling her face, her rose gold hair bouncing with each step she takes. When she gets halfway to the bottom step, she launches herself at me. I don't expect it, but I'm ready anyway, catching her midair and swinging her around.

Monroe's arms wrap around my neck as she kisses me. When Chaos and Sin found their old ladies, I let myself imagine what it would feel like to have someone's face light up when they saw me. I never thought it would happen. Especially not from someone as pure as Monroe.

"I missed you," she whispers against my lips. "It's unfair you get to watch me all day, and I don't get to watch you." My eyebrows arch at her as I set her back down on her feet.

"That can be fixed, pixie girl. Are you good with Maggie's today?"

"Yes! I am craving a BLT like you wouldn't even believe," she groans, and it's so fucking cute. Monroe laces our fingers together as we head down the cobblestone street toward Maggie's.

We don't make it far before a voice snaps from behind us, demanding our attention.

"Hey!" I stop in my tracks, slowly turning to face the fucknuts who won't leave Monroe alone. I crack my neck from side to side as annoyance rears its ugly head inside me. Monroe grips my hand tighter, her thumb swiping back and forth to calm me.

"Yeah?" I say.

"You need to leave Monroe alone. She's not some victim you can just pluck from her life and steal away. You're going to ruin her."

I go to open my mouth to speak, to put him in his place, but Monroe takes a step forward, beating me to it.

"Don't talk about me like I'm not standing right here, Zach!"

"Maybe if you had a fucking backbone, Roe, I wouldn't have to. You're gonna fuck up the life you get to live if you don't walk away from this nutjob."

"Newsflash, Zach, it's my life! I get to choose how I spend it, and I am done living in the shadow of Tyler, Nora, and Javier! I don't owe you or anyone anything just because I survived. I love him, and he is far better a man than you'll ever be. So judge me all you want, but stay the hell away from us!"

Zach opens his mouth, but I step forward, draping my arm protectively over Monroe's shoulder and shaking my head. "No, no. The time for talking is over now, buddy. You can move along. A piece of advice, though, she has made it clear she wants you to stay away from her. Next time you violate that, you'll have to deal with me and my brothers, and I promise we won't be so nice."

Zach stares at Monroe with venom that has my blood boiling, but Monroe nudges me forward, clasping my hand and pulling me up the street.

"He's such a dick, I'm so over him."

"I'm proud of you for standing up to him. It's not easy to do after what you've both been through."

"It was long overdue. I'm ready to live, Crew, and I can't do that with him constantly reminding me that it should have been his brother who lived instead of me."

I stop in the middle of the sidewalk, my hands threading through her short pink hair and angling her face upward to look at me. "I've walked my entire existence in the dark. I convinced myself there was no good inside me, but you showed me how wrong I was. They brought you back to life, and in turn, you did the same to me."

"Church!" Chaos yells the word through the clubhouse, and I have a moment where I want to dig my heels into the ground and refuse to go. I don't want to leave Monroe alone out here in the clubhouse hangout room. She's acclimating as best she can, but she still feels out of place and clings to me like a baby sloth. Not that I'm complaining.

Bristol must read my turmoil because she and Kinsey move closer, taking a seat on either side of her as I stand up.

"I'll be back in a bit. You okay?" I ask her. She nods, and I tsk, leaning down to tuck her hair behind an ear.

"Words, pixie."

"I promise, I'm good. Go!"

The girls laugh as I walk away, and my chest loosens some. I head into church, taking my seat next to Chaos, across from Sin. My eyes automatically drift to Rolo's empty chair, and the loss hits all over again. Rogue pats me on the back, pulling my attention to him.

He and his old lady, Kinsey, got in this morning from Aspen Ridge, and it's always nice to have them here. The club feels like the divorced parent who has to split their time with the kid, but it works better this way. For Rogue at least.

"Happy you found your queen, brother," he tells me.

"Fuck knows why she decided to be with me, but she did."

"Aw, don't talk like that, buddy, you're a catch," Sin adds.

"Fuck off with that shit. Why are we here?"

Chaos speaks up from the head of the table. "Wrath and Otto pulled info on Rolo's blood brother. Cain, whose legal name is Joshua Davis, just got out of the slammer after doing time for grand theft, rape, assault with a deadly weapon, and a slew of other shit last year. Seems he really hit the ground running when he got out, didn't take him long to take over a club."

"It's not sitting right with me that this club was respected, that they were like us, keeping the peace, living their lives, and then this piece of shit comes along and takes it, destroys it. Garrett may have pulled that trigger, but Cain is the one who sent the order. I want him," I demand.

Wrath nods his head, and I know he's got my back on this. He's not one to sit back and let shit go, just like me.

"I've been in touch with Saint. He's got bad news and asked for a favor," Wrath shares. All eyes are on him.

"Another one? He's already asked us to get his club back for him."

"According to Saint, Cain has eyes on his sister, Sienna, and will stop at nothing until she's in his bed. Saint has been moving her from place to place the last two weeks, trying to keep her hidden, and Cain is burning shit to the ground to find her."

"So what's the fucking favor?"

"He wants us to take Sienna in under our protection. I already said yes."

Chaos slams his fists down on the table, hard. "For fuck's sake, Wrath! Another one? We can't take in another fucking woman here!"

"We don't turn them away, either! I'm meeting him tonight to pick her up."

"And where the fuck is Cain?"

"Saint doesn't know right now. Looking for Sienna."

"Bring Malice and Rogue with you. Don't get yourself fucking killed in the goddamn process."

Well, this shit just got more complex. I don't want to leave my little pixie, but I'm not about to let Wrath head into unknown territory without me.

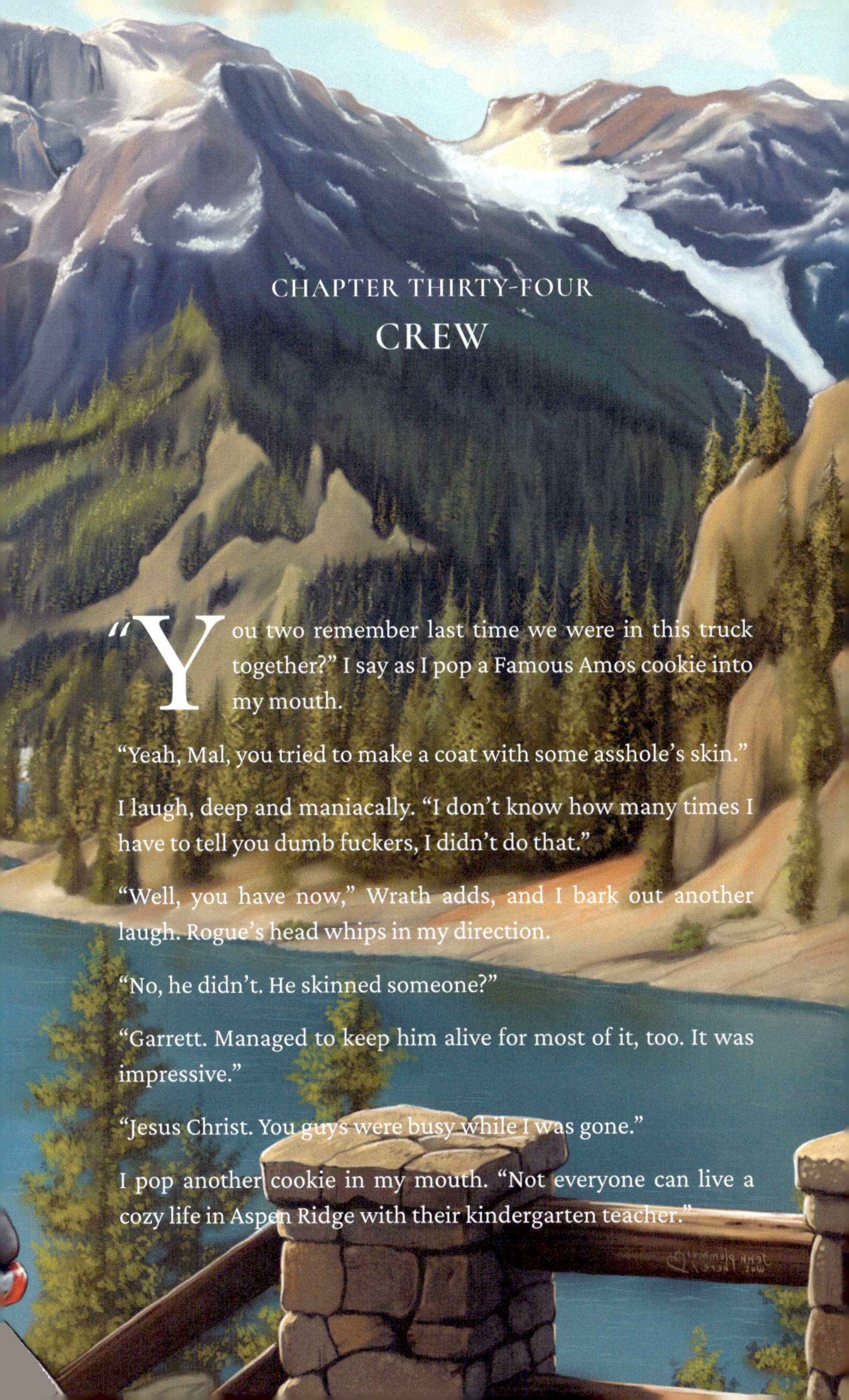

CHAPTER THIRTY-FOUR

CREW

"You two remember last time we were in this truck together?" I say as I pop a Famous Amos cookie into my mouth.

"Yeah, Mal, you tried to make a coat with some asshole's skin."

I laugh, deep and maniacally. "I don't know how many times I have to tell you dumb fuckers, I didn't do that."

"Well, you have now," Wrath adds, and I bark out another laugh. Rogue's head whips in my direction.

"No, he didn't. He skinned someone?"

"Garrett. Managed to keep him alive for most of it, too. It was impressive."

"Jesus Christ. You guys were busy while I was gone."

I pop another cookie in my mouth. "Not everyone can live a cozy life in Aspen Ridge with their kindergarten teacher."

"Shut the fuck up, Mal. She's more than a teacher. She's fucking everything."

"Oh, we know, maybe we all wish you came around more often."

"I see you two weekends a month! Not to mention any of the in-between you all need. Don't give me that shit. And when did you become so in touch with your feelings?" he snaps, making me laugh. I love pushing their buttons.

"He got soft when he found Monroe, in a fucking mortuary of all places."

"Jesus Christ. Well, that tracks. Is she as morbid as you are?"

"No, surprisingly. Just been through some shit and loves all my broken pieces." I crumble up my trash and put it back in the grocery bag.

"How are things going with Kinsey, anyway?"

"Incredible. We've been babysitting our goddaughters a lot. Her brother, Sawyer's, you remember him?"

"Uh, yeah. Chaos hates him," Wrath adds.

"Yeah, 'cause he's jealous because he thinks he's your best friend and not him," I say. Rogue just rolls his eyes.

"There's no fucking competition. Jesus Christ. Anyway, he's got a fucking breeding kink or some shit, and he won't stop knocking up his wife, Ivy. Which is fine, 'cause Kinsey and I are getting a lot of practice with babies by having them all around the family. Hoping for a baby of our own."

"No shit, you want to be a dad?" I ask.

"Yeah, Kinsey wants a few, and I want to build a family with her. Plus, the baby-making process isn't a hardship."

"Fucking is never a hardship. Where is this fucker, Wrath?" I say, just as a set of headlights pulls up in front of us on the side of the road. The three of us nod at each other, checking our guns, and then climbing out.

Saint steps out of the driver's seat, with two other men getting out of the SUV as well. I don't see the woman yet, but that doesn't mean she's not in there. But that doesn't mean she is, either.

Wrath feels more confident than I do because he marches forward, meeting them in the middle.

"Saint," Wrath greets.

"Wrath, Malice. This is Deacon and Creed."

We give them a head nod. "This is our road sergeant, Rogue."

I watch the three of them closely, and I know Rogue is doing the same. The two men flank Saint, and there seems to be something deeper there than club brotherhood. They're just as on guard as we are, but they don't seem like a threat.

"Your president agreed to take her under your protection?"

"We wouldn't be here if he hadn't. She'll be safe with us. Both Rogue and Malice's women live at the clubhouse, as well as two others. Patch bunnies are all there of their own free will and all under our protection. No harm will come to your sister while she's with us. You have my word." *My* word. My eyes flick to Wrath for a brief moment. He should be speaking for the club, not just himself.

"This isn't an easy fuckin' choice, but I'm out of options. I'll owe you. Whatever you need, when the time comes, it's yours." Saint nods at either Deacon or Creed, and they walk back to the car, opening up the back door. A woman steps out of it, her white-blond hair striking compared to Saint's now that they're next to each other. Huh.

I take a duffel bag from one of them and nod. She looks fucking frightened, and I don't blame her. But I also see a strength simmering just under the surface, like she's pissed about the situation. Us, too, sister.

"Hey, Sienna, you ready?" Wrath says, his voice dropping slightly.

"As ready as I'll ever be." She turns to face Saint, who wraps her up in a huge hug and kisses the top of her head.

"Remember, zero contact. No phones, don't try to reach me. I'll reach out to their burner when I can. Stay put and be safe, you understand?"

"Yeah, I know the drill. I love you." He cups the back of her head and pulls her in for one more hug, and I feel uncomfortable watching. I can't imagine what it would be like to have to send someone away that I love just to keep them safe.

She hugs Deacon and Creed, and I don't know why that surprises me. The three men really do give off something deeper than brotherhood, but I can't put my finger on it. It's not sexual, it's just a connection that seems deeper.

I'm annoyed that we don't have Cain, but I know someday, he'll get what's coming for him. At least we gave Garrett what he deserved.

The four of us walk back to the van and climb in, Rogue taking the wheel this time, and me in the passenger like usual. Wrath gets into the back with her, and Rogue pulls onto the road, taking a sharp U-turn back toward Amberwood.

"Put your goddamn seatbelts on," I snap when I realize none of them have theirs on.

"When did you become the seatbelt police?" Rogue asks.

"When someone close to me taught me how important they are. So fucking wear them, or you'll get my fucking knife next time."

"You're fucking insane, Mal. But, okay."

When we arrive back at the clubhouse, I've got a one-track mind and head right into my dungeon, stripping myself of my clothes as I go. It's late, and I'm sure Monroe has been sleeping for hours by now.

I creep easily into our room, hiding in the shadows, finding my sleeping woman in our bed . . . naked. Just as she should be. She left the bathroom light on for me, the door cracked just enough to illuminate her like a beacon.

The sheet is draped over her body, but one of her bare tits peeks out. My mouth waters at the sight of the perky, pink bud. I slowly pull the sheet back, exposing her naked body to me. She's so fucking sexy. I've watched this woman at work, at home, while she sleeps. I've seen her play with herself multiple times, but I've never snuck in and played with her while she sleeps.

The thought alone stirs something deep in my stomach, my cock rising to attention and throbbing like a desperate asshole. My eyes roam over her body, all sharp lines and delicate features. She's a work of art.

Monroe shifts slightly, her leg spreading as she lifts her knee outward. I delicately comb the tuft of hair at her pussy, as I drop to my knees next to the bed. My mouth finds her nipple, lapping ever so gently until it's a stiff peak. When she doesn't wake up, I take my chances, leaning forward and dragging my tongue through her slit. I'm licking her sideways, and this angle gives me a new way to explore her.

Monroe stirs slightly, her hips moving ever so slightly as I gently tease her clit, slowly working her up. It's so fucking hot, her body responding to me, even when she's dead asleep. I swipe across her slit, lapping at her lower lips, giving her just a bit more pressure.

Her pussy starts to weep, and too tempted not to lick it up, I dip my head lower, stuffing my tongue into her hole, fucking her with it. Monroe starts to wake, her legs shaking, little mewls escaping her lips.

"Crew," she moans, her hands scratching down my back. "Let me taste you." Fucking hell, woman. I quickly shuffle us, pushing her further into the bed as I flip her on her side. I lay next to her, upside down, and get us positioned as easily as possible.

I grip her smooth thighs with both hands, stuffing my face into her pussy, as she feeds my cock into her warm mouth. She sucks me down her throat like she's done it a million times, even though she's only done it once before. It feels so fucking good, her sweet tongue flicking at my piercings, rubbing the underside of my head.

I lick down her slit, all the way to her ass, rimming the puckered hole with the tip of my tongue. Her arousal continues to leak from her pussy, and I lap it up like I'm starved for it. Her moans flow freely against my length, the vibrations shooting up my cock and into my balls. Her perfect little mouth feels so good wrapped around me like this, especially when I'm suffocating between her luscious legs.

I move back up to her clit, taking two of my fingers and sliding them inside her, curving up toward her belly button. Her hips buck and her legs shake around me. Goddamn, I'll never get enough of her taste, her scent, the feel of her in all ways. I never knew sex could be so much more than a physical release, but this? Every single thing Monroe and I do is a connection; it's so much deeper than a meaningless fuck.

I lick her pussy, rubbing my fingers against that sweet spot inside her that has her toes curling and legs shaking. I feel the moment she starts to come, her velvety walls tightening around my fingers, fluttering and spasming as her clit swells against my tongue.

I'm right behind her, my balls drawing up, a tingling sensation working its way through me as my cock hardens further. Then I'm spilling inside her mouth, my eyes closing as she wraps her lips around the head and sucks, her hand jerking up my length in tight strokes.

Monroe takes me to the fucking stars with her.

When we've both come down, I move back up to face her, gripping her face in my hands and capturing her lips. I kiss her sweetly, the taste of our cum mingling between us. It's perfect.

"I love you, Monroe. You've given me so much more than I could ever ask for. Thank you for loving me."

"You never have to thank me for loving you, baby. You're my person. You've given me just as much. We may look like opposites, but we were both walking through life the same. We were made for each other."

"I'm glad you think so, pixie, because I'm never letting you go now that I've found you."

I drop a kiss to her forehead and pull her into my chest to sleep. Then I look up at the sky and send Rolo my thanks for one last gift.

EPILOGUE

MONROE

SIX MONTHS LATER

Dear Diary,

I want to marry him. I know we haven't been together long, but I don't want to wait. I want to live. Finally. I've always wanted something special, like what my parents and my grandparents have, and now that I've found it, I want to celebrate it. How lame would it be if I proposed? Would he hate that? Why is being a woman so hard? Why does society say that we have to wait for the man to decide when we can be engaged or when we can get married? Isn't that outdated? Damnit, I want to ask this man to marry me, so I'm going to do it. Enough waiting.

Time to live, right?

EPILOGUE

CREW

I pick up Monroe from work like I do every day, waiting in my truck now that it's the dead of winter and there's snow and ice on the ground. I miss the days of riding with her, and I'm ready for spring to thaw out this bullshit that's surrounding us this year.

I pull out my phone when I realize she's ten minutes late, just as a text comes through.

Pixie: Come inside

Curious, I hop out of the truck, my boots crunching over the bullshit snow, and make my way to the door. I hate coming in through the front door and regret it the moment I start sneezing through the lupines and other shit George has littering the place in wreaths and vases.

I slow my steps, easing my footfalls so that I'm silent as I get closer to the preparation room, wanting to get a glimpse of my girl before she sees me. To my surprise, she's changed out of her winter work clothes and is wearing the dark green dress I first met her in, the fabric covered in white daisies. Her dusty pink hair frames her face, her fresh cut keeping it right under her chin. She's so beautiful. She paces back and forth with her back to me, muttering something under her breath. She seems nervous, and I don't like that at all. My heart rate picks up as I step into the room, needing to know what's wrong.

"Crew," she gasps, as if she were well and truly lost in her own head. "Hi."

"Hi, pixie. Are you okay?"

"I'm better than okay." She shakes her hands to the sides and smiles up at me. "I know this is unconventional, but nothing about us is normal or conventional. We work, we make each other whole. This is me, choosing to live. I wish I had the words to express how much I love you. Of the healing you've brought me since the very first moment you walked into my life. You have brought me so much good and love that I never thought it would be possible. You are brave, and resilient, smart, and witty, and so funny. You're kind and gentle, and there hasn't been a single day since you walked into this room that I didn't feel how you felt about me. I love you. I love you. I love you. And I want to spend the rest of my life with you. So, Crew, will you please marry me?"

I stand there momentarily stunned, my gorgeous girl holding out a single daisy to me, asking me to marry her. Me. The human who was born and then discarded, who's always felt unlovable. This magnificent creature wants to spend the rest of her life with me. My face is damp, and I don't register that it's the tears that are streaming down my cheeks.

She stands there so hopeful, so in love, and then I'm moving to her, wrapping my arms around her waist and picking her up. I bury my face in her neck and breathe in her sweet sunshine, and I know I'm home.

"I'll marry you. I'll marry you in every lifetime. You saved me. I love you, Monroe, more than anything."

SNEAK PEAK OF COMPLETE ME

"Take me with you! Please! You can't leave me to Mom and Dad's snoozefest tonight!" my sister begs as she grips my bicep with both hands, pulling me to a stop. She's two years younger than me, and we've been attached at the hip since she was born. She also hates being told no and being left behind when she'd rather go out and have fun with me.

"Hell no, Lena. This is no place for you, and you know it. I mean it, stay home."

"What? Why? I've been to the clubhouse plenty of times before! They like me!"

"That's because you followed me, brat. What was I supposed to do? Leave you outside the gate? You're too curious for your own good and you know it." Lena is notorious for sneaking out and finding trouble, and it's been my job for as long as I can remember to keep her out of it.

When I went in for my first tattoo appointment four years ago and met Ink, the owner of the shop, who's also a member of a motorcycle club, an entirely new world opened up for me. One with open roads, family, and freedom. The only expectation is that your loyalty is given freely to the club, which I happen to have in spades when something is worth it. I skipped college and started my tattoo apprenticeship with him not long after, much to my father's dismay.

A few motorcycle clubs call Washington State home, but I had never been intrigued until I was spending all my time with Ink at Heathen Tattoo.

"I wouldn't have to follow you if you just took me with you. Reeeeeeid, c'mon!" she begs, her hands clasped in front of her, bottom lip pushed out in a pout. For a moment, I don't see my twenty-year-old sister; I see the little girl she used to be. Her brown hair falls around her face in large, beachy waves, and green eyes that are identical to my own stare back at me, bright and pleading, and I almost give in. *Almost.*

But I know tonight I've got club business, and I'm finishing some tattoo work on a member's sleeve. I can't bring my sister along for that because I wouldn't be able to watch her like the personal bodyguard she needs when she's there. As much as it pains me to leave her behind, I've got to think about myself from time to time.

"Sorry, brat, not tonight."

"Ugh. Fine. Whatever. I'll just have to find something to do to occupy myself," she says in a tone that is more of a threat than a statement. I roll my neck, trying to ease some of the tension she's putting there.

"Stay out of trouble, k? Tomorrow we can do whatever you want," I try as a way of a bribe, hoping like hell it's enough to keep her from doing anything other than staying put tonight.

"Wait, you mean it? I can plan the entire day?" she squeals in excitement, and I can't help but laugh at her. When Lena smiles, it fills her entire face, her eyes crinkling, lips tugging upward, all toothy and genuine. It's the same smile that gets her in and out of trouble. She didn't get her nickname without a reason.

"I'm good with that. We can even go to the coast if you want to." The first thing Lena and I did when I got my license at sixteen was take the top off my old, rusted-up jeep and drive to the coast. I spent a few years before she could drive toting her and her friends around, but I didn't mind. Anything to make her happy. I know how lucky we are to be best friends on top of siblings, and I want to always keep it that way.

"Yes! Okay, okay. I'm excited to have you all to myself! No club business?"

"No club business," I promise.

My sister's arms bound around my waist in a huge hug, her head resting against my chest. I wrap my arms around her in return, dropping my cheek to the top of her head.

"Be good, brat. I'll see you tomorrow."

"K. You be safe!"

"Always."

I slide my arms into my cut at the front door, *Hell's Heathens* stitched on the back, before walking out of my parents' house and heading to my bike. It's nothing fancy, but it's mine and I love it. I throw my leg over my motorcycle, settling into the leather seat, my fingers flexing over the grip of the handlebars. The engine purrs to life under me as I start it up, loving the vibrations and the weight of it in my hands. The first time I was on a bike, it became part of me, gave me a freedom I hadn't yet learned existed at eighteen. Now, I can't imagine my life without it. It's therapeutic on my bad days, energizing on my good, and all I need in life can be found on the back of it.

Before heading out, I take one last glance up at my spitfire sister standing in her bedroom window, flipping me off like the little shit she is. I chuckle under my breath as I pull out of the driveway, ready to start my night with my brothers at the clubhouse.

My sister and I have always been close. We were inseparable as children, and even though I've long since moved out of our parents' house, I still hang out with her multiple times a week. I've managed to keep the motorcycle club separate from my parents over the last four years to preserve our relationship, but Lena was harder since she's stuck to me like glue.

Unbeknownst to my parents, Lena's been to the clubhouse a few times for some BBQs and when I was patched in, but I try to keep her from it, especially since the members are all a bunch of horny bastards and throw parties that are filled with debauchery everywhere you look.

Even if they know Lena is off-limits and they respect that fact, she thrives under their attention, and I don't like it one bit. She may be twenty, but she's still my little sister, and I'm not down for letting her have free rein of the clubhouse. It's too much work to bring her with me. There's no unwinding, it's all big brother mode, and the need to keep her safe is front and center —even from my club brothers, whom I trust with my life.

The night air is cool on my skin as I ride through our small town of Amberwood, Washington. I love riding alone, always have, and the road conditions in this small part of our state provide me with exactly what I need. I coast through town, but as soon as the road opens up and it's just me, the purr of my bike and the late summer air, I gun it. I've always enjoyed the solitude of the open road, and this evening is no different.

I lean into every curve, feeling free and untouchable. My dad is a big shot lawyer and had hopes and dreams that I would do something just as prestigious as him, and even though his disappointment is strong, his love for me is fierce. At least he isn't a prosecution attorney because that would make for some tense family dinners. While all the businesses the club is involved in are legit, some of the shit we get pulled into is more seedy and questionable. Especially lately.

The dim lights up ahead signal my approach to the Hell's Heathens' compound. The perimeter is surrounded by a fence with a dozen or so prospects doing twenty-four-hour checks with four guards at the main gate—our only entry point at the moment. We've had an ongoing turf war with another club that has been flexing its strength lately, and our new president has put us all on guard and ready to be prepared for an attack.

The Iron Wolves deal in the flesh and drug trade, and they're looking to take over our territory and push us out of business. We're not going to let it happen. Their club is run by a monster named Damon—road name: Grim—and he runs it by instilling fear. He picks up the lowest of the low of society, preying on addicts and convicts to fill his ranks. His club is full of sick fucks, and it's clubs like theirs that give the rest of us a bad rap. As one-percenters, they don't live by the same rules as us. They're outlaws.

Hell's Heathens may not look like it from the outside, but we're a family. We live and die together. We have core values that each of us believes in, and when we patch in, it's for life—because we choose it. Not because someone is forcing our hand, not out of desperation or coercion. It's a deep, unwavering loyalty to the club, its values, and each other.

After passing through the gates, my bike rolls to a stop, the music blaring from inside, and a steady thump of bass that consumes your heartbeat and throbs between your ears reaches me as I cut my engine.

It's a typical Friday—the boys looking for a reason to celebrate, and the patch bunnies looking to spend their night in someone's bed with hopes of becoming an old lady.

The doors are pushed open, and people spill out onto the porch, drinks in hand and having a good time. The open room is filled with leather cuts and half-naked women. Brothers play pool and darts, letting loose and having a good time, while others are already getting their dicks wet with patch bunnies out in the open.

I head to the bar to show my face before I need to set up in the back. Tonight, I'm tattooing instead of partying, which is much more my style anyway. Any activity that I can do that empties my head and frees my soul, I'd prefer. Despite my large size, I've never been the loudest in the room, preferring to keep to the back in the quiet. That's not to say that I don't know how to have a good time, given the right circumstances.

"Hey, Rogue. What can I get ya?"

"Hey," I say in greeting to one of our prospects working the bar tonight. "Jack and Coke. Tattooing tonight and gotta keep my head straight. You want anything done? Know you've been itching to add some more."

"Nah, Prez has got me working the bar all night, then I'm on cleanup duty."

I wince on his behalf. Cleanup duty sucks after a rager. "Damn, man. I feel for you. I hear the vote is soon, though, so keep doin' what you're doin'. You'll be patched soon enough, and all the shit duty will be in the past and for some new prospect to deal with."

"You think?"

I give him a nonchalant shrug, but my face is all smiles as I sip on the cool liquid he set in front of me. He's a good guy, and I have a feeling the vote will go in his favor. The noise is thunderous all around me, and I know I need to head to the back to get set up before I get pulled into it.

I stand up and adjust my cut before walking through the main part of the house, trying to avoid any patch bunnies who will be giving it their best shot to convince me to claim them as mine for the night. Most of them are fun, sexy things that satisfy a completely primal urge, but tonight I'm working and need to focus; the last thing I need is the distraction of pussy.

Just as I'm about to step into the hallway off the main area, my path is blocked by a blonde bombshell in a red dress and heels.

"Hey, Rogue," Callie purrs as she drags her manicured nails down my chest. Nails I know all too well, having felt them rake down my back in the past. Maybe my focus can wait. I bend my knees so I can wrap my arm around her back, my free hand grabbing her jaw as I move us to the closest wall. She hitches her leg around my hip as I grip her ass hard with my palm, squeezing just enough around her throat with my other to get her attention.

I've hooked up with Callie on more than a few occasions, and I know she's hoping I'll make her my old lady someday, but it's not going to happen. She's hooked up with me enough to know that I have two rules: no kissing on the mouth, and I won't be making you my old lady. After a few failed attempts, she no longer tries. Which makes things easier on me.

A hard hand slaps the back of my shoulder, pulling Callie's mouth from my neck, where she's sucking on me like a fuckin' vampire.

"Rogue. I'm ready, let's get going."

I drop Callie's leg to the ground, her face pinching into a pout as she whines.

"Sorry, babe, duty calls. Maybe next time," I say with a wink, taking a step back and putting space between us.

"Don't worry, sweet thing, I'll keep you warm," Noose chuckles as he wraps an arm around Callie's shoulder. She perks right up, her glassy eyes shining bright and looking at him like he hung the moon.

When I was brought into Hell's Heathens, I learned real quick that sharing the patch bunnies was common. All of them are here of their own free will and can come and go as they please. Most of them sleep with patch members, and none of us have ever given it much thought. We're all clean and test regularly, and there's no jealousy. It's not a bad setup when you don't have the time or energy to date.

But that's a huge reason why—those of us who care—won't make one of them our old lady. It's the same reason I don't kiss any of them on the mouth. I reserve that right for the person I'm in a relationship with, whenever that time comes. There's something more intimate about kissing than fucking. I'll fuck someone one of my brother's has been inside before me, but I'm not going to kiss her or make her mine permanently.

Sin and I head to the backroom where Ink and I have set up a makeshift studio for the club. While he works the majority of his time at Heathen Ink, one of the club's legitimate businesses, I tattoo here. I'd love to own my own shop one day and am saving every extra penny to make that dream happen.

"You ready to get this sleeve finished?" I ask him. We've been working on a long-term project of fine line work that covers every inch of his arm, fingers to pec, and the next several hours should finish him up. The guy is about my size—six-four and 260 pounds—and is one of the toughest assholes here, but he hates needles. We should have had this work done in two eight-to-ten-hour sessions, but here we are, session six.

Sin shrugs, looking slightly green as he takes off his cut and hangs it on one of the hooks on the wall.

"Let's get this shit over with."

I laugh at him. "Why even do it if you hate it so much?"

"Love the ink, you know what it means to me. Just hate the process. Any chance Stitch got his hands on some Propofol?"

"Believe it or not, he couldn't. You're gonna have to stay awake for this." I continue to shake my head and laugh at him. I move through my routine, opening new tools and setting up my ink, getting the green soap ready, and opening a new roll of towels. The room is painted deep black with my tattoo table in the center, and overhead lights pour directly over us, giving me the lighting I need.

I lay out all my supplies on the black rolling table and grab my pens and markers to get started.

"Ready?" I ask him after everything's been drawn on and prepared for me to make permanent.

"Get it over with, Rogue."

I swipe some Vaseline over the area and get started, focusing on my task and losing myself to the steady vibrations that hum through my hand, and the resistance as I press the needle into his skin. I fall into a hypersensitive trance as I work my way through the project. I'm attuned to his every movement and the quiet grinding of his molars as I work over the sensitive area on the inside of his wrist.

I lose track of time, progressing further and further, checking in with Sin periodically as he scrolls his phone and fights for his life.

Just as I'm about to wipe Sin down, the door to the room slams open, the force bouncing it off the wall. Sin and I both jerk up, wondering what the hell is going on. Chaos stands in the doorway, his face void of the stony features he typically wears, and I'm immediately on guard.

"Reid," he gasps in a hurry. My body is on high alert at his use of my legal name. It's rare and reserved for situations that call for it. "It's Lena. I'm so fucking sorry, I didn't know."

My blood turns to ice in my veins as I quickly stand, dropping my machine to the table, a feeling deep in the pit of my stomach that almost brings me down to my knees. A whoosh of lightheadedness passes through me. His tone is all wrong. His typical, stoic calmness is missing, and putting me on edge. The anger and fear in his voice are palpable.

"What do you mean it's Lena? Where is she?"

"Reid . . ." he says my name like he's delivering a death announcement, but that's impossible. My heart stops as the breath is stolen from my lungs, and Sin grips my bicep.

"No. No, you're wrong. She's at home. Camden, tell me you're fucking wrong."

"She was with Lucas. They've been sneaking around. I didn't know."

Was.

My thoughts race with explanations. Lena and I don't hide things from each other, and she's been seeing Lucas? For how long? I knew I should never have brought her here to begin with. What the fuck was I thinking? She's twenty, for fuck's sake; she doesn't need to be around a motorcycle club with a bunch of testosterone-fueled men, no matter how well-behaved they are or how deep their loyalty runs.

"Where's your brother then? Where the fuck are they?"

My president's face falls further, and I know it's worse than I could have imagined.

"The Iron Wolves have them. We need to go. Now."

Fear like I've never felt before clutches me. There's no love lost between Hell's Heathens and the Iron Wolves, and hurting one of our females is a line none of us will allow to be crossed. The fact that they just did means war.

"I want wheels on the pavement in less than ten minutes!" Chaos yells into the open room, sobering everyone quickly. Everything else happens in a blur. My gun is strapped in its holster behind my back, and we're all on our bikes, a massive show of force as we head to the last place the Iron Wolves have been known to hide out.

We don't have the element of surprise; we don't have a plan or coordinated attack. Just going in guns blazing on a hope and a prayer that we can get Lena and Lucas out of their clutches. We ride in formation, only the loud rumble of our bikes to be heard. Anxiety and fear roll through me in equal measure, my hands shaking as I grip my handlebars. My brain wars with itself, unable to comprehend that my sister could be anywhere but home right now.

She has to be okay.

She's okay.

What feels like hours later, but in reality was under thirty minutes, we roll up to a shitty neighborhood on the outskirts of a town I've never been to. At the end of a long cul-de-sac sits a rundown, decrepit house with fire erupting from the first-floor windows. I skid my bike to a hard stop at the front of the house as Camden is jumping off his and racing inside with other members hot on his tail. I pull my gun and move to rush in when Malice and Wrath grab my shoulders, hauling me backward.

"Let me fucking go! I need to get to her!" I do my best to fight them off, but they hold strong.

"Nope, not happening, brother. Prez' order. We're to keep you back. We don't know what awaits inside, and it looks like their crew is long gone."

I know he's not wrong; the lack of bikes out front was the biggest clue. Whatever happened inside, they've left it and tried to torch the evidence. But that doesn't mean Lena is in there. She could have been taken by them as a hostage, or something worse.

Minutes go by but it feels like fucking hours as I stand by my bike and fucking wait. Wrath and Malice each hold me back by an arm, like they don't trust that I won't book it inside the moment they release me. They aren't wrong.

I should have been with her. I should have fucking taken her with me. She would have been safer if I had just given in and kept her by my side. She fucking begged me to bring her with me tonight. I put my own selfish wants above hers, and now I'll live with that. Regret pulls me under, suffocating and debilitating me.

She has to be okay.

She's okay.

I repeat the words out loud, unintentionally. A mantra, a prayer.

The front door is kicked wide open as fire rages behind Camden. He walks out of the house with my sister's limp body cradled in his arms. Her head hangs back at an angle that's all wrong, arm hanging lifeless toward the ground, the clothes left on her body ripped and dirtied, and I know the truth before they get any closer.

All the life drains out of my body. I crumble to my knees, an animalistic wail echoing through the night as my soul is torn in two and my heart shatters into a million pieces. Like the devil himself plunged his cold, dead hand into my chest and obliterated everything good that was once there, I'm left empty and devoid of any light, any good.

She can't be gone. My sweet Lena. So full of life. Her sweet, infectious smile. The laugh that could turn anyone's mood around. She had her entire life ahead of her. My vision is clouded, darkness creeping in at the edges as he walks toward me. Everything is silent around me, moving like a slow-motion picture, while I spiral out of control. I heave in lungfuls of air, my knuckles rubbing the spot where my heart used to beat.

Camden's leather boots stop in front of me, and he drops to one knee as he places her in my arms. I sink further into the hard ground as I hold my sister close. My eyes trace over her lifeless body, taking in the bruises marring her once-flawless skin, the blood that tracks down her thighs, the cuts, her busted lip. I push the wet strands of hair out of her face, looking into familiar green eyes that life no longer dances behind.

I run my hand over her eyelids to close them. Screams rip from my body as I rock her in my arms. Begging, praying to whoever will listen to take me instead. For whatever being that exists above to bring her back to this plane. To let her live. She deserves to live.

The fear she must have felt as they raped and beat her before stealing her precious life from her slams into me. Sobs wrack from my body. I was too fucking late. Too preoccupied with my own shit to realize she had gone out. I didn't even know she was with Camden's brother; I would have stopped it.

I could have prevented this.

Why didn't I prevent this?

How did I not protect the one person on Earth I would gladly die for?

"Wh-where's Lucas?" I don't recognize my own voice as the words struggle to come out between labored breaths.

Camden's face pales further as he finally stands, but he holds stoic in his position as our leader, even though it's his brother I'm asking about.

"He can't be recovered. They burned him alive."

"FUCK!" I scream until my voice runs hoarse.

Tears continue to pour down my face, dripping onto Lena's, the wet droplets leaving track marks over the dirty flesh of her body.

"We need to move, Rogue. We gotta get out of here before the police arrive."

Camden moves to reach for Lena, and I jerk out of his way with a snarl, pulling her closer to me, an inhuman growl leaving my chest. He puts his hands up defensively, and I know he means no harm, but no one will take her from me. No one. Camden squats down to my level again, and I know what he's gonna offer before he says it.

"We've got two options, and you need to make a decision quick or I'll make it for you. One, we take her with us, we give her a proper burial on our grounds or somewhere pretty, but she's just gonna be a missing person from here on out. No one will know what happened to her but us. Two, we leave her here for the cops to find, and your parents will get closure and eventually find peace. But they'll know every terrifying, brutal detail of what happened to her tonight."

I look down at my sweet little sister, and I know I would rather die than leave her in the hell that took her life from us. I also can't bear my mom's pain of knowing the truth about her only daughter's fate. I would rather her live with hope in her heart that someday Lena would be found. It wouldn't bring them closure; it would kill both of my parents just like it killed me.

Forcing my legs to work is a strength I pull from some unknown place as I cradle her close. Chaos helps me get situated on my bike with her wrapped tight in my arms. It takes all my strength and balance, but I follow the rest of our crew out of this shithole and back to our clubhouse on autopilot, holding my lifeless sister—my best fucking friend—in my arms. I'll never recover from this.

I feel like I'm drowning, the weight of Lena's death holding me under the water like an anchor, knowing I'll never be able to come up for air again, but not putting me out of my misery and ending it. I walk into church and am thankful to find that it's only me and Chaos right now.

I drop my cut onto the table in front of him, and the seriousness and finality of what that represents sucks the air from the room.

"I want out."

Chaos stands, resting his hands on the table as he peers down at my cut.

"You'll never be out, Rogue. You know what you joined. You're a Hell's Heathen. Only way out is through Hell's gates, and you're not dying today."

"Camden . . ."

"No!" he snaps loudly, slamming his fist down onto the table. "In here, I'm your president. You aren't the only one who lost a sibling that day. I feel the weight of that shit every single moment. Lucas was . . . fuck!" His spine straightens as he pushes his hair out of his face.

I know this eats up Camden every day, but he and I both know it's different. We all know it could have been any one of us. Lucas had earned his cut, and he knew the risks just as each of us does. But Lena? Lena was innocent. Lena was pure light and everything good in the world.

"You'll never be *out,* Rogue. Ever."

"Chaos . . ." I plead.

"When I gave you your road name, I didn't think it would mean what it's about to. You're not out, but I'm letting you go. Show up for church when I need you, be there when we call, but you can leave," he says, pushing my cut back into my arms.

My eyes widen in shock; I was prepared to put up a harder fight. I nod my head in agreement, the emotion choking me up and preventing words from forming. I knew it was a long shot that I'd be released, and I was prepared to beg. I can't live here anymore, not when it serves as a constant reminder of how I lost everything. The reason all the light was sucked from my life, shrouding me in complete darkness.

The only girl who would ever mean anything to me is gone, and it's all my fault. If I hadn't been involved with Hell's Heathens, Lena would never have been exposed to this world. If I had just taken her with me that night, she wouldn't have been out alone with Lucas. I turn to walk out of the room, reaching for the heavy wood doors as Chaos' voice rings out.

"Oh, and Rogue? Don't stray too far from your family. We're here for you."

THANK YOU FOR READING

Loved Crew & Monroe's story?

Please consider leaving a review! As an indie author, reviews are so important. Thank you so much for your support!

Stay up to date with Jenn Plummer by joining her Facebook readers' group, Jenn's Harlots. Ask questions, get first looks at new books/series, and have fun with other book lovers!

https://www.facebook.com/groups/jennsharlots

BOOKS BY JENN PLUMMER

Aspen Ridge Series

Unravel Me

Crave Me

Love Me

Wreck Me

Complete Me

Aspen Ridge Holiday Novellas

Ready or Not (Halloween)

Sweet Girl (Valentine's Day)

Daddy Issues (Father's Day)

Queens & Heathens

All's Fair in Love and Sin

All's Fair in Love and Malice

All's Fair in Love and Wrath

Wicked Games

Nothing to Fear: A Dark Academia MM Romance

Nothing to Hide: A Dark Academia MMF Romance

Nothing to Lose: A Dark Academia MM Romance

Standalones

Not a Holiday Romance

ACKNOWLEDGMENTS

Wow. What a story. When my editor, Katie, and I plotted this one in the fall of 2025, I didn't think it was going to put me through such a rollercoaster of emotions. We both knew Crew had trauma, but it wasn't until I started writing that I realized how deep it went. Then Monroe stumbled in. This bright, sunshine character that I really struggled to write at that time in my life. I knew she wouldn't understand Crew unless she could relate, even a little bit. These two were written in the stars, and I feel honored to tell their story. It's one of so much pain, and suffering, of grief, and self-doubt, but there's so much hope, so much recovery, and healing. I hope it gives just one of you hope to keep moving forward, to not live stagnant, to push past whatever is holding you still. Life is so beautiful and so precious, and we all deserve to feel the warmth of it on our skin. Sending you all love from the bottom of my heart.

To my readers,

Thank you. There are so many incredible stories out there to read, and you chose to pick up mine, time and time again. I couldn't do this if it weren't for you.

My editor and friend, Katie,

The last few books have been rough. I questioned my ability, I questioned my sanity, I questioned my choices. I lost some of myself and my joy in the process, but you stuck beside me through all of it. This book made me fall back in love with storytelling, with writing, and creating. Getting to do this with you, so authentically and so genuine, is such a highlight of my life and my career. Thank you for holding me up when I can't do it myself. Thank you for helping create characters that we are passionate about and love so thoroughly. Thank you for the million and one things you do for me and these stories. I love you, now and always.

My team, Anja, Samantha, Emily, THANK YOU!

A huge thank you to my content team for all of your help pumping up these stories! I'm so grateful for every post, share, comment, graphic, edit, and early review. You all are amazing, and I'm in such awe of you!